DRAGON SLAYERS

K.A. PENDRAKE

Author's Note

I've chosen to publish this book under an anonymous pen name,
as some of its themes may be controversial to powerful people,
but more importantly, to let the story speak for itself.

This is not a call to arms or a manifesto, only a work of fiction that I hope you
enjoy. I do not condone violence of any kind and believe that violence only
undermines a cause, whereas thoughtful discourse creates lasting change.

To all who knew about this idea and supported me
along the way, I am forever grateful.

Your help made this journey possible.

Especially to my mother, whose love and support not only helped
with this book, but made me the person I am today.

CHAPTER 1

THE PROMOTION

"Greed is the root of all evil, which slowly suffocates all those who blissfully play within the devil's playground."

-RALPH HARLOW

"YOUR FATHER WOULD be extremely proud of you, Charlie."

FBI Director Bill Cartwright says, beaming with satisfaction.

"James Grayson was a remarkable soldier and hero. I recognize his traits in you as well."

His praise helps me to relax just a bit.

"Thank you, sir. Just doing my job."

Bill lifts a folder with my name on it, Charlotte Grayson, and casually flips through the pages.

"Intercepting a terrorist attack in your first year. Dismantling an entire weapons smuggling network. Medal for Meritorious Achievement.

"Charlie, most operatives don't come close to those achievements in their entire career, but I'm not surprised. It's in your blood; you're a Grayson, after all. You have your father's focus. His resolve to accomplish whatever needs to be done to achieve victory."

I smile, masking the uneasy truth that my father's untimely death opened as many doors as it has closed. At times, his legacy is a badge of honor. Other times, it's an elusive shadow I can't outrun.

Bill's office is lined with esteemed mementos. Photos of him alongside generals, presidents, foreign dignitaries, and even the Pope. Rows of crisp uniforms decorated in polished medals, each frame a tribute to status and power.

One picture stands out. It looks out of place, a worn snapshot of two young men in boot camp. No medals. No titles. Just Bill and my father, grinning like fools, arms over each other's shoulders, mud-splattered faces from field training.

My dad's death was a sacrifice that etched his name into the legacy of service. Bill became my father figure, filling the void of losing a parent too soon. A mentor, lifeline, and a constant reminder of the legacy I strive to live up to.

Bill shifts forward as if he is about to share a secret.

"That's why I'm promoting you to Deputy Director of the FBI," Bill exclaims. "Working for me... well, Charlie, we'll be a tremendous team."

"Thank you, Director Cartwright. This position is everything I've been striving for."

He waves it off with a playful smirk.

"Let's not get lost in titles, Deputy Director Charlotte Grayson. It's me, Bill. And I hope I can still call you Charlie."

"Of course you can, Bill. I wouldn't have it any other way."

I release a genuine smile, my eyes revealing gratitude. Any other excitement on my part is kept in reserve, as rumors about my promotion had been spreading. I worked hard and made many sacrifices to achieve this level of success. It's been my one goal, a step closer to continuing in my father's footsteps.

"Charlie, you've earned this all on your own. And you know that I'll always support you. Now, let's get down to business."

He slides a thin file across the desk.

"We have a case. One of those tech mogul playboys has disappeared."

"Yacht party gone wrong?"

"That's what we assumed at first, but I think it could be more complex. His crypto holdings worth fourteen billion dollars have disappeared. Accounts are completely drained."

Opening the file, the page heading reads: Lucian Voss. Innovator, venture capitalist, and notorious party host.

"The money landed in flagged accounts, ones we've been tracking," Bill continues. "This could be the biggest theft of all time. I'm assigning it to you. Unfortunately, we have nothing substantial.

"The last time anyone saw Voss was almost two months ago. He's been known to disappear on a bender and turn up months later. However, the issue is all of his assets were only recently transferred, so that's why you'll be looking into it."

"Appreciate your confidence in me. I'll need a team and full access to Voss's finances, associates, travel schedule."

Bill lifts his hand, cutting me off with a reassuring grin.

"I've already put together a team of our top agents for you. But for now, Charlie, you need to enjoy your special achievement. It's time to celebrate."

As we enter a packed assembly room, the cork of a champagne bottle explodes. My fellow colleagues let out a cheer as a glass is shoved into my hand, their faces lighting up with pride.

"To Charlie!" someone yells.

"To Charlie!" the group echoes.

Stepping forward, I raise my glass.

"Thanks, everyone! My success is because of all of you. Such incredible colleagues. Here's to all of you... this is ours."

A ripple of applause floods the room. I smile, just for a moment, then take my seat. The champagne glass feels heavy in my hand. The realization is sinking in that now I must prove that I am worthy of my new position. Me. FBI Deputy Director.

The music thumps, causing the table to vibrate. And then I see her.

Across the room, Lex. She's standing at the bar, wavy auburn hair cascading over her shoulders, talking with her usual animated charm. She is effortlessly captivating, and her bursts of laughter indicate a cocktail... or three.

Lex notices me and, with her signature grace, makes her way to my table, turning heads as she works her way through the crowd. She nails the natural boho-chic vibe, always picking outfits that highlight her stunning figure.

"Well, well, Deputy Director," she drawls. "What's the woman of the hour hiding for or should I say, from?"

"Hey Lex. I'm not hiding."

My eyes lower as if she has caught me in a little white lie.

"Been a while," I timidly reply.

"A while? Only you would call a year a while."

Lex grabs a chair and strategically places her elbows on the table.

"Come on, Charlie, that face of yours is not giving off any party vibes. You got what you've been chasing for years. You should be the one celebrating."

Lex's voice softens, dipping just enough to land.

"I'm really proud of you. You stayed focused. You made it happen. I know the sacrifices you made. It wasn't easy."

"Thanks, Lex. Really. I just… need to stay grounded right now."

"Grounded. That's so you, Charlie. Always so prim and proper. Meanwhile, I need a couple of drinks just to get the courage to come over here."

Lex's voice is sweet and sensual, her eyes filling with nostalgia. Her words unsettle me more than I expect, as she was one of the sacrifices I made for my career and this promotion. Guilt constricts my thoughts, a quiet ache of knowing what we used to be.

There's no question our relationship was unique. Two fresh-faced FBI agents thrown into the fire together. It was inevitable we'd fall hard for each other.

I cared deeply for Lex, and still do. But unlike her, I chose my career over love. Every late night, every missed call, every time I prioritized a mission over Lex made our relationship suffer. Eventually, the space I had created between us became impossible to bridge.

There would be no compromise on my part. Lex deserved more than stolen moments, more than me always being half-present. And in the end, I made the decision for her.

"Lex, I'm sorry…" I whisper.

She silences me with a lifted finger. Her hazel eyes entrap mine. A provocative smile plays on her lips.

"Shhhh. Come on, Charlie. You made it clear from the start that your work is your main priority. You have this flame, this passion that I have always loved about you. I could never hold that against you."

She edges closer, her fingers brushing mine, holding me captive in the moment.

"And besides… you were worth more than a little heartbreak. So yeah… I'll always be here for you."

"Lex, I really appreciate that…"

She squeezes my hand before I can finish.

"Always, Charlie. Now, don't be so serious. You're supposed to be celebrating."

Lex's warmth melts any remaining friction between us, her presence consuming all of my concerns. Her fingers brush lightly against my cheek, her magnetic aura drawing me towards her.

She bats her eyelashes and wickedly teases me.

"How about we sneak out of here and really celebrate at my place for old times' sake?"

Her remark catches me off guard, tumbling down the walls of my solitary fortress. Tonight, with her warm hand embracing mine and the undeniable signs of a second chance, I find myself asking how I can even consider saying no, as the painfully familiar voice in my mind slams the brakes on saying yes.

My voice cracks as I struggle to remain firm.

"Lex. That's not a good idea."

She laughs devilishly, moving in closer until her shoulder nudges against mine. Her scent is impossible to resist.

"Come on, Charlie. Don't make me your greatest missed opportunity… just one night… no strings attached."

"Fine," I whisper. "No strings attached."

She wastes no time, gripping my hand tightly, pulling me towards the door. Suddenly, she freezes, tilting her head to one side with a saucy grin.

Imitating a toast, she pretends to take a sip, winking at me.

"Deputy Director. You're driving. I might've had… just a little too much."

"Of course, you did."

"Just partying for the two of us… like always."

The drive to her apartment is far from silent. Lex snuggles into the passenger seat, drawing patterns on the window with her finger, singing along to one of her favorite playlists. She taps an offbeat rhythm; her carefree spirit captivating me, her scent intoxicating me.

This girl knows how to use her charm and wit like a weapon, of which I have been on the receiving end many times. Our gazes lock.

"What?" she says, her voice teasing, a slight flush appearing on her cheeks.

"Nothing. Just having a great time, aren't you?"

"Of course, this is what I do, Charlie. I find beauty in the little things. Someone must, don't you think?"

Her words sting as I try to stay focused on the road. Lex's here-and-now attitude is her greatest asset, a counterpoint to my future-oriented planning. Despite all that I put her through; she remains unwavering.

Still, even with Lex next to me, my mind wanders. The promotion, the accolades, all the sacrifices… it should be more than enough. But here now with Lex, this feels more fulfilling than any ceremony or title.

Arriving at her apartment, Lex beams as she opens the door. Inside, nothing has changed. Her place is Bohemian, warm and, as always, a bit disorganized. It embodies her essence. Radiant and chaotic. A stark contrast to my own meticulously organized structure of life. Doubt I could ever embrace her gypsy lifestyle.

She tosses her keys onto the counter and turns to greet me seductively.

"Welcome back to my paradise. So, what'll it be? Beer, wine, or something stronger?"

Lex retrieves two glasses from the cabinet, making the choice for me. She sets a glass into my hand, her eyes flashing with mischief.

"Charlie, you always do this."

"Do what?"

"Keep yourself in reserve. Hold everyone at arm's length as if you're too busy being the flawless FBI agent to ever truly allow yourself to feel carefree."

"Ouch… that's not fair."

"It's true. Just chill. Let people in. You deserve more than you are willing to accept."

"Lex, you're right. I know I need to slow down. I know it takes a toll. On me. On everyone around me.

"So yeah… I owe you more than a few apologies."

Lex's face reveals an emotional jumble of hurt, understanding, and acceptance.

"Charlie, stop. I've said over and over again, I get it, I get you. Always have and always will. You were honest from the start. Career first. I could never hold that against you.

"And look at you now. The youngest deputy director in FBI history. You set your sights on reaching the top. And you made it, Charlie.

" I'm so, so, so proud of you. Not because of the title. Because I know what it cost you to get there. And that matters the most to me."

"Thank you. Lex. You've always understood me. And the fact that you're happy for me… it's just one more reason I'll never stop being grateful for you. But I still feel guilty."

"Enough Charlie. Let's not waste tonight on regrets, okay? You look so…"

Lex stops mid-sentence, choosing to continue our conversation with a physical touch. She lightly traces the features of my face, spinning me in a sensual web as we collapse on the couch. Our bodies melt into one.

She brushes her lips on mine, bold, unapologetic, electric.

For the first time in what feels like an eternity, all my inhibitions disappear.

No legacy. Just Lex.

Our kissing becomes more intense, her hands on my waist, pulling me in closer. My heart races as she tilts her head, her breath hot against my skin. This is what I truly need... and it's her.

The sound of my phone ringing shatters our sensual bliss.

Lex moans, her sweat-beaded forehead against mine.

"Fuck... of course this would happen. Please be scam-likely."

The screen displays an incoming call. Bill Cartwright.

"It's Bill," I whisper, guilt welling up in my voice. "Sorry. You know I have to."

"Probably needs you to put your superhero cape back on."

"Bill?" I stand up straight as if he were in the room with us.

"Charlie. We have something. I need you at HQ. ASAP."

"Yes, sir," I reply, already reaching for my coat. "On my way."

Lex doesn't move. Doesn't say a thing. Her expression says it all. If looks could kill, I would be dead.

"Lex, I'm really sorry. It's my duty. I have to..."

"Charlie, just get going. But I'm demanding a raincheck."

"You have my word," I reply, pressing a firm kiss on her lips to seal the deal.

"Now go save mankind," she says smugly.

Lex's words play in my head as I drive into the morning twilight. Serving my country is my life, and that affirmation banishes any desire for Lex, at least for now.

Inside FBI headquarters, the usual comforting hum of activity has ceased, and an unsettling quiet reigns. Fluorescent lights cast long shadows down empty corridors, contributing to the tension that tickles the back of my neck. I've spent countless hours here, but the vibe this time feels more intense.

The conference room glows like a beacon. Analysts cluster around laptops, their faces lit by the blueish glow of the screens. One of them glances up as I approach.

"Deputy Director Grayson," he says, jerking his head down another corridor. "You're needed in the DEFCON room."

"DEFCON?"

"Yes, ma'am. Director Cartwright requires you there ASAP."

My chest constricts as I step into an unfamiliar hallway. I've been in nearly every room in this facility, but not this one. The DEFCON room is a maximum-security space reserved for the most sensitive missions, some of which ultimately can decide the fate of nations.

Straightening my spine, I quicken my pace, shoving my nerves aside. Whatever awaits, I am ready to handle it.

As I enter, the gravity of the moment hits me. The room is cavernous, dominated by an elongated steel table surrounded by screens. Streaming data swirls on the walls, bathing the room in cold light. There is muted tension, broken only by panicked keyboard clicks.

Two people are in the room with Bill and two more on the massive screens at the sides of the table. No introductions are necessary as my FBI assessment training kicks in.

Lanky frame, hunched in a worn hoodie, fingers flying across the keyboard, detached from his surroundings. Most likely cyber ops. Young... maybe too young... but analysts like him don't land in this room by accident. If he's here, it's because he is a critical asset.

My eyes shift to the monitors. Both figures are definitely White House staff.

Middle-aged man, cue ball head, stuffed in a custom-made suit... Washington elite. There is something not quite right about this administration lackey. He emits an attitude of arrogance that even the top generals keep in reserve.

Another screen displays a mature woman, sharp-faced, dressed in an impeccable designer suit. Her glasses reflect the glow from the screen, her eyes unnervingly fixed on me.

I can't get a read on her. It feels as if she's not just sizing me up; she's calculating exactly how I might serve her purpose.

Finally, the soldier. Military build, upright posture, tugging at his collar, obviously uncomfortable in civvies. A thick mustache masks his expression, but the moment it clicks, my breath catches. Graham Cross.

In this line of work, his reputation is well-known and held in high regard. The leader of the FBI's elite tactical ops, the ones who risk their lives every time they step into chaos.

Though I've encountered him during combat training sessions and occasionally at the FBI's gym, witnessing him here feels entirely different. He is flawless, and his success rate is unmatched. If Graham is at the table, it signifies that whatever is transpiring is serious.

Bill sits at the head of the table as tension emanates from the room. He gestures for me to come in. His voice is authoritative.

"Deputy Director Grayson, welcome, thanks for coming in so quickly."

Graham glances up at me, eyes narrowing as recognition dawns. Respect in his eyes, as well as amused curiosity. I have witnessed this reaction many times before, the Grayson legacy. My father's elite soldier reputation always overshadowing me.

My eyes are drawn to the screens behind Bill. At the center, a symbol stands out, all gold, a sword driven through the body of a coiled dragon, wings spread wide, frozen in mid-flight. The design is sharp and deliberate; a haunting image clearly designed to make a permanent impression.

My question is direct.

"What's the situation?"

Bill's posture stiffens.

"We've received a video. It's related to your new case. Missing billionaire, Lucian Voss. A group has taken credit, calling themselves the Dragon Slayers."

I find their name amusing. "Dragon Slayers" sounds more like comic book characters than a group of terrorist extremists.

Bill motions to the screens with urgency.

"We found their video on the dark web. It's not live yet, but we think they're getting ready to launch it. When they do, it'll spread like wildfire.

"They're claiming they have Voss's money. All of it."

A scoff crackles through the monitor before the man speaks.

"And you actually believe that?" the man shouts. "For all we know, it's a scam. Some offshore shell game to cover up tax fraud, probably for Voss."

Hearing him speak triggers my memory. Victor Hargrove. The administration's shadowy advisor. If Victor's here, it's not to ask questions. He's already calculating how to spin this into something manageable. Damage control in a pin-striped suit.

But he has a valid point. Extremist groups love to make bold claims just to grab attention. I've seen it before, bluffs, misinformation, anything to stay in the headlines.

The young man hunches over his laptop, barely glancing up.

"You don't move fourteen billion dollars into ten thousand wallets just to dodge the IRS. That'd be child's play compared to what they pulled off here."

"Thanks, Diaz," Bill replies. "And Victor, you might be right. But for now, we need to take full precautions until proven otherwise."

Diaz, of course, Carter Diaz. That must be him. Everyone

knows his name; few have met him. Keeps to himself, the epitome of an expert cyber analyst.

Bill turns to me, gesturing to the main screen.

"Grayson, you need to watch the video before we continue with the briefing."

In the corner, a technician presses a key, and the room goes silent. The screen flickers with static before settling into an image that grips everyone's attention.

A figure stands in the center, face obscured by a black-and-gold mask built for battle and to demand attention. Faceless in structure, the mask captures a blistering stare, an unyielding soul-piercing presence.

His armor gleams in the dim light; striking colors of black and gold exude both power and precision. The intricate design, while functional, allows each segment to move freely, radiating an undeniable authority.

Across the chest, the same golden emblem, a dragon perfectly encircled, pierced by a sword. An ominous warning.

A baritone voice, slightly augmented to avoid any detection, cuts through the quiet with the precision of a razor.

I am Lancelot, leader of the Dragon Slayers.

His words hit like lightning bolts, vibrating with a power that commands attention. He pauses, allowing the gravity of his introduction to sink in deep before he continues.

Mankind has talked of dragons for centuries.

Monsters of unimaginable strength and boundless greed.

*They accumulated riches, burned the earth,
and left destruction in their wake.*

But dragons never existed. They were an allegory.

A metaphor for the wealthy and powerful who are blind to the destruction they leave behind.

The camera zooms in closer, its focus settling on the figure's mask. Expressionless yet authoritative, it possesses a living quality of its own.

Dragons are still among us today.

Not fire-breathing beasts but billionaires who accumulate wealth while the world burns.

They are the makers of war, the source of pollution. The reason so many hunger.

Their greed is the cause of humanity's misery.

He tilts forward, his voice dropping an octave.

But this is not about who you are. It's about what you choose to be.

Billionaires aren't decided by race, religion, or class; they're not bound to their wealth by fate.

They are dragons by choice.

Lancelot times his pause perfectly.

You have 72 hours.

After that time, the names and locations of every billionaire will be made public.

All you have to do is repent.

Surrender the fortune you stole from the backs of the people.

Strip your wealth below a billion dollars, and you are free.

Those of you who continue to hoard your wealth,

Who refuse to acknowledge your sick-
ness will be known for what you are…

Foes of humanity.

Greed is your sickness, but you will be cured.

Shed your wealth that was gained by exploit-
ing the work and innovation of others.

Let go of your hoard. This is not punishment… it is redemption.

The camera closes in, Lancelot's presence overwhelming, his voice hardening into steel.

For those who refuse, know this: we will come for you.

We will find you.

And when we do, you will understand
the cost of the disease you carry.

The one that feeds on greed and spreads suf-
fering to everyone but you.

To the rest of the world… our time has come.

Assist us in revealing the dragons.

Provide information and assist with their capture.

For every tip, for any assistance, you will be rewarded.

We will use the only power these dragons have
against them… their excessive wealth.

We have already secured 14 billion dollars, which
will go directly to those supporting us.

Together, we will show them what they already know.

He pauses for a moment, then speaks with undeniable certainty.

We are the masses.

We are everywhere.

We will not stop until the dragons fall.

CHAPTER 2

THREADS OF CONTROL

"A government big enough to give you everything you want, is big enough to take away everything you have."

-THOMAS JEFFERSON

THE LOGO OF the Dragon Slayers lingers on the screen, its faint glow casting eerie shadows around the darkened briefing room.

Lancelot's words ring in my ears, mingling with a sense of doubt on my part. Most terrorist groups act out of hate or ideology, targeting nations or cultures. This feels different; it's requesting the direct support of the public.

Bill's voice snaps us out of the silence.

"Now that you've seen the video, Charlie, let's get you up to speed on the team we've assembled. First, from the administration. Victor Hargrove and Dr. Evelyn Hart."

Victor jumps right in.

"Let's cut the bullshit. This whole revolution is smoke and mirrors. If it's tied to the missing money at all, it's just a distraction designed to waste your resources while some jackass laughs offshore. And judging by how quickly everyone here took the bait, I'd say the con is working."

His remarks are textbook politics… dismiss an issue until it is too big to ignore. Bill lets him babble on.

"No one's getting paid. These assholes will rile up a bunch of desperate losers, they'll trip over themselves, and then we round 'em up," he says. "These Dragon Slayers will deliver the anarchists to us on a gold tray.

"And don't forget… President Tuff is a billionaire. This threat is a goddamn assault on our entire nation!"

He settles back in his chair, self-satisfied.

Bill clears his throat.

"Thank you, Victor. Evelyn, you have incredible insight and experience in shaping the message. Any thoughts?"

The administration's PR tactician is deathly still, her eyes throwing darts at Bill.

"Doctor… Hart," she replies harshly. "As for Lancelot's message, it taps directly into the desperation of the weak and the poor, the ones who feel abandoned by the system. To them, it sounds like hope. Like justice. And that makes it incredibly potent."

She lets the silence harden, setting the stage for the pivot she's about to make.

"But if this isn't fake, it's also an opportunity. We can frame this as the inevitable result of extremist ideology. If we tie the Dragon Slayers to our opposition leading into the election, it will make them the face of chaos. We then become the answer. The party of law and order."

We haven't even confirmed that the Dragon Slayers are real, and Dr. Hart is already plotting how to weaponize the situation. The ease of her cunning is disturbing.

"Thank you, Dr. Hart," Bill replies. "On our FBI team, we

have the head of Cyber Ops, Agent Carter Diaz. He's the one keeping our digital eyes open and our systems two steps ahead of whoever's behind this mess."

Carter speaks before being asked.

"Yeah, so here's the deal, people. Whoever it is, they are serious about doing something. No question about it."

"How can you be sure?" Victor asks suspiciously. "All we have is a damn video of some loser anarchist."

"Oh, yeah?" Carter snaps. "The amount of work this loser put into moving these funds is the most advanced funneling via crypto networks I've ever seen. This isn't some half-baked hoax or a single job. This Lancelot dude is setting something up.

"What I'm saying is, these aren't basement-dwelling wannabes fumbling around online. They know exactly what they're doing.

"So, unless anyone else in this room has even a remote understanding of multi-layered blockchain forensics and off-chain linkage, I recommend you listen to me."

Bill shoots a 'stop being a wise-ass' look to Carter, who stretches his legs out, unfazed.

"Thanks for your insights, Diaz. That brings us to ground operations. Leading that component is Agent Graham Cross. His team will provide the boots, eyes, and muscle we'll need to track these people down… if they're the real deal."

Graham Cross's deep voice interrupts.

"The gear Lancelot was wearing isn't easy to get. Looked like advanced special ops prototypes. If that equipment is legit, we're looking at someone who's highly trained and well-resourced.

"My opinion? These individuals are ex-military or… hell, possibly even active."

Everyone turns to look at him. A seasoned war vet, his dark

eyes are still fixated on the blank screen where Lancelot's face captivated us.

"Listen, Cross," Victor says. "Every other prepper on You-Tube has military equipment these days. Doesn't mean they have any idea how to use it."

"This isn't weekend warrior nonsense," Graham answers sternly. "I know genuine experience when it's in front of me."

"Military or otherwise," Dr. Hart interrupts tersely. "Their true weapon is the story these Dragon Slayers are weaving. The tactics are secondary. The gear is irrelevant.

"What matters is the narrative, and if we control that, the rest becomes background noise. Collateral damage is unfortunate, but if we shape the perception, we shape the outcome."

Graham unfolds his arms, his expression adamant, stance unwavering.

"With all due respect, Dr. Hart, that 'collateral damage' you're brushing off? Those are American citizens. If even a fraction of them take the Dragon Slayers up on their offer, we're talking about blood in the streets.

"The message is the bait. The money is the hook. And if we don't take them seriously, it's only a matter of time before they start reeling people in."

Graham's practical wisdom is appreciated. He is not a fan of drama, but when he speaks, people listen. This soldier knows his stuff.

Bill steps forward, his voice steady and deliberate. He surveys the room, ensuring he has everyone's full attention.

"Graham, your point is taken. We'll assume this is a high-level threat until we can prove otherwise.

"Deputy Director Grayson will lead this task force and serve as our primary liaison with the Administration. If anyone can steer this operation, it's her."

His words catch me off guard.

"She is new to her deputy director role, but she has been an outstanding agent with the FBI for nearly a decade. I have watched her rise through the ranks, and she is the right person for this mission."

I had assumed that I would only be working on the Lucian Voss case. Bill just handed me the lead role in what could be the most sensitive domestic counterterrorism mission in years.

The main screen shows Victor leaning back slightly, not hiding his surprise. Dr. Hart tilts her head just enough to register calculation. Her eyes question whether I'm ready to handle an operation this big.

I've seen that look before, and I've proven them all wrong. Across the table, Carter and Graham sit composed. No doubt there. Just quiet readiness.

I straighten and speak, finding my voice before anyone else can fill the space.

"Thank you, Director Cartwright. I can assure everyone here that I am more than ready to stop whatever this turns out to be. And we have the perfect team to accomplish this assignment."

I meet the webcam head-on, addressing Victor and Dr. Hart.

"At the FBI, we never underestimate potential threats. Until proven otherwise, we'll operate under the assumption that the Dragon Slayers have the funds… and the intent to use them. Any updates on the legitimacy of that claim will be relayed to you directly."

No one interrupts.

I turn to my new team, the ones that really matter.

"Agent Cross, field operations are yours. Your team needs to be prepped for rapid response."

"Copy that," Graham confirms.

"Agent Diaz," I say. "I know you and your team are probably

already deep into it… but I want to be fully up to speed. I'll meet with you in thirty."

"Sounds like a plan, Deputy Director Grayson. I'll keep the internet on a leash for you."

"Perfect. Your schedules will be updated shortly with our new meeting structure."

Victor's expression shifts from irritation to satisfaction, smugness settling in.

"Naturally," he states. "The White House will require regular briefings, and we'll see they receive them."

"We better," Dr. Hart replies coolly. "Though the administration's priorities will probably need more attention as this develops."

Their message is obvious. Their intention is to see how they can benefit from this incident. There is no doubt in my mind that if push comes to shove, they'll do what's best for themselves.

This mission is ours, mine, Bill's, Carter's, and Graham's. With the entire might of the FBI at our disposal, we have every tool, every resource, and every ounce of authority we need to bring the Dragon Slayers down.

I take a last look around the room. The people in front of me can make or break this mission.

My words are definitive.

"We do this right the first time. If anyone has questions, ask now."

No one speaks, as they intently process their assignments.

"Good," I reply firmly. "Let's get to work."

Monitors disconnect Victor and Dr. Hart from the room.

Lancelot gave a seventy-two-hour deadline in this video.

If they push his message out there, then every second between now and then matters. We need to act fast or we'll lose the lead.

Bill remains, placing a hand on the back of my chair.

"Are you sure you want me leading this?" I ask hesitantly. "Shouldn't you be in charge of such an urgent assignment?"

He lets out a soft, tired laugh.

"I haven't solved anything important in years, Charlie. That's not my job anymore."

He moves around my chair to face me.

"My job is to be the lightning rod… to handle the political hits, the press, all the noise… so people like you can actually get things done. You've got the instincts. The grit. You've earned this, and I have full faith you can handle it."

He steps closer, his presence grounding me, steady and sure.

"Victor and Dr. Hart? They'll test you. Try to push you around. Don't let them. You show them your resolve, and they'll figure out real quick who's running the show."

He turns, then pauses, a dry grin tugging at the edge of his mouth.

"And if you can't do it… well, hell, then we're all screwed. Because I don't know anyone else better."

I look up at him, searching for any trace of doubt, and find none.

Just faith. Unshakable and absolute.

He leaves without saying another word.

This much is clear. The stakes are high.

But failure has never been an option for me.

CHAPTER 3

ECHOES OF THE VOID

"The test of our progress is not whether we add more to the abundance of those who have much, it is whether we provide enough for those who have so little."

\- Franklin D. Roosevelt

THE CYBER ANALYST room is always animated. Monitors line every wall, their constant glow illuminating the exhausted faces of operatives who seem to live here.

I navigate through islands of desks, each one practically copy-and-pasted, uniform, and indistinguishable from the next.

At the far end of the room, a dim glow spills from a partially open door. Carter Diaz's office. I knock once and ease it open. The second I step inside, the contrast is jarring. While the rest of the Bureau feels sterile and uniform, his space is the complete opposite.

It looks more like a college dorm than a workspace. Posters line the walls, countless cables snake across the floor as three monitors display rotating code. A half-eaten protein bar sits next to an energy drink. The foul odor of burnt coffee, stale clothing and overworked circuitry mingle in the air.

"I told you I'm busy," he mutters without looking up, fingers clacking across his keyboard.

Carter swivels, catches sight of me and immediately straightens.

"Deputy Director Grayson, sorry. I thought you were… someone else."

"Don't worry, Agent Diaz. Sorry to have interrupted you."

He seems flustered, so I hold up a hand, easing the formality.

"And call me Charlie. We're going to be in the trenches together, so we can skip the formality."

"Well, boss, call me Carter. Agent always sounds way too dramatic. I'm not running ops or clearing rooms. I mostly stare at code and chase breadcrumbs across the internet. It's not exactly glamorous, but I enjoy the pursuit."

"Trust me, I know it can be tedious. All those hours staring at screens, chasing dead ends to find one lead… it's exhausting. But it's also important to any mission.

"Graham and his team can't do much if they don't know where to go. You give us the roadmap. Without that, we're in the dark."

Carter smirks.

"Spoken like a true fellow nerd."

"Well, I did start as an analyst."

"Yep, I took a look at your file once word got out. And honestly? It's great to see someone like you in command. Usually, it's just some old guy hanging in there long enough to get the position."

"Thanks, Carter, and I won't tell Bill you said that," I say jokingly. "And while I started as an analyst, cyber was never my

strong suit. I'll be depending on you to assist with that defi-
ciency.

"You okay with this kind of pressure?"

"Honestly? I've been waiting for something like this for a
long time. Everything else I've worked on... bank fraud, ran-
somware rings, black-market crypto... that's all child's play.

"But this? What these Dragon Slayers are doing... it's a different level. Cloak and dagger. It's terrifying, but yeah... I'm all
in."

"Good to hear; now, bring me up to speed."

Carter sighs dramatically, flopping back into his chair.

"Everything, huh? Alright, short version, we have nothing.
It's like they're playing counter-counterterrorism."

"Counter-counterterrorism?"

"Basically, they're adding extra layers for no reason just to
run circles around us. Whenever we think we've got a lead, it
disappears. Information is shifted around, signals rerouted. It's
like a game of digital whack-a-mole, only the moles all have
comp-sci degrees and no social lives."

"Okay, what about the blockchain? If they're moving money,
there has to be a ledger we can trace."

"Yeah, that'd be nice if they were using an ancient relic like
Bitcoin."

"So, they're not using Bitcoin?"

"Nope, these people are using Monero, Zcash... maybe
something even worse. Privacy coins built to lock people like
me out. There's a ledger, but it's buried under layers of encryption and tricks. Trying to follow it is like chasing a speck of dust
in a sandstorm."

He rolls a pen between his fingers, focus narrowing as he
works through the logic.

"Right now, we can only see the money going into the start

of these laundering machines. If this video's fake and they're just here to steal and vanish? Then yeah, that might be it… no more trail.

"But if they're serious, if this is real, they'll have to keep paying out. Which means they'll have to keep moving funds. And that's where I have a plan, the genius that I am."

"And that would be?"

"Anyone in IT knows the biggest issue in a system is the people using it. Someone slips up paying or getting paid… well, that's how we nail the Dragons Slayers to the wall."

"Do you think your team can actually track all of these transactions if they start paying out? If a single payment's being funneled through a dozen channels, won't that waste critical time before we find anything useful?"

Carter smiles, then pushes up from his chair.

"Oh yeah."

He steps out into the hallway, pointing toward the bullpen. Rows of analysts hunched over glowing monitors, typing furiously, faces glued to their screens.

"Look at these beautiful introverts," he says. "A mix of caffeine, Adderall, and autism. It's a terrifying power. God bless the USA."

I try to hold back a laugh.

"Well, it's good to see that you have so much faith in your team. Because I do, too.

"If the Dragon Slayers start moving money to supporters, that would mean the video is already out there, so what's the strategy to contain it?"

"Honestly, it shouldn't be too tricky. If it gets uploaded, taking it down will be a lot easier than tracing its source."

"And why's that?"

"The moment that video hits public view, it's going to be

labeled terrorist content. No platform, genuine or otherwise, wants to bear that kind of heat. The free-speech guardrails? They'll be gone. Every single one. As soon as the label is applied, it's open season on takedowns.

"If the video gets posted, we choke the signal. And without the reach, they're yelling into the void."

Carter throws his arms up in triumph.

"Boss, don't worry. This is my life. Finally, I get an op that really challenges me. You wouldn't believe how monotonous the typical cybercriminal hunt is.

"This… me… art in motion."

"Good to know you're living the dream, Carter. Keep working on the tracking side. I'll loop in Bill and the others about ramping up takedown protocols. Keep me posted, and thanks again for all you've done here. I know you will figure this out. You're the best the Bureau has."

"Geez. If you keep saying things like that, I'm liable to get a big head."

"Pretty sure that ship sailed a long time ago. Now, get back to work. We're depending on you and your team."

Pausing at his door, I turn to look back at Carter leaning over his keyboard, a wicked grin balanced by an intense focus. He might not be the poster child for the ideal FBI agent, but in this cyber conflict, he is definitely the one for this mission.

Heading to my office, my phone buzzes, yanking me back to reality as I read the text message.

It's Victor. Call me now.

I dial immediately.

"It's Grayson."

"We need to meet with you online now. The President requires a briefing on this crisis in four hours, and we need to be ready."

"Understood. On my way."

Yet another one-sided briefing to look forward to, another opportunity to navigate the treacherous waters of politics. It's a waste of time managing optics instead of hunting down the Dragon Slayers.

Squaring my shoulders, I head toward the conference room.

This case isn't just the biggest of my career; it's the first time I'm dealing directly with the administration.

No chain of command to hide behind. Just me, face-to-face with the people who care more about optics than outcomes.

As deputy director, politics unfortunately comes with the territory.

I don't get to opt out.

If I want to lead this team, I must play the administration's game.

CHAPTER 4

THE POLITICS OF POWER

"Those who make peaceful revolution impossible
will make violent revolution inevitable."

-JOHN. F. KENNEDY

I WALK TO the conference room, reviewing some intel on Victor Hargrove and Dr. Hart. I'm all too familiar with their reputations. They're the architects of President Tuff's rise, fluent in the new language of power.

Victor Hargrove is a disgraced former businessperson with a trail of lawsuits, bankruptcies, and failed ventures behind him. After burning every bridge in the private sector, he reinvented himself as a ruthless political fixer.

For the right price, he is more than willing to get his hands dirty.

Victor's history makes him too toxic for any official cabinet role, but that hasn't stopped him from bulldozing his way into the White House. Branded as a trusted advisor to President Tuff, he wields more influence than most sitting officials. Ethics are a foreign concept to him.

Dr. Evelyn Hart keeps a low public profile. A former academic, she built her reputation through groundbreaking studies on human behavior and mass psychology, research that caught the attention of political operatives looking for an edge.

But theory wasn't enough for Dr. Hart. She left academia and quickly carved out a role as one of President Tuff's most effective campaign architects. A behind-the-scenes force in shaping public perception.

While she rarely appears on camera, Dr. Hart is the one scripting the lines the talking heads repeat. She excels at orchestrating narratives with surgical precision, ensuring every message serves the administration's agenda.

Victor and Dr. Hart represent the vanguard of a new age of politics where message control is more important than the truth. Fact checks are just background noise meant to be ignored. It might look like chaos from the outside, but I've been around them long enough to know better. Every move is deliberate. Every spectacle is calculated.

The one thing you can't question is their loyalty. It's blind, absolute, and the main reason they are always given a seat at the table.

The FBI's work is about protecting citizens, not politics. But these days, the line blurs with every decision, even more so with the upcoming election looming over our heads. Tuff won the presidency fair and square, giving him the right to shape policy. It's hard not to wonder how much bending is left before something breaks, especially if a second term comes with even stronger mandates.

Reaching the conference room door, I inhale deeply, trying to shake off my frustration.

Stepping inside, I steady my nerves before switching on the secure line. Hargrove and Hart appear at once, like predators catching the scent of blood.

"Grayson," Victor says smugly, reclining back in his chair. "It's about time you joined. We have a situation."

"Victor. What sort of situation?"

"President Tuff knows about the Dragon Slayers' video. He needs to be certain that this issue is contained. It cannot get out of hand."

The implication is obvious. Failure is not an option.

"We're doing everything we can. My team is rapidly sorting through all the case scenarios."

Victor pounds the table.

"No what-ifs, Grayson! The President desires specific outcomes. He needs to know this is a blip or a hoax, and it will be taken care of fast and discreetly."

"A blip? Agent Diaz thinks we can trace and disable the video, but he's also said that there's a good chance that it'll spread given the viral nature of the content and their networks."

"Government inefficiency at its finest. If a private company were doing this, someone with some actual initiative, this wouldn't even be up for debate. It would already be accomplished."

There it is, Victor's signature duplicity, denouncing the very system he benefits from, basking in its privileges. I'm not going to bite. My gaze instead falls on Hart, whose expression is unreadable.

"Dr. Hart, you know how difficult it is to contain something like this. Once it gets out, there's no possible way to stop it completely."

"Deputy Director, your assessment is accurate. Which is precisely why contingency narratives are already being developed. However, shaping public perception falls within my domain. Your responsibility is operational containment. I trust you'll execute accordingly without requiring intervention from my end."

"This is why merit ought to count, Grayson," Victor sighs

dramatically. "Ingenuity, intelligence, actual success. Look at the Dragon Slayers, failures bent on destroying what they could not create. Jealous losers, bottom-feeders clawing for a taste of what real success looks like."

I resist the urge to engage in this type of debate. His disdain for anyone not in his privileged circle is blindingly apparent.

"Victor, we can reserve the philosophy for later. For the time being, we are prepared to take the necessary appropriate action if the video is uploaded.

"Diaz's team is monitoring the major social sites around the world. Agent Cross' team is poised to bring down physical sites as necessary. It may not be ideal, but it's our best shot."

Victor's smile is bitter.

"Hope your best shot doesn't end with us having to mop up a catastrophe that destroys all this nation holds dear."

"Ms. Grayson," Dr. Hart says dryly, "allow me to remind you of our primary objective... securing the President's re-election. With that in mind, you must recognize the level of chaos and uncertainty this Dragon Slayer situation could generate.

"It cannot be allowed to spiral. It cannot spread. And above all, it must not be permitted to damage President Tuff's public standing in any measurable way."

I try to reassure them.

"Understood, we'll do all we can to make this not be a problem for the nation's election."

Victor places his hands behind his head, snickering.

"Good. We're counting on you. The President doesn't like surprises, and neither do we.

"A little lesson in messaging. When we speak to the President, we'll assure him there's nothing to be concerned about; all is under control. And do you know why we'll say that?"

I remain silent, withholding from them both the satisfaction of a reply.

"Because it's your fucking job! You're here to make President Tuff and our billionaire donors sleep well at night. If you don't, if you don't so much as suggest that any of this is more than a minor irritation or completely fake, then the promotion you've just secured will be the briefest in FBI history.

"I'll personally see to it."

His words drip with venom, laced with the assumption that I'll fold under pressure.

I don't flinch. I expected this. Bill made sure I did.

I lean forward, holding his gaze.

"Listen, Victor. Don't think for a second that my team and I are not doing everything feasibly possible to stop the Dragon Slayers. They're not only a danger to United States citizens but to the world. We take this op much more seriously than you possibly could.

"More importantly, I don't deal in fantasies or fiction. I deal in reality. And the reality is, there's no guarantee that Lancelot's message won't get out. My role is to provide you with the facts, unvarnished, not sugarcoated to suit your contributors."

Victor tries to interrupt, but I continue. My voice is strong and steady.

"You have my word. We're doing everything we can to locate the Dragon Slayers. Hopefully, before the video has a chance to be released to the world. But if it is released, we still will find the Dragon Slayers, break up their syndicate and end their game."

Victor goes quiet, not expecting my pushback. I'll find out soon enough if that earns me his respect or his wrath.

Dr. Hart speaks, her voice brittle.

"Well, that's all nice and good, Deputy Director, but the President does not want to hear probabilities; he wants assurances."

I turn my focus back to her, resolve unwavering.

"In that case, perhaps the President needs to reconsider who he's listening to. Assurances aren't going to stop terrorist networks. Action will."

Victor crosses his arms with a look of exaggerated tranquility.

"Grayson, I appreciate your confidence. But let me make one thing crystal clear for you. In three hours, you and Director Cartwright will be with President Tuff at the Oval Office. When you enter that room, you'd better not make this issue bigger than it actually is."

He sharpens his tone, dropping the pretense, every word now aimed like a bullet.

"We will not let some bullshit fake terrorist fantasy revolution fuck us in this election, and you're the one who is going to make sure that doesn't happen! Understand?"

"Trust me, Victor. If the Dragon Slayers turn out to be a fraud or a front for stolen funds, I'll be the first to celebrate. That would mean no one's been hurt.

"But until we have definitive proof, I won't ignore the other possibilities."

Victor's smile stiffens, arrogance curdling into something sharper.

"Fine. The President will see you at 10 a.m. Let's see if you've found something real by then."

The screens go dark as Victor and Dr. Hart log off without another word. I stare at the empty monitors for a beat, letting the silence settle.

The pressure is already too intense, and we are still very much in the dark.

What happens if the Dragon Slayers are real?

CHAPTER 5

THE WEIGHT OF COMMAND

*"The more laws, the less justice… and
the more wealth, the less virtue."*

- CICERO

THE EMBLEM OF the Dragon Slayers continues to intrude into my thoughts, mercilessly taunting me. I shake off the image and turn my attention to the illuminated screen before me.

The clock displays 6:30 a.m. My team and I have been operating since early morning in overdrive. The President's briefing takes place at 10 a.m., and I need to be well prepared.

I stretch my shoulders, open my laptop, and go to work. Orders need to be dispatched: gear analysis, combat assessments, blockchain leads, dark web surveillance, and linguistics.

First one: To: Gear Analysts. Subject: Priority

Identify everything: helmet, armor, gloves, boots. I want manufacturers and military contracts. If it's restricted, it narrows our list. If not, follow the purchases.

To Carter. Subject: Tracking

Keep an eye out for any major cryptocurrency movements, especially from new wallets. They've got to be shifting funds somewhere if they're gearing up for something.

To: All Mission Analysts. Subject: Dark Web

Monitor for chatter regarding the Dragon Slayers, Lancelot. Look for recruitment and planning.

To: Graham. Subject: Target list

Start a list of probable targets. Focus on billionaires with public linkage to scandal. The Dragon Slayers will likely prioritize those that everyone loves to hate.

Three hours to go before my meeting with the President. Sitting around and waiting is never an option for me. Brooding will not do. I grab my gym bag, craving the release only sweat can bring.

The gym smells of rubber and bleach, quiet except for the ring of weights. It used to be a chore, but this space slowly became my sanctuary over the years. A place to focus, to rebuild piece by piece.

I wrap my hands around the pull-up bar, exhaling as I start. Two reps in, Graham's voice echoes across the room. He's wearing faded clothes, a towel slung over his shoulder, clipboard in his hand.

"Deputy Director. Figured I'd find you here."

I drop down onto the mat and roll my shoulders as I look up at Graham.

"Thought it would be a good idea to get a workout before the circus starts."

Graham waves his clipboard.

"Already on that suspect list you wanted. Will have it to you shortly."

"Appreciate it, Cross, feel free to call me Charlie."

"Deal, as long as you stick to Graham, cause I'm not one to

37

break the chain of command. And hey, congrats on your promotion. I gotta say it's nice seeing you here; higher-ups tend to be glued to their chairs."

"Think I'm just a pencil-pusher now, huh? Let me remind you that I've trained and thrown your men more times than I can possibly remember."

Graham lets out a soft laugh as he sets the clipboard on a nearby bench.

"True. One of my team's favorite things is watching the new guys go up against you. They have no clue what they're in for. Seriously, I'm not here to question your skills. I'm here to figure out what this whole Dragon Slayer debacle is going to cost."

"Cost how?"

"The collateral damage could be disastrous. These Dragon Slayers are tossing money around like confetti, hundreds of millions, possibly billions. That's a massive incentive.

"My squad will be in situations where anyone, even innocent civilians, might become a target. Desperation makes people lethal. I don't like the risk of losing anyone because someone decided they could get rich by taking a shot."

His words linger, heavy and immovable. Beneath the rough exterior of this weathered soldier lies a depth, a man who cares for more than orders and outcomes. He is concerned about his crew, but he also fears the chaos that could be unleashed.

"I'm not going to lie to you, Graham; it's something I've been worried about too. But I promise you this, I'll do everything I can to keep your unit, and everyone else, as safe as possible if this group is legit."

"Fair enough. I'll expect you to come through on that, Charlie. Give me names and addresses, and I'll give you heads. Figuratively speaking."

"Figuratively, huh?"

He shrugs, grabbing his towel and clipboard.

"Mostly."

As Graham heads out of the gym, I get a sense of satisfaction knowing he is on our team. Solid and dependable, if he makes a promise, he will see that it is fulfilled.

Collateral damage. Those two words resonate in my head, sharp and relentless. If Lancelot and his Dragon Slayers have $14 billion, and if they intend to spend it, there's no estimating the fallout.

Vast sums of money do more than buy guns and ammo. The Dragon Slayers can shift balances and spark mayhem.

My arms tremble, and my muscles burn as I complete another set. As I finish my workout, the idea sneaks in again: What if Victor is right, and it's a bluff? A ruse designed to paralyze the FBI, incite panic, and get us running after illusions.

But even though this may be some type of sick charade, the fear generated is enough to ignite a global catastrophe. Folks act rashly when money's involved, families in jeopardy, futures hanging in the balance.

I wipe my towel across my face, trying to get my head clear. Bluff or no bluff, we can't afford to hesitate.

The gym is quiet, but my mind is racing with questions that have no answers.

Who are the Dragon Slayers? What can they really do? Where's Voss?

I've studied terrorist cells, and crime syndicates, but this is different. They're actively arming society. It's a tactical plan, and the devastation will extend much further than their intended targets.

I catch my breath, steadying myself. One thing at a time. I cannot let the enormity of this mission cripple me.

We will beat them; we must.

If we don't, billions of dollars will fuel a war, and it won't be just the billionaires who will pay. Everyone caught in the crossfire will be hurt, one way or another.

I step back from the bar, checking the time. I need to get a move on and hit the showers.

Minutes later, steam fogs the bathroom mirror as I step out, wrapping a towel around myself. The hot water helped, but the tension hasn't left my shoulders. This day started under a cloud of uncertainty, and there's no space for comfort. I dry off quickly and slip into a navy tailored suit.

When I close the last button, my phone vibrates. Lex. The name stings slightly, shame rising before I even read the message.

Hope you're okay!!

I type back a hasty response.

Doing okay. Getting ready for a meeting with President Tuff. Talk soon.

You're welcome. Just let me know when you want that rain check.

Lex is great at slicing through the static. She's not angry… at least, not yet, but I can sense the weight of her patience hanging over me. She deserves more than hollow promises. For now, though, it's all I can spare.

I pocket my phone and hurry back to my desk, booting up my laptop. Emails flood in, each a small piece of nothing. I scroll quickly, sorting updates into mental categories.

The gear specialists confirm Graham's suspicions; most of Lancelot's equipment seems to be prototypes. Some pieces are military-issue, may be connected to private contractors. It's a lead, but not conclusive.

Carter's email stands out.

"Hey, Boss. Got some traction on their dark web operations.

Identified a few nodes that could take us back to their source. Also, Big Tech is ready to cut them off if this video comes out."

Carter's impressive, and he's getting ahead of the right problems. If he's already engaging with the platforms, that's one less headache to deal with.

I rapidly fire back.

"Good work, Carter. Keep monitoring the nodes."

I sit back, stabilized by the sense of relief that a plan is being executed. For the first time this morning, it feels like progress is being made.

The team is mobilizing. Resources are deployed. It's enough for the time being.

Now comes the hard part.

The White House and President Tuff await.

CHAPTER 6

THE ADMINISTRATION'S AGENDA

*""The forest was shrinking, but the trees kept
voting for the axe because the axe was clever
and convinced them that because its handle
was made of wood, he was one of them."*

-TURKISH PROVERB

THE BUILDING IS alive with motion, agents barking into
phones and the distant thud of hurried footsteps. I cut through
all the noise as I head to my next meeting.

The director's office sits at the heart of the seventh floor,
a fortress of glass, steel, and authority. Every detail about it
reminds you of who he is: William Cartwright, Director of
the FBI.

For me, it's familiar ground.

I knock once, firm, and direct.

"Come in," Bill calls out.

Entering the room, I clock the two figures instantly. One
is Simone Wallace, CIA Director.

Early fifties, built like a soldier who continues to embrace a military lifestyle. She stands with perfect posture, hands behind her back, expression unreadable.

Next to her, slouched in the chair with a two-day stubble and bloodshot eyes, is Donovan Pierce. CIA Deputy Director. Early sixties. Looking like he just came back from a black bag op, or a bottle of something strong.

Simone's reputation is carved into the agency's history, a prime example of excellence in service, discipline, and leadership. She shattered ceilings and rose through a system designed to keep someone like her in check.

Her presence commands respect, as she earned it the hard way.

Donovan, on the other hand, is a leftover from a different era. A relic of the CIA's shadowy years, when the agency operated as a rogue autonomous machine instead of a loyal government branch. Times when the lines of power blurred and accountability was never more than an afterthought.

He's the result of when someone's too effective to fire and too dangerous to put on camera.

Bill gestures casually.

"Charlie, you're just in time. Director Simone Wallace and Deputy Director Donovan Pierce have stopped by."

Simone steps forward first, sizing me up like a field report, handshake extended.

"Well, Ms. Grayson, hell of a first day. Welcome to the big leagues, Deputy Director."

"Thank you, ma'am."

Donovan doesn't rise to greet me. He remains slouched in the chair, legs stretched out like he owns the place. He gives me a slow nod and a mock two-finger salute.

Bill continues addressing me.

"We were just wrapping up. Charlie, we need to bring you up to speed on our briefing. Simone?"

"We've confirmed the video is spreading internationally on the dark web. Translated, mirrored, and uploaded across every forum and encrypted messaging network. Whoever's behind it wants it to spread quickly for maximum impact."

I cut in.

"Do you think it's foreign-backed? State actors?"

"We don't think so because of who's reaching out, and that's our adversaries. China, Russia, Iran. They're pinging us directly and through back channels, trying to figure out what the hell's going on. They seem just as confused as we are."

Donovan lifts his head and speaks without looking directly at any of us.

"Even my dirtiest connections are shitting bricks over this."

Simone picks up the thread, as if she's used to his off-the-cuff interruptions.

"The gear in the video is U.S. military surplus, and the currency is U.S. dollars in all the videos. We're not ready to call it domestic yet, but that's where the arrow's pointing."

Bill leans back.

"Keep us looped in. We're flying blind, and I'd rather not crash without warning."

"We'll push what intel we get, but at the moment, this is unlike anything we've ever encountered before.

"Let's go Donovan."

As they leave, Donovan walks past me, close enough to smell the acrid scent of cigarettes trailing off his jacket like a warning label. Before he closes the door behind him, I catch his low, offhand mutter.

"Good luck, kid, you're gonna need it."

Their departure shifts the energy in the room.

"Charlie, talk about hitting the ground running. When I first started, I spent three weeks just shaking hands before anyone needed me."

I manage a weak smile, shaking my head.

"To be honest, I'd rather be busy. I prefer action to inaction. Even if it's a mess."

He laughs, turning to face me.

"That's what I like about you. Always diving right in. That's how I know you're going to make a great deputy director."

"Bill, I've got some files ready for the briefing. Key points we could review together, so you're set to present."

He looks at me quizzically.

"Oh, I'm sure they're perfect... but you won't be handing them off to me."

"What do you mean?"

"You're going solo, I want President Tuff to hear it from you. You're the lead on this, Charlie. The administration needs to hear directly from you.

"Listen. I've got a full day of wrangling with the other agencies and setting up favors in case this thing spins out. This is your briefing. Show them who's in charge."

Bill picks up his suit jacket and starts sliding it on.

"Charlie, if you want the administration to take you seriously, show them you're not just my shadow. Walk in there like you own it... because you do."

I swallow hard, gripping the file a little tighter.

"Are you sure? If what we're seeing is even a tiny fraction accurate, this case could be massive. Victor and Dr. Hart both made it very clear that the last thing I should do is even suggest that to Tuff. But it's a real possibility."

Bill stops and gives me his full focus. For a moment, the

weight of his years settles across his face, softening the usual fire in his eyes.

"Charlie. Administrations change. Policies twist in the wind. Priorities shift depending on who's in the room. But what doesn't change is the work... the values we carry into it. That's what matters.

"You just work the case. Say what needs to be said and don't waste a second worrying about fallout.

"I'll handle any blowback. That's about all I'm good for these days. A human punching bag, absorbing hits and smoothing the political landscape so the real work can get done."

His assurance is an invisible shield, stabilizing my doubt.

"Thank you, Bill."

"Of course. I've got to get moving, and you've got a big meeting coming up. Let's get going."

Bill stops me at the door and rests a firm hand on my shoulder.

"And Charlie. You've got this. You're the best person for this mission."

"Bill... thanks again. For everything."

He pulls me into a warm hug, the kind that says I've got your back, no matter what.

"Don't you worry. This meeting will be a breeze for you; don't overthink it."

"I hope you're right."

"Trust me. I know how to work with Tuff. If I didn't, I'd have been out of my job three years ago."

With that, Bill gives me a departing smile and heads down the hall, lost in the Bureau's noise.

I head out to the black SUV, waiting at the curb. The door opens before I reach it, and the agent inside gives a respectful nod as I slide in.

The drive to the White House is quiet, city blocks blurring past the window in a stream of gray and gold. My mind drifts, uninvited, to the only other time I made this trip. I was sixteen. Navy blue dress and my first pair of heels, flanked by men in uniform who kept calling me "ma'am."

That day, my father was awarded the Medal of Honor. Posthumously.

It should have been a day of honor. Instead, I remember standing in that room, numb, barely able to breathe, cameras flashing as my mother squeezed my hand too tightly.

Everyone called us brave, heroic. But all I felt was hollow. A prop in someone else's story.

Interesting, the memories we keep.

But this time… this time is different.

Now, I'm going back as a leader on a mission with purpose.

The SUV pulls off the main road and takes the side entrance reserved for high-level briefings. A uniformed agent opens the door, and I step out into the cool morning air, my heels clicking sharply on the pavement.

Security checkpoints come in rapid succession… badge scans, facial recognition, pat-downs, escorts. It's a gauntlet designed to remind you where you are and who you're about to face. I pass through each one with silent efficiency, my mind already turning over the key points of the briefing.

Rounding the last corner toward the inner hall, I catch sight of a small group ahead. For a second, I assume they're staffers, maybe aides or advisors.

But something's off.

As I draw closer, the illusion breaks. They're billionaires and corporate titans, faces I've seen on magazine covers and financial broadcasts.

I doubt they're here because of the Dragon Slayers. The

administration is doing its best to keep that quiet. More likely, they're here to make a deal. Campaign support for policy guarantees. All just part of the political game they now play.

Men and women who've publicly attacked each other's politics, tech philosophies, tax structures… laughing and patting each other's backs, like old friends at a country club.

Ideology is window dressing. In the end, they all bend toward the same goal: power and influence. Whatever it takes to keep their world intact.

I keep walking past them, posture tight, steps steady.

Entering the Oval Office waiting room, I immediately spot Victor and Dr. Hart already seated. Their posture is rigid, faces drawn tighter than I've ever seen them, sharp edges carved by tension and control.

Victor scowls at the sight of me.

"Where's Bill?" he asks, clipped and impatient.

"Director Cartwright has other matters to attend to. More importantly, I'm the one leading the Dragon Slayer case."

I take a seat without waiting for permission.

Victor's eyes narrow, voice laced with condescension.

"See? Even your boss doesn't think it's important enough for his time. So tell me, Deputy Director. Have you finally come to your senses? Realized it's a hoax? That this whole thing is being blown into something it's not?"

"Actually, Victor, I'm going to outline exactly what we're prepared to do for every scenario."

I reach into my bag and pull out the case folder, placing it on the table between us.

"Whether this is a hoax, a smokescreen for stolen funds, or a credible threat, we're treating each scenario with the seriousness it deserves."

"First day in the big seat, and you're set on walking into the Oval Office with bad news?"

Victor shakes his head, disdain dripping from his words.

"Your funeral, kid."

Before I can respond, Dr. Hart interjects, her tone crisp and clinical.

"Deputy Director," she says, eyeing the folder as she adjusts her glasses. "I'm sure your analysis is thorough, and I'd be very interested in reviewing it myself.

"However, some advice. President Tuff is a man of action. He has no patience for background data or supporting evidence. Keep your report focused, one or two bullet points at most. Anything more, and he'll stop listening."

Her comments catch me off guard.

Victor's contempt is expected; he's been actively rooting for me to fail since the start of this mission.

But Dr. Hart… her tone isn't kind, but it isn't cutting either. Calculated, maybe. Cold, definitely. But not cruel. Not yet.

And for the first time, I realize… she's actually trying to help.

I nod once, slowly, keeping my expression unreadable.

"Noted."

Victor chuckles.

"Yeah, I've got two bullet points for you. One, the Dragon Slayers are not real. Two, it's not a problem."

"Thanks for your input, Victor."

Before he can fire back, the door to the Oval Office opens with a soft click. A staffer steps in, eyes scanning the room.

"The President will see you now."

I rise, folder in hand, and walk toward the door, every step sharpened by purpose.

Entering the Oval Office is an experience in itself. The space is larger than I remember, elegant, restrained, and brimming with the kind of history that demands reverence.

But I'm not here to be impressed. I'm here with a purpose, with a mission. To protect the country my father served and the one I've dedicated my life to.

President Tuff stands near the Resolute Desk, larger than life in every sense. He's big and broad, built like an aging linebacker who never let go of the weight room. In his early sixties, his suit is crisp, tailored within an inch of perfection, his silver-streaked hair combed with care. Polished. That's always been part of his brand.

Despite the billions behind him and the elite circles he was born into, he's crafted the image of a man of the people, a populist juggernaut. And it's worked. The charm, the swagger, and the straight-shooting rhetoric bought him loyalty in places his résumé never could.

Tuff deserves credit. That kind of influence doesn't come cheap, and it doesn't come easy. He's dangerous in his own way. While the rest of us play by the rules, he knows how to bend them until they break... in his favor.

President Tuff turns as we enter, a broad grin already on his face.

"Ah, Victor, I have to look at your mug this early in the day? I must've pissed someone off."

Victor chuckles, striding forward to shake his hand.

"Always a pleasure, Mr. President."

Tuff clasps him on the shoulder before shifting to Dr. Hart.

"Doc, good to see you too. You catch those new polls yet? That immigration pivot... brilliant. You spun that narrative like a damn maestro."

Dr. Hart gives the faintest reaction.

"Of course, sir."

Then Tuff's eyes land on me.

"And you must be Bill's new deputy."

He walks toward me, extending his hand with the same simple confidence that's made him a media darling for years.

I shake his hand, firm and steady.

"Bill's a dear friend of mine. He said you were sharp as a whip. And if Bill likes you, I like you.

"Just make sure you tell me what I want to hear," he says with a wink.

"It's a pleasure to meet you personally, President Tuff. Though I wish it were under different circumstances."

He lets out a sharp laugh, shaking his head as he moves behind the Resolute Desk.

"Oh yeah, no kidding. Can you believe this crap? Who the hell do these whack jobs think they are? Of all the people to pick a fight with, they go after billionaires?

"Idiots. Absolute idiots. You don't attack the people who make the damn world spin."

Victor is quick to jump in with a well-rehearsed comment.

"Exactly, Mr. President. That's why this Dragon Slayer mess can't possibly be real.

"Right, Deputy Director? Surely, we're not giving serious weight to a bunch of gangsters playing dress-up and making silly threats online."

I can feel their eyes on me. Victor's smug anticipation, Dr. Hart's composed stillness, and President Tuff's subtle scowl, not angry, but expectant.

This is the moment. The kind Bill's mastered for years. Now it's mine.

"That very much could be the case, and at this stage, it's the most likely explanation. We haven't seen any definitive actions aside from the video."

Victor eases back in his chair, clearly pleased. Dr. Hart offers a small, approving tilt of her head. Tuff's scowl softens slightly, but his glare at me doesn't waver.

"However," I continue. "We'd be irresponsible to ignore the possibility that there's more beneath the surface. Which is why we've already implemented precautionary measures... just in case this group is more than talk."

I make it land, not as a warning, but as preparation. I didn't make it a threat. I made it manageable and easy. That's the only language they respect.

Tuff stares at me for a moment, eyes narrowing just enough to make me wonder what's going on in his big head. Then, a grin slowly spreads across his face.

"See? Bill knows how to pick 'em. I tell you... you just reminded me that he still owes me a visit to the clubhouse."

He chuckles, then locks eyes with me again.

"I've got no doubt you'll do an amazing job here, won't you, Deputy Director Grayson?"

There's fake warmth in his words, layered, equal parts charm, expectation, and testiness.

"Of course, Mr. President. My team and I will do everything we can to stop any threats and keep America safe."

"Good... good... good. Because I don't need to tell you how important billionaires are, right? How the hell do you think you win an election without them on your side?

"They fund everything. They shape the narrative. And they know I'm the winning side."

His tone lowers, but the intensity rises.

"If we can't protect them, and the Dragon Slayers aren't a farce, it won't just be a tragedy; it'll be devastating to my reelection. You understand?"

He jabs a finger toward the door behind him.

"I've got some of them already outside, lined up and ready to beg for what they want in my second term."

He straightens, the pressure doesn't ease.

"Don't mess that up, Charlotte. Don't give them, or the markets, any reason to panic from now till November."

"Understood, sir," I say, holding his gaze. "The FBI's mission is always to protect this country, and we'll do exactly that."

He nods slowly, lips pressing into something that's not quite a smile.

"And remember, if you help me, I'll help you. Your career depends on it. You're not irreplaceable. No matter what Bill thinks.

"But hey, you're a sharp cookie, you get that. I can tell. So, I don't need to say anything else, do I?"

"No, sir. I've prepared a full briefing for you outlining our response strategy should the threat escalate."

Tuff waves a hand, already half-turned from the desk.

"Fine. Fine. Nothing I need to read. Just work with Victor and Dr. Hart on whatever."

He casually stretches, straightening his cuffs.

"I've got some executive time before I meet with those check writers for the rest of the day. Always good to make them wait so they understand who's in charge."

He flashes a grin over his shoulder.

"SLY News is doing a segment about the positive poll support I have going into the election. Should be a good one. They're saying they've never seen numbers this high, it's looking like a landslide reelection."

It didn't take the President long to make national security take a backseat to optics.

Victor and Dr. Hart rise as Tuff waves us off, already reaching for his remote, dismissing us without another word.

We leave the Oval Office together, the door clicking shut behind us.

Victor is the first to speak, his voice filled with smug satisfaction.

"See, Grayson? That's how it's done. A man of action is always in control. Follow his lead, and you'll go far."

Dr. Hart doesn't bother looking at me as she pushes her glasses over the bridge of her nose.

"I'll review your briefing documents this afternoon. I want to make sure they align with the tone we need to project."

I give a tight nod, keeping my expression unreadable as they walk away.

By the time I'm back in the SUV, the silence is a welcome shift from the thinly veiled power plays of the West Wing. It doesn't bring comfort... just a quiet space to think.

If the Dragon Slayers are not a bluff, the White House briefings will quickly become exasperating. Political, theatrical, annoying.

This morning's meeting was just the beginning.

Right now, my team is the only thing standing between calm and chaos. We're ahead of the story, barely.

But once it's out there... once fear spreads, markets dip, and billionaires start scrambling for safety, what happens then?

What happens when we're no longer chasing shadows but trying to stop a storm already in motion?

I don't know, and all I can do is be ready for it.

CHAPTER 7

THE WAITING GAME

"The measure of a society is found in how they treat their weakest and most helpless citizens."

-JIMMY CARTER

RETURNING TO THE operations room is like breaking the surface after being submerged for too long in the suffocating politics of the administration. Here at the FBI, everyone works towards the same goal.

This is the way it is supposed to be: a group of individuals concentrated on their tasks, not indulging in posturing or politics.

"Well, Charlie," Bill asks with a knowing smile. "What do you think of Tuff?"

"It was interesting… I came armed with reports, contingencies, and the works. He didn't want to see any details; he just wanted to make one thing clear: we can't mess up.

"There's no room for mistakes with his focus on the election."

"Yeah, Tuff likes to keep them short," Bill says, a hint of

amusement in his voice. "Sounds like you've already figured that out. Keep it high-level, give him the headlines, and you'll be fine."

He stands, straightening his jacket.

"Now it's time for you to get back to what you do best."

He clasps a hand lightly on my shoulder, then moves toward the door without looking back.

I clear my throat and step forward. The room quiets as I look around.

"Alright, everyone. Lancelot's video is still our top priority. It could drop at any moment, and when it does, we need to be ahead of it. So, let's have some updates."

Graham speaks first.

"We've got coverage plans in place for all potential targets. The second it hits, we'll have response units ready to move in."

"All set on my end, boss," Carter says, then hesitates. "That said, one issue. The dark web forums are already starting to light up. There's even chatter bleeding into more public channels.

"If the Dragon Slayers video drops and goes mainstream, we're gonna be in a bind. My team can shut things down fast, but if we're too busy pulling content, we'll lose the ability to track its spread in real-time."

Carter's warning is on target. If we're chasing down copies all day, we won't see their overall strategy until it's too late.

And that's what scares me most. The Dragon Slayers' offer to pay out millions will catch fire, especially with the economic struggles so many people are facing. If that message gains traction, we'll have full-blown crowds turning into accomplices.

My gaze finds Graham, and he's already reading my mind. This was our concern from the start that the citizens we are supposed to protect become collateral damage if war breaks out.

The only way to stay proactive is directly through the social media wave. Someone needs to track the raw pulse of it all.

And I know who that someone is… Maya Lin.

Just an intern a year ago, fresh out of a behavioral analytics program, Maya has uncanny instincts and skills. She is credited with flagging the circulation of a meme that led to the arrest of three domestic terror suspects.

Maya deciphers patterns no one else can find.

If anyone can help us keep up with the tempest brewing, it's her.

"I know just the person that can help us," I say, already moving for the door.

My team needs no further explanation as I hastily head down the hallway. If there's any chance of staying ahead of the Dragon Slayers, I'm taking it.

I spot Maya near the end of a corridor, weaving through a cluster of analysts.

Dark hair pulled into a neat ponytail, her black suit is crisp and no-nonsense, except for the white sneakers that somehow don't undercut her presence. A laptop's tucked under one arm, the other holding a green tea, like always.

"Maya!"

She turns and then lights up.

"Oh my God, Charlie, congrats again on the promotion!"

Maya throws her arms around me in a quick hug, then pulls back with a sheepish laugh.

"Wait, is that, like, not professional? Are we handshakes only now?"

I shake my head, already smiling.

"You're fine. But I have something I need to show you."

"Okay, sure."

I lead her into a side meeting room, shut the door behind us, and motion for her to sit. She settles in, setting her laptop and tea aside as I cue up the video.

"It's best if you just watch," I tell her.

As it begins to play, her eyes narrow with interest. I don't say a word; I just study her reactions.

At first, she's focused and curious. But as the video continues, her posture shifts, and by the time Lancelot finishes speaking, she's still. Her face is pale.

The screen goes black.

Maya blinks and slowly turns to me.

"Holy fuck. Is this real?

"We don't know yet, Maya. It could be. The Dragon Slayers might actually have the fourteen billion. And if they really plan to do what they say…"

Maya cuts me off, eyes wide.

"Then it would be devastating. Oh my God, Charlie, there would be no way to stop this. The sentiment out there right now; people are barely scraping by, while the rich just get richer.

"This concept, with that kind of money behind it? This is bad. Really bad."

"Exactly. Which is why I want you on my team… starting now. I need you tracking sentiment, monitoring the shift in real-time."

"Wait, really? Me?"

"I've worked with hundreds of analysts over the years, and you stood out. Not just because you're sharp but because this is your lane. You're wired for it. Social patterns and trends this is where it'll start, and I think you're the best we've got to handle it."

"Wow, really? Okay, sure. Anything you need, Charlie."

"Perfect. We'll talk about your pay bump and new title later."

She almost spills her tea.

"Wait, what? I get a promotion too?"

"Yeah. This is the biggest case we've got, Maya. Grab your laptop and come with me."

Maya falls into step beside me as we head back toward the operations room, her expression shifting from shock to focus. She clutches her laptop tight, surging with fresh energy as if she has just been let out of a cage.

Back at the ops room, Graham and Carter look up at us, curiosity spreading across their faces.

"I want to introduce you to our newest team member on this case. This is Maya Lin. She'll be playing a critical role moving forward tracking the social narrative."

Graham offers a respectful, steady look.

"Welcome aboard, Maya."

Carter grins, spinning slightly in his chair.

"Ooh, I remember you. The social media savant who helped us take down that one drug syndicate."

Maya shifts under the attention, cheeks blushing.

"Thank you," she says, noticeably flustered. "I just want to say… it's an honor to be working with all of you. I'm happy to be here, and… just tell me what I need to do, and I'll do it."

"Thank you, Maya. Your task is going to be difficult. If their message gets out, and if the Dragon Slayers start paying people, we're going to be facing something we've never seen before.

"You'll be tracking the spread of the message and the people acting on it. Right now, we're in the calm before the storm. But when it hits, we need to be ready."

Carter lets out a low whistle.

"Now that sounds crazy; data is easy. People don't make any sense."

"You're right, they don't. But I see people the way you see data. All the quirks and contradictions buried under noise. It's messy, sure, but that randomness is exactly what makes it traceable. Especially now, with how much people give away online, there are entirely new ways to track and shape behavior. You just have to know where to look."

Carter laughs, faking a drumroll.

"So, what's the strategy, Maya? TikTok dances and memes?"

"Not quite. The trick is to discredit the messengers, not the message. If the public questions the legitimacy of the Dragon Slayers, they'll hold back. Hesitation will work in our favor."

"Doubt is hard to sell when you're brandishing that sort of cash," Graham states. "Lots of people I know would take the gamble for a payout like that."

"Correct, which is exactly why we make them fully aware of the risks. Consequences are built into the message. No one gambles with their future if they think it ends in jail time, or much worse."

"Okay," I say directly. "Looks like we have all the bases covered. Maya, we're glad to have you on the team. Now let's get back to work."

Everyone returns to their desks while Maya pauses, sending a nod in my direction before she exits. She may be young, but her insight is exactly what we're missing.

For the first time all day, there's nothing left to do but let them focus on their assignments.

My mind drifts the second the urgency fades, and the first person that surfaces is Lex. I reach for my phone and text her.

Hey, want to get lunch? Cafeteria?

The response is nearly immediate, a barrage of texts coming back:

YES!

On my way!

I'm so hungry!!

Typical Lex, always ready for whatever if I am there. Her catch-all energy tugs me in like a lifeline.

The cafeteria is overflowing with activity. I spot Lex waving me over to a window table. She's already got her lunch, and mine too, all my favorite things lined up like she read my mind. Her smile is as infectious as ever.

"Hey, boss. Surviving the apocalypse or whatever top-secret mess has you sequestered?"

A mischievous spark dances in her eyes.

"Is it… aliens?"

I let out a low laugh, grateful for the way she could downplay the turmoil.

"Lex, you know better than to call me boss. And no, not aliens, but still classified for now. What have you been up to?"

"Not much. But a bunch of us are heading to Finn Henry's tomorrow night. College basketball playoffs. Drinking, yelling at TVs, it's the ideal way to unwind."

"Lex…"

"Don't Lex me. You've been buried in this case. You desperately need a break. Just one drink. Please, Charlie. Worst case, you leave early. Best case, you get to see Kyle get too drunk and freak out when he loses his bets. It'll be lots of fun!"

I consider her invite, but the gravity of the day has exhausted me.

"I don't know. Things are… strained at the moment. Something big might happen; I need to be ready."

"Okay. I get it. But if you decide to break out of your personal jail cell, I'll be sure to save you a seat."

"Thanks, Lex. If I can't be there, I promise I'll make it up to you."

"No need. Gotta head back. And Charlie… all work and no… well, you know. See you at Finn's."

Lex flashes a grin before slipping away. She's right; letting off some steam wouldn't hurt. But the thought barely has time to take root before that familiar voice inside me shuts it down, cold and sharp:

You don't deserve a break. Not with the Dragon Slayers out there.

Reluctantly, I make my way back to my office, every step dragging me closer to the reality of my immense responsibilities.

It's well past the end of the workday, and I have no companionship except for Lancelot, frozen on my computer screen. It must be my hundredth viewing of him.

This job isn't what other people imagine; they think of action and the thrill of the hunt. It's less exciting and more tedious.

Patience is required. Baiting the trap, setting the pieces, and waiting for the ideal moment to attack. It feels like the Dragon Slayers have learned this skill, pushing us to react instead of acting.

Every tick of the clock that we remain motionless is a win for them.

I shut my laptop down, sending Lancelot's face into darkness. The silence is more oppressive this evening, punctuated only by the late-night cleaning crew. It's been time to go home for a while now. Today dragged on, forged from tension and unresolved issues.

At home, I collapse onto the bed, my body a weighted blanket. I crave sleep, but my mind refuses to comply.

Everything in my head is tangled, turning over and over. The heaviness of what is coming presses down on me like a rock on my chest.

Maybe we'll keep waiting.

Or maybe tomorrow everything breaks.

Ultimately, fatigue prevails, and my mind slips into a restless quiet.

CHAPTER 8

A MESSAGE IN GOLD

"Poverty is the parent of revolution and crime."

- ARISTOTLE

I TRY TO sleep, but my brain won't stop chattering about Lancelot and his broadcast. Endless questions swirl in my mind, needling me...

Charlie, what's the plan? Charlie, don't screw this up. Charlie...

This voice has always been part of my life, fueled by the high standards I have set for myself.

"Enough," I say out loud to myself, checking the clock.

There's nothing that can be done right now. My team is in place, and our strategies are set, but my mind couldn't care less. It keeps spinning, searching, prodding me to move, to do something, even when there are zero options.

It's the same damn voice that tells me to avoid career distractions... fun, rest, even things that might be irreplaceable, like Lex.

The voice that says ambition is my top priority. That success only comes to those who stay sharp, stay busy, and stay ahead. This mentality serves as the foundation I built myself on.

Stillness only makes the self-inflicted taunts louder. Rest is needed but remains elusive. So, I fall back on the only thing that's ever worked.

When I can't settle my mind, I force my body to catch up to it.

A quick look at my phone first. No voicemails. No texts. No missed calls. No news is good news. Ironic.

Dressing quickly, I grab my earbuds and head out the door. It's still dark as my feet hit the pavement, the air refreshing every part of me. Upbeat music playing in my head distracts me from brooding as my body finds its pace. For the time being, it's just me.

The streets of D.C. are half-asleep, washed in that bluish haze that appears before sunrise. Streetlights buzz overhead, casting long, stretched shadows across the pavement.

My body aches from undue stress, but the rhythm of my steps starts to break it all down. Each stride frees me as the city blurs into motion.

There's a welcoming early-morning peace. Just my breath, the pavement, and the steady pulse of a world ready to wake up. It feels like I could outrun my exhaustion, I could keep running forever.

Instead, the alarm on my watch alerts me that it's time to head back.

By the time I shower and dress, the edge has worn off my anxiety. I feel clearer and more grounded. Still tired, but steadier.

Driving to FBI headquarters, I consider the possibility that the Dragon Slayers are all smoke and mirrors. Just a well-crafted lie, meant to throw us off the actual crime and keep us chasing shadows. A ghost story designed to distract.

I've always arrived at work early. There's something about the stillness before the day starts that helps me focus.

The FBI building is almost empty, except for the early morning housekeeping crew shuffling through the halls. As I approach the analyst area, Carter's door is open, and his office is lit up like a Christmas tree.

I pause at his doorway. Carter is completely fixated on his monitor. Still wearing the same clothes, hood covering his head, chewing on the drawstring to self-regulate his stress.

He didn't get in early. He likely never left.

"Still working?" I ask, already knowing the answer.

Carter rubs his eyes, voice dry and scratchy.

"Boss, you're in early."

"According to my watch, Carter. It's seven fifteen."

He gives a lazy shrug, clearly having lost track of time.

"Huh. Not that early, then."

"You didn't leave, did you?"

"Couldn't. The video's one thing, ominous for sure, but that's not what's keeping me here."

Carter turns toward me, eyes bloodshot, face drowning in fatigue.

"It's the money. Fourteen billion dollars. Moved fast, laundered through hundreds of thousands of wallets, broken apart, mixed, cleaned, perfectly.

"Then nothing. Total silence. No trail, no further activity, just gone. And you don't pull something like that off unless you've mapped out every action.

"It's like the best you can do, theoretically speaking."

He takes his glasses off to rub his eyes before giving me a half-smile.

"When something gets under my skin like this, I can't sleep. It doesn't matter how late; my brain just locks onto it and keeps turning the gears until something clicks. It's a good thing… mostly… nothing for you to worry about. A few energy drinks and some eye drops, and I'll be as good as new.

"It may sound odd, but do you know what I mean when you get obsessed with something and the voice just won't stop?"

"Trust me, Carter. I know exactly what you mean. You should try running. It helps."

"I run my mouth. That's about it."

A smile tugs at my lips.

"Got it. Morning briefings in two hours."

Carter gives me a thumbs up and goes back to work, snapping back to his screen without missing a beat. Clearly, his mind is fully committed to our mission, and with his skills, he is an irreplaceable asset.

Back in my office, I slide into the quiet rhythm of work… emails and reports. Some things are moving forward. Some things are in a holding pattern.

A knock on my door with a familiar rhythm interrupts me. Soft, two taps, unhurried.

I don't need to look up to know who it is.

"Come in, Bill."

He steps in, calm as ever, carrying that sense of quiet gravity that always radiates around him. He shuts the door with the same deliberate ease, taking a second before he speaks.

"Morning, Charlie. How's everything looking?"

"Surveillance is active. Response teams are ready. We're positioned for movement. Still no signal or real chatter. Just the video and the missing money.

"Fourteen billion dollars didn't vanish by accident. So maybe… it could all be a smokescreen."

"God, I hope it is."

He deliberately pauses, the kind that hints whatever's coming next isn't going to be good.

"Anyway, Charlie, I've got an update for you from my side. Dr. Hart and Victor would like to start sitting in on the morning briefings. Just to keep the President advised in real-time."

Irritation starts to swell up in me, but I don't say a word. I keep my expression flat, my hands motionless.

And still, Bill notices the emotions I am keeping in check. Of course, he would.

He softens his tone just slightly.

"Listen. If it gets to be too much, if they start slowing you down or stepping on toes, tell me. I'll handle it."

"This is how the game works, Charlie. It's a give-and-take. If they feel like they're in the loop, they stop pushing for access in other ways. And that makes your job a hell of a lot easier."

Dr. Hart and Victor hovering over our every move will turn briefings into political theater, but Bill has a point. This is how the game works. Access buys patience. Inclusion keeps the wolves at bay.

"Bill, you're right. If keeping them in the room makes everything else run smoother, I can deal with them… and all their B.S."

"That's the way to look at it. You're doing great, Charlie. Don't forget that."

He leaves me with renewed confidence, the kind that comes from knowing Bill's in my corner. My team can take anything thrown at us from all sides and channel it for motivation.

My phone remains blank. No new intel. Just static and silence. Except now, politics has a front-row seat.

With my focus sharpened, I make my way to the briefing room.

One by one, my team filters in.

Carter's first, eyes shadowed, coffee in hand. Maya follows, hair still damp, probably from a rushed shower. Nods replace words, quiet acknowledgments of exhausted individuals who've seen too much of each other.

Then there's Graham. Sharp, alert, posture locked in like he just walked off a training floor. It tracks. His job doesn't allow for half-speed... he's the one who must be ready when everything else breaks. Rest isn't optional for him. But even with that edge, I can tell he's been pushing the limit. We all have.

No one says it out loud; no one wants to admit it. But the feeling is unmistakable... the Dragon Slayers' plan may be in motion, and if we don't swiftly unravel it, the fallout will be devastating.

My voice cuts through the gloom.

"Alright, we have no major updates. Nothing transpired overnight.

"There is one change going forward. We'll be implementing a new component in these briefings. Victor Hargrove and Dr. Hart will be checking in each morning. This will allow them to keep the White House looped in."

The screen flickers once, then stabilizes. Their faces are waiting patiently. Cold and observant.

"Good morning," I say with all due respect.

Dr. Hart responds first.

"Good morning. Thank you for letting us join you."

Victor doesn't bother with the formality.

"Enough small talk," he snaps. "Have you found anything that proves the Dragon Slayer video is anything but bull crap... a big hoax?"

He gets right to the point, and to his credit, he may be right.

"As of now, Victor, no, we haven't."

Smugness creeps across his face, claiming his victory.

"But that doesn't change the fact that we have to be prepared. Fourteen billion dollars didn't vanish by accident. And if the Dragon Slayers' claim is real, then we're dealing with something built to scale."

"I'll tell you what we're dealing with," he barks. "That Voss playboy didn't want to pay taxes, so he staged the whole thing. Hires some hackers, drops a creepy video, and makes himself the victim.

"Worst-case scenario? No money was stolen. It's a bunch of Voss' dimwit friends, off in Thailand or Dubai, burning through it all. Boats, clubs, new identities.

"I mean, if you had fourteen billion dollars, would you really turn yourself into a terrorist? Go to war with the most powerful people on the planet?"

"Victor, we have a special unit team working the Voss angle. No updates from them at this juncture. Those possibilities you just shared are on the table... but none of them impact what we're doing here."

Victor sits there, self-satisfied.

"Please let President Tuff know that we'll continue to keep you both briefed as things develop. But as you mentioned, Victor, we can skip the small talk. That's all we've got for this morning, so unless there's anything else, we need to get back to work."

"Fine," he says. "Keep running in circles, Deputy Director."

Dr. Hart interjects smoothly and precisely.

"We need to be reassured that your team is already drafting a response plan... messaging strategy, targeting protocols for potential threats. Please ensure I'm copied on any related reports or documents moving forward. You'll find I have Top Secret security clearance."

Their disconnect is quick. There was no time for me to respond.

My team lets out a synchronized sigh of relief.

"Well, this is gonna suck," Carter mutters, dragging a hand through his hair. "Morning briefings are bad enough without Hart and Victor adding their negativity to them."

Graham doesn't say a word, just shifts in his seat, expression, as usual, unreadable.

Maya says what we all feel.

"Dr. Hart gives me such a weird vibe."

"Second that, "Carter says. "Hey, boss. Just curious. How long do we keep this up if nothing moves?

"I mean, I'm convinced the Dragon Slayers are real. But timing-wise... it's all on them. If they don't push the video, we could sit on this for weeks. Months, even."

"Kid's got a point," Graham says candidly. "Bill's keeping this front and center for now. But a few weeks with no movement? No new leads? This won't stay in focus. Not with how fast the world moves.

"We'll get buried under the next fire. That's just how it works."

All eyes are on me, waiting. I need to choose my words carefully.

"Graham, you're not wrong. That would be the best outcome for us. A large-scale theft with no casualties.

"But the reason Bill's keeping this a priority is because if the Dragon Slayers really have that money, and they plan to use it the way the video implied? To incentivize violence and weaponize public anger?

"That won't end with one event in one city.

"This is about preparation. If this fizzles out, great, we move on. But until then, we assume it's real. We assume that whomever we are dealing with is capable of achieving their objective. And we must stay ahead of them."

I meet each of their eyes in turn.

"So, until we're told otherwise, we stay on high alert. We treat this as a legitimate threat. Understood?"

One by one, they nod. They're all in.

"Perfect. I know you're all doing your best. Keep me posted on any updates, no matter how small."

The meeting breaks without any further fanfare. Everyone heads out to their respective offices, ready to dive back into their work.

By the time dusk settles, I make sure that my team heads home for a much-needed rest. Quiet goodbyes, tired looks, postures slumped by the unspoken burden of having no answers.

I languish behind, attempting to shake off my ongoing uncertainty. The Dragon Slayers stand ready, and here I am, trapped in limbo, waiting for the opening of the curtain. It's always not knowing that incapacitates me the most.

Despite the constant motion, progress is elusive. The team is running on fumes, and I'm no exception. Every step forward feels like ten steps back with no clear direction.

Hope cannot factor into this equation. If the Dragon Slayers are real, the fallout will be devastating. It will be an underestimation on my part. Why didn't I see more, accomplish more, been faster?

Doubt becomes rampant. Each dead lead is a personal failure; every incorrect decision adds to my uncertainty. Victor and Hart's skepticism hangs over me, mocking my deliberation.

What if they're right? What if this is all smoke and mirrors?

Exhaustion has taken up residence in me. My workplace is less of an office and more of a solitary cage. I'm staring blankly into space when my phone buzzes to life, illuminating Lex's name on the screen.

Hey! You think you can make it?

March Madness playoffs. Finn Henry's. You know you want to…

GO SPORTS!!!

Please? We've saved you a spot :)

Lex's text decompresses me. She always knows how to pull me out of my work mindset. But I won't forgive myself if I join her and miss something important here.

I stare at my phone, weighing my options. Another message appears before I can even begin typing:

Last text. So, I know it's classified, and I don't know the details. However, I know you, and I think there's nothing more you can do right now. So, you might as well do nothing over here. With me. Cashing in that raincheck.

A gentle laugh escapes me. Lex has a good point; the team is established; the processes are in place, and leads are being pursued. I've done everything I can, haven't I? But none of it will make any difference at all if I burn myself out before the actual battle begins.

I text her back:

Fine. But only for a little bit.

Yay! I'll see you there in an hour. Don't make me come get you ;)

I let the phone fall onto my desk. It feels like a mortal sin to be going out tonight, a betrayal of the seriousness of what is happening. But Lex is right; I can't be on hold waiting for a break in the case.

It could go on for weeks, maybe months. No one can stay in fight-or-flight mode indefinitely. Not even me.

A subtle joy engulfs me while I gather my things. Lex awaits, offering a rare chance for me to feel human again. The Dragon

Slayers could be out there, so that familiar voice breaks to the surface again.

Don't go. You can't. Not now.

But I choose to ignore that part of me, knowing it will never be satisfied. If anything happens, I'll be ready.

The moment I walk in, I'm enveloped by the spirit and noise of the bar. It is jam-packed with laughter and expectations, as the faint aroma of fried food and loud chatter ensure that this will be a fun night. TV screens are full of life with pre-game highlights promoting the Gators vs. the Tigers.

I spot Lex at a table in the corner, surrounded by acquaintances. Her face lights up the moment she sees me, and she waves me over like she's been anticipating my arrival all evening.

"Charlie!" she says, sliding a drink across the table to me. "I'm so happy you're here!"

I smile despite myself, pressure fading, breathing normally. Former colleagues are enjoying the night's revelry around me, telling stories and jokes over the noise. Their congratulations on my promotion come more naturally now than at my official party.

Lex gives me a gentle nudge with her elbow.

"See? I told you this was way better than pouting in your office."

I don't reply, but she's right, so I take another sip from my drink.

Somebody starts telling a disastrous training drill story, and the group erupts into laughter. In this moment, I disappear completely, slipping into the crowd, hiding from the lurking Dragon Slayers, the ramifications. Most importantly, hiding from the voice in my head that keeps telling me to do more.

As the night wears on, I bask in the feeling that this is the best time I've had in ages. And Lex, she's the reason for it. Her easy, unrestrained laugh tugs at something deep inside me. It's stupidly effortless the way she commands a room without trying.

It was delightfully natural to fall for her. It wasn't dramatic, wasn't some whirlwind affair. It was simple. We fit. Maybe I was too naive to realize how rare we were… or maybe I was smart enough to know that we could not be. Not with my unquenchable desire to succeed.

And now?

Now, I'm here, sitting in the thick of everything I chased, everything I thought I wanted, and I can't stop the question from gnawing at the edges of my mind. If I finally have what I worked for, why does it feel like something's still missing?

If this moment, this feeling, is what makes me feel alive, then what the hell have I been running toward all this time?

Lex. The warmth of her shoulder brushing mine as she leans in to tell me something undoubtedly reckless. Tonight, I will not fight it… I will not fight us getting closer again.

For once, I'm having a good time, a really good time. Just noise, cheap beer, and the kind of laughter that comes easy.

Finn Henry's is packed, wall-to-wall bodies, a sea of jerseys and half-empty pitchers, everyone locked in for March Madness. The energy's loud and reckless, every shot drawing either a cheer or a groan. The place is alive.

Then, without warning, the screens flicker a few times. A couple of people notice, groaning softly, but it's nothing major, barely enough to raise concern.

Then, every TV cuts to black.

A wave of confused shouting breaks out.

"What the hell?"

"Fix the damn game!"

Bartenders scramble, jabbing remotes and checking wires.

My heart is pounding against my chest, deafening all the sound around me as an image appears on all the TV screens, engulfing us in his presence.

Lancelot.

At first, it feels like a night terror, a cruel trick being played by my overworked mind. But it's all too real. Dressed in his polished black-and-gold combat armor, Lancelot fills the frame with the same calm intensity that has haunted me for days.

His voice cuts through the bar like a blade, firm, deliberate, utterly commanding.

Mankind has talked of dragons for centuries,

Monsters of unimaginable strength and boundless greed.

Lex grabs my arm, her hand clenching tight.

"Charlie, what the hell is this?"

I can hardly hear her words.

Everyone in the bar is transfixed, wide-eyed with shock, jaws dropped open.

They are the makers of war, the source of pol-
lution, the reason so many hunger.

Their greed is the cause of humanity's misery.

Lancelot's words boom, each syllable uttered with intent, each pause deliberately planned. I scan the patrons, taking in the stunned faces of strangers, colleagues, and Lex.

The murmurs begin again, a subdued buzz of incredulity making its way through the gathered crowd.

Someone near the bar shouts out, "Is this a fucking joke?"

Lancelot's mask pierces through the screens, captivating the world with his somber words.

We are the masses.

We are everywhere.

And we will not stop until the dragons fall.

The screen cuts to black, and for a second, nobody stirs. The bar falls into a steady stream of awestruck whispers.

Each pause, each line resonates with a quality of unavoidable truth.

It's the same video that I have memorized word for word, but now it's come to life.

Lex turns to me, her face pale.

"Charlie. Is this… is this… your secret op?"

I just look at her, my eyes releasing a silent yes.

The panicked chatter around me dies down, replaced by the overwhelming pressure of this new development. Millions of people will replay that video as I grasp at straws.

The Dragon Slayers have awakened.

Their message is impossible to ignore.

Seventy-two hours.

The countdown has begun.

CHAPTER 9

WHEN WORDS IGNITE

"It does not require a majority to prevail, but rather an irate, tireless minority keen on setting brushfires of freedom in the minds of men."

-SAMUEL ADAMS

THE DRAGON SLAYERS' broadcast opens Pandora's box, and there's no closing it now.

Noise swells around us, panicked bar patrons, pushing, shouting, swearing. Voices talking over each other as if anyone here has answers. Phones are out, notifications pinging, people recording, calling, texting.

But for me, it all narrows.

This is the confirmation we were bracing for, the first shot has been fired.

I look at Lex. She already knows.

"I have to go," I say with no hesitation.

Lex's face shifts from panic to concern, and I know then that she will not stop me.

"Be safe," she whispers in my ear.

One last look, then I turn pushing through the side door into the street, as a blast of cold shocks life back into me. My phone is burning up with calls and texts.

Right now, there is only one person that I need to talk to... Carter.

He picks up on the first ring.

"What the hell happened, Carter!" I exclaim. "How the hell did they hack the feed?"

"Boss. That's the thing," he declares tensely. "They didn't. No hack, no digital breach. Everything's normal for the networks. Which means..."

"Shit. They took the uplink site," I affirm, finishing his sentence.

"Yeah. That's our best theory, especially since they aren't responding. We've already got local PD en route, and Graham's team is closing in."

"We knew the Dragon Slayer video could get out. I don't think we expected it on this large of a scale. How's our response plan holding?"

"We're on it. Total shutdown protocols in place, every platform and outlet. We're removing and tracking every upload in real-time.

"This is it; the Dragon Slayers are finally moving. The good thing is this gives us something to track them."

"Carter... that's good, but it's out now. Their clock's started. We've got to stop this. Fast. Get ready for a full briefing soon. I'm on my way back to HQ. I'm sure it's going to be living hell."

The call with Carter ends as Bill's name lights up the screen.

"Charlie, you're on your way here... right?"

"Will be there shortly. Bill, we knew this could happen. We planned for it. Set the contingencies. But that doesn't mean it's going to get any easier."

His background noise is a low roar of phones ringing and voices colliding. He's already in the fire at FBI HQ.

"I've got numerous calls coming in. This is going to trigger big moves from the administration. Just… be ready, okay?"

"I will be. And I'm not letting the Dragon Slayers get away with this."

"Charlie, it is going to be a long day tomorrow. Let me know if you need anything. I'll be tied up most of the day. Press conference, briefings… well, you know the ropes."

"Understood."

Our call ends, and for now, I only have to maneuver the road in front of me. Traffic lights flickering green to red, sirens threading through the distance, the city shifting beneath the weight of something it doesn't understand… yet.

There is no pulling back. The world has seen Lancelot's' message. Maybe that was the whole point.

Doubt on my part remains. I can't help wondering if this is just a cruel tactic.

Threats are easy to make when no one's bleeding. Talk about revolution while dressed in myth and hiding behind masks is effortless.

But what if the Dragon Slayers meant every word?

It's one thing to claim you'll tear down the most powerful people on the planet. It's another to do it using the system built by these billionaires, buying silence and access. Funding your war like a corporation funds expansion.

If the Dragon Slayers are serious, then they will be able to purchase the necessary tools needed to destroy the framework built by these same plutocrats.

Then there's no stopping what comes next.

I pull into the parking lot, making a mad dash to the

entrance. Security is already tighter; extra guards are posted at the doors, faces somber.

This broadcast has triggered every alarm the FBI possesses.

Inside, it's the same, agents flood in, phones pressed to ears, quick conversations layered with urgency.

I head straight for the DEFCON room as my phone buzzes mid-stride.

Of course. Victor.

I answer, assertively.

"Victor."

His voice barrels through the line, sharp and loud.

"What the hell happened? How could you let that fucking video get out there?"

"Victor. You were advised that this could be a possibility. And my team is responding with every feasible protocol."

"Full update in ten minutes from you," he snaps. "Dr. Hart will join us."

Victor hangs up on me before I can confirm his request.

The pressure is mounting on their end. And it's only going to get worse... a lot worse.

I have just a few minutes to prep for Victor's meeting. Hopefully, my team has some much-needed updates, so I quickly head that way.

The DEFCON operations room is in high gear. Carter shifts just enough to speak without breaking focus.

"Hey, boss. We've been waiting for you. Graham's patched in. He's airborne, fifteen minutes out. Local PD should beat him there."

"Thanks. The Dragons Slayers' message is out. Now it's a question of whether they will deliver or if this is still some kind of bullshit propaganda.

"Since intel points to them physically securing a satellite

uplink site, we must take them at their word. Which means we treat the seventy-two-hour warning as active.

"Graham, once you hit the facility, I want a full sit-rep. Prioritize any signs of staging, signals, or on-site equipment."

"Copy that, Charlie," he says through the static.

My commands continue.

"Carter, your focus shifts to the payouts. Anything large. If they move money how the video implied, we'll have multiple opportunities to catch someone in motion. Maybe even trace it back up the chain."

"Already on it," he affirms, pulling up another window.

"Maya, stay on social. I want live tracking of the narrative... any accounts showing an organized push or sympathy. Anything that smells like coordination, flag it. Tag known bot networks but prioritize real traction."

"Got it, Charlie. So far, lots of people are calling it fake. Fed trap, psy-op, whatever spin fits. Which, honestly, works in our favor, for now. Keeps people cautious."

She pulls up a scroll of trending keywords, the blur of hashtags and looping reposts accelerating by the second. One post's comment section flashes across the screen:

Nice try, Fed Daddy.

Not clicking that cursed link.

Anyone who thinks this isn't a one-way ticket to jail is an idiot.

Maya looks at me, her face flushed with concern.

"Charlie, there's another narrative gaining traction. It's not about the threat. It's about the target. They don't care if the Dragon Slayers go after billionaires. Some of them are cheering it on."

She taps a few posts that scroll across the upper display.

I hope they're actually real.

Billionaires need to be held accountable.

Good. They deserve it, and everyone knows it.

Maya narrows in on a longer post, climbing fast in engagement, shared by a mid-tier political influencer.

"Wake up, people. Billionaires do not become extremely wealthy through their efforts alone. They steal their wealth from people, from you. They use the backs of collective labor to increase their wealth. Its human exploitation. The only minority destroying America is the billionaires.

"EAT. THE. RICH."

She turns toward me.

"That one's already been reshared by three other verified accounts. It's not fringe, but most people think it's too good to be true. They support the idea in theory, but they don't believe it can happen, so they are dismissing it as fake."

"Okay. Thanks, Maya. Focus on the major accounts pushing that narrative. Prioritize traction and reach. I want eyes on anything that could escalate sentiment.

"Stay on it, everyone. It's going to be a long night and an even longer morning."

A glance at the time, two minutes until the call with Dr. Hart and Victor.

The walk to my office is short, but the noise in my head doesn't let up. I close the door behind me, drop into my chair, and open the laptop.

The feed connects instantly.

Two windows load. Victor in one, pacing in what looks like a conference suite. Dr. Hart in the other pane, seated in a pristine office, hands folded, motionless.

Victor is shouting, his footsteps echoing faintly through his mic.

"Futures are down nine percent, *nine*, and that's trillions evaporating because of some stupid video! A fake video, no less, and there's still no proof anyone's getting paid. Just fear and the markets are bleeding over it."

His rant doesn't slow when I connect; if anything, it sharpens the second he sees me.

"There she is," he roars, spinning toward the camera. "Grayson, explain to me how you let this happen! How something this destructive went live under the FBI's watch."

His tone spikes, indignation masking panic.

"We are hemorrhaging value across every major sector because the public saw a theatrical manifesto stitched together by cybercriminals in Halloween costumes. How the hell did you let them hijack a signal like that? Was no one at the Bureau monitoring the feeds?"

"Victor, it wasn't a hack. The Dragon Slayers physically took over the uplink facility. That's how they broadcasted it, they were there."

For a split second, his expression falters, just long enough to register what that means. But it's gone as fast as it appeared.

"Then clean this up! Here's how this goes. Whatever you find, we call it a cyber-attack. A glitch in the system that allowed a breach. I don't care. What we're not doing is letting anyone think there was a coordinated assault on U.S. soil. That kind of story doesn't get out. Understood?"

I don't respond right away.

It would be a lie. A deliberate one. True, letting the public believe this was done remotely, that it's just another faceless hacker breach, would take the edge off their fear.

The alternative? That the Dragon Slayers executed a flawless physical assault on a hardened comms site and vanished without a trace? That makes them real. Legitimate. Capable in a way that changes the equation entirely.

And right now, that's the last thing we need.

My response is direct.

"I understand. We'll keep the administration posted. Updates are coming in every minute."

Victor drags his hand down his face, rapidly scrolling through his phone.

"This is a complete nightmare. Government agencies can't stop a damn video from airing? Useless. Absolutely useless."

It's ironic coming from him, considering how tightly he's wrapped around the system's throat, but that's always been his angle. Disdain sells. Rage wins.

Dr. Hart's facial expression hasn't changed since the call started. Flat. Reserved.

"Now that the message is out," she says curtly, "my role takes precedence."

"First priority is locking the narrative. These individuals are to be labeled anti-American repeatedly. That association must be immediate.

"Any public debate about inequality can be reframed as destabilizing rhetoric. If they question the system, they're sowing doubt in a time of crisis, potentially aligning with domestic threats. That framing must be present in every communication moving forward. The message needs to be clear: the country can't risk a change in leadership during a threat like this. If we manage the response effectively, it positions the administration as the only stable option."

Of course, Dr. Hart's main objective is pitching strategy. It's impressive how fast she pivots. To be fair, she's worried about the same things as I am. The difference is she sees the threat and smells opportunity.

Dr. Hart doesn't blink as she continues.

"Ideally, the correct management of this crisis will require competence from your team. We could position this as a platform of stability. Law and order. And if executed properly, that narrative could secure the President's re-election."

She says it as if it's a weather report. No emotion or hesitation.

Just another outcome to shape. Another story to sell.

My reply is simple.

"To be clear, Dr. Hart. Our top priority is validating that the Dragon Slayer threat is real, and if so, taking them down.

"If they're serious about pulling this off, they'll need infrastructure. That means movement, which means they'll leave tracks. That's how we locate them and put a stop to their scheme."

Victor cuts back in, his voice cracking through the feed.

"Oh, you fucking better stop this, Grayson. Because if you don't…"

He stops himself and then points straight at the screen.

"We're meeting with President Tuff tomorrow morning. And you had better have what he wants to hear. Real intel. Real progress. Or else…"

The call disconnects. Classic Victor.

His pressure is one thing. Dr. Hart's spin is another. Next up to bat, President Tuff. Demanding answers, demanding certainty. And I'm the one expected to deliver the perfect pitch.

This is a different scale. A different game. Nothing I've done before even comes close, never this public, never this critical, never in my wildest career dreams.

My genuine hope now is that this is still some kind of misdirection. If not… then this wave of terror will turn into a tsunami.

I switch lines, my pulse steadily rising.

"Graham what's the update from the site?"

"Charlie. It's bad."

"Christ, how many casualties?"

"None… but that's actually a problem.

"The Dragon Slayers pulled this off perfectly. No casualties. Every employee was tied up. They got the drop on everyone without firing a single shot.

"That kind of precision? It screams inside support. And there are five people unaccounted for."

"Staff?"

"Yeah. Confirmed shift logs show they were supposed to be on-site. They're gone. No signs of struggle. I don't think they were taken hostage."

He doesn't have to say anymore.

I already know.

"These five employees, they helped them. They must have been paid. This is exactly what the Dragon Slayers are promising."

"Charlie, that's what I'm thinking too. There's more, and you're not going to like it.

"Most of the system data's been wiped. Whatever they used to push the signal, it's clean. Maybe Carter can dig something out, but whoever did this knew what bases to cover."

"And the surveillance?"

"That's the thing, they left it. Full feeds, multiple angles."

He's quiet for a second.

"Charlie, I'm sending you something now. You'll want to see it."

The file pings through. I open it without a word.

Grainy security footage fills the screen. Standard angle, fixed overhead, the entrance hallway of the uplink facility. Nothing at first. Just static hum, timestamp flashing in the corner. Footage you'd scroll through a hundred times without blinking.

I watch anyway, bracing myself for what will show up next.

And then he appears.

Lancelot.

Center frame. Full battle armor, black and gold. Moving with purpose like he's done this a hundred times before. Other Dragons Slayers line up beside him, each in matching gear, weapons in hand, formation tight, flawless.

Their message is not one to be lost in the digital void.

They wanted to be seen.

They wanted to be heard.

No longer a myth.

The Dragon Slayers are real.

CHAPTER 10

THE MYTH BREAKS

*"Property monopolized or in the possession
of a few is a curse to mankind."*

-JOHN ADAMS

I AM COMPLETELY captivated by the surveillance video; the footage grows more alarming with each replay.

Lancelot stands on screen, an almost godlike figure encased in black and gold armor. Every tiny detail burns itself into my mind as I incessantly analyze it for any hidden clues.

The Dragon Slayers wanted to be seen.

Enough, I tell myself, turning my attention to the call with Graham.

"I have to brief President Tuff first thing in the morning. I'll be flying right out to the facility link after the meeting. We'll start interrogating the staff as soon as I land."

"Copy that. We're already coordinating with local PD, doing everything we can to get intel on the five missing employees. If they helped the Dragon Slayers, they're priority one."

"Roger that. Everything hinges on what they know."

I kill the feed, push away from the screen, and head for the DEFCON room. Carter, Maya, and Bill need to see this. Any doubts have now been ruled out.

The Dragon Slayers are no longer a myth.

The second I step inside the room, Carter and Maya look up, searching me for a glimmer of hope. Bill's at the back monitor, arms crossed, locked in position.

"They're real," I say bluntly.

"How real?" Bill asks, his voice skeptical.

"Full footage. The Dragon Slayers. Lancelot. Clear as day."

Carter pushes his glasses up, blinking fast.

"Wait, really them?"

I pull up the file on the central monitor.

"Take a look for yourselves. It's them, casually walking through the uplink facility. They purposely didn't delete the footage. They wanted to be visible. Wanted us to know that they're not just some masked anarchists posting propaganda videos."

Bill seems detached from us, rocking back and forth as he watches every move the Dragon Slayers make with their unshakable presence.

"This is bad, the broadcast, the coordination, the message. All of it.

"Now the only thing left is whether they're going to pay up, because if they start distributing billions to people helping them, that's when this becomes insurmountable."

Bill has always been the rock in every storm, the one who never doubted that the Bureau would win. No matter the threat, no matter the stakes, he believed the system would sustain the load.

I've never seen this level of concern in him. Not once.

He turns to me, his voice low but steady.

"Charlie, I know you understand how even more critical this op has become, and what will happen if we don't stop the Dragon

Slayers. I need you and your team to step up to this challenge. The entire nation, maybe even the world, depends on a successful outcome from us.

"I need to prepare for press conferences and meetings tomorrow. You all need to act. Push. Fight. Find any leverage you can. I'm counting on all of you here, especially you, Charlie."

His directives are like verbal blows.

"Of course, Bill. We will not let the Dragon Slayers get away with this," I say, unwavering, despite the whirlwind inside me.

Bill gives us a rigid look, a show of absolute resolve, and without another word, leaves the room.

"Boss, we've taken down tens of thousands of uploads, but for each one removed, three more appear in its place. They knew exactly how we would respond."

Maya's expression is grim as she interjects.

"It gets worse. They have this new VPN, and darknet guides are all over the place. They are actively teaching millions how to use their secure systems."

Carter swivels in his chair, fingers tapping a restless rhythm against the console.

"If they follow the Dragon Slayers' playbook to the letter, it's going to be almost impossible to catch anyone. Seriously, full encryption, burner devices, dead drops, decentralized comms, it's airtight.

"But they're going to be working with a lot of people. And the more people involved, the higher the probability is that someone screws up. That's when we get them. My team's hyper-focused on it, chasing every signal, every mistake, the second it happens."

The room feels like it's tipping, momentum sliding in the wrong direction.

Asking the next question is like volunteering for bad news, but I don't have the luxury of avoiding it.

I turn toward Maya.

"How's public sentiment trending?"

Maya taps a few keys, pulling up a live stream of trending keywords, the graphs climbing fast.

"It's ramping up. People have had just enough time to start digesting it now. Thankfully, a good chunk of the country's still asleep, but the ones who are up and paying attention are splitting into two camps.

"The first group thinks it's real. They see it as a legitimate threat, and they're not scared. If anything, they're pushing the message that it's about time. That finally someone's doing something. So yeah, the Dragon Slayers are already starting to build solid support.

"The second group thinks this is either a trap set up by the government or a hoax. They're still dismissing it, mainly from disbelief in the execution."

She pauses, scrolling through a wave of posts piling up by the minute.

"Charlie, no one appears to be against the Dragon Slayer concept. The only pushback so far is from accounts tied directly to the administration, and even they haven't started spinning serious anti-Dragon Slayer messaging. At least, not yet.

"If they really start paying out, it's going to be devastating. Even if the platforms ban posts, shadow accounts, and lock people out just for liking or sharing the content, it won't matter.

"Once people believe there's actual money behind it, they're going to see the Dragon Slayers as the ones helping the common people. The administration will be perceived as protectors of the elite. That's a war we can't win if it breaks wide open."

Maya's right. And she's not pulling any punches, laying it out exactly the way I need to hear it. It's one of the reasons I'm grateful she's here.

"Thanks, Maya," I say sincerely. "Carter and you are both doing a fantastic job.

"Now let's regroup. You two stay on this as best you can. I need real-time updates for the report with the President tomorrow.

"I'm going to grab a few hours of rest in the dorm. After the meeting tomorrow with Tuff, I'm flying out to the uplink site to meet Graham. We're going to start interrogating the on-site staff.

"Our focus remains on the five missing employees. They're either collaborators or hostages."

"Boss, Graham already sent me the list. I'm digging into them now. You'll have a file ready by the time you land."

"Appreciate that. If anything happens, anything at all, wake me up."

I leave the DEFCON room behind, my steps echoing faintly in the quiet halls.

As hard as it is to even think about getting sleep right now, my meeting with Tuff will demand that I am sharp and on point. There can be no mental lapses.

The dorm area includes a repurposed wing of offices, with a few cots thrown in for agents who have to stay on site. It's no better than crashing on a gym mat, but at this point, anything will suffice.

I find an open cot wedged between two walls and drop down without ceremony.

As I lay there, I wonder if the CIA might have some updates, so I enter Donovan Pierce's number.

It rings twice before a gruff voice picks up.

"It's Pierce..."

"Donovan, it's Charlie."

"Who?"

"Charlotte Grayson.

"Who?"

"The Deputy Director of the FBI. We met in Bill Cartwright's office."

He pauses, then coughs out a dry laugh.

"Oh. Right. G.I. Jane. Yeah, I remember you."

I ignore the nickname.

"The Dragon Slayer's video went live. It looks like they physically seized an uplink site for the feed."

There's no panic in his voice.

"Well, shit. Those crazy sons of bitches actually did it."

"They did. Any intel on your end? Anything that could assist us?"

Donovan lets out a faint grunt.

"Listen, kid, I don't really do the intel thing. I'm more of a… facilitator of desired outcomes. Plus, we both know the CIA's main purpose isn't always to stop chaos. Most times, we're the ones lighting the damn match."

He lets that sink in for a moment.

"But hey, it's admirable, what you FBI scout types try to do. Real commendable. So good luck."

The phone disconnects.

What the fuck.

How is this guy a deputy director?

Either he's been collecting dust in enough back rooms to fall upward… or he's really good at something the rest of us don't see, but it's definitely not inter-agency cooperation.

I tap Carter's name on my phone.

"Something change, boss?"

"I need you to check out an agent for me. Donovan Pierce. CIA."

"Damn. What a twist. The Dragon Slayers are in the CIA now?"

"Not quite. I just need to know who we're dealing with. That guy is either a washed-up prop or a dangerous menace, and I'd like to know which it is."

"Copy that. I'll see what I can find."

After hanging up, I keep checking my phone; I find a text from Lex, time-stamped hours ago.

Hope everything's alright. Sorry for the bad timing.

Carefully, I select the words I will type back.

Hey. Things are a little crazy. I promise I'll check in as much as I can.

Also, last night at Finn Henry's. One of the best nights I've had in a long time. You have nothing to feel sorry about.

I stare at the message a second longer before hitting send.

Those few precious hours at the bar with Lex made me feel human again. That sensation begins to fade as I lie on the cot, coaxing myself to sleep.

Micro-sleeping has been a personal survival skill of mine. Small bursts of deep rest when full sleep isn't an option. I honed this skill years ago, blending in meditation and deep breathing to wipe my mental slate clean.

Right now, I need this sleep routine to work, to re-energize me for what comes next with Tuff. I close my eyes, focusing only on the inhale, the exhale. In, slow. Out, slower. As still as I can manage.

The faint image of the Dragon Slayers' emblem, the dragon pierced by a sword, overwhelms me. I push it away, instead coercing myself to chase the rhythm of my breathing.

In.

Out.

In.

Out.

Slowly, the edges of my consciousness start to blur. My surroundings fade into oblivion as I drift into sleep.

But rest will not erase my burdens.

CHAPTER 11

A BILLIONAIRE'S EGO

"Behind every great fortune is a crime."

-Honore De Balzac

IT WAS NOT a refreshing sleep. I check my phone; the alarm is ready to chime with just one more minute before I need to rise and confront the next crisis that awaits me.

Still, it's more rest than I expected to get. Rubbing the fatigue out of my eyes, I force myself into motion. No time to waste.

The dorm area is not even close to standard lodging, but the showers have hot water and high pressure, which is enough for me. Dressing quickly, I grab the spare clothes I keep stored here, another habit from years of living at work more than anywhere else.

My level of preparation goes beyond what the FBI expects from its agents, but it's how I've always operated; it's who I am… or at least what I've molded myself to be.

Always ready. Always moving.

Time to see the current state of affairs.

I enter the DEFCON room, noting that nothing appears to have changed.

Carter's still at his station, bloodshot eyes locked onto the monitors, fingers hammering away in perpetual motion. Maya is out cold in one of the side chairs, wrapped in her oversized hoodie.

"Any updates?" I whisper to Carter.

"Hey, boss. Right now, no big movements. It's nonstop damage control for my team; we're scrubbing the Dragon Slayer's video every time it surfaces.

"People are getting crafty now. Re-editing it, splicing it into other footage, trying to dodge auto-filters. But so far, we're handling it."

Behind him, Maya stirs, pulling her hood back and yawning herself awake.

"Charlie, sorry, I just… I was just resting my eyes."

I wave her off immediately.

"Maya, first thing you're going to do is go get some actual sleep. Don't worry about any schedule other than what works best for you on this. I know you'll give it your all."

"Okay. Got it. Honestly, I could crash for a few hours. My brain needs to recharge."

Maya scoops up her things, and before heading out, gives me a quick update.

"Charlie, the same general trends are still holding. People are watching and waiting. The big variable now is what the administration's going to do. That's the piece that will trigger public reaction."

"Understood. We'll have a much better idea about that in about an hour or so. Don't worry, Maya, I'll keep you posted."

She gives a weak thumbs-up and slips out.

I turn back to Carter.

"So, no big shifts yet?"

"Nothing major. Still digging into the five missing staff. We have some leads, but it's going to take time to piece it all together."

"We're moving in the right direction. Carter, I really, truly appreciate what you're doing here. I know how hard you're pushing. Make sure you get some rest as well."

"It's what we do. And don't worry about me, I'm basically a functioning insomniac."

Leaving Carter alone to continue his caffeine-fueled hunt, I make my way up to Bill's office. Reaching his door, I knock lightly, half expecting no answer.

His voice calls out, low and gravelly.

"Come in."

I push the door open to find Bill at his desk, wearing the same suit as yesterday. The deep lines carved in his face are more pronounced.

"Morning, Bill. You were here all night, weren't you?"

"Yep. Just like I know you were too, Charlie. Don't worry about me. The makeup team will work some miracles on this old mug before they shove me in front of any cameras today."

"Any idea how you're going to spin things?"

"I've already received my orders. We're going with a hack. Digital breach. No physical intrusion. The Dragon Slayers aren't real; they're just a bunch of online terrorists stirring the political pot."

"Bill, we know that's not true."

"Charlie, you know we don't always tell the complete story to the public. Sometimes it's about preventing panic. Sometimes it's about preserving operations. Sometimes, it's just because we need misdirection. This isn't new. And it's not pretty. But it's necessary."

The truth is, he's not wrong. It's something I've known for years but never liked admitting out loud. Within the Bureau, facts are filtered, shaped, and sometimes even inverted depending on what a situation demands. We classify, we redact, and we twist timelines because the truth, raw and unvarnished, doesn't always serve the mission at hand.

"Bill, I get it. I do. If people knew the Dragon Slayers pulled off a full physical breach, and if they knew about the money, it would be mass hysteria."

He exhales slowly, the kind of breath that carries years of compromise. For a moment, his eyes lose focus, as if he is daydreaming about every trade-off, every line he crossed in the name of duty.

Bill catches himself and blinks whatever he was thinking away. With a firm voice, he continues to address me.

"You're right about a lot of it. And now, Deputy Director, you have to walk into the lion's den. Dr. Hart, Victor, Tuff. It's not going to be as easy this time.

"You know what you need to do. Tell them what they want to hear. Bend when you must, but don't break."

"Bill, I understand and appreciate your advice. I won't let you or the Bureau down.

"After my meeting at the White House, I'm flying straight out to the uplink site. Graham is already there. We'll start talking to the staff, see if we can determine what really happened. Hopefully, we can get our hands on those five missing employees."

"Great to hear. It'll get you back to the serious work. This mess in D.C. is just theater compared to what you're doing."

"Exactly, I just have to survive today's briefing with Tuff first."

"Trust me, Charlie. You'll do great. I'm just concerned about what's going to happen next. But if I had to pick anyone to have standing beside me when this gets worse, it would be you.

"Now, get a move on. Tuff doesn't tolerate tardiness, except of course, if it's his own."

As I make my way to the lobby, Bill's words resonate deep, his pep talk sending a rush of fortitude through me. Everyone should be so lucky to have a mentor and leader like him.

An unmarked SUV waits by the curb to take me to the White House. I climb inside, settle down, and force myself to focus on the meeting.

I have no updates for the administration. I'm walking straight into the Oval Office as a designated punching bag.

But that's not what's gnawing at me the most.

It's the reaction.

As Maya said, it's not just what the Dragon Slayers do that matters. It's how the administration responds. And if the wrong choices are made, it will add more public fuel to the Dragon Slayers' cause, more than anything they broadcast.

Given President Tuff's dismal record at handling crises, I don't have high hopes. His default move has always been to overpower, to bully, to crush anything that pushes back. It's worked for him against smaller threats and weaker opponents. Against people who couldn't afford to fight back or were simply too scared.

But the Dragon Slayers are different. They're here to make a point.

If Tuff tries to strong-arm them the way he does everyone else, it's not going to end well. There will be serious consequences for everyone.

The SUV glides through the White House gates, tight security waiting for my arrival. A staffer waves me through without ceremony, ushering me toward the security checkpoint inside.

I tighten my jacket, steadying my breath. The second I clear security and step into the main corridor, he appears.

Victor.

He's pacing with a phone pressed tight to his ear, speaking in a low, clipped tone.

"I don't care what the models say. Do not let the markets open like this. You hear me? Keep the circuit breakers ready. No headlines about free falls. We get the message out that this is under control. President Tuff will issue a response shortly. That's all anyone needs to hear."

Whoever's on the other end clearly isn't appealing fast enough because Victor's jaw tightens like he's about to break the phone in half.

His eyes lock on me instantly, narrowing into cold, accusatory slits.

"I'll call you back," he grumbles and abruptly hangs up.

Victor strides toward me, every step radiating uncontrolled fury.

"Deputy Director Grayson. As you can see, I'm putting out fires started by your inefficiency.

"Come this way. Tuff wants to meet with you. Now."

I fall into step beside him, matching his pace.

"I'm ready, Victor."

He doesn't acknowledge me as we walk through the final hall to the Oval Office. The President's secretary meets us at the door.

The moment I step inside, the temperature turns icy from Tuff's demeanor.

He stands behind the Resolute desk, arms crossed, face crimson with rage, his temper barely kept in check. Ready to launch every one of his political nightmares directly at me.

But he's not the only one in the room.

The second I see the other person, I have to fight not to cringe.

Alan Schmutt.

The richest man in the world, a so-called genius innovator, has recently become a living billboard for everything that's broken about power in this country.

Schmutt is perched casually near the window, his wiry hair a tangled mess, unsuccessfully projecting some bizarre image of brilliance. The challenge for him is that I know the truth. Everyone in the administration probably does too, but they are afraid to openly admit it.

Alan Schmutt built nothing. He bought them and rebranded them, taking full credit.

A rich kid from another country, riding a tidal wave of money pulled straight from a diamond mine littered with human rights cases. Daddy's fortune paved the way for everything, paying for his way into an Ivy League school, buying a seat at the table he never honestly earned.

There, he latched onto real innovators, using his wealth like a crowbar to pry open doors he could never have unlocked by himself. He leeched off their ideas, wrapped himself in their brilliance, and spun it all into an impostor tale.

A well-timed exit gave Schmutt the cash and the audacity to buy into a rising car company. He merely saw it as his next attempt to stroke his ever-inflating ego.

However, it wasn't a friendly acquisition; it was brutally hostile. Schmutt used his fortune and leveraged the money of others to amass enough control for a takeover. The resulting legal battle dragged on for months, fueled by his chronic insecurity and need for validation.

In the end, he won, and even demanded to be officially labeled a co-founder, holding the payout for the real inventors hostage until they agreed. As a final act of self-worship, he stamped his name on the company, Schmutler Motors.

Alan Schmutt, the second coming of Einstein.

In reality, all he ever did was get lucky by being born into wealth, use it to ride the backs of smarter, more talented people, slap his name on their work, and cash the checks. That warped strategy allowed him to build a global empire.

Signs of his insecurities are even clearer as he moves behind Tuff and nests himself on the edge of a window. His weirdly smooth skin, the patchy hairline that seems to shift in every photo, the subtle distortions in his features all hint at too many cosmetic procedures.

What makes it worse, what makes Schmutt so dangerous, is that he's here because he bought himself a place at the table. He is the biggest donor to Tuff's campaign by millions. This has given him a seat in every backroom conversation, a say in decisions no private citizen should ever be privy to, least of all, him.

If Alan Schmutt is involved in this, if he is the devil sitting on Tuff's shoulder, then the Dragon Slayer situation will get much worse. Incompetence combined with unchecked ego is catastrophic.

The moment the door is closed, Tuff registers my presence and slams his hands on the desk.

He hollers at me, his face is flushing into a dangerous level of red.

"What the hell happened here, Charlotte? I thought you and Bill had this under control! I'm being inundated by my donors panicking that these Dragon Slayers are going to hunt them down if they don't cough up their cash! What the hell is happening here?"

I hold my ground, shoulders squared, bracing for the blowback.

"Mr. President, we knew this was a possibility. Since they've acted, we have more to work with. We've identified five missing employees from the uplink site. Based on the Dragon Slayers' message, we believe these individuals may have been turned into accomplices."

Before I can finish, a loud, theatrical scoff cuts across the room.

Schmutt.

He pushes off the window ledge, flailing his hands in some exaggerated, aimless gesture as he steps forward.

"Oh, this is just this is just," he stammers, shaking his head like the brilliance of his thoughts is simply too much to process. "I just don't understand how... how anyone could ever... ever do something like this. Hurt someone... just for money. I mean... that's just... terrible."

He lets out a long, wistful sigh, pressing both hands to his chest like he's been personally wounded.

"Look at how much money I have," he continues, his voice climbing into a nasal whine. "And all I've ever done... is good! I mean, I'm trying to save humanity by getting us to Mars!

"I'm trying to help President Tuff win! And yet... they hate me? They hate us? I just don't get it! How the ones we create jobs for... can be so angry at us for helping them!"

Each word grates like fingernails dragged across a chalkboard.

Fundamentally, Alan Schmutt doesn't believe he's done anything wrong. He can't even comprehend why people might resent him. In his mind, the billions he's amassed are a public service, and any outrage directed at him is just proof that everyone else is broken and jealous.

And somehow, now, he's sitting at the table during one of the worst crises in recent history.

Tuff holds up a hand, cutting Schmutt off mid-ramble.

"That's enough, Schmutt. You want to vent, do it after we solve this goddamn problem."

Tuff refocuses, stabbing a finger toward me.

"So, what are you going to do, Grayson?"

"Mr. President, I'm flying out right after this meeting. We've identified the missing staff, and we're going to find them. One way or another."

"Better do that. I spoke with Bill, and he knows our stance. This was just a hijack of the digital feed. No Dragon Slayers were on site. Do you understand me?"

"Yes, sir."

"Damn right you do! You need to find something, and fast. This is a disaster. People are losing their minds. And let me be clear, don't hold back.

"I've already signed off on labeling the Dragon Slayers and anyone working with them as terrorists. So, whatever you need to do in those interrogations, do it. For all I care, they're not U.S. citizens if they believe in what these bastards are preaching."

Tuff is ready to destroy anything that threatens his reelection.

He continues speaking, as if nothing he has said is unconstitutional.

"Bill's about to go on camera to set the tone. Then I'll address the nation, calm the markets over this Dragon Slayer bullshit. But it's on you to deliver results. Find those bastards and take them.

"And since Alan knows what's best for this country and runs in all the right circles, you'll keep him updated. Same way you keep Dr. Hart and Victor in the loop.

"Because this isn't just about keeping billionaires safe, Grayson. It's about keeping their wallets open. Do you understand me?"

"Yes, sir, Mr. President."

"Good. Now get the hell out of here and go bring me some damn Dragon Slayers!"

I turn and walk out, every step pushing down the anger bubbling under my skin. The moment I'm outside the office, Victor is there, arms crossed, a smug little smile playing at the corner of his mouth.

"Told you, Deputy Director, you're not ready for the big league, kid. Sooner or later, everyone gets chewed up and spit out."

"Victor, don't you understand we're on the same damn side?"

I leave him standing there with his sarcastic smile slipping from his face, the scowl crawling back where it belongs.

The meeting was brief, but the impact looms large. It didn't provide any clarity. Just added more undue pressure.

But it's over, and now I can focus on the op that really matters.

I return to the SUV without a word. The driver opens the door, providing me with an escape from the madness of the outside world.

"Take me to the airfield," I order.

He nods and pulls away from the curb.

The second we're moving, I de-stress. The noise, the posturing, the billionaire theatrics are behind me now.

Ahead is the real mission.

Graham's waiting. The five missing satellite employees are still out there.

And if there's anything left in this job I still believe in, it's the part where we chase the truth, not just the story we're told to sell.

Time to get to work.

CHAPTER 12

SILENT ALLIES

"Overcoming poverty is not a gesture of
charity. It is an act of justice."

- NELSON MANDELA

THE SUV'S TINTED windows protect me from the commotion of the outside world, as we head to the airfield, leaving D.C. and all its turmoil fading behind us.

The calm rumble of the engine is accompanied by the gentle tapping of my fingers against my knee. In here, all is quiet. It stands in stark contrast to the turmoil slowly eating away at me with each tick from my watch.

Settled into the seat, my eyes close briefly as the driver takes a tight turn to the runway. An anxious notion bothers me, an itch I cannot scratch. Earlier, I had envisioned my Deputy Director promotion to mean strategic planning, the occasional high-stakes meeting, and navigating bureaucratic politics.

Now, I'm tracking terrorists on U.S. soil with the entire world frozen in fear.

The silhouette of the plane takes shape as we approach, its

glossy surface catching a beam of sunlight. Ground personnel move in practiced operations, a tiny maelstrom of motion in the airfield's calm radiance.

It's a good feeling that I'm getting out and about, not stuck in some conference room uncoiling bureaucratic spin.

My phone buzzes, and I see it's Carter calling.

"Hey, boss, got that background intel you wanted on Donovan Pierce."

"And?"

"Redacted as hell. At first glance, it was just one giant black box. No joke, half the documents were nothing but bars."

I raise an eyebrow.

"So… basically useless?"

"Come on, boss, you know me. I'm a miracle worker. Started pulling threads. Cross-referencing known ops, leaked cables, off-book timelines. And yeah, his name, or his ghost aliases, keeps popping up."

"What's he linked to?"

"Yugoslavia in the '90s. Bogotá during the cartel crackdowns. Iran-Contra mop-up crew. Rendition flights. Black sites. Even tied to some of the early cyber warfare programs that never made it past DARPA files."

"Christ."

"That's not even the worst of it. I found ties to Benghazi post-fallout, shady movements in and out of Afghanistan during those unofficial JSOC runs. You know, the ones no one wants to talk about."

"So, he's been in the center of every CIA scandal for the last forty years."

"Pretty much. Every time the agency needed something done off the books, Donovan's fingerprints show up."

"And they're still using him."

"Looks like it. He's too useful to let go, too dirty to let off the leash. So, they keep him within reach for when something goes sideways."

"Doubt he's going to help us stop the Dragon Slayers."

"Sorry boss. Donovan is in the business of making sure the machine can spread out as far as it can."

"Alright thanks Carter, I'm getting to the plane now, I'll keep you updated."

"Sounds good."

The SUV stops, tires crunching on the gravel. Agents are waiting to escort me to the Gulfstream jet. The engines purr softly, soothing me, as I take the airstairs two at a time.

Inside, the cabin is small and functional. Dark leather seats paired with polished steel provide a sleek, professional appearance. A coffee tray remains untouched on the table.

The jet takes off smoothly, leaving the turmoil on the ground behind, bathing it all in dull grays and blues. My ears briefly ache as we ascend, a familiar pain that I barely register as I take out my tablet.

I scroll through the briefing materials, consisting of files on the five missing employees.

Carter and Graham have been diligently stitching together any available intel they can find. Backgrounds, timestamps, job roles. It's not fully complete yet, but close.

Graham texted me before takeoff, shedding light on their progress.

Working with site staff. Filling in some holes. Update when you land.

No reason on my end to dig any deeper until I have a better picture.

I move on to the live feeds, checking public chatter. The

headlines are all over the place. Some echoing panic. Others are spinning doubt.

Exactly what Maya warned me about.

One headline catches my eye:

FBI Director William Cartwright Issues Statement on Dragon Slayer Threat

I tap it, and the screen shifts to Bill's face, filling the frame.

Stoic. Measured. Exactly how the nation needs him to look right now.

That's always been one of his gifts, the kind of presence that makes you feel safe just by him being there.

Bill stands at the podium, American flag behind him, a sea of reporters in front.

"Welcome, everyone. The FBI is aware of a hijacked broadcast feed used by a terrorist organization threatening specific individuals within the United States. These anarchists call themselves the Dragon Slayers."

He lets the line sit before continuing.

"At this time, we believe this is nothing more than a hoax and a fraud, an opportunistic act by a fringe group seeking attention. I want to emphasize that we are treating their threats as credible until proven otherwise.

"Let me make this perfectly clear to each and every one of you. It does not matter what your net worth is. The FBI will protect and defend every citizen of this great country.

"So, for those considering working with these individuals, whether or not you receive money, it is still a crime. Helping them in any way will not be tolerated. You will be arrested, labeled as a terrorist, and given a swift sentencing.

"We will find whoever is behind the Dragon Slayers video and all their accomplices. So, think carefully of the repercussions if you aid and abet them. You will be held accountable."

It's the right message, stern, patriotic, and smart. The kind that plants seeds of doubt in people tempted to take the Dragon Slayers up on their offer.

Bottom line. Don't do it. It's not worth it.

I pause the video and absorb his speech.

Director Bill Cartwright.

It's easy to forget, watching him up there, just how many battles he's fought behind closed doors. How many impossible decisions he's had to make without ever revealing his true feelings.

Bill carries himself with a casual, unshakable calm, quick to joke, quick to praise. However, beneath his stoic façade, lies a man who will never disclose the true weight he carries for his country.

And now he's out front again. Taking the heat before the administration provides its take on the situation.

Their response will not have Bill's restraint.

Maya is right. If Tuff overreaches, overreacts, and labels anyone interacting with the Dragon Slayers as enemies of the State, he will be fanning the flames.

Because here's the truth no one wants to say out loud:

It's hard to despise someone who's desperate. Hard to villainize people with no options. The public may not agree with the Dragon Slayers' methods, but they're going to understand why someone would take the offer.

People drowning in debt, pushed to the margins, overlooked and demoralized by a corrupt system. Public sympathy will feel compassion for those disadvantaged individuals more so than for the billionaires hiding behind compound gates.

If the White House handles this situation with brute force instead of managing it tactfully, the Dragon Slayers movement will not be shut down.

Instead, it will be given oxygen.

And the worst part for me?

I can handle the Dragon Slayers. I can track them, maybe even stop them.

But how do I stop this administration if they go too far?

Right now, this is something I refuse to consider.

The plane touches down on the runway, snapping me back into reality. I collect my gear and emerge into the predawn darkness. Another FBI SUV idles at the curb, its engine quietly purring. Graham's massive shape in the back seat, the screen of his tablet etching a white glow across his hard features. A thermos of coffee remains untouched next to him.

Not lifting his head, he palms a bottle of water into my hand.

"Long flight?"

"Long day." I twist off the cap and take a quick drink. "Graham, have anything?"

"We've run profiles on the five missing employees. Tyson McKay is our primary suspect. He's the head of security. Right before this happened, he called an 'emergency briefing' to get all the guards off their posts and unarmed."

"So, either he's dirty, or they have something on him."

"Exactly. Kyle Becker, gate access security. He was supposed to be on break during the breach, but his login was still active. Someone let the Dragon Slayers in, and it was likely him."

The SUV rumbles onto the main road, the tires drumming in a continuous beat as Graham shuffles through more profiles.

"Then we have Paula Nunez and Derrick Hoffman. Control room techs. Graveyard shift vets. They know the uplink systems inside and out. If the Dragon Slayers needed a clean feed, these two were essential."

"And the fifth?"

"Juan Rivera. Facilities tech. Cameras, alarms, power... he's the guy who'd sever the strings to keep them concealed. The man's a ghost, kept a very low profile."

Glancing out the window gives me a chance to process his intel. Snowflakes blur the scenery, erasing any trace of the world beyond the glass.

"Head of security, gate access, two control room operators, and a facilities tech. Wonder who needed the Dragon Slayers' money the most?"

"Charlie, wish I had an answer for that. What we do know is that they had every point of control that mattered. Those employees had the facility wrapped up like a Christmas present for the Dragon Slayers."

"Do you think they're still alive?"

Graham looks at me thoughtfully, giving me a chance to brace for his response.

"If they didn't kill them, they bribed them. This seems to be their modus operandi. Clean, strategic, no mess unless it is absolutely unavoidable. Bribing five people allows them to go in and out without firing a shot.

"And, Charlie, if the Dragon Slayers had wanted to, they could have killed everybody in that building with ease."

"So, until we uncover bodies, we go with the idea of them being bribed."

"Right," Graham confirms, "If the Dragon Slayers are looking after them, there will be a trail."

"What about their families and close contacts?"

"Our missing five don't have many connections. Which makes sense, they're the perfect candidates to disappear, with no one to hold them back. If they offered a way out, those employees would have every reason to take it."

"Okay. We'll start with staff interviews. Someone might've seen something out of place."

The SUV slows as we reach the police station, and what I see ahead adds more mayhem to the mix. Blinding cameras, reporters crowding the entrance, their voices punctuating the chaos of an overflowing parking lot. This will not be low key.

The door opens, and the roar of reporter questions hits me like a rogue wave.

"Deputy Director Grayson! Is the government withholding information about the attack?"

"Was the breach a sign of systemic failure?"

"Is the FBI treating this seriously enough?"

"Is this somehow tied to Lucian Voss going missing?"

"What if the Dragon Slayers are real?"

I maintain a neutral expression as I step onto the asphalt, cameras flashing around me like fireflies in the night. The press is unyielding, wild hounds snapping at my heels. I've navigated crises before, yet this intense scrutiny is overwhelmingly suffocating.

The police stand firm on the steps of the station as they move the reporters behind their barriers. Graham moves forward, appearing taller than usual, unperturbed, his composure slicing through the clamor. I wrap my coat around me and follow him up the path, the sound fading only when the glass doors shut firmly behind us.

Within the station itself, there is tension. Faulty lights buzz intently, revealing the need for bulbs to be replaced. The air smells of stale coffee and pastries. Officers stride purposefully; their faces somber, acutely aware of the seriousness of their job.

The man waiting at the front desk has a solid build that commands attention. He extends his hand toward me.

"Deputy Director Grayson. I'm Chief Reynolds. We're glad to have the FBI's support for this matter."

"Thanks for pulling everything together so quickly, Chief. I know this hasn't been easy."

"Easy will not be in my dictionary this week," he says, rubbing the back of his neck. "We've started interviews with the staff who were on site that evening, anyone who might've seen or heard something off.

"We've got initial statements and timelines pulled together, but I'll be straight with you, Deputy Director, we're a small district. Real small.

"We don't usually get much more than bar fights and the occasional drunk driver trying to outrun a stop sign.

"This? This is a whole other kettle of fish.

"Having your team here means a hell of a lot. We don't have the resources or training for something like this. And I think we all know that whatever this is, it's really big. So yeah. We're grateful you showed up so quickly."

"Thank you, Chief. It goes both ways. What you do here is just as important.

"It'll be a privilege working with your team."

Before he can respond, Graham steps in beside me.

"Chief, just so you know, your officers have been incredibly helpful. Sharp, cooperative, and swift to move. You've got good people."

Reynolds nods, relaxing his posture.

"Well, we try our best. It's good to hear it counts for something.

"This is how it's supposed to be, Deputy Director. Local and federal, side by side. One team. I didn't take this job for politics or power.

"I grew up here. Always knew if I was going to wear a badge, it'd be right here in the town that raised me. All I care about is protecting our citizens. Doesn't matter who they are or how much money they have, that's my job."

It's refreshing. More than I expected.

Something is steadying about hearing it said so plainly. It's clear the Chief gives a damn about the job.

I've spent too much time around those who treat leadership like a throne, barking demands from above and expecting others to handle the fallout. People who contribute nothing but pressure, who measure success by what they can extract, not what they build.

When in reality, it's not them who make the world run.

It's the people on the ground, the ones in uniform, on factory floors. The ones showing up day after day in government or the private sector, making things happen, making things work.

"Chief, I understand this is a lot to process. We're dealing with an unknown threat here, too. But your team's remarkable efficiency hasn't escaped our notice. We genuinely appreciate it."

Reynolds offers us a weary smile.

"Well, anything you need, just say the word."

"Right, let's start with the interviews."

Reynolds nods and gestures toward a nearby door.

"We have them ready to go for you in this room. I'll let my team know. We'll bring them in one at a time."

"Thanks, Chief."

With that, he turns and walks off down the hallway. Graham watches him go and then shifts back to me.

"Alright Charlie. Let's talk to the people who've seen a Dragon Slayer. Find out what they know."

He strides toward the door, and I follow behind, centering my attention on the interrogations.

No more theories.

Time to get some straight answers.

CHAPTER 13

TIES THAT BIND

*"The paradise of the rich is made
out of the hell of the poor."*

- Victor Hugo

THE INTERVIEW ROOM is intentionally stark, with one frosted window, three worn wooden chairs, and a scratched metal table. The overhead light emits a visual effect of rolling waves. Someone's attempted to clean up the area. The pine-scented floor cleaner is still noticeable in the air.

Graham sets his tablet down, glances around, then pulls the door shut behind us. We take the seats facing the door. Recorders and files are strategically placed on the table. He reaches for the small buzzer on the wall and presses it once.

A second later, a voice comes through the intercom.

"Ready for the first one?" an officer asks.

"Good to go," Graham replies.

The first interview begins. Quick and clinical, there's no room for unnecessary words.

"What did you see?" I ask.

The young guard across from me, barely in his twenties, shifts uncomfortably in his seat. Sweat breaks out on his forehead as his fists clench on the table.

"I didn't see much. Tyson called for an emergency briefing; he told us we had to review some new procedures. He's the security chief, so we complied. Then… then those masked guys just appeared out of nowhere."

"They?" Graham questions him.

The guard nods hastily.

"Yup, six guys. Black and gold tactical gear. Each one had a slightly different mask, but hey, I barely got a good look. They were too quick; everything was one big blur."

I probe him further.

"Did they say anything… anything at all?"

"They weren't shouting. They were oddly quiet. One of them stepped in front of me, calm as anything, and said, 'put your hands behind your back. You're not the enemy in this war. Nobody's going to get hurt.'"

The guard swallows hard.

"And that was it. No screaming. Once we were down, they didn't say another word."

"And you trusted them?" Graham prods him.

The guard bows his head, shame creeping into his expression.

"We didn't have a choice. We put our guns away for the meeting. Nothing we could do. Tyson told us to stand down, said that no one was going to get hurt. He was right.

"They had us restrained in seconds, like it was routine. One of them even apologized. Said it was just an inconvenience, that they'd be gone soon."

"They apologized?" I confirm.

"Yeah, all of them were polite. Exceptionally polite for terrorists. Like they really didn't want to scare us. Just kept their voices low, gave simple instructions. Routine for them, scary as hell for us."

Graham glances at me, and his unspoken message is clear. This is the Dragon Slayers' core message. Ordinary citizens are not their target; it's only the billionaires they are hunting.

Each interview provides the same information. And the next. And the next. Facts merge seamlessly, creating a pattern that, while clear, provides us with nothing.

Six masked men. Heavily armed. Minimal communications.

The Dragon Slayers moved with inconceivable accuracy. There was no unnecessary verbal or physical intimidation used to overwhelm the employees.

We interview the janitor next, a wiry man in coveralls with tired eyes and calloused hands. He shifts in his seat, fingers tightly clutching his hat, waiting to be chastised.

"Those guys told me the same thing. You're not the enemy. We're on the same side here. I… I don't know what exactly that side is, but they seemed sincere about it."

I jot it down, turning his words over in my mind. Propaganda, expertly designed to disarm and manipulate. The Dragon Slayers have succeeded; none of these employees seem to harbor any ill will for being bound and restrained.

By the time the last interview ends, the air in the room is murky. I close my notebook, the soft thud resounding louder than it should.

Graham presses his lips together, his thick mustache twitching.

"Those Dragon Slayers walked in like they owned the joint."

"I agree with you on that, Graham. And Tyson McKay? He was way too quick to urge his staff to comply. It's clear he helped them, clearing the way. Called the meeting, kept the guards calm."

"McKay made it way too easy for the Dragon Slayers. They must have paid him for his cooperation. Plus, the Dragon Slayers didn't hurt anyone. They're playing a more formidable match.

"Charlie, this mission they pulled off. It's a solid statement of their cunning. Every move calculated and well-executed."

I exhale sharply.

"The Dragon Slayers know collateral damage will only hurt their image. The moment they kill civilians, they lose the 'we the people' versus the elite angle. They need to be seen as righteous, not overzealous monsters."

Graham remarks dryly.

"Yeah, well, they're doing a hell of a job selling it. I've never seen a group of hostages this... grateful to their captors.

"You heard them. Oh, they were so professional. So polite. One of them even apologized. This shit isn't normal Charlie."

A mental clutter is spinning in my mind. Sparing the guards looks like mercy, but more likely, it was strategy. Designed to build trust with the very people they're counting on for support.

Winning a battle is one thing, but winning a war takes more than force. It takes hearts, minds, and beliefs.

After a few hours, we've exhausted the list.

Every employee has been questioned, prodded, pressed from every angle; despite that, we have nothing solid. Just the same vague fear and carefully worded uncertainty.

Graham pushes back from the table, and I follow suit, gathering the last of our notes.

The moment we leave the interrogation room, I hear a heated debate between investigating officers rising above a familiar voice in the background.

Another group of officers gathers around a small television

on the wall. The President's boisterous tone is heard through old speakers, as one of the police officers struggles to turn up the volume.

On screen, Tuff stands confidently at the podium, perfectly staged between an oversized American flag and heavy gold-trimmed curtains. Every part of him is carefully curated for the cameras, America's made-for-TV strongman.

The President roars, thick with gravitas.

"My loyal citizens! We're the greatest country in the world. We're the richest, we're the strongest, we're the smartest. And you know why? Because we've got the greatest people."

His voice booms, deep and rehearsed, dripping with the same unwavering command he's always projected. He's a performer. Always has been.

But something's off this time.

It's subtle, just a beat too long between lines, a hint of something behind his eyes. I sense the pressure catching up with him. Even Tuff, for all his bravado, is starting to feel it sink in.

He points a finger at the camera, freezing for dramatic effect.

"And do you know who those great people are? The billionaires have been our saviors. The ones who create jobs, finance innovation, and enrich the economy to make the United States of America the most prosperous country in history.

"Without them, where would we be? Who would we be?"

The officers watching the broadcast react differently. Some shift with discomfort, their faces tight with unease, while others exchange quiet nods, relief flickering in their eyes.

Tuff continues, intensifying as he thumps his fist on the podium.

"Billionaires are the backbone of this nation. They are the reason the stock market is booming; they are the reason we're all richer, safer, healthier, and happier."

Tuff shakes his head in a demonstration of over-the-top incredulity.

"And now, a bunch of pathetic losers, maybe North Korean hackers, or China, or even my many political opponents who don't want me to win re-election. Those fools know that if I do, America's only going to get greater.

"Those Dragon Slayers think they can scare you. They want you to believe they can bring this country to its knees. What did they really do? Hijacked a video feed during a basketball game. That's it. A cheap stunt. Do they really think they can frighten us?"

He leans too close, appearing to almost swallow the microphone, his voice dropping to that pseudo-grave whisper he adores so much.

"Let me tell you something: I won't let them; I will defend you as I've always done!"

The media is silent, cameras clicking as journalists scribble notes. Tuff stands tall, chest thrust out as if challenging viewers to disagree with him.

"Our bloated government agencies are slow. Our private leaders are fast and ready to act, and I am ready to help them.

"That's why, starting now, we'll be announcing a massive package of subsidies to stimulate the economy and ensure we're prepared to deal with threats of this nature. We'll be working closely with top business leaders and the brightest professionals in the country, bringing the private sector into the loop like never before."

Graham takes a sharp breath, his tone harsh.

"Of course, he would promise this, more gifts on a silver platter for his donors."

Tuff turns heated, his next words popping like gunfire in all directions.

"Let me be clear, these fraudsters? They're gimmicks. A joke. Anyone dumb enough to fall for this trick, anyone who tries to help them, spread their message, or get involved in any way, will be labeled a domestic terrorist. No exceptions.

"The Dragon Slayers aren't real, but the crimes they're convincing people to commit are. And those crimes will be punished to the fullest extent of the law."

Tuff pauses, letting the silence hang. And then he creepily smiles, before he delivers the coup de grâce.

"We're even exploring how to strip citizenship from homegrown terrorists. Because if you don't believe in our values, freedom, liberty, and capitalism, then you don't belong here.

"It's your choice. But don't expect to stay. We'll be more than happy to throw you out."

The reporters move aside, pushing one another, as Tuff steps out, his ringmaster performance completed.

My mind is panicked knowing that everyone's rights are being eroded. Yet around me, the reaction is anything but uniform. Some officers shake their heads, holding back their frustration while muttering curses. Others are quiet, their expressions unreadable, absorbing what they just heard.

And then there are the ones who don't look angry at all, the ones who nod in agreement, arms ready to salute their fearless leader.

What happened at the uplink site leaves no room for doubt. Whatever they are willing to believe doesn't sway them from acknowledging that Tuff was lying. The Dragon Slayers are a genuine threat.

One by one, the officers return to their tasks, the station settling back into tense, focused movement. Next to me, Graham retorts sharply, his voice barely above a whisper.

"If they actually crack down, it's going to make this much worse."

Graham is right; the implications of the President's words sink deeper under my skin.

Tuff doubled down; he doused the flames with gasoline. He portrayed billionaires as saints. And worse, he gave the Dragon Slayers what they most desired. Another reason people should pay attention to them.

He can't seem to get past the real problem: People are listening, and now he's dared them not to.

Back in the interrogation room, I slide the employee files in front of me.

One by one, I review the missing employee profiles again. It's clear that the local PD did its part. They reached out to families, relatives, former coworkers, and anyone who could be a possible contact or could share crucial information.

But the answers given were uniform, no one had anything viable to share.

Most hadn't even realized they were missing, which says a lot.

We're spinning our wheels again.

Then my tablet pings.

New message. Maya Lin.

Subject line: Nunez's boyfriend

I tap it open.

Hey Charlie,

Just ran a deeper scrape on Paula Nunez. No mention of any relationship in the file, but I found a comment trail buried in an old post string. Traced it back to one Evan Marshall. Not a ton of photos together, nothing obvious, but the interaction's consistent. Pretty sure it's him.

My pulse quickens. A boyfriend.

If Nunez has a boyfriend, there's a chance he's involved. Trusted him. Told him something. Maybe even took him with her.

I stand up quickly, causing my chair to scrape on the floor.

"Graham. Maya found something. Nunez might have a boyfriend, Evan Marshall. He's not in the initial report, but Maya pulled it from comment traces."

"Could be a lead?"

"Possibly, it's more than we've had all day."

Pulling out my phone, I dial Carter.

"Yeah, Boss?"

"Carter, I need a full dive on someone named Evan Marshall. Maya just flagged him as Paula Nunez's boyfriend. He's not in any of our files, but there's a digital trail. Could be nothing, could be everything."

"Hang tight. Let me pull his profile."

The wait for a response from him is excruciating.

"He's clean," Carter eventually replies. "No priors or flagged associations. Not even a speeding ticket."

"That's it? That's all you got?"

"On paper? Yeah. He seems pretty boring."

There's a pause, then Carter speaks, his voice drier than usual.

"Boss, I don't know if you saw Tuff's... well, I guess it was a press conference? A speech? A patriotic crash out? Whatever that was."

"Carter, I saw it."

"Yeah. So technically, if you say the magic word terrorist, a lot of options open up for us."

He's not joking. If I say the word, if I flag Evan Marshall as a potential domestic terrorist, doors open. The legal hurdles vanish.

And under Tuff's new directive? It's justified.

The President made it clear, any interaction, any support, any hint of alignment with the Dragon Slayers qualifies, even if the group itself isn't proven real. Even if the crime hasn't technically happened yet.

So, I'd just be following the administration's playbook.

Granted, it's not how things are supposed to work. It cuts out due process and everything I believe is sacred for this job.

Still, if I can stop the Dragon Slayers using this tactic, if we can get ahead of this before it spirals further, it might save lives.

Graham is studying me carefully. He knows what I'm thinking. He knows exactly what comes next.

"Carter. This is an order. Label Evan Marshall a terrorist. Do a full dive into phone records, location pings, and surveillance feeds. Anyone he's even remotely associated with; I want it all flagged."

There's a pause on the other end. Then a low whistle.

"Copy that, boss. Digging in now."

Evan Marshall isn't a person under the law anymore.

He's the justification for breaking it.

CHAPTER 14

PAWNS AND KINGS

*"We do not commonly find men of superior
sense amongst those of the highest fortune."*

- JUVENAL

INTERROGATIONS COMPLETED; WE sit immersed in silence.

Graham continues analyzing the employee profiles, as the tension from my choice to flag Marshall permeates between us.

Labeling him a terrorist was a decision made in seconds, but the repercussions of it could last a lifetime. He could be guilty or complicit. Or he could just be an unlucky guy, associated with the wrong person who has swept him up into the perfect storm.

I try to rationalize it. Tell myself it is tactical, not personal. The gravity of the situation called for it. That I'm following protocol.

There's a stark difference between acting on intelligence and acting out of desperation. I'm unsure of which one this was, perhaps a combination of both.

All I know is that no other op has ever pushed me this far.

No other case has me frantically pursuing leads, dissecting angles, pulling micro threads just to catch the faintest trace of a possible target.

I need fresh air to reset myself.

Without saying a word, I leave the room and step out into the dreary hallway. The front doors of the station creak open, releasing a burst of cold that brushes against my skin.

A flurry of snowflakes slowly drifts down, soothing my flushed face with cold dots that vanish in seconds. The setting sun hurls streaks of gold and violet at the sky, unwilling to disappear into the horizon.

It'll be dark soon. And with it, the end of the first full day since the Dragon Slayers seized the world's attention.

One whole day of chatter, speculation, silence, and half-answers.

When tomorrow arrives, will I have produced any tangible results?

I check my phone for updates from Carter. Nothing.

With a sigh, I slip it back into my pocket and head back inside. Settling in for another long night, I brace myself for the grind ahead.

Combing through my inbox, reviewing every update, every lead, I search for anything that might push this case forward. It's all in vain. Marshall remains our only chance to uncover anything of merit.

A ping from the phone breaks my focus.

Victor's name illuminates the screen, his message as curt as ever:

Tuff and Schmutt require an update. 15 minutes. Don't be late.

Terrific. Another episode of optics and ego-stroking.

Alan Schmutt's voice sneaks into my thoughts, self-satisfied, repeatedly auditioning for the role of smartest man on earth. He is bound to suggest some sleek, tech-based solution for the Dragon Slayers, something overly complicated that misses the heart of the issue entirely.

A perfect example of this is when he bought Chipper, the social media app, for billions. He immediately re-titled it *Y* and watched it spiral into something dark, and entirely off the rails.

When people ask why, he just smiles and says, *"Y... exactly,"* as if that answer should suffice.

Whatever he is trying to achieve remains a mystery.

What bothers me the most are the individuals with infinite resources, influence, and spare time. People who could be saving lives, lifting communities up, and funding solutions to actual problems. Instead, they chase vanity projects. Take over news outlets. Launch themselves into space. Build bunkers on islands just in case the rest of us can't keep the mess they made together.

Wouldn't you want to help if you could?

Wouldn't that be the natural thing to do?

People like Schmutt, well, it never crosses their mind.

And that's why the Dragon Slayers' message resonates so deeply with ordinary people.

It's been brewing for decades, the widening gap, the mounting pressure, the way everyday citizens are told to accept less, while billionaires keep raking in more. And every time someone questions it, the blame circles right back to the people who are struggling the most.

Work harder. Hustle more. Maybe don't buy that latte or avocado toast.

As if that's the real problem.

Is personal failure the reason rents keep rising, or why education costs more than a down payment on a home, or why basic healthcare has become a luxury item?

Meanwhile, stock portfolios of the wealthy explode as executive bonuses hit record highs.

No one dares ask what the one percenters are doing with their wealth. So, when the Dragon Slayers show up, to some people it doesn't feel like terrorism; it feels like representation.

Chief Reynolds' voice startles me. I glance up, his imposing figure blocking the light from the hall. His expression is serious, a bit too focused.

"Deputy Director, the room is ready for you. A secure line is available. Anything else you need, just ask."

"Thanks, Chief."

My boots squeak on the polished tile floor as I step into another sparsely furnished room. Table, two chairs, a screen on the wall, and an intercom on the table. Fluorescent lighting bounces starkly around the room, creating foreboding shapes.

The screen crackles to life, revealing President Tuff in all his self-satisfied glory. Leaning back in his chair, he exudes the smugness of a hero who has just saved the world.

Tuff's grin is wide, his face flushed as laughter ripples faintly through the line. Victor and Schmutt chime in with giggles grating in sycophancy.

He spreads his arms wide, like an actor basking in applause.

"What'd I say? Nobody can handle a crisis like me. Stock markets are up, what a bounce they said, everybody's okay. Best president ever… right here. No doubt about it."

Victor, never far behind when it comes to stroking Tuff's ego, chimes in with ease.

"Absolutely, Mr. President. Masterful. Your subsidies were genius. Markets are soaring again, and our friends have pledged even more donations for your re-election."

Tuff thrusts a finger towards the screen.

"That's what happens when you have somebody who genuinely

understands what they are doing. The markets have confidence in me. Not bureaucrats or politicians. Me, the only leader this country needs."

I clamp my lips shut, trapping my desire to release a scream. The Dragon Slayers commandeer a satellite uplink site and are looking to plunge the nation into anarchy, while these men are having a victory parade because the Nasdaq went up.

Tuff's voice drops, his tone becoming conspiratorial.

"And those subsidies... military contracts, private prisons. Hell, let's throw in oil for kicks. Enough pork to go around. This is how we guarantee a fully funded campaign."

Last but not least, Alan Schmutt joins in, tilting awkwardly forward into the camera. His semi-stuporous enthusiasm is as unnerving as always.

"This... uh... this is why you're so smart, Mr. President. Leadership like yours... it's how you make such great strides for Americans. And the subsidies, they're brilliant. Really, really, really brilliant."

Tuff's face displays boredom, the heaps of Schmutt's ass-kissing a bit too much even for him.

Schmutt continues to babble on.

"With the right investments, we could make this... galactic. Like my planetary Mars missions. All that, literally I mean seriously, I can save the world."

My eyes widen.

Alan Schmutt, locked in a permanent personal sprint for relevance, leaping from one grand delusion to the next. One month it's protecting free speech, the next it's saving foreign democracies or ensuring the survival of mankind itself.

On paper, they sound noble. Up close, they're just vehicles for what he alone desires.

Attention and approval, which when bought, don't feel quite right.

Schmutt persists, barely pausing for breath.

"Did I tell you? Our cars will drive themselves soon. Everyone's going to have robots. Household AI, autonomous everything. All of it. From one guy, me."

He jabs a finger toward the screen, beaming.

"You and me, Tuff, we're the same. Powerful. Smart. People don't get it, but we do, right?"

He's vibrating with excitement, eyes wide, words piling on top of each other, pushing to get out first.

Tuff grins, sharp, territorial, the way he always does when someone dares to stand on his level.

"You can say that when you win an election. Oh, wait, you can't. Not a real American, you immigrant."

Schmutt starts to fidget, his shoulders twitching as he constantly adjusts his posture.

"Well, I... I am the most followed person on Y, and I have the most money in the world, so... that's gotta count for..."

Tuff doesn't let him finish.

"Alan, you're ridiculous. You think you can do what I do? You think it's easy? You think you can win an election? Hell, try getting through an interview, or even a handshake, without making it weird. Just look at the polls. Everyone thinks you're a rich asshole."

Victor doubles over in laughter at the President's remarks.

Tuff just sits there; his trademark sneer stretched across his face. In his mind, he has won another verbal victory, kicking Schmutt out of the sandbox.

Schmutt hesitates, eyes darting around the room, and then lets out a strained laugh of his own.

It's too loud, to off-beat, the kind of laugh used to try to fit in with the cool kids.

Right now, he can barely keep himself together, let alone save the world. The signs are so blatant that even a casual observer could see that this man is deeply disturbed.

This call is supposed to be about a terrorist group, but it has veered way off course. The Dragon Slayers just issued the highest-profile threat in modern history, and here we are, watching a billionaire beg for validation while the President plays kingmaker.

Typical Tuff behavior. For all his absurdity, he has something that no amount of money can buy, and that is the talent to sway people. That's what keeps the billionaires in check. Pure and simple, it's public opinion.

He is the weaponizer in chief of the nation's citizens.

Victor irritatingly clears his throat and addresses me.

"Grayson. Give us something worthwhile."

I push down the annoyance that tries to creep into my tone.

"The Dragon Slayers were extremely coordinated. They executed a methodical plan."

"And the breach?"

"They had help entering from the workers there. We think the five missing staff were bribed. Their positions were essential in carrying out the Dragon Slayers' operation so successfully."

Tuff interjects, biting and scornful.

"Bribed? Naturally. Poor losers will do anything for the cost of a cup of coffee and some eggs."

Victor cuts in.

"Precisely, Mr. President. They are stupid because they have nothing. That's why billionaires are scandal-proof. You can't bribe someone who already has everything."

Schmutt eagerly jumps in, trying to reclaim his status in the conversation, nodding a little too hard.

"Yeah! Billionaires are, uh… always the good guys. And funny too. Like, the best meme lords."

His delivery wobbles unconvincingly, and then he starts laughing, an awkward, forced cackle that somehow manages to be even more unbearable than humanly possible.

I neutralize my expression as professionally as possible.

"Okay, picture this right…," he says, gesturing wildly. "Uh… It's that classic distracted boyfriend meme, right? For the guy, it's like, the American public. The girl he's with? Terrorist sympathizing. And the hot girl walking by? Capitalism. Boom. Perfect. It tells the whole story."

Tuff exhales sharply, turning his head.

"Alan, just shut the hell up already."

Schmutt gasps and swallows whatever quip he was about to make, shifting awkwardly in his seat like a little schoolboy.

Victor interrupts Tuff's reprimanding.

"Anything else, Grayson?"

"No, sir. We'll update you as soon as there's any further intel."

Tuff waves his hand dismissively.

"Yeah, yeah. Don't screw it up, Deputy Director. Keeping the markets calm is the priority right now."

The screen abruptly cuts to black, leaving a heavy silence in its wake.

I'm mid-thought, trying to map out the next viable step, when a sharp buzz slices through my concentration.

Carter.

I answer immediately.

"Boss, we got him," he says straight away.

I jolt upright, as if a live wire just shocked me.

"What do you mean? How?"

"Just made a call to his sister. Said he needs to lie low for a bit. I pulled the signal and got a location. It's the Mountain Inn Motel."

Adrenaline courses through me.

"Can you see any movement? Anyone else coming or going?"

"Negative, boss. Satellite shows the location is quiet. If Marshall is there, I can't imagine the Dragon Slayers just leaving him there for us."

"Copy that. Carter, we're on the move."

Graham looks up at me from across the room. I give him a thumbs up, and he's on his feet, moving with a set purpose.

Rushing into the breakroom, I spot Chief Reynolds mid-conversation with his officers. He turns, reading my urgency as I approach.

"Chief!" I exclaim. "We have a location, Mountain Inn Motel. I need every available unit, armed and ready."

Reynolds doesn't waste a second. He looks to his team.

"You heard her. Move."

The room erupts into motion as everyone rushes out to make the necessary preparations. The staging area springs to life with methodical mayhem. Officers in motion check their guns and load equipment.

I fasten my tactical vest, cinch my comms, and pat my sidearm twice. Muscle memory asserts itself, even as the fringes of fatigue loom in my visual field.

Graham tosses me an earpiece, his expression stern.

"Helicopters en route. Chief's sending squad cars for support. We'll have air support before we get there."

"This could be the link we need."

"Charlie, it could be a trap; we still need to stay vigilant."

I nod in agreement. The Dragon Slayers have demonstrated their tactical skills, but that can't deter us. Whatever happens next, we need this. We need a win.

Outside, the whine of rotors grows louder. The Black Hawk helicopter descends below the lot, its sleek body shining in the floodlights. Snowfall has increased; heavy flakes are swept sideways by the downwash. The wind tears through my hair and stings my face as Graham and I move forward.

The cabin hums with raw power as I climb in first. Graham follows, buckling himself in, checking his rifle with military expertise.

The pilot looks back at us.

"We'll be over the site in twenty."

I get on the comms.

"Carter, keep feeding us information. If anything moves at that motel, I want to know."

"Roger that. And Boss, be careful. Marshall could be in cahoots with the Dragon Slayers. Worse, he's a loose end they don't want alive."

"Will do, Carter. Just keep the feeds active. If anything changes, I want to know immediately."

"Copy that, boss."

I glance over at Graham, rifle still steady in his grip.

"This could be our only chance to stop this madness."

He glances up at me with unspoken understanding.

Airborne, I look outside to see snow starting to cloak the mountains in a blanket of white. The glow of rotor lights forges a path through the darkening sky. The helicopter banks gently, tilting toward the ridgeline, buildings below appearing as an array of colorful miniature models.

Ahead is nothing but emptiness, dark and menacing.

Then, out of that void appears a twinkle of lights.

A faint white glow clings to the edge of a snowy hillside.

The Mountain Inn Motel.

Somewhere within the motel walls is Evan Marshall.

He's the strand we dare not lose.

CHAPTER 15

INTO THE FIRE

"An imbalance between rich and poor is the oldest and most fatal ailment of all republics."

-PLUTARCH, 53 AD

THE HELICOPTER DIPS lower, pushing through the wind as the terrain beneath us becomes more distinct. Snow continues to sweep past the windows, flurries thick enough to mask the ridgeline, but not enough to hide what we are seeking.

The Mountain Inn Motel.

There is no mistaking the weathered structure tucked against the side of a hill. A battered metal neon sign casts a weak orange halo onto the snow-covered roof. It's the only thing that indicates any sign of life.

The unknown of what lies ahead presses down on all of us. Whether this mission succeeds or fails will have repercussions far beyond our personal circumstances. One mistake could set in motion a cataclysmic chain reaction.

A jolt of static in my headset heralds Bill's sharp and direct commands.

"Charlie, if any Dragon Slayers are anywhere near that location, don't hesitate. Let them know the FBI doesn't play games. You got this."

"We'll get this job done. The Dragon Slayers will get the message loud and clear that we mean business."

"Roger that."

The line drops into silence as I turn to find Graham steadily observing me. His solitary raised eyebrow says it all.

"Charlie, we need to stay sharp here. The Dragon Slayers have shown that they are well prepared."

I give him a thumbs up, as Carter's voice crackles in my ear.

"Boss, the drones are airborne. We've got eyes on the motel. It's quiet. Nothing so far."

"Escape routes?"

"Just the main road and one back trail; everything else is mountains. They're boxed in with nowhere to run. We've got units covering all angles."

"Keep the drones close. We can't let anything catch us off guard."

"Copy that. No one's getting past us."

The building looms ahead, and from a distance, it's unremarkable. A faded, typical trucker lodging with peeling paint and a blinking sign. A dimly lit parking lot reveals a few cars surrounded by mostly empty spaces.

"Lights on," Graham advises the pilot.

Floodlights erupt in a blinding display, illuminating the motel in an unrelenting white glow. Shadows stretch and contort, spreading across cracked asphalt. The place feels suspended in time, the only movement coming from the snowflakes, dancing in the wind.

Graham grabs the comms mic, his voice blasting out across the vast emptiness.

"This is the FBI. Remain in your rooms. Attempt no departure from the grounds. Repeat: Remain in your rooms. Noncompliance will be answered with hostile force."

I scan the motel, waiting for the parking lot to fill up with activity.

"Hovering," the pilot announces as the helicopter settles, its blades churning a maelstrom of dust.

Red and blue lights materialize in the distance, sirens piercing through the gap between us. Squad cars screech into the parking lot, engines snarling ominously as they spread out to seal off all points of escape. Officers burst out, guns drawn, their movements tense with resolve and determination.

I signal to the pilot that the perimeter is secured. The helicopter drops down, its floodlights dimming as we close in. Dust and gravel are whipped into a frenzied whirlwind as the tactical team pours out, dropping one by one with mastered precision. Once the last team member has jumped out, the helicopter rises again, resuming its vigilant position in the sky.

Chief Reynolds' cruiser screeches to a stop. He leaps out, knowing that the stakes are incredibly high. This could be the most important night of his career.

"Grayson. My men are ready to roll. What's the plan?"

I pull out a picture of Marshall from my pocket and hand it to Reynolds.

"This is our suspect. He's priority one. Close the perimeter. If anybody tries to leave, arrest them on sight. And instruct your officers that this isn't a firefight unless there's absolutely no other choice."

"Got it. We'll keep it cordoned off."

My gaze drifts back to the building. Within those walls, Marshall could be hiding. And maybe if luck favors us, he is not alone.

In the motel's head office, fluorescent tubes flicker overhead, illuminating every wrinkle of the yellowing wallpaper. A vending machine in the corner vibrates noisily as its compressor struggles to keep working.

A young man behind the desk tenses as the door flings open. His hands rise into the air, face pale and pinched against his rumpled, stained uniform.

"Jesus Christ! Don't shoot me!" he pleads, trembling. "Please… don't shoot!"

Graham lunges in first, rifle raised but not aimed, eyes moving with controlled precision around the room. I follow behind him and then approach the young clerk.

"It's okay. We only want to ask you some questions."

I slap a photo of Evan Marshall onto the counter, my movement abrupt and forceful. The clerk jerks his rounded eyes, darting apprehensively back and forth between me and the tactical squad.

"Do you recognize this man?" I press urgently. "Is he here?"

"I… I've been here for maybe fifteen minutes. Haven't worked in four days. This is my third job. I take shifts whenever they need someone to fill in."

"What's your check-in process? Guest registry? PMS system?"

"Lady, what system? We're lucky if the credit card machine doesn't freeze. Most of the guys that stop here pay cash, truckers, loners, folks who don't want receipts. If we're lucky, they scribble their real name."

Graham cuts in, causing more friction.

"What about suspicious individuals? Military uniforms, odd behavior. Anything out of the ordinary?"

The clerk shakes his head wildly.

"No man! I swear! I just got here. Please, I don't know anything!"

I shoot a look at Graham, irritation boiling just below my placid surface. The clerk's fear is real, and his inability to provide any information is making things more difficult for us.

"Just stay where you are," I order him.

Leaving the shaking clerk behind, we step outside into a steady blanket of snow, the icy wind numbing us.

Graham gets into a squad car, moving the mounted loud-speaker easily aside.

"This is the FBI. Evan Marshall, come out with your hands up. We know you're in there. Don't make us have to come get you."

The motel is eerily still, the quiet becoming a physical presence. The only sign of life is the neon vacancy sign, which seems to blink a SOS code for help.

"Evan Marshall," Graham repeats "This is your last chance. Vacate your room at once, or we'll come in with our guns drawn."

There is a deep silence, dense, tangible, as the tension builds with every tick of the clock.

I whisper to Graham.

"He's either too scared to come out, or he's not alone."

"Charlie, we don't know who or how many are in there. This could be a trap. We take it slow."

"Got it. No one's going anywhere. They're boxed in. We do this right."

Graham gives the signal.

The tactical team tightens, starting at the far end of the lot, weapons ready, each step carefully gauged.

Without warning, the loudspeaker is activated, shattering the stillness of the snow-covered night.

"Room 1, open your door and slowly come out with your hands up. Lie on the ground, face down."

The door creaks open, revealing a young couple tightly holding hands. They step out slowly, terror twisting their features. Officers rush to encircle them, verifying their identities before leading them to safety.

The process repeats itself for room 2, a grungy trucker, room 3, a woman with the appearance of an aged sex worker. Out of room 4 comes a family, two small children clutching their mother as she whispers frantic reassurances.

With every room we clear, the tension builds. By the time we get to room 5, the air is so thick with apprehension it's becoming hard to breathe. The loudspeaker makes its call, but there's no response.

"Breach it." Graham orders.

With one solid blow, an operative slams the ram against the door, breaking it wide open.

Unlike a standard breach, fast, aggressive, built on surprise, Graham is taking a much more controlled approach. His men move slowly and methodically, clearing the room like it's rigged to explode. Every corner swept, every shadow checked, leaving zero chance of missing anything.

The same unnerving sight awaits us in rooms six and seven, each of them unoccupied. The slow pace is increasingly maddening as we move along, but no one breaks rhythm.

By the time we reach room 8, something feels off. The blinds are closed, a strained silence emanates from the room. Graham holds up his fist, calling for quiet.

"Room 8," the loudspeaker thunders. "Open the door and come out slowly with your hands up."

Nothing.

"Breach," Graham yells.

The next door is approached just like the rest, every angle covered.

Then the ram hits, cracking the door open.

We move, flooding the room with practiced precision, guns covering every quadrant.

It's empty.

Then we see it.

Spray-painted across the far wall, bold and unmistakable, is the emblem of the Dragon Slayers.

Everyone freezes.

"Hold your position," Graham orders over the comms. "This is the room."

We move in slow motion.

The breach team clears the threshold first, flashlights piercing the darkness. Every inch of the room is treated like a threat, under the bed, behind furniture, the ceiling corners, no space too small to miss.

I follow at the rear, my boots careful, deliberate.

The light catches scuffed floor tiles, a cracked lamp, and a half-empty bag of chips on the counter.

An acrid smell hits me as one of the agents mutters.

"Gasoline."

Everyone stiffens, posture shifting as the tension spikes.

Flashlights scan intently now, slower in their sweep but deeper in their focus, pausing on every vent, every outlet, every object large enough to hide a device.

"Bathroom," another agent calls out.

Graham and I approach the half-open door, rifles raised. One swift kick sends it crashing open, and what's inside stops us cold.

Evan Marshall.

He's slumped on the toilet, wrists and ankles cinched tight with thick zip ties; a ragged gag knotted deep across his mouth. His face jerks up, wild-eyed and pale, drenched in sweat. He tries to scream through the gag, a muffled, panicked plea for help.

Then he sees our guns drawn, and he loses it.

Marshall's head thrashes, his shoulders lurch, and he starts desperately kicking in one direction. His eyes shift frantically toward the counter next to him, where a small rectangular metal box is placed.

Graham doesn't hesitate.

"Everyone out! Now! Get EOD in here. Go, go, go!"

A torrent of motion fills the room. Agents spill back through the doorway, pushing out fast, leaving Marshall behind, helpless. I move out with the other agents, instincts clawing at me.

Evan Marshall. The key to breaking open this case. We finally found him, and now we're leaving him behind.

From experience and training, I know we need to let them handle this threat.

There's no such thing as certainty when you're staring down a bomb and your single lead is strapped to a toilet, praying that we don't get him blown up to smithereens.

The EOD tech moves in, weighted down by his blast suit. The rest of us hold back outside, our breathing suspended.

"Moving in now," the tech says, voice steady through our comms. "I have visual. Single box. No visible wires. The device is positioned close to target.

"No clear tripwire, but the proximity is tight. Removing the subject may trigger detonation."

He's covering his words: Marshall could be the failsafe.

The Dragon Slayers set a trap for us.

We finally have someone who can provide valuable evidence. The Catch-22 is that touching Marshall might kill him.

"Approaching device," the tech advises. "No visible trigger. Opening now."

We are riveted in place.

Then.

"It's…" the tech pauses. "It's just a letter. No device. No explosives. Repeat. Box is clean. It's a letter inside."

For a second, none of us speak. We were braced for detonation.

And instead, the Dragon Slayers left us a note.

Graham exhales slowly.

"Get Marshall out of there. Carefully."

The team moves strategically back into the hotel room, eagle eyes matched with steady hands.

Marshall is still paralyzed with fear. He is barely able to lift his head as an agent cuts the zip ties and gently pulls the gag from his mouth.

I kneel beside him and place my hand on his knee.

"Evan. You're safe now. We're here to help, okay? We're going to get you out of here. You're going to be alright."

Marshall doesn't say a word. He is in a catatonic state, his eyes fixed on the wall.

I signal for some assistance.

"Get him back to the station and make him comfortable. We'll question him when he snaps out of it."

Marshall is lifted by two agents who support his weight as they guide him out. He doesn't resist, his body limp, lungs filled with harsh vapors, mind still trapped in the hell he just experienced.

The smell is heaviest here, suffocating. I peel back the stained curtain, and behind it, the tub is loaded with cash.

Tight stacks. Row after row of hundred-dollar bills, drenched in gasoline. The chemical sheen glistens under the overhead light.

It has to be close to a million. Maybe more.

This must have been Evan's cut of the bribe money.

All of it could've gone up in smoke with a single spark.

All of it just inches from him.

My stomach tightens as Graham joins me.

I step over to the opened box, left on the counter. The letter inside is crisp, formal stationery, folded neatly in the center, inviting me to take it.

I remove the letter cautiously and start reading it.

Good thing you don't have a billion dollars,

We're on the same side here. You just don't know it yet.

"They're fucking toying with us," Graham groans, his voice low and strained. "They wanted us to find this. They wanted us to know they're way ahead of us. Bastards.

"Graham, I need fresh air."

I hand him the letter and head outside.

The cold is now a welcome relief to the burning sensation flowing through my body. I look up at the nighttime sky, which is always soothing for me. My mind is suspended between the comfort of the heavens and the turmoil here on earth.

How am I supposed to stop the Dragon Slayers?

They're organized and so well-funded that they can drown an entire city in bribe money or burn a million dollars just to make a point.

How does one fight that?

It feels hopeless, but whatever it takes, I have to stop them.

Because if I fail to stop them...

I don't know who can.

CHAPTER 16

ONE STEP AHEAD

*"When the rich rob the poor, it's called business.
When the poor fight back, it's called violence."*

-MARK TWAIN

A GUST OF freezing air jolts me back to reality, grounding me just enough to regain my footing.

I turn back toward the parking lot, making tracks in the fresh snow that covers the cracked asphalt. Ahead, a patrol car idles low, the steam from its exhaust pipe curling lazily into the night.

A thermal blanket wraps Evan Marshall, who hunches over in the back seat. He is somber, bowed low, still disconnected from the world.

As we approach, he looks up apprehensively. His words slowly trickle out, tears welling up in his eyes.

"Fuck, thought I was going to die. Those assholes said it was a bomb next to me wired to blow once someone came to my rescue. I... I thought I was done for..."

"Evan, it's over. I'm Deputy Director Grayson with the FBI. We have everything under control."

He doesn't reply, just pulls the blanket tighter around his body.

I give a wave to the officer at the wheel.

"Take him in. No lights. Straight to the station."

The cruiser rolls forward, and I watch it leave until the red taillights disappear into the dark. Graham steps beside me and puts a comforting hand on my shoulder.

"Charlie, if Marshall cracks for us, then we have a real shot at the Dragon Slayers. Right now, they are in control, but that can easily change with the right info.

"He must know something, and we will find out whatever that is."

We head back to our SUV, and once inside, nobody speaks. The driver is concentrating on the winding roads, slippery with snow. Graham scrolls through his phone, while I stare out the window, wondering where to begin again.

It's one thing if someone helped the Dragon Slayers by sharing intel, unlocking a door, or looking the other way. But this? To take Marshall hostage, plant him next to a gas-soaked fortune and then plant a taunting letter is extreme intimidation.

The question now is, what do they want Marshall to share with us? As we pull into the police station lot, I know that the answer will be ours soon.

Reynolds is waiting near the side entrance for us. Marshall is already tucked safely inside.

"Chief, thanks for your support tonight," I say quietly.

"Glad you got your man, Deputy Director. Hopefully, this helps turn the tide a little."

I wish I could honestly tell him it will, but the odds are not in our favor.

"Priority one," I tell Reynolds. "No leaks. Keep him locked up tight until we're ready to talk with him."

"Understood. He'll be put in isolation and closely monitored."

I watch Marshall forlornly disappear into the station, fear and shock still engraved on his face.

"We interrogate him the moment he's stable," I tell Graham. "He's our best bet."

Graham grunts in agreement; his mind is already considering our next move.

My comm beeps. Bill connects over the link.

"Charlie, update."

"We've got Marshall. No Dragon Slayers are present. They had gasoline everywhere; they were hoping we went in hot. The suspect is shaken and in custody."

There is a pause before Bill's tone comes down hard.

"Good. But we're running out of time. Two days left, Charlie. We can't keep following their shadows. We need a victory, something big."

"Understood. Evan Marshall might give us that something."

"Unfortunately, we need more than 'might.' Tuff's growing more impatient. The public is jittery. Billionaires are freaking out. Pursue every lead, no more playing defense."

The comm cuts off, but the heaviness of his words is choking. Breathe, I firmly tell myself, rubbing my hand over my face. Time is marching by too fast… enough for all of us to panic.

Another buzz. Victor's name displays on the screen. My answer is quick.

"Grayson," he says, his voice seeping with contempt, "Tell me you've got something worthwhile."

"We located our lead suspect, Evan Marshall, alive, but no Dragon Slayers were present."

"And what do you propose we do with this Marshall character? Have a nice, friendly chat over coffee and donuts? He needs to go to a black site now. Enhanced interrogation. Get everything out of him… no holds barred."

"Victor, Marshall's actions make little sense for someone who's supporting terrorists. He was bound, gagged, and left in a trap. That doesn't scream willing accomplice."

"I don't care what it screams! I care about results. And so far, Grayson, you've delivered none. If you can't manage this, we'll bring in private contractors, men without your damn moral hesitations."

Unshaken by his attempts to rattle me, I keep my voice firm.

"We're pursuing every lead. You'll have results soon."

"You'd better. Time's running out, and if you continue to mess things up, this failure will fall squarely on your shoulders."

The line goes dead, and anger brews beneath my skin. Victor's threatening rhetoric and private contractor menace could make this operation a catastrophe.

The comm buzzes again before I can shake off my concentration. Carter filters through, tense but even.

"Boss, we've got a problem."

"What is it?"

"Chatter on the dark web. Dragon Slayers are gearing up. Might be a second video or something larger. Either way, activity is spiking."

"Carter, what sort of chatter?"

"Encrypted forums and burner accounts are solidifying into logistics centers. They're writing a playbook for collaborators, for anyone who wants to cash in. It's like a help desk for their revolution."

"You're saying the Dragon Slayers are planning out in the open?"

"Pretty much, it's mass recruitment. Guides are starting to appear. Kinda like how to get cash and avoid the slammer. The more the Dragon Slayers' message spreads, the less we can control it."

"They're building infrastructure. This system of terror is taking shape."

"Right. If this continues to escalate, it's game over. They'll have a worldwide platform we can't touch."

"Can we infiltrate them? Track down the sources?"

"We're working on it, but they've encrypted it in layers. We'll crack it, but not soon enough to prevent the harm if this leaks out."

The severity of what he says chokes me. With under 48 hours remaining, the ticking clock sounds louder than ever.

"Keep digging. And Carter?"

"Yeah, boss?"

"If the Dragon Slayers make another attempt at anything, we need to stop them before they strike. Bill made it clear we might not have much time before the administration takes this into their own hands."

"On it."

The line dies, and I'm left pondering my own decisions as I make my way to the station's interrogation room. Marshall is seated there, his hands trembling as beads of sweat glisten like dewdrops on his face. His eyes dart anxiously between Graham and me as we walk in.

I sit opposite him, my hands clasped together on the table.

"Mr. Marshall, please tell us from the beginning. How did you find yourself in this situation?"

Graham stands still, hand tracing his mustache with measured patience.

"Help yourself by helping us. Right now, you're our only

lead to the Dragon Slayers. Don't waste this opportunity we are giving you."

Marshall clears his throat, words cracking.

"I didn't intend this to happen. It was Paula. She told me someone had called her a few weeks back. Said they were going to change our lives."

"Who?" I press. "How?"

"I don't know. Paula said they tracked her down. Gave her an offer of ten million dollars for an easy opportunity. Paid fifteen grand just to discuss. Paula was in deep financial trouble… gambling, bad investments. She thought this was her way out."

"And then what?"

Marshall's voice squeaks.

"The video. By the time it went live, it was too late. They wired her another fifteen million via some crypto thing, told her she had to leave the country and that I had to come too. She pleaded with me. New identities, new lives. But I couldn't. I told her no. So, she went by herself."

Graham steps closer.

"And what did you do next?"

"Nothing, man. Like a dumb fuck, I panicked and went straight to the motel. I didn't know what else to do, so I called my sister. Five minutes later, the door opened. Three of them… Dragon Slayers."

"And then?" I ask.

"They tied me up. Dumped the money in the tub. Covered the cash with gasoline. One guy wanted to shoot me, but another one told him, 'No. That's not how we win.'"

"They spray-painted that symbol on the wall and told me, 'If they come in hot, the gas will take care of everything. And if not, then the bomb will.'"

"Fuck, I almost shit myself over a box with only a damn letter in it. I thought I was dead for sure."

I glance at Graham, and our eyes lock in silent understanding. The same awful realization between us: if we'd entered quicker or used a single flashbang, that room would have been a ball of flames. A sharp wave of reality ripples through me.

Graham's team saved us by making sure we kept our emotions under control.

My questioning continues.

"They left you bound, with the gas, the cash, everything?"

Marshall swallows hard, his face pale.

"I just… waited and prayed. When I heard you guys, I hoped maybe it was finally over."

Graham steps forward, his tone a controlled whisper infused with menace.

"Mr. Marshall, better hope you didn't send Paula to her death. From where I'm standing, it's much easier for them to kill her than provide her with a new life."

"I know. That's exactly why I couldn't do it. But Paula, she was so desperate. She didn't see any other way out."

"Desperation is no excuse for helping terrorists.

"You know what happens next, Marshall? You become the face of traitors. The idiot who got caught working with the Dragon Slayers. Your name, your mug shot, plastered everywhere.

"You'll wish you were forgotten because you'll be remembered as a terrorist from now on. If there's anything you haven't told us, now is your last chance."

Marshall starts to shake uncontrollably, his hands gripping the edge of the table like it's a life raft, keeping him afloat.

"I…I don't know anything else," he stammers. "I swear, I…"

I step in, keeping my tone calm but firm.

"Evan, listen to me. Right now, you're classified as a terrorist. But if you help us, if you give us anything. Anything at all, you have a much better chance of walking out of this as a victim instead of an enemy. Do you understand?"

Panic engulfs Marshall, and for a moment, I think he's going to pass out. His shoulders sag as he lets out a defeated sigh, until something clicks. His eyes sharpen as he straightens up, suddenly remembering.

"Wait, there is one thing. One of them mentioned a 'save something.' They said once they had it, something would be locked in, and they could capture a bunch of billionaires. One of the other Dragon Slayers told them to shut up since I was there. Think they thought I couldn't hear anything with the gag and hood on."

Graham sends a shrug my way, an unspoken question forming between us. Save something? This could mean anything... Marshall doesn't know, and that means we don't either.

Forcing a small, reassuring smile, I touch Marshall on the shoulder.

"Okay, this is enough. Thank you. If you remember anything else, you need to tell us immediately."

He nods too quickly, eager to please, trying to believe he's done enough. But then, as we move toward the door, his voice catches.

"Wait. What's... what's going to happen to me?"

I hesitate. Just for a second. Long enough that I know he sees it.

"Don't worry. It'll be okay."

Marshall lets out a deep sigh. He wants to believe me, but I know he doesn't.

I don't let my expression shift, because I know I can't guarantee a damn thing I just said.

To Tuff and the administration, Marshall's life doesn't matter. It never did, and never will. What matters is the optics. The headline. Another convenient face to slap on a podium and declare victory, even if it's premature, empty, and loud. As long as it drowns out the truth.

My thoughts circle back to those two words: 'save something.'

What did he mean? A location? A password? A message meant for someone else?

To help Marshall and the others who will get swept up in Dragon Slayer euphoria, I need to figure out what save something actually means.

Could be a code. Could be secret location. Could be the next phase of whatever the Dragon Slayers have planned.

The possibilities are endless.

Unfortunately, our time is not.

CHAPTER 17

RECRUITMENT GONE VIRAL

"The great bulk of the wealth of the country is in the hands of a few men… and they are using it to build up a class government and destroy democracy."

-Ulysses S. Grant

GRAHAM AND I step outside, mentally and physically depleted from the past 24 hours. Behind us, the station remains a fortress, locking Evan away into whatever grim fate awaits him. It's out of my control now, and his only chance of redemption might be if we can stop the Dragon Slayers.

I let out a moan. *Save something.* That's all we have, and it's not enough.

The words rattle around in my mind, hard thoughts bouncing off dead ends.

It could be anything, and that's the problem. It's the only real clue we have, and it's nothing.

My fingers twitch at my sides, restless.

"What are you thinking?" Graham asks beside me.

"I'm thinking we have next to nothing."

"Yeah, going nowhere fast."

"Nothing's going to change. We're done here."

Graham jerks his chin toward the lot.

"Let's head back to HQ."

I step beside him, pushing past gnawing frustration as we load up to leave. The pieces aren't interlocking yet, but eventually they have to.

Fifteen million dollars. That's what the Dragon Slayers shelled out to two people. Paula Nunez and Evan Marshall. Ordinary, desperate people. I do the math in my head: ten million split between fourteen billion.

Nine hundred.

That's how many more Paulas and Evans they could buy, and they'd still have lots to spare.

I gaze out the SUV window, my reflection a dim shadow in the pane. For billionaires, money is their greatest weapon. They've used it to silence, crush, and insulate. Now, that wealth is used as a turnabout for fair play, buying loyalty to the Dragon Slayers.

If they actually paid all five of the missing employees, if they provided a way out, how do we stop them?

What can compete with a suitcase full of money and the assurance of true freedom, when compared to working the rest of your life just to barely survive?

My phone buzzes, halting my racing thoughts.

Carter.

"Talk to me."

"Boss, we have a problem. I'm sending you a link. Just watch it."

The dashboard chirps, and I glance at my tablet.

"Carter… another Lancelot video?"

"Honestly, somehow, it's worse. You gotta see it."

The file unfolds, and I hesitate before clicking to open it. The screen erupts with the image of a female figure wearing a mask; it is smooth, gold and ivory, contoured to evoke softness, almost inviting. It cuts off just above her mouth, so you can see her smile. Her warm eyes and long blonde hair lend her the appearance of a pinup poster, captivating yet deeply unsettling.

Soft white sheets accented with delicate gold floral designs create a serene background. At the center, bold and unmistakable, the Dragon Slayer emblem anchors the frame.

Everything about the woman's elegant surroundings is intentionally staged to capture viewers' attention. And she holds it effortlessly.

"Good tidings, Resistance!"

The voice that comes out is playful and welcoming. It's one you'd trust for customer service instead of a terrorist manifesto. It's intimate. She's inviting each viewer in for a hug instead of issuing a threat.

My name is Guinevere.

And I'm here to help.

Together, we're building a better tomorrow for everyone.

It starts with destroying the greed-based systems that have controlled us for far too long.

I am drawn in, captivated by her words. This is a lesson in psychological manipulation.

Guinevere subtly tilts her head, a calculated, playful gesture.

My role is straightforward.

I'm your guide, your news source, your ally in this struggle.

I'll update you and make sure your valor is properly rewarded.

You've toiled away your whole life. Now,
it's time for that effort to pay off.

Literally.

The screen blinks, revealing a QR code on a blurred webpage with encrypted chat logs.

Guinevere continues, warmly disarming.

Intrigued by how to get started?

It's easy.

Number one, get yourself a VPN.

Number two, use the QR codes we've pro-
vided or visit the links we're sharing.

They'll lead you to our untraceable network.

There, you can access everything you require to help
with the revolution and earn your keep.

To the people who have already offered their help, thank you.

The five courageous souls who stood with us at
the satellite uplink were compensated.

Fifty million dollars is not bad for a day's work.

But even one day of work is more than most billionaires ever do.

Our new friends are now leading finan-
cially secure, brand-new lives.

You need not bear the burden of others greed any longer.

Join us, and your contributions will be cherished, and rewarded.

Her voice narrows a fraction, but not by much, maintaining radiance and warmth.

To the billionaires watching, it's not too late.

Prove to the world that you can change.

Do the right thing, and we'll make your transition seamless.

*But cling to the deadly sin of greed, and it
will consume you, as it always does.*

Remember, we still have billions at our disposal.

To put that in perspective:

a million seconds is twelve days.

A billion? That's over thirty-one years.

But the median person on this planet only has two hours.

That's the scale on which we're operating.

The scale of your greed.

The scale of the suffering it's caused.

And now, the scale of what will be used against you.

The choice is yours. But let's be honest,

*you don't stand a chance against the masses
you've oppressed, now do you?*

If I were you, I'd be very worried indeed.

Guinevere smiles, playful, patient, and undeniably certain.

*So, billionaires, we'll make it easy for you
to reach out to us,*

we'll show you all the ways your ill-gotten wealth can redeem you.

The video concludes with Guinevere moving closer to the camera; her smile radiating an undeniable charm. She reminds me of a sophisticated influencer than the face of a terror organization.

I'm Guinevere.

I'm here to help.

And I look forward to seeing you again soon.

Good tidings, Resistance.

The screen fades to black. I am paralyzed, the gravity of what I've just seen squeezing me like a vice.

Carter snaps me out of my trance.

"Boss, you still there?"

"Christ, Carter. That Dragon Slayer… Guinevere… she's going to be damn effective.

"How is your team handling this?"

"We're doing our best. Tor traffic spiked the second this went online, and we've been tracking it ever since."

"Did we succeed in closing her video down?"

"Most of the large sites, yes. But there is one big problem."

"What is it?"

"Alan Schmutt's fucking Y. It's filled with uploads. Content moderation isn't even responding… which, given that he fired 80% of the staff a few months back, isn't exactly surprising."

"You're saying someone at Y is helping the Dragon Slayers? Maybe bribed?"

"Perhaps, but in all honesty? More likely incompetence. The site's a shitshow. The Dragon Slayers probably figured it's a prime target. No one's monitoring Y, it's basically an echo chamber filled with bots and incels."

"Of course, another one of Schmutt's ego trips. He took a global stage and turned it into a disaster, and now it's a megaphone for terrorists."

Carter responds with a dark laugh.

"Exactly. That cesspool is paying off for them. It's trending everywhere. We take down one post, and three more appear. The system's so broken it's not even funny. We'll get it under control, boss. Promise."

"Thanks, Carter. I'll see what I can do on my end. Keep me updated."

Reluctantly, I pull up Alan Schmutt's number, because as much as I hate it, the fastest way to cut through this mess is to call him directly, but dealing with him is aggravating no matter the hour.

It rings twice, then goes directly to voicemail. Heroic orchestral music blares out, flamboyantly absurd, and is followed by Schmutt's smug tone:

"Hello! You've reached Alan Schmutt. Visionary, entrepreneur, space cowboy. Leave a message, and I'll call you back when I'm not busy saving the world. Tootles!"

I pull back the phone, agitated as though it's mocking me. Of course, that would be his voicemail. I hang up and call Victor.

"Grayson, not surprised, you need help again?" he retorts arrogantly.

"Victor, where's Alan? Y is hosting Dragon Slayer propaganda, videos, guides, the whole manifesto, and no one appears to be taking it down."

"Oh, Alan? He's here. Crashes at the White House occasionally. He sleeps on the floor here, pretending he's so busy. One of his endearing habits. Hold on."

Victor's shoes squeak in the background, followed by shouting in the distance.

"Alan!" Victor yells. "That Grayson girl needs you!"

"What? I'm in the middle of a game! Top 10 in the world on hardcore. She can wait!"

"Apparently not. Something about your platform harboring terrorists."

Silence, then Alan's voice draws closer.

"What do you want, Grayson? I'm busy dominating the matrix."

I want to get back to work, to focus on something that matters, but instead, I force myself to stay calm and address Alan directly.

"Alan, Y is flooded with Dragon Slayer propaganda. Videos, instructions, everything. They're recruiting openly, and your team isn't responding. What's going on?"

Schmutt snorts.

"Y is about free speech. Innovation. You know, the good stuff. But don't worry, I'll handle it. Easy fix for a coding god like me."

Victor interrupts, his overzealous voice dripping with reverence.

"See? That's why Alan's the man. He's got this under control. Watch and learn, Grayson."

Schmutt merges our call.

"Yo, Bob. We've got some heavy biz on Y. Kill the switch or whatever. Call me back.

"Huh, Bob's not answering."

"Do you have someone else?" I ask gruffly.

"Uh, no. I've fired the rest of the moderation team. Why would you want a team preventing free speech? Look, I'm the visionary here, there, everywhere. Silly details such as off switches aren't exactly my forte."

Victor, the perpetual brown-nosing toady, croaks in.

"Damn that, Bob! He's spoiling such a wonderful system. Don't worry, Alan. You'll get it sorted out. You always do!"

"You know what? This is actually good! The Dragon Slayers

walked right into our ambush. My code is so tight that we'll follow them back to their lair. Everything is completely under control."

"Under control?" I retort. "This is a PR nightmare. They're recruiting in real time, and you're allowing it to happen."

Schmutt's voice strains for nonchalance but lands somewhere between defensive and clueless.

"Come on, shutting down Y would cost me millions in ad revenue. Do you even know how much interest on the loans I took out to buy it cost me? Maybe we just, I don't know… spin this as extreme free speech? Lean into it?"

"Extreme free speech? Alan, you're endangering lives here."

Schmutt lets out a nervous chuckle, then immediately overcorrects with a scoff.

"Lives of terrorists, maybe. I mean, really, who's siding with those losers?

"Anyway, Grayson, I'll fix this. I always do. And I need to… uh, climb the ranked ladder… I mean… work on an important project. Yeah, real important. Slashing government waste. Did you know how many kids were getting a free lunch before we took over? Disgusting waste of taxpayers' money."

He hangs up mid-sentence, realizing he's said too much or perhaps simply losing interest in the conversation. I glare at the phone, reminded yet again of the incompetence that thrives in wealth's protective bubble.

My gaze drifts to the city lights beyond the window.

The word is out now.

The Dragon Slayers will live up to their promise.

Destruction is about to be unleashed.

CHAPTER 18

THE SYSTEM TURNS

*"Every gun that is made, every warship launched…
signifies a theft from those who hunger and are
not fed, who are cold and are not clothed."*

-Dwight D. Eisenhower

OUR FLIGHT BACK to FBI headquarters gives us the chance to catch up on some much-needed sleep. It's not a deep rest, but enough to make me feel human again.

By the time we land, the sun is low, the days have become one big blur. A car is waiting to take us straight back to HQ, leaving no time for Graham and me to return home for a quick visit.

Back on-site, there is just enough time for a shower and a change of attire. Hot water and clean clothes help to rejuvenate me, but the headache of dealing with Alan Schmutt will not go away anytime soon.

My phone buzzes.

A text from Maya.

Hey, can you come by and see me as soon as possible?

A small spark of hope ignites within me. Perhaps she has a solid lead, something that I can actually work with.

Stepping into her office, I scan her multiple screens, live feeds flickering, social media panels open and video clips ready to be played. Her attention is vigilant, but there's a hint of urgency that gets my adrenaline pumping.

"Hey Maya, what's happening?"

"Charlie, we have a situation. A few of the billionaires are donating some of their wealth. And now they're going public with it."

"Wait. What?"

She clicks to open the first clip, and when the video starts playing, what appears is alarming. I feel like an invisible opponent has blindsided me.

The first man appears to have stepped out of a 90s dot-com startup, older, with the demeanor of an engineer who, by some divine intervention, made a fortune. He is seated in front of a drab backdrop, with no PR makeup or canned answers. Just a man speaking his mind.

"I pledged early on that if I were ever to make billions, I'd give most of it away later in life. Honestly, it can do a lot more good now. I started a great company, and it took flight. That's all. I was fortunate.

"My employees made it what it was, my customers made it what it was. And now? Now I get to make good on my promise."

I cross my arms, watching him intently. There's no strained look on his face, no fear in his voice, just a quiet kind of conviction. He displays no signs of coercion, as if this has always been his intention.

Apparently, this man already has a charitable foundation, a structure in place. Maybe he's sincere in saying that he did mean to help, eventually. The question is, was it truly his choice?

Or did the Dragon Slayers motivate him enough to take the step he'd been delaying for years?

Maya promptly clicks to the next clip. The next man appears younger, perhaps in his mid-forties, with a heavyhearted look on his face, as if his fortunes were an unwelcome burden.

"I mean, I just wanted to create a cool product. My company went public, and now I'm sitting on billions. It's really sort of insane how little work I did to achieve this compared to, you know, a firefighter or a nurse.

"And trust me? The Dragon Slayers aren't wrong. I don't need that much money, and neither does anyone else."

His words are unexpected and consequential, the narrative taking a U-turn. The first man had made it a matter of a personal badge of honor.

But this guy? This is an explicit validation of the Dragon Slayers' entire radical message.

Maya clicks again, revealing the latest billionaire waving the white flag of submission.

She's lounging in what appears to be an over-the-top studio, with an expensive pedigree cat curled on her lap. Far too charismatic for this to be anything other than genuine.

"The past several years have been the best ones of my life with my massive tour success," she says, her eyes glistening with appreciation. "And it's all due to my fans, my team, and the wonderful crew that helped make all this happen. So, I'm giving back... because it's not just about me.

"I've already rewarded my team with millions and now I'm going to extend my generosity by launching a Fandom Foundation. This will allow me to support my team and my fans much more efficiently.

"Plus, I'll still have all of my worldly possessions, with more than enough money to see me through the rest of my life. Giving back doesn't equate to giving it all away; it's about looking after the people around you, as well."

Maya doesn't hold back.

"You know where we're headed now, Charlie, don't you?"

"I do. Tuff, Victor, Schmutt and Hart are going to completely lose their minds."

Without hesitation, I send the clips directly to Victor, with a concise message:

Victor, have you seen these videos?

It takes less than a minute for my phone to start ringing.

Victor's voice thunders through the speaker, his anger unchecked. There is no hello, no preamble, just rough, guttural outrage.

"Grayson, what are these traitorous bastards up to?"

"You watched the clips?"

"Of course I saw them! Billionaires giving up their money now? Don't they know how bad this appears? It makes the Dragon Slayers' cause look credible. This is fucking disgusting!"

I visualize Victor pacing back and forth like a caged animal, face red, clenching his phone as if it is responsible for this mess.

His words become labored.

"You need to take a call in five minutes. President Tuff must be briefed on this immediately. We cannot allow this abomination to continue."

He hangs up before I have a chance to respond. Clenching my jaw tight, I glance at my watch, five minutes 'til showtime.

I turn to Maya.

"None of this is good for us. These are prominent billionaires caving to the Dragon Slayers. How many other billionaires are doing the same thing but in secret?"

"What's even worse, Charlie, is the estimate of $23 billion in donations. Hard not to notice that figure when the positive effects start kicking in. Life has already changed for so many people.

"Ironic, isn't it? The same billionaires who built the social media ecosystem thrived on capturing our attention for profit. They designed it to hook as many people as possible, to make addiction the default. Now, that same system is turning on them."

Trying to process the extent of the war I'm facing is becoming more difficult. How do you fight for the side associated with blatant greed? It's a grave thought that I need to reject, at least for the time being.

My attention turns back to Maya.

"Good work. Let's stay on top of this story to monitor the message that these billionaires are doing the right thing."

"Carter and I are taking charge. The challenge is that it's a viral concept. We can throttle the views from them posting it, but the reaction videos are infinitely more difficult to control."

She's right. The problem lies not with the message itself, but with its magnification by others, which renders it unavoidable to any viewer.

"It won't be easy, but everything helps. I have to go, Maya. Let me know if anything else pops up."

"Will do, Charlie," she says without even looking up.

I hurry to my office for the call with the administration cavalry. Tuff is screaming as I join in.

"Traitors! Sniveling, backstabbing, ungrateful traitors! I don't care how much they made; if they just give it away, they didn't deserve it in the first place! We need to take those funds back... damn it!"

He is having a complete meltdown.

"Mr. President, I don't believe we can dictate what other individuals do with their own money."

Tuff strikes out at me instantly.

"Well, if it's aiding the Dragon Slayers, of course we fucking can!"

The intensity of his shouts makes me almost push back from the screen. I fortify my nerves and lock eyes with him.

His sharp tone is erratic, bouncing between rage and frustration. A man built on excess, furious at the idea of anyone even daring to reject anything he demands.

Victor jumps in fast, his voice in damage control mode.

"Mr. President, I understand your frustration... we all do. This is unacceptable, and we're already moving to address it."

Dr. Hart cuts in next.

"We need to discuss narrative containment immediately. If we permit the perception that billionaires are willingly relinquishing their wealth under no outside duress, it contributes to the perception that wealth concentration at their hands is itself unfair."

A new face flickers onto the screen, pale, clammy, and unmistakably smug.

"I can be of assistance."

The oily confidence in his words hits first. Then the face finishes the confirmation. Damp skin. Bulbous nose. A twisted smile tucked beneath thick glasses.

Eugene Lasky.

Tuff's top legal counsel. Known for twisting legal language into whatever shape best protects his clients, no matter how grotesque.

"We're already exploring legal ramifications," he says, his tone syrupy with false patience.

"There are loopholes. If their donations are funding a group that's under investigation, we can seize assets, freeze transactions, even prosecute them as co-conspirators."

Tuff smiles, very satisfied.

"See, that's why I like you, Lasky. I want you working on every angle. Find me a way to make this stick fast and hard. I want charges drafted before the next briefing. I want people arrested for even flirting with this ideology. I want to make them suffer, damn it!"

I keep my tone measured, but I can't ignore the obvious.

"If we start clawing back donations from charities, it's going to look like we're punishing people. That kind of move could backfire and burn trust we can't afford to lose."

Tuff growls, nostrils flaring.

"Listen, Grayson. If I say what they're trying to do is a terrorist act, then they're goddamn terrorists, okay? And your good-for-nothing FBI is supposed to take out terrorists! Are you listening to me, Deputy Director! Because I swear to God, if not, I'll have your ass off this case in an instant."

His threat lands hard. I fall silent for a moment, my mind weighing options. I could fight back. Call this what it is, an outright abuse of power, a subversion of the very system we claim to serve.

But if I'm off this case, who fills my shoes? Someone worse. Someone who'll do whatever Tuff commands.

What is best for me may not be in the best interest of the nation.

I swallow my pride, forcing the words out.

"Yes, Mr. President. I do."

Tuff exhales hard, like a pressure valve popping.

"Fine. If the people want to believe that the Dragon Slayers are heroes, then we'll show them exactly how bad things get when you let a terrorist group like that gain traction.

"Victor," Tuff yells. "Get all my CEO buddies on the phone. We're going to jack up prices. Big time."

I feel heat marching up the back of my neck, but my face reflects composure.

Tuff's next statement is filled with triumph.

"We're going to blame the Dragon Slayers for inflation. That all this money that's being handed out to people is the reason why prices are going up.

"We will make sure the public thinks their hardship is because of the Dragon Slayers. Just like we did when we blamed the last administration for skyrocketing prices, when it was just our donors making record profits."

Tuff unleashes a colossal grin, rubbing his hands together like he's about to feast.

Victor endorses Tuff's scheme.

"A market shock scenario, perfect. Americans won't bother thinking through the fallout; they'll just want someone to blame.

"And our base? They'll fall in line fast as always, hell they do and think whatever you tell them at this point. The damage, the fear, it all lands on the Dragon Slayers, not the White House."

Dr. Hart is already processing the rollout.

"Brilliant, Mr. President. We'll tie in illegal immigration, claim they're aiding the Dragon Slayers."

Laskey chimes in smoothly, seizing the moment.

"Even better, Mr. President, now that we've labeled them terrorists, legally speaking we can invoke national security. That gives us full justification to accelerate deportations. And anyone who protests? We flag them as sympathizers. Once tagged, they lose voting rights in the upcoming election."

Tuff grins wide, eyes gleaming with cruel delight.

"Great idea, you two. I like your thinking."

Schmutt, who has been silent, finally speaks up.

"Er, well, I mean, like, you could also... I don't know, like, crowdsource a solution? Like a hackathon? Or, like, we put some kinda, uh, blockchain thing on it? You know, AI, deep learning, that kind of thing?"

Victor rolls his eyes ostentatiously. Dr. Hart disregards him completely. Laskey's mouth curls just enough to suggest disgust.

"You're fucking useless, Alan." Tuff jeers.

Schmutt's head nods as if he has learned something new.

"Right, right. Yeah. Got it."

Tuff claps loudly.

"Okay, people. Get to it. Victor, you get the CEOs. Hart, you draft the message. Laskey, I want every legal angle locked in. Schmutt, shut your mouth and just keep signing over checks to me. And Grayson… you know what to do. Get these fucking terrorists."

"Yes, Mr. President."

This administration blurred every legal line it could the moment it took office, but this? This is outright economic warfare on their own citizens, all to protect their election and power.

The screen goes dark as the meeting ends, but I just sit there, unmoving. The silence only makes the question louder: how far, and how fast, is this administration willing to turn on its own people?

And when will they expect me and my team to follow suit?

I need to find Carter, and he is exactly in the same spot. A man with a confirmed mission, his fingers haven't stopped tapping at the keyboard, his eyes darting between multiple windows.

"Carter. What's the latest? Any luck?"

"If by 'luck' you mean that I've lost all faith in humanity and would rather burn the internet to the ground, then sure. It's a major success."

"That bad?"

Carter spins around and pushes his glasses up.

"Boss, we're searching for 'save' and something."

I move in, looking over the disorganized mess in front of him, codes, highlighted chat, and report upon report.

Carter slumps back in his seat, frowning.

"Save file, save point, save route, save code, it could mean anything. And the word 'save' shows up constantly in encrypted chatter on the dark web. It's one of those terms that sounds innocent enough but can hide behind a hundred meanings."

"So, we're looking for a nonexistent black cat in a dark room."

"More like trying to find one particular needle in a haystack full of arbitrary needles nestled in even larger haystacks, and we don't even know the color of our needle. And never mind that for now, since I have something even worse."

"Well, this is great, Carter. I love bad news."

He taps a few keys, and a new window appears.

"I saw unusual traffic on gig and task apps yesterday. Now, a pattern is occurring."

He points to a screen full of data. Thousands of transactions. Payments, places, times. A lot of it looks like nonsense, but Carter wouldn't be showing it to me if it were inconsequential.

"What kind of pattern?"

"People are getting paid double, triple, quadruple the normal rate for simple tasks."

"Like what?"

"Moving boxes around town and making deliveries. But as we approach the Dragon Slayers' deadline, these tasks have become more frequent."

"Are you saying that the Dragon Slayers are employing gig apps?"

Carter lets out a brief, humorless chuckle.

"Boss, it's fucking genius. Anonymous burner accounts for making payments. No clear chains of command."

I exhale sharply.

"Checks out with their style."

"Yeah, here's the worst part. Most of the people completing the gigs have no clue what they're actually doing."

"Some of them must."

Carter shakes his head in disagreement.

"One individual believes he's merely delivering a package, but he's inadvertently handed off a burner phone."

"Jesus. These gig workers are going to be flagged as terrorists, and they'll have no idea why."

"Yup. Once their names are in the system, it's all over for them."

It's overwhelming for me to comprehend the Dragon Slayers' brilliant rollout. They're utilizing the same one that billionaires created to take advantage of people, and now it's another tool to bring them down.

Carter grins, twirling his pen around his fingers.

"Yep, it's nearly poetic, isn't it? Those tech behemoths spent decades paying individuals a meager pittance, ruthlessly stripping them of benefits and reducing human labor to algorithms on an app.

"They did so while hemorrhaging cash, groveling for funding from billionaires, wiping out their competitors; the ones who actually paid living wages and honored unions."

I shake my head in disbelief.

"The Dragon Slayers are using the exact machinery that was established by the oligarchy that they say they are fighting. But in doing so, the question has to be asked: will it actually be effective or will it end up dragging more and more people down with it?"

"Boss. It's going to get ugly out there. Really ugly."

"Carter, we have to continue to push for anything 'Save'-related, regardless of how futile it is. If we can find even the slightest crack, a single lead, we may have a chance at halting this before the administration tramples over citizens, stripping them of their rights along the way."

"Dark days, Deputy Director. Dark days. At least we don't have a billion dollars."

I shoot him a sharp glance, but he's not wrong. Technically, we're not the targets of the Dragon Slayers. They are outsourcing their success to the public, and it is those unsuspecting people who have the most to lose.

The Dragon Slayers will push their plan forward.

Billionaires will not be the only ones paying the price.

It'll be everyone else, too.

CHAPTER 19

ZERO HOUR

" The existence of inequality is the cause of revolution."

- NAPOLEON BONAPARTE

IT'S 4:02 P.M.

A little over thirty hours remain until the Dragon Slayers' deadline arrives.

I stare at the red digital clock above my desk, mocking me for being so far behind. Every second that ticks away is a constant reminder of my failure. Hundreds of leads, thousands of tips have all proven to be worthless.

There is only one number that now matters the most. Time. And we're running out of it.

Sitting here in my office won't change anything. If there's even a spark of progress, it'll come from Carter. If anyone can turn digital noise into a signal, it's him.

Their deadline is approaching fast, and we're not even close. Carter and his team have been in overdrive, and they are running on fumes.

"Hey, Carter. I just wanted to thank you and your team

for going above and beyond for our agency and the American people."

"Damn, boss. Finally, you're admitting that I am your most valuable asset. Took you long enough."

"You already knew that; just take the compliment."

"Accepted. This whole Dragon Slayer thing is terrible for you. For me? It's sorta fun."

"Carter, you're kidding… right?"

He waves his hand like a wand at his screens, a haze of data, coded messages, and everything else in between.

"This mission is a real challenge for me; sure, it can be frustrating as hell, but that's what makes it motivating too. You, on the other hand? You're out there massaging egos and juggling politics. It's a mystery to me how you can keep putting up with all their crap."

"Well, it's the worst part of the job; unfortunately, it comes with the territory."

"Whatever you say, boss. Go attend to your optics. I'll be here, drowning in encrypted nonsense."

Carter is a kid in his own candy store, so I leave him alone and dial Graham.

He's been coordinating directly with high-risk targets and their private security teams, making sure everyone on the list has a plan in place, assuming a plan will even matter if this thing escalates.

He picks up right away.

"Charlie, if this is you coming to rescue me from babysitting duty, I will respectfully do any mission you request."

"Sorry, Graham. No get out of jail free card for you. Just checking in."

"Then let me bring you up to speed: I despise this. I despise every single solitary minute of this crap. I'm here with my team babysitting the most paranoid billionaires in the nation, keeping them safe from what? Their own panic attacks? And guess who I despise the most?"

"Hmmmm… tough question?"

"BlackSteel."

"Agent Cross, how could you not be a fan of a private military contractor?"

"Not when they possess the tactical awareness of a wrecking ball."

I imagine him stuck there, watching BlackSteel agents take over, replacing protocol with brute force and calling it progress. Every time they mention "containing the threat," it sounds more like permission to shoot first and sort it out later.

"These are trigger-happy mercs, and I've got to prevent my team from getting steamrolled by their nonsense."

"Understood, and Graham you know that it's only going to get worse."

"Charlie, should I be concerned? You sound like you've got something else on your mind."

"Whatever transpires with the Dragon Slayers' deadline tomorrow changes the course of the whole mission."

"Yeah, I feel it too. So does the team. No one's saying it, but it's thick—like everyone's holding their breath, waiting for something to snap. With BlackSteel in the mix, it's not about genuine threats anymore. It's about shielding the rich, no matter the cost."

My response is depressing, but true.

"The more power they get, the more likely civilians are going to get caught in the crossfire."

"That's what I'm worried about. You know me, Charlie; I don't want to pull the trigger unless necessary. These corporate cosplay fools. They're searching for any excuse."

What unsettles me most is knowing that some of the people caught in the middle will be innocent. Others will consider the risks, the danger and still choose to support the Dragon Slayers. That kind of conviction has a ripple effect. It complicates the fight. It deepens the fallout.

"Graham, we need to stay ahead of this. Keep your men alert. I'll do what I can on my end."

"Roger that. But ever since the subsidies rolled out, BlackSteel has been spreading its tentacles deeper into every component of the Bureau."

"That might be true, but it's the reality we're working with, and it sure as hell isn't going to slow us down."

"You're damn right, Charlie, just let me know if you need anything."

"Thanks, Graham, enjoy babysitting."

Graham is another valuable asset to the FBI and especially to me. Only he knows how many lives his team has saved in the course of their operations. My concern is that he is exhibiting signs of apprehension with every new phase of our mission.

At my office, I collapse into my chair, rubbing at my eyes as the laptop screen stirs to life. Its soft light casts elongated shadows across my desk. Again, there is nothing. No news on the horizon. Clearly, nothing with Save something. No strings to pull on the Dragon Slayers as the clock ticks ever closer.

They're always one step ahead, always in motion. We're chasing phantoms, grasping for shadows that vanish the moment you think you've finally caught them.

Before I can spiral any further, a knock at the door stops me in my tracks.

"Come in." I bid, bracing myself for more bad news, another crisis, another reason why this entire operation is a losing battle.

Rather, Lex walks in, smiling, holding in her hand a recognizable white bag.

"Hey, you. Figured you probably haven't eaten since I last saw you. So, I brought us some Shakai."

The smell instantly gets to me, and my stomach twists in pain. It's only now that I realize how empty I am, how long I've been running on nothing but stress and caffeine. I don't even know the last time I ate a real meal.

"Lex, you don't know how happy I am to see you."

She smirks, playing with the bag clutched in her hand.

"Me or the sushi?"

"A little bit of both."

She puts down the food, opens the containers, as the savory aroma of soy sauce, wasabi, and steaming rice fills the air. The stale smell of my office disappears beneath the respite of something warm, something ordinary.

We eat in silence for a few moments, the only sound coming from the soft crunch of chopsticks against plastic boxes. Peace is such a rare thing. I allow it to go on longer than I ought to.

Lex turns slightly, facing me as she eats, each bite measured like she's studying me instead of the food, reading my posture, my tone, the way I'm holding myself back.

"Charlie, you look exhausted. I can't even imagine what you've been through. Please level with me. What's going on in that head of yours? What do you think about all this?"

"Think about what?"

"The Dragon Slayers. Their deadline. The whole damn mess."

Setting down my chopsticks, I let out an exhausted sigh.

"To be honest, Lex? No clue. We don't have much to work with on the Dragon Slayers. They are always one step ahead of us. Even if we can scrape something together, there's no guarantee that we can act in time. This is the most difficult mission I've ever had to handle."

Lex's soft eyes scan over me as she continues chewing thoughtfully. Then she shifts backwards, crossing her arms.

"Yeah, but I mean, what do you really think?"

"I just told you, Lex..."

"No, you outlined how Deputy Director Charlotte Grayson is involved in the case as if you were providing me with a briefing update. What I am asking for is your opinion of this Dragon Slayer shit."

I pause, recognizing that she's asking something else entirely, something that, honestly, I haven't even permitted myself to reflect on.

"I'm not too worried personally," she continues.

"Excuse me?"

"I mean, yeah, I suppose some people are going to get hurt, but let's be real, most people aren't billionaires. We're talking, what, a few thousand ultra-rich getting targeted?"

"Lex, there are consequences when someone defies the law. Tuff and his administration are going to throw the book at the people supporting the Dragon Slayers. They'll be jailed as terrorists. You know that."

She pauses, carefully considering my words. Then she asks the one question that has hung in the balance for way too long.

"I don't know, Charlie. If this many people are in support of what's happening, isn't it possible that it's... not as terrible as they're portraying it?

"It just feels like the government is so clearly defending these rich bastards and letting the people suffer who are just asking questions to stay informed."

My body stiffens as I gaze at her, my expression unchanging.

"Lex. You know what you are saying, right?"

She raises an eyebrow, but I don't stop as the familiar voice inside rushes to defend the legacy of service.

"We're the government, Lex. We're part of the administration. You don't want to be saying that."

That should settle the argument. But this is Lex.

She only smirks.

"Yes, sir, Deputy Director Charlotte Grayson, sir. I will never speak ill of this wonderful country's government again."

She smiles, holding up her hand in a mock salute, yet there is another glint in her eyes, one that suggests discomfort.

"Come on, Charlie. Ordinary American citizens are the real backbone of this country. They make up the government, corporations, small businesses, the law and all that other stuff, including the FBI.

"And 99.99% of ordinary citizens are not being pursued by the Dragon Slayers."

She nonchalantly shrugs.

"Charlie, it's billionaires. And the administration is fighting for billionaires more than they are fighting for ordinary American citizens, like us. That doesn't sit well with me, and I have freedom of speech.

"So, they can go fuck themselves."

In perfect Lex fashion, she isn't even fazed by what she said, instead, she simply scoffs down another piece of sushi and continues.

"So, yeah, I don't know. I'm sort of wondering what's going to happen, like it's a movie or something."

Lex stops. And then I notice it, genuine concern.

She reaches across the desk, her hand over mine. Her eyes locked on mine.

"The only one that I'm genuinely concerned about is you."

I hold my breath, my eyes locked on her. Lex squeezes my hand gently.

"I don't want to see you get caught up in this. That is what truly frightens me."

She breathes sharply out. Her voice is soft, but resolute.

"Because I know you, Charlie. I know just how much you'll do to save everyone."

She maintains my gaze with unwavering solemnity.

"And I just need to know that if you're going to do it, it's for something that truly matters."

The words hang between us, weighing more than anything else she's told me tonight. I need to say something, anything, but it's as if my brain won't function.

Lex waits, eyes not blinking as I swallow hard, searching for the courage to gaze at her.

The words aren't easy, yet somehow, I manage them.

"Thank you, Lex. I'll be careful. I promise."

She gazes at me for an extra second, then, either satisfied or maybe wanting to keep going, nods.

"Good."

She pulls her hand back, deftly retrieving her chopsticks, not realizing she has just rocked my core. The tension dissolves from her face as she transforms back into the real Lex. Easy, effortless, and out of reach.

"Anyway, I have to run. I need to round up more evil citizens who clicked on the wrong link. Internet jaywalking will not be tolerated on my watch."

Another mock salute followed by a wink, and then she heads for the door.

I watch her walk off, my mind set on her words.

Lex is concerned for me, to the extent that she's also bringing up points I stubbornly refuse to hear. I'm reminded that my duty is still ironclad, that my obligation, my dad's honor, and my loyalty to this nation are unshakeable.

But the same principles that made me who I am, that I'd believed were indestructible, are now seemingly crumbling faster than I can grasp.

If anyone else had dared to make those same statements, I know a fire in me would have been ignited to defend everything I've given my life for so far.

She is barely gone before I thrust myself back into the case, restlessly cycling through reports, decrypts, chatter logs, anything that might crack the riddle of "save something."

The answer is right in front of me, hidden in heaps of data. Every fragment is just a bit shy of being useful. Hours spent behind glowing screens, caffeine overloads, and half-scribbled theories were all for nothing.

As the weight of the deadline creeps closer, the drumbeat in the back of my skull pounds louder, faster. The idea of sitting still, of doing nothing, is intolerable.

I take a sneak peek at the clock. 11 p.m.

There is no putting the brakes on the countdown. We're all bracing for the inevitable plunge into dark waters.

I crave the comfort of my home, my own bed, my safe space, even if it is only for a few hours.

It's an indulgent feeling, an almost foreign concept. For a second, Lex comes to mind; the warmth of her company would help ease my guilt and distress. I crave her touch, but once again, the timing for "us" is off.

The streets are quiet when I leave HQ, and before I realize it, I am home.

Dropping my bag, I crawl under the covers and retreat into silence.

My alarm goes off at 6:00 a.m. Fourteen hours left.

I roll over and cover my head with a pillow. This could be the day everything breaks wide open. Or burns down. Either way, there's no going back.

The stress is palpable the moment I walk into HQ. It spreads like static in the air; everyone feels it, no one names it. The deadline countdown ticks louder with every passing hour.

I meet with Bill, and we revisit worst-case scenarios, fine-tuning emergency responses. It's all the same loop. Rehashed theories intermixed with backup plans that feel more like busy-work than delivering outcomes.

We're paralyzed. Waiting for the Dragon Slayers to strike again.

There are no other options than to keep working, even if it is meaningless. A part of me still believes this case will crack open under pressure. It's happened before in dozens of cases. The pieces just… click.

But this? This is different. I've never had such limited intel. No momentum. Just an incomplete phrase and an unstoppable deadline.

The PA system announces what we have all been dreading to hear.

Thirty minutes. All necessary personnel to the DEFCON room.

It's animated chaos when I enter.

Carter, Maya, and Bill are already at the central table, their eyes fixed on their screens.

Side screens stream Victor and Hart's images at the White House.

I drop into a seat and survey the room. The tension is unmistakable, fatigue etched into every face; everyone is braced for whatever comes next.

My nerves are in overdrive, yet I stay remarkably composed.

The FBI has the force and readiness to strike back, and I bear that in mind.

Graham's unit stands by as our QRF, locked and loaded for immediate raid deployment. Carter's digital watchdogs are monitoring the web for the faintest blip of Dragon Slayer activity. Maya stands ready to track every shift in the public pulse.

I interrupt the tension, stepping forward as every eye in the room turns to me.

"This is it. I know the pressure's real. I know we've been chasing shadows and second-guessing every step. But listen to me; we are the best this country has to offer. Every single person in this room has earned their place, and no terrorist is going to make us forget who we are.

"They want chaos. They're about to find out what happens when you provoke the full force of the United States FBI. We will stop them. And we will show the world what it means to go against us."

My words resonate.

I can see it on their faces, grim nods, straightened backs, a flicker of fire returning to tired eyes.

Then, a snort.

The source of the sound is Victor. Head bobbling, smirking as though this whole ordeal is a practical joke.

"Cute speech, Deputy Director."

I don't give him the satisfaction of an acknowledgement. Victor doesn't matter. What matters is my team and being able to handle whatever comes next.

He can mock us all he wants. He doesn't know what it takes to be in this room.

All eyes drift toward the main screen. The timer ticks down.

00:00:05

00:00:04

00:00:03
00:00:02
00:00:01
00:00:00

The room falls silent.

Nothing happens.

"Updates. Sitrep checks," Bill commands.

Graham is the first to speak.

"All quiet here. No movement."

Carter frowns, furiously typing.

"Blockchain is normal, no sudden transactions."

Maya shakes her head.

"Nothing major on social, aside from people asking if anything happened."

And then Victor laughs. He is grinning like a man who's just won a big wager.

"I knew it!

"These fools! These pathetic, stupid fools! It was all a bluff! A joke! A ruse! They couldn't pull this off!

"And you, Grayson! All of you! Hook, line, and sinker! How could anyone think of attacking billionaires?

"You all should have known that the Dragon Slayers would never be able to do this; they scammed some poor people and sent us a video. What a revolution!"

It's obvious he's trying to save face, taunting us that he was always one step ahead of the rest of us. But he has no idea.

Something is coming. I just don't know when.

The deadline may be over, but this is far from finished.

The Dragon Slayers are real.

The only question is what they are truly capable of?

CHAPTER 20

BILLIONS IN MOTION

*It's truly unfair that some people should
have so much while others go hungry.*

-DALAI LAMA

THE DEADLINE PASSED, but this is far from over.

I scan the DEFCON room with a slow, measured look, an unnerving feeling forming within me. It's the sort of emotion that lurks just beneath the surface, wound tight and waiting to snap.

Everybody here knows what's at stake as Victor lets out a loud, sarcastic cackle.

It's jarringly out of place, smashing through our focus like a hammer, shattering the windows of our concentration.

I shoot a brief look at the real-time feed of Victor and wonder whose plush, taxpayer-paid office he is sitting in. He lounges back in his chair as if he's at the beach, watching some comedy on his phone, instead of a national security briefing.

"Oh, this is rich," Victor snickers. "You pay off a few desperate nobodies to upload a video, promising them the world.

Hell, I seriously doubt those nitwits got even a fraction of what those fake terrorists promised. In fact, I wouldn't be surprised if they just killed them to shut them up for good! Tie up loose ends, right? Either way, what's the big payoff?"

I stay still, resisting the urge to react. He is a pompous ass, and I will not let him rattle me.

Nor will I make his day by even acknowledging any of his moronic comments. Victor is a politician, not an operative, who does not need to be correct; he merely needs to appear that way. He's only playing the part of a man much too clever to be duped.

I feel irritation vibrating throughout the room as everyone tries to ignore Victor.

But he just won't shut up.

"I mean, come on," Victor says, his hand waving in the air. "They've scared a few billionaires and stirred up some basement-dwelling fan club. That doesn't make them a threat; it makes them pathetic.

"Now we're supposed to think they're about to bring down civilization? This is a fucking scam. That's all it is. You're all just wasting time hunting phantoms."

"Premature gloating isn't a strategy, Victor. Nothing's happened yet," I snap.

"Yet? What a joke. You really think those Dragon Slayers have the logistical knowledge and skills to do something this big?

"Let me tell you precisely how this plays out. The money gets shifted around, they keep a low profile, and six months down the line, someone stumbles upon that knight in shining armor, Lancelot, unconscious in a jungle camp, burning cash on prostitutes and fine scotch."

Carter mumbles a slew of four-letter words, barely audible, and then he explodes.

"Right, because tracing fourteen billion dollars through six tumblers, three privacy chains, and a mesh of cold wallets across continents is just a wild-goose chase to kill some time."

Victor plays deaf. I can't have him wasting our time anymore.

I keep my tone strong, unbending, facing Victor's smug expression without flinching.

"We can't afford to underestimate the Dragon Slayers. They have already shown themselves to be well-organized and efficient, and until we can ascertain their next move, this is far from finished.

"Victor, know this: if it is revealed to be an elaborate hoax, I will be the first to rejoice that no lives were ever in danger. In the meantime, we must continue our efforts and remain vigilant."

"Another waste of taxpayers' money, Grayson. Go ahead and keep chasing your boogeyman. Let me know when you've caught him. Now you can keep playing pretend, but some of us have actual work to do."

With that, he reaches forward and with a click, fades into black.

Graham's voice comms in, calm and unrushed.

"Status report. My men are good. No movement, no sign of a breach. If the Dragon Slayers are planning on doing something, they're strategically waiting."

His words should be of some comfort, yet fear prickles my skin. I tap beats with my fingers and momentarily think of Lex doing the same the night we drove to her home. It seems like a lifetime ago, instead of a few chaotic days.

Stay centered, I implore myself as my eyes dart back to the incessant data streams. We can only lie in wait for something to happen.

To say the hours were dragging on is an understatement. Waiting for the powder keg to blow is agonizingly cruel for my team. Anticipation itself is bearing down on everyone; anticipation in every movement, every breath, every unspoken word… the dormancy, a pressure cooker about to explode.

Maya leans back in her chair, her hands massaging her temples.

"So, what exactly is the plan? We're just going to sit here, waiting for the apocalypse to start?"

Carter looks up from his screen, cracking his knuckles.

"That's part of our job. Wait and hope, just like Edmond Dantès did."

His words were just what we needed to break up the mounting tension. Who knew Carter enjoys classic literature.

"Alright, everyone," I say begrudgingly, "Let's break, monitor the situation from your stations. Keep sharp."

They rise in unison, stretching, shrugging their shoulders, gathering their things. I remain seated, waiting for the Dragon Slayers to strike the match.

Drained, it takes every ounce of energy for me to head to my office. My mind is still filled with misgivings. What if Victor is right? What if the Dragon Slayers were just a scam, a well-planned scheme to fleece some billionaires and nothing else?

Collapsing down in my chair, I twist a strand of my hair a bit too tight, exorcising dark thoughts before they overwhelm me. No. I saw the uplink facility footage with my own eyes. I saw the precision and the coordination of the Dragon Slayers.

I saw Evan tied up in that motel room filled with gasoline fumes, waiting for a match that was never struck. And I know for a fact that fourteen billion dollars doesn't just lie dormant. It gathers momentum.

There is something happening here. It just hasn't raised its ugly head yet.

Reclining back, my eyes count the ceiling tiles, as memories of my father overwhelm me. I wish he were here to advise me. My thoughts darken. His missions always had clear, concise objectives: execute without casualties.

But this op? This is painfully slow. It's like playing chess with a sloth.

My mom said he lived for that rush, for the clarity of action. She, however, had to live for survival. Cancer is a bitch and when you're the wife of a dedicated soldier… at times you're basically a single parent.

In many ways, she was stronger than he ever was, and I promised her I would stay out of the front lines. It was her one ultimatum. She would support my FBI career if I stayed clear of any direct enemy engagement.

No combat action, that was the deal. Intelligence was safer. Smarter.

To quiet the part of me that craves more, I threw myself into every active training course I could sign up for, firearms, close quarters combat, field strategy.

Anything that could let me feel like I was ready.

When my mom passed, my role in intel had already solidified. However, there's still some part of me that never stopped wondering what it would've been like to prove myself on the battlefield.

I stretch my arms out over my head and release the strain from my shoulders as I softly press my fingers into my eyes.

It's late. Or early. Whichever you prefer.

Heading back to the dorm room, too tired to bother with anything else today. The area is never comfortable, but it's familiar, and tonight, that's more than enough. I kick off my boots and stretch out, letting the quiet hum of the vents pull me under.

My eyes close as I think of Lex, her silhouette easing me into a deep sleep.

Suddenly, I am jarred awake.

Carter is shaking me, his voice panicked.

"Boss, wake up. It's happening."

For a second, I can't process his words. My brain lags, tangled in the heavy weight of exhaustion, my body sluggish as I blink against the dim light of the dorm.

Then his words sink in, and I jolt upright.

"Jesus, Carter. What? What happened?"

Carter's face is sharper than I've seen it in days, none of his usual smirks, no easy sarcasm. He is wired and jittery.

"Right now, I don't know the specifics. But the blockchain's going insane. Billions, maybe trillions in transactions. It's moving. Something fucking big is happening."

Gathering my gear in haste, we hustle out of the dorm, Carter keeping pace beside me. My heart pounds against my chest as we cut through the quiet halls of headquarters. The stillness of early morning makes it feel like we're running through the eye of a hurricane.

I check my phone as we move.

Posts are still saying nothing happened.

The Dragon Slayers were bluffing.

It was just a publicity stunt.

Knew nothing would happen!

Stupid communist cosplayers

Where's that dude Lancelot?

They're wrong. I know they're absolutely, positively wrong.

If the Dragon Slayers are disbursing payments, that means they are in business. And by the time the world realizes what's transpiring, it'll be too late.

We push into the DEFCON room. The main screen glows with untouched feeds, global alerts still in a cautious yellow instead of full-blown red. It doesn't sync with what Carter just told me.

Maya steps in just as we do, coffee in hand, hair still damp from another rushed shower. She frowns, barely awake.

"Someone, tell me what's going on. Everyone says it's nothing."

Victor's face pops onto the main screen, groggy and irritated.

"Why am I awake for this? What is this nonsense? We've already been over this...this isn't real. You're acting like the sky is falling, and all I see are a bunch of numbers on a screen for Christ's sake."

Carter cuts in before I can.

"You can say it's not real all you want. All I know is that someone is getting paid to do something. And the Dragon Slayers said that something is to kill billionaires. So that's what we're going with."

"Excuse me, sonny, but...?"

"Enough, Victor, we need to focus," I sternly warn him. "I'll give you an update when we have one."

"You better, Grayson, because..." and with a quick click, I cut his feed.

The drop-dead stillness that veils the room is unnerving. Refocusing on my team is all that matters right now.

"Everybody listen up! We need all eyes on this. If the Dragon Slayers are moving money, there's a reason.

"Maya, continue to track public chatter, especially anyone saying they got paid. Carter, I need every wallet linked to a major transfer in the last hour flagged now."

Then I switch comms, hitting the channel for Graham.

"Graham, anything on your end?"

"Nothing on our men. But I reached out to BlackSteel."

"And?"

"They said they're having complications."

"Complications?"

Graham says exactly what I already know.

"Son of a bitch, it's really happening, Charlie."

Carter sucks in a sudden breath and lets out a shout.

"Oh, for fuck's sake!"

His words fire across the room like a gunshot. All heads turn, but I'm already in motion, whipping towards him.

"What?"

"Boss… it's another video."

"Pull it up. Now."

Carter doesn't hesitate. His fingers blaze across the keyboard as the main screen shimmers. The whole room holds its breath as the picture clears, and there he is…

Lancelot.

The lighting is harsh, sending out long, ominous shadows on the bleak industrial backdrop behind him. His black and gold combat gear is spotless, with the golden dragon insignia on his chest, a gleaming war crest.

Lancelot's mask gives nothing away. He delays speaking, just stands still, allowing the crushing silence to impale us. And then, he speaks in an authoritative voice.

The war for humanity has started.

His words strike like a hammer, syllable by careful syllable, blow by careful blow.

*For too long, the greedy have grown rich while
the rest of our people have suffered.*

They've constructed their palaces on our backs.

Feasted while we've starved and thrived even as we died.

But those days are at an end.

We are the masses. We vastly outnumber them.

And now, we have the resources to bring suffering upon them.

He waits long enough for his words to resonate.

*To all those who have already stood with
us, we give our sincerest gratitude.*

As promised, we are giving more than just our thanks.

*Over eight hundred million dollars has been real-
located to those who have assisted us.*

*Those who gave us details needed to locate
and slay these beasts of greed.*

Then the camera pans.

Ten figures appear, kneeling in an aligned row behind him. Each is dressed in an orange jumpsuit, their heads hidden beneath black hoods.

Lancelot continues, unshakeable and confident.

And now, ten Dragons kneel before you.

*They had fortresses. Vaults of lawyers and layers
of lies. But they couldn't outrun the truth.*

*Their maids, chefs, drivers, butlers, and nan-
nies were those they thought they owned.*

Those people have turned against them. And why wouldn't they?

*They accepted indignities for a wage. For
a simple chance to survive.*

But what do you do when a better offer comes along?

What do you do when the free market speaks?

The answer is obvious.

Loyalty to the billionaires is not real.

Loyalty is earned, not bought.

I seize the side of the table, struggling to maintain my composure.

*The wealthy have constructed a system that
makes a profit out of your suffering.*

that flourishes in your despair,

and that gets rich from your hunger, your illness, and your fight.

So, we're investing five billion dollars as a start to reverse the harm.

The harm they have wrought on you and your loved ones.

*Because we are not your enemies. We are
on the same side of this struggle.*

And when a dragon is slain, the village does not mourn; it prospers.

True prosperity is coming. And it begins with justice.

Lancelot's message is a siren song, weaving something intoxicating, something irresistible.

*This is what happens when the people reclaim
what was wrongfully taken from them.*

*We are the 99%. We are the masses. And
we will rebuild for the masses.*

He moves forward, coming closer to the camera, encompassing the whole frame.

To you, billionaire scum,

the choice is still yours.

You will be found, like the others.

Betrayed not by us, but by those around you,
because you are rightfully despised.

The people have awakened.

They will no longer tolerate your greed while they suffer.

Even when you are captured, we will offer the same chance:

Relinquish your hoarded wealth.

Because your stolen wealth is the fuel that feeds our fire.

And if you give it up, you won't have to die.

There is a pause, a silence that lasts just long enough to allow for a sense of reflection.

But some among you will not change.

Some will cling to their riches until their last breath.

And for you, there is but one destiny.

The screen goes pitch black.

No one speaks or moves. We have been turned into stone.

"If they even give a fraction of that five billion to people? Public support is going to skyrocket," Maya gasps. "This is economic warfare. People aren't just going to sit back and watch… they're going to start choosing sides."

The severity of the situation takes hold of me in all the wrong ways.

If the Dragon Slayers start doing what governments refuse to do, if they start proving that wealth redistribution works, then the entire economic system could collapse.

"You have to be kidding me," Carter retorts, his words sharp enough to cut through the chaos of the briefing room.

My head snaps toward him.

"What now?"

"Another video."

"Pull it up."

The screen flickers, and there she is…

Guinevere.

She stands against a dark, wooded backdrop, the early morning sun filtering through the trees behind her. Her attire is not as sleek or polished as before. Instead, she's wearing an orange jacket, the kind hunters wear when they're tracking deer. A rifle rests in her hands, and for a second, she just smiles at the camera, rocking back slightly on her heels like she's enjoying the moment.

Good tidings, Resistance. It's officially dragon hunting season.

Then… BANG.

Guinevere fires into the air. The recoil jolts her shoulder back, and she laughs, wide-eyed, grinning as she steadies herself.

Good Lord! That kicks more than I thought!

She giggles, shaking out her arm as if she's just getting used to the weight of it. Then she looks straight into the camera, her expression shifting into something warm, friendly, and then deadly.

So, let's talk about our dear, sweet billionaires.

The ones who decided that even 999 million dollars wasn't enough.

Now, let's put that in perspective.

The median wage in this country? About forty thousand a year.

*Do you know how long it would take that
person to reach a billion dollars?*

Guinevere pauses.

Just a quick 25,000 years, without spending a single penny.

*So, if you've been working every day since the last
ice age, then congrats, you've earned it.*

But these billionaires?

*They need more. More than they could
ever spend in multiple lifetimes.*

And why?

She shrugs. Her tone dips more seriously.

Because they're sick, and their illness is greed.

Their illness is literally causing the suffering of mankind.

*Their greed is killing people, forcing families into
debt, hoarding resources while others starve.*

Destroying our planet.

Guinevere takes a slow breath, her gaze sharpening.

And if they're sick? Well…

She lifts the rifle, tapping a finger along the barrel.

Sick people need treatment. Sick people need a cure.

And it's a cure we will be more than happy to administer.

With practiced ease, Guinevere swings the rifle behind her,
letting it settle against the sling at her shoulder. She claps her

hands loudly, beaming, as if she's just unwrapped an expensive gift.

Now, just look at how many people are already standing with us.

I just love hearing all these stories about billionaires getting stabbed in the back.

Oh, wait. 'Stabbed in the back'… that's what they say.

Her grin falters for a split second, just long enough to shift her tone.

But tell me, dear friends.

If someone's been abusing you, starving you,

stealing from you every single day of your life,

and you finally hit back,

Is that betrayal? Or is that justice?

Guinevere claps again, regaining her chipper, enthusiastic energy.

The shackles are off, friends!

And we're just getting started.

She glances over her shoulder as if she's checking for someone or something. When she turns back, her menacing grin is still there.

You heard the big man,

five billion dollars already going out the door, no strings attached.

Real help, right now.

Medical debt. No one should die just because

a company wants more money.

The insurance giants have fed on your pain long enough.
Education? They turned learning into a trap.
They chained you to debt so you would be forced into their system.
We're cutting those chains.
Food. Housing. The basic right to live. They hoard, we starve.
They buy up homes to sit empty while you fight to make rent.
They throw out more food daily than you'll see in a week.
That's not a system, it's a sickness.

She gives the camera a sly smile, turning just a shade more playful.

Oh, and there's one more little thing,
if you want to get more involved.
We thought let's have some more fun.
We are now placing a bounty for anyone who
wants to destroy their precious assets.
Take their empty houses. Take their barely
used yachts. Take their cars.

Guinivere drops her words to a whisper.

Burn them. Break them. Destroy them.
Send us the footage, and we will pay you handsomely.
Friends, we are not greedy. We are not hoarders.
Together, we will win this war.

The video cuts out.
The war has arrived.

CHAPTER 21

MANDATE OF POWER

"The means of defense against foreign danger have always been the instruments of tyranny at home."

-GEORGE WASHINGTON

"THIS IS BAD." I whisper to myself, but dwelling on it won't help. Swiping the thought aside, I focus on the next steps.

I cut a sharp look towards the team.

"Carter, keep monitoring for payouts. We should expect to see a lot more transactions come through, especially after those videos. If they try to convert to USD or any fiat currency, that's where we'll catch them."

He pauses and looks up, his face aglow with the light of the screens.

"Smart thinking, boss. If they get sloppy, that's our in."

It's not much, but it is progress. If the Dragon Slayers are paying out as much as they claim, they are bound to leave openings.

I continue with my directives.

"Graham, I want a complete list of all the billionaires Black-Steel hasn't accounted for."

"Doing my best, but they're not sharing shit, Charlie. We're getting stonewalled by them. They're only looking out for themselves. Trying to camouflage their mistakes."

Of course, BlackSteel mercs are in cover-up mode already. Their reputation is based on being the gold standard of private security contractors. The fees they charge their clients are exorbitant, small fortunes that the average person can't even begin to grasp.

"Keep pushing them. Do what you have to do to get the information."

"Charlie," Maya interjects, "The Dragon Slayers' message has gone viral. It's only been twenty minutes, but we're already seeing a surge in support."

She hands me her tablet.

"Here, take a look."

Lol, just saying how can you not hate billionaires, who the fuck cares?

*Dragon Slayers murder billionaires. *Grabs popcorn*.*

The Dragon Slayers aren't the disease. They're the cure.

Lancelot, you're my hero.

Guinevere… you slay.

"Even worse. They're asking for the going rates of damaged assets. How they get paid. What else can they do to help."

The Dragon Slayers are triggering the reaction they desire; people are eager to join their crusade.

The flip side is that the more they open themselves up, the more chances we have to track them.

Time for my team to do what they do best.

"Listen up, everyone," my words demanding attention. "The Dragon Slayers are escalating their operation, and when they do, they are bound to make errors. That's what we'll capitalize on and put a stop to this."

My phone vibrates. It's a text from Bill.

Come to my office. ASAP.

I turn and make a beeline for the door.

Bill's office immediately feels off the second I step in. The blinds are drawn closed, and a hint of whiskey permeates the air even though it's early morning. A half-full glass remains on his desk, contents stagnant and unmoving as if he just poured it for admiration.

He doesn't greet me with a smile, doesn't offer the same even-keel calm I've grown accustomed to. Instead, he raises his eyes to meet mine, offering a deeper emotion on his face, a look I have never seen before.

"Charlie, this is very serious. I'm sure you already know this."

"Bill, my team is doing everything we can."

"I know you are, and I wouldn't have anyone else on this, but that's not the issue."

I study him intently, trying to see beyond his words. Bill has always been a rock, the sort of leader who conceals everything, no matter what pressure he bears. The sluggish rhythm of his breathing and the undrunk glass beside him suggests that this time it's different.

"The thing is that the administration isn't happy. Everything is falling apart."

"I hear what you're saying, but right now, there's nothing more we can do."

"I know, I know. But Charlie, there are forces in motion that will change the very nature of the Bureau. The straw that broke Tuff's donor's backs were the recent kidnappings."

"Bill, I don't like where this is going."

He lifts the glass, letting it slip between his fingers, entranced by the flow of light in the amber liquor. He doesn't take a drink; he merely continues to gaze at it, soothed by its presence.

"This administration bought their way through the House and the Senate; crony capitalism. They have them by the balls. When people like that get power, they use it."

"That's not very reassuring. use it how?"

Bill looks up, the strain carved deeper into his features than I've ever seen. Sitting across from me is a man weathered by responsibility, his posture heavy with the burdens he keeps to himself.

My mentor is time-worn; the years of overtaxing stress have finally caught up with him.

"The administration is going to capitalize on the Dragon Slayer chaos. They're planning to take this opportunity and mold it to suit their own agenda."

"What does that have to do with the FBI and with us?"

"Charlie, the administration wants private corporations to exert greater influence on the management of the government."

"Privatizing government abilities for corporations? Bill, that's crazy."

"No, it's not crazy when you own the people making the laws. Indentured public servants."

The meaning behind his words is harsh.

"Charlie, we can fight the system or work with it. I'm sorry, but I need you to work within the new parameters."

There's no anger in his tone, no frustration, just a quiet surrender.

Bill Cartwright has survived more administrations than I care to count. He's always been the kind of man who could easily read the shifting tides of power before they even moved, the one who knew exactly when to push and when to pull back.

I've had the privilege of watching him navigate impossible

situations and negotiate with people who hold our country's fate in their hands. I watched him maneuver his way through political landmines. It was all second nature to him.

Now, in all the turmoil, our captain doesn't know where to point his ship. He seems rudderless in this situation.

"If we don't stop the Dragon Slayers now, it's going to get worse... Charlie..."

There's something unspoken in the way he says my name. A plea, a warning or worse, an expectation.

A shadow covers his face.

"Perhaps I will not be able to protect you. Or any of us."

"Protect us? Bill, please, I don't understand."

"I don't know what's on the horizon for the Bureau. I don't know what I'll be able to do anymore."

"Are you saying I'm being removed from the mission?"

Bill studies me, reading my reaction as I'm certain he has done many times before. His words are dangerously close to becoming a threat.

"You have to understand something. If we don't stop the Dragon Slayers, the administration will, and it won't be pretty. This could change the nation forever."

My expression stays neutral despite the maelstrom churning within my brain, spurred on by all that Bill has disclosed. His cautionary words prey on my spirit, but I will not be disheartened.

This is not the time for doubt, no room for hesitation. The administration will move forward, and if I don't keep ahead of them, the guillotine's blade floating over my head will fall.

"Understood." I reply solemnly.

Bill looks at me for a moment, debating whether I really do. I offer him nothing else.

Rising quickly, I exit his office, my steps echoing down the hall.

Regrettably, Bill's correct. It's in times like these, when nations are stumbling, when fear travels quicker than facts, that the balance of power shifts. Sometimes for the better. Most often for the worse.

History doesn't recall the gradual declines, the incremental losses, the slow erosion of control. It recalls the turning points, the moments when everything pivots because someone was bold enough or ruthless enough to make a difference. And now, being thrown into the midst of it, I feel the magnitude of the role I'm playing.

The Dragon Slayers have driven America to the brink, but they are not the only ones ready to exploit the opportunities that instability offers.

My phone pings, breaking my troublesome thoughts. I look down at the screen.

Fucking Victor.

"Grayson, what the hell? How could you let this happen? I told you this was a serious threat. Now, more of our donors are panicking. I told you this couldn't happen, and now look at what you did!

"Tuff is furious. The administration is furious. The markets are bleeding red, and guess whose fault that is? Yours!

"Deputy Director, you are a failure. A complete failure. I knew we never should have put a woman in charge of this operation."

I move my phone away from my ear, letting him wear himself out.

When he finally stops screaming, I bring the phone back to my ear again.

"Victor, this is precisely what we cautioned you about. We

anticipated that something like this might occur, and we're already taking the appropriate action."

"It's goddamn not enough. It hasn't been enough since day one. But don't worry. You're going to learn what enough is. Because now the administration is going to mop up the mess you've made.

"Get on the fucking briefing. Now."

The line goes dead before I can even reply.

I quicken my step, striding towards the briefing room, logging in remotely. By the time the screen flickers on, Tuff is already speaking, or more aptly put, he is losing his shit.

"I have never witnessed such ineptitude! You people can't do one damn thing right. You allow those bastard Dragons Slayers, those criminals, those terrorists, those nobodies to turn my great country against me.

"And worse, you allowed them to abduct some billionaires right under your nose. My donors are all panicking about their contributions! Now I'm supposed to sit and wait for you to fix this?"

Tuff's fist crashes against the desk, making objects on its surface tumble over.

"And this," he goes on, stabbing the air with an invisible knife, "this is the exact reason my administration is going to shake things up. We're done with bureaucracy. We're done waiting. We're done with the FBI!"

I straighten up, my heart racing.

Tuff shouts.

"We're introducing a new bill today, and it's already as good as passed. No one dares vote against me now."

It's true. His greatest talent has always been reshaping the system to serve him, bending senators and congressmen into voting against their own constituents.

What makes it even worse now is that parasitic leech, Alan Schmutt.

His billions carry weight, and he never hesitates to use them. Any lawmaker who dares push back gets buried under a wave of targeted spending, smear campaigns, and handpicked challengers. Schmutt treats political destruction like a sport, and no one wants to be his next target.

The screen opens in half, revealing three more faces.

Tuff acknowledges them; his anger transmutes into something far more perilous and certain.

"This is Jackson Kane, CEO of Black Steel," he states like a king introducing his court.

I recognize Kane immediately. Military stance, sharply tailored suit topped off with a cowboy hat that shades his impassive face. His company, BlackSteel, is the unholy fusion of black ops efficiency and corporate savagery, strategic brilliance with a polished façade.

"And this." Tuff points to the left. "Is Margaret McMullen, head of Continental Containment."

Margaret McMullen looks like she would be more comfortable in a cozy kitchen than at the helm of a corporate empire built on incarceration. Her silver hair is neatly curled, her soft features crinkling with warmth as she offers a gentle, practiced smile. She radiates the easy charm of a grandmother who bakes cookies and pinches cheeks.

For all her charm, Margaret McMullen is no kindly matriarch. Her company doesn't just run private prisons; it feeds them, padding the palms of judges to ensure a steady supply of inmates. She's the architect of a system that turns human beings into revenue streams, wrapping corruption with a warm, welcoming face.

"And finally," Tuff confidently boasts. "Alexander Sorin, founder and CEO of Sorakin Technologies."

Sorin appears on screen with the relaxed precision of someone who doesn't chase attention. Mid-fifties, with a slender frame and an air of quiet authority. His silver hair is intentionally wild, tousled yet somehow deliberate. Horn-rimmed glasses frame eyes that study more than they see.

Sorakin Technologies has become the backbone of modern surveillance infrastructure. Originally developed to help with counterterrorism efforts in the early 2000s.

Over time, those same capabilities found their way into the private sector, quietly expanding as AI and digital networks became inseparable. Today, Sorakin powers everything from real-time analytics to predictive threat models.

It's become more than just a company now. It's the next generation of a global powerhouse, laying the foundation for how AI and robotics govern the modern world.

That's when a slow realization creeps in, heavy and undeniable.

BlackSteel, the private army. Continental Containment, the private prisons. Sorakin, the intelligence and surveillance machine.

Each one is a piece of the puzzle that will allow for a new level of governmental enforcement never seen before. And with these three corporations, the administration has all the tools to get the job done.

Tuff continues sharply.

"We're done waiting. Detention criteria, enforcement scope, it's all expanding. Laskey, explain how the hell you pulled this off."

Laskey adjusts his collar and speaks with a slow, deliberate cadence that makes everything sound reasonable, even when it isn't.

"The issue is scale," he explains. "They're flooding the system. Sympathizers, payouts, decentralized activity. Traditional law enforcement simply isn't equipped to keep up. The government was never designed to respond at this speed or volume."

He taps the folder in front of him.

"That's why we drafted the Protection of Freedom Bill. It reallocates funding from underperforming and non-essential programs. Social services, healthcare subsidies, educational grants. All of it redirected into high-priority stabilization efforts.

"That includes the creation of Freedom Zones. These are designated safe regions for high-net-worth individuals. Protected by three strategic partners. BlackSteel, Continental Containment, and Sorakin Technologies. Each has been granted expanded authority under the act. Detention, asset seizure, surveillance, enforcement. They now operate with federal backing and without the usual bureaucratic lag."

A faint, knowing smile creeps in.

"To further incentivize relocation and cooperation, the act also includes targeted tax relief and legal protections for qualifying donors and billionaire partners. It ensures capital flows inward and stays loyal.

"And to make it even better, Mr. President, all the key goals from your second-term economic package have been folded in. The tax cuts, the elimination of wasteful spending, the restructuring language, it's all there. No one's going to vote against this. We took full advantage of the timing."

Tuff lets out a satisfied breath.

"Beautiful. My donors are chomping at the bit over that."

The House and Senate are both under Tuff's control. Every

member of his party knows what he's promised. If this act doesn't pass and he wins reelection, anyone who opposes it is finished.

Not just politically. Financially. Socially. Everything tied to the machine vanishes the second they step out of line.

So, they'll make their wager. They'll decide who's more dangerous to bet against... the people or Tuff.

And most of them are not choosing the country. They're choosing their careers and safety.

Standing firmly behind the President doesn't just keep you in office... it makes you rich.

McMullen interjects, her expression warm like a good friend offering kind words.

"Anyone who has taken so much as a penny from the Dragon Slayers will be detained. Now, I know that sounds harsh, but really, it's for their own good and the good of our country. Some of these misguided people, well, don't always make the best choices, do they?"

McMullen's Botoxed smile doesn't waver. Her tone never loses its softness, even as she speaks about mass detention like it's nothing more than tidying up a house.

"We'll give them a nice, structured environment where they can rethink their decisions. Re-education centers. A second chance, if you will! And of course we'll be very fair about it. The moment they learn their lesson... and we do expect them to... they'll be free to go. With proper oversight, of course.

"A safe society needs order, after all. And I'm simply here to help make sure everything runs smoothly."

Tuff rubs his hands together, an overzealous grin spreading across his face as if he's just heard his personal manifesto.

"Thanks, Maggie. Isn't she the best?"

Jackson Kane chimes in, calm but laced with the discipline of a man always in command.

"With the immediate funding outlined in the bill, we're prepared to expand our operations tenfold. Recruitment starts with your base, Mr. President. We'll be drawing directly from your supporters, loyal and ready to enforce order. They'll form the backbone of our new domestic tactical response.

"BlackSteel will scale as fast as needed." Kane tips his hat, just slightly, like it's all part of the service.

Tuff nods in agreement.

Alexander Sorin speaks last, his intentions precise.

"Our AI infrastructure will not require additional funding. However, given the increasing likelihood that this movement spreads among the general population, we will need substantial investments to accelerate our robotics program. Automation becomes essential when containment is no longer a question of a few, but of the many."

I feel the weight of his words settle before the implications catch up.

There have been talks about this program. It's been circling the edge of feasibility for a while now. A blend of tactical drones and four-legged robotic dogs, more prototype than production. The designs have firepower and, even worse, approval to use it.

President Tuff nods slowly, almost impressed.

"Perfect. You're a smart guy, Sorin. Whatever you need, you'll get it. Now, back to the real problem at hand: these terrorist traitors looking for a payday.

"Do our citizens really believe that they can accept money from terrorists and just walk away? No! These individuals are going to get arrested. They're going to be held without bail. They're going to lose their vote in this election and their goddamn citizenship to my great country."

Tuff is creating cataclysmic shifts. His personal vendetta is now about eliminating everyone who might even begin to question him, his administration, and the system.

Then his gaze targets me.

"Your assignment, Grayson?" Give these amazing leaders anything they need from the FBI so you can finally stop these goddamn Dragon Slayers."

His order lands hard. This has nothing to do with stopping terrorism. This is turning fear into power, and I'm supposed to help create the machine that will carry it out.

Tuff lets the moment hang, his beady eyes sweeping the room.

"Does everyone understand me?"

A chorus of agreement follows. No questions, only obedient understanding.

"Good. Now let's restore our control over this nation and my re-election from those bastards and their paid minions."

There is no time to waste as I hurry back to the ops room, incessant activity enveloping me. Physically and emotionally fragmented agents are everywhere.

Carter perches on the edge of his seat as he speaks without raising his head.

"We're still watching, boss, but there's simply too much data. Nothing solid yet."

"Thanks, Carter. Continue digging."

Graham crackles over the comm, frustration in every word.

"Still on the line with BlackSteel. Giving me nothing but corporate PR crap. Not a peep about whether some of their clients were the ones kidnapped."

"Graham, they're going to play a much larger role in this going forward."

"Charlie, what the hell does that mean!"

"Sorry, but it appears the administration is going to pass a new bill to deputize BlackSteel."

"You have to be fucking kidding me."

"I wish I was. It's going to get ugly, Graham. Keep pushing for any information if you can, but honestly? Just get back to HQ. We need everybody here."

"Copy that. On my way."

Maya gestures to one of the upper screens.

"Charlie, Sly News is spinning this event. They're scrambling to make sure the billionaire class retains narrative control."

She lifts the feed, and as soon as the broadcast flashes on, I cringe.

Rocker Callahan.

His trademark bow tie is more like a pinned tail on a donkey, his over-starched shirt choking him. Rockers' face is nauseatingly smug, ready to deliver another divine revelation.

He drips with condescension and feigned bewilderment.

"Why are there so many Americans who hate billionaires? What makes poor people so poor, and why are they so angry now? Who would have the audacity to kidnap the wealthy, the only ones that make America the best!"

This professional village idiot is adding fuel to the flames.

"These same people owe their jobs to billionaires. They have opportunities because of rich people. And where is the gratitude? Where is the respect for men and women who have built whole industries for them? I honestly don't think I've ever heard them say thank you."

He shakes his head, exasperated, like an aggrieved parent.

"What kind of woke, elitist, socialist brainwashing have we undergone in our educational systems that has transformed this country into one that no longer respects success?

"What's wrong with Americans when our business leaders, the genius minds who innovate, are criminalized?

"Why are everyday citizens acting on everything The Dragon Slayers are preaching?"

He takes a sip from his monogrammed mug, rolling his eyes for a more dramatic effect.

"This is beyond disgusting. Taking money that comes from the suffering of others. What could be more unpatriotic?

"What could be viler than lining your own pockets at the direct expense of your fellow Americans?

"The real heroes of this nation are the ones who create opportunity, the ones who build corporations. And yet, some people, some opportunists, see pain, see destruction, and instead of standing against it, they cash in.

"They take blood money, stolen wealth, and for what? A bigger TV? A few extra luxuries? At the cost of their own neighbor's well-being?"

His voice sharpens, brimming with righteous disgust.

"It's shameful. It's parasitic. These people aren't just betraying their country... they're betraying their own communities. All because they couldn't say no to money?"

Rocker's frustration builds, sharp and unavoidable.

This man, this squawking parrot in a bow tie, is a marionette with strings looped tight around his neck. A hypocritical preacher sermonizing to people who will peddle their virtues for money.

Rocker has every minute of his life scripted by billionaires' teleprompters, changing his talking points based on whoever fills his pockets for his broadcasts. This man has the audacity to call other people traitors for taking money simply to survive.

Maya gasps, her head shaking disapprovingly.

"Charlie, this is going to backfire. Hard."

She's right, and it should be obvious to anyone not sucked into this level of propaganda.

The more they spread this fairy tale that billionaires are victims and the working class should be grateful for whatever meager pittance they receive, the worse it will become.

My team has not been fully briefed about the Protection of Freedom bill. Americans will receive the mandates soon enough.

And when it all drops...

All hell is going to break loose.

CHAPTER 22

PRIVATIZED TYRANNY

"That's the standard
technique of privatization: defund, make
sure things don't work, people get angry, you
hand it over to private capital."

- NOAM CHOMSKY

THE DEFCON ROOM feels small. I should review security protocols and prepare for the next phase, but my mind is stuck in a continuous loop of disarray.

The Dragon Slayers might have started this war, but the administration will end it in a way no one can foresee.

Bill's warning to me was unsettling. Tuff's administration is now fully exploiting this situation for their gain.

BlackSteel gains power, Continental Containment acquires lives, Sorakin Technologies tightens control, and the Constitution heads for the shredder.

I let my hands fall, folding and unfolding them in a restless cadence. So many questions remain unanswered.

If the Dragon Slayers hadn't sent out that initial video, would we even be in this political situation?

Would the government still have decided to turn the keys over to private military forces?

Would we still bear witness to the erosion of American democracy, but at a slower and more mundane pace?

There will never be an answer or a solution to these questions.

The badge I wear is a burning reminder of the debt I owe to Bill, the Bureau, to my team, to my country. My scarlet letter. These obligations replay in my core, yet my foundation no longer feels firm.

I'm standing on a fault line, observing cracks spreading out like spiderwebs, waiting for the instant when the earth splits open, plummeting me and everything I hold true into the void.

Five minutes remain until showtime.

Tuff will appear live to make his agenda official. Five minutes until he heralds to the world that this isn't about stopping terrorists anymore. It's about the administration taking total control to fix America's latest problem, making it safe again.

Agents move decisively, muted dialogue overlapping, boots hitting the tile with brusque efficiency. Everybody knows something major is about to be announced, unaware that it will change the world forever.

The main briefing room is filling up quickly. A row of screens blink on, showing live feeds, news broadcasts, security cameras, and various data metrics.

But the most dramatic change in the room?

All the new faces.

BlackSteel operatives are gathered in front, their black-and-red patches distinguishing them as uniquely different than us. They are not FBI for now, but soon they'll have just as much authority.

The tide is turning. BlackSteel will be given unlimited power, and we will be pushed aside or, worse, become a tool for them to flush out the Dragon Slayers and innocent civilians.

The Presidential Seal flashes on the main screen in the front of the room as whispered conversation between agents stops. Everyone warily looks forward.

Tuff seems like a magician without a cape, telecasting live from the White House. His makeup is too heavy, mocking the stern, stately presence he is trying to portray. It's a leadership mask that he seldom wants to wear.

He leans forward, hands clasped on the Resolute desk, staring into the camera, self-assured that this will be the most important speech of his presidency.

"My fellow Americans. Make no mistake about it. We are in the midst of a war."

No off-the-cuff rambling. His teleprompter script cuts straight to the chase.

"This is not a conflict of nations. This is a battle for civilization itself. A battle between those who build and those who destroy.

"A terrorist group, the so-called Dragon Slayers, have declared war on America's finest. And who are the finest that they are targeting?

"Not soldiers. Not politicians. Not agencies. No, these terrorists are hunting down the best of us. The job creators. The wealth builders. The innovators. The men and women who've made America the greatest country on earth.

"These Dragon Slayers are monsters who think they can threaten, intimidate, and murder their way into power. They think they can make us bow, give up our way of life, betray all that has made this nation a beacon of freedom and prosperity."

His hand slaps the desk, slightly jerking the camera, the intensity of his conviction shaking the room.

"Allow me to be perfectly clear. America does not engage in negotiations with terrorists. We do not yield to radicals. We do not forsake the American Dream simply because a mere handful of cowards desire to see us afraid."

I can sense the palpable shift in everyone's mood. The agents surrounding me are rigid, their faces frozen, eyes glued to the screen with a mix of skepticism and terror.

Tuff adamantly continues.

"This nation was created by the daring, by the strong, by those who risked and achieved something greater than themselves. This is the America that I love, and as we know from the last elections, America really loves me back."

The President pauses, savoring his words as if they are proof that anything he does is already justified.

"And that is why it is my duty as the leader and protector of the Citizens of America that I am expanding our crackdown on anyone who aids the Dragon Slayers. They will be arrested as terrorists.

"To bring an end to the Dragon Slayers and their followers, we need to act decisively. That is why, as part of the Protection of Freedom Bill, and with the full backing of Congress, we are granting federal authority to BlackSteel Security Solutions, Continental Containment, and Sorakin Technologies. This legislation ensures that our nation's enemies will be tracked, contained, and eliminated without delay.

"Under this bill, BlackSteel operatives are authorized to arrest, interrogate, and if necessary, terminate any individual suspected of assisting the Dragon Slayers."

There it is. The transfer of power. The privatization of national security. A collective gasp breaks the silence. Some agents shift in their seats; others stay completely still.

Tuff continues, his tone growing darker.

"This includes anyone who has accepted money from these terrorists. Anyone who's spread their propaganda. If you liked, commented, or shared one of their posts, you're no different than someone aiding domestic terrorism.

"BlackSteel will find you. And let me be absolutely clear, if you support the Dragon Slayers, you lose your right to vote. Your rights as an American citizen are nullified if you are working against your country."

Tuff raises his tone again in triumph.

"This is the law. The House and Senate are moving this bill through with overwhelming support. No one is standing in our way. We are united in stopping this threat to our great nation and its greatest citizens."

He pivots quickly, swelling with pride.

"We're protecting the future. The Dragon Slayers have already kidnapped members of our billionaire community. We will not allow another one to fall. Their safety is the foundation of this country's strength.

"Which is why I am proud to announce the establishment of our new Freedom Zones."

A graphic fills the screen, gold-rimmed city names with bold patriotic lettering:

New York, NY
West Palm Beach, Florida
Houston, Texas
Dallas, Texas
Scottsdale, Arizona
Washington, D.C.

"These secured communities will be available exclusively to our Patriots of Prosperity, America's billionaire class. Other wealthy contributors committed to our economy may also qualify.

"Each zone will be guarded by advanced AI systems, drones, and robotic enforcement, ensuring only authorized individuals can enter. These cities are designed to allow our wealth creators to live and work without disruption.

"We must send a message that our greatest patriots will not be targeted or harassed. That's why the Protection of Freedom Bill also includes the Creators of Prosperity provision.

"Under this clause, any assault, physical or financial, against a billionaire or their property will be treated as an act of terrorism. No exceptions.

"And let me say this again so no one misunderstands, it's retroactive. If you've taken a single dollar from those Dragon Slayer terrorists, don't bother hiding. BlackSteel is coming for you. Door knock first. Cuffs second."

I tighten my fingers into a fist, my knuckles bleach white.

Maya turns to me; color drained from her face.

"Charlie, millions of people might have just lost their rights. The President is ensuring that billionaires control the future. Forever."

Tuff sits back, smug, content on his golden throne.

"This is happening now. We have the votes; this will be law. And let me remind you: when I win, America wins."

With those final words, the President fades away from the broadcast.

I stare into the blackness of the screen, the vacant space in which democracy has just expired. There may be no coming back from this tyrant's rule.

"Charlie, what the hell is going on?" Maya's whisper is panicked. "Like, this is freaking insane.

"If they go through with this, oh my God, how the hell are they going to do it?"

"Maya, it could be more of a threat than a course of action.

A way to scare and intimidate people into obedience. Mass detainment on this scale might not be possible…"

My thoughts trail off before I can even finish what I was saying.

Under the new law, they have the means to do it.

Empowered to act swiftly and at scale, BlackSteel, Continental Containment, and Sorakin Technologies now have everything they need to execute the most expansive domestic crackdown in modern history. A mere knock on the door could mark the beginning of a state-sanctioned purge.

Maya looks at me, her eyes pleading for more, a conclusion, a solace, anything.

I have nothing.

Carter moves towards me, his face a mix of frustration and incredulity.

"Holy shit. Who's excited to crack down on these dangerous civilians?"

I snap at him.

"Carter, enough."

"Boss, seriously. This doesn't sit right. We just sat here and watched some guy go, if you mess with a billionaire's yacht, we'll treat it like a murder case and have a corporation arrest and maybe kill you. Like, holy fuck! This is bat shit crazy!"

"Carter, the administration may be pursuing its agenda, but we're still here doing our jobs. Keeping peace and order."

It doesn't sound genuine even to me. I can sense the skepticism rising in my team.

Graham marches over, fuming, so I just know that this is going to get worse.

"That's some fucking bullshit. That's how you hijack a country.

"I don't know if I want any part of this, Charlie. Black-

Steel? Private prisons? Taking away people's rights for viewing the wrong video?"

He is not mincing words, a loyal soldier's honest point of view.

There is a dual fire burning inside. I need to regain my composure, but I can't. Instead, I raise my chin as my tone falls into a robotic, unwavering rhythm.

"You're right, all of you. This is terrible. It really is. At this moment, I don't know what to say.

"I talked earlier with Bill, and he told me that this was going to happen. That this is the way things would go down. He knew that there was nothing he could do to stop it."

Drop-dead silence surrounds me.

"So, what are we going to do?" I ask.

"Are we just going to give up? We could. We could all just walk out right now.

"Or we could actually do something while we still have a chance. Unlike the administration, our mission isn't to seize as much power as we can. We're here to put an end to the Dragon Slayers."

"Know this. If we stop the Dragon Slayers, then we stop the crackdown. And maybe, just maybe, people will finally see how insane Tuff and his administration have become.

"We could return to some form of normalcy."

The quiet that follows is like the wait before a verdict is about to be read.

Maya speaks first.

"I mean. I don't know if we can stop the crackdown, Charlie. But yes, we certainly can stop the Dragon Slayers and hopefully find the other missing billionaires."

Carter releases a contained sigh.

"Yeah. Okay. I'm in boss."

Graham just stares at me for what feels like an eternity, long enough to make me suspect he may just turn and leave.

His expression hardens, eyes narrowing.

"Fine. But I promise you, Charlie, if they try to use us to start rounding up regular citizens, I'm out."

"Graham, I hear you. That is not who we are. That is not what we stand for at the FBI.

"We may operate under this administration, but we don't serve its political agenda."

"Everybody!" Maya shouts. "Dragon Slayers just released a new video."

Carter utters a low moan.

"Jesus, that didn't take them long."

Before anyone else can react, the screen in front of us flashes, and a figure appears.

Guinevere.

She sits with an unconcerned demeanor; her smile a playful dare, as though she knows some joke the rest of the world has yet to hear. The background behind her is dark and featureless, providing no clues about her location.

Guinevere's gold and ivory mask shimmers in the studio lights. There is no tension, no suggestion of anger, only a sense of amusement.

Good tidings, Resistance!

Guinivere stops. Her head tilts as if she's having second thoughts. Then she claps her hands together, applauding her viewers.

"Oh, wait… whoops! I guess I mean, Good tidings, terrorists?"
Wasn't that just wild?

Look how fast things change when it's about defending billionaires?

See how quickly the government moves to pass new laws?

Laws to make sure their precious oligarchs
must never experience a second of fear.

She leans in, enticing listeners to lean in as well.

Let us all pause and reflect.

How long does it take for something, anything,
to be done when it's good for the masses?

How many years do we wait? How many elec-
tions do we go through?

How many promises do we watch disappear into the ether?

Your elected officials say, it's complicated or
we just don't have the money for that.

She shakes her head slowly, disgust creeping in.

Feeding hungry children? Ah, that requires years of debate.

Better schools? Sorry, that's impossible within the budget.

Healthcare? It's just too expensive.

Wages? Well, we can never hurt corporate prof-
its; think of the poor shareholders.

Guinevere's smile fades as her tone becomes more piercing,
cutting through the hiss of the feed.

But the second billionaires get scared?

Her fingers snap, a sharp sound that reverberates through
the room.

Emergency powers, overnight. BlackSteel is given carte blanche.

Sorakin robots, built to neutralize the power we hold in numbers.

Private prisons are expanding by the hour.

Civil rights? Suspended.

And you?

She gestures gracefully to the screen.

You're labeled a terrorist.

*Why? For having the audacity to oppose
having your rights destroyed.*

They say you are the problem, that you have become the enemy.

*They say that if you take even a penny from us,
you are giving aid and comfort to terrorists.*

Now, let's discuss heroes.

Oh, our heroes!"

Guinivere muses, drawing out the word as if savoring an ancient memory.

*Do you remember the time when you were
branded as essential workers?*

*When billionaires barricaded themselves
inside their extravagant mansions?*

*While you, the insignificant ones, kept the
world turning amidst a global crisis?*

Do you remember when you stocked the shelves?

When you drove the trucks?

When you delivered the food and worked in the hospitals?

*When you had to deal with entitled customers yell-
ing at you for simply following orders?*

"And do you recall what they promised you in return?

A few checks from the government?

Sounds like a cheap thank you to me.

Guinevere offers a soft tsk, tsk, tsk.

Meanwhile, these so-called creators of prosperity literally made trillions.

Look it up, it was the biggest theft of wealth under
the guise of keeping the economy alive.

Billions in corporate loans? Quietly written off like rounding errors,

while they raised prices, blamed inflation, and
posted record profits as you suffered.

But fear not, my friends.

The Dragon Slayers have not forgotten your efforts.

Since your government sees fit to ignore the real heroes,

we will take matters into our own hands.

Her eyes sparkle behind the mask.

I know they're attempting to frighten you,

intimidating you into believing you can't have our money.

Saying you'll be branded a terrorist if you try but here's the catch.

She pauses as we all hold our breath.

We're good at what we do, and they can't
stop all of us, now can they?

That's the power we have. And we will use it.

So, here is our proposal.

If you were told to risk your life during the pandemic and earned under $200K,

we urge you to contact us.

A QR code suddenly pops up on the screen.

Our stimulus check for you is much, much bigger.

With all the money we've freed from those sick with greed,

well, we want to give back the money to each one of you.

Consider it a Dragon Slayers Real Hero kickback.

No strings attached.

Just straight-up giving you,

the working class that holds this country together, what you deserve.

They have billions of dollars.

We have billions of people.

Let's see what's harder to replace, shall we?

She slowly fades into darkness, leaving her question unanswered.

The room is shocked into silence. No one breathes. No one moves.

Carter lets out a nervous laugh.

"Holy shit. People are going to take that money and run."

Maya chimes in.

"If they start funneling money like this, we'll never be able to track all of it. Not in real time and they know that.

"The Dragon Slayers are forcing the government's hand. They want people to take their money to provoke more action."

She's right. Guinevere is tempting the government to enforce their threats. One video, one promise of cash, and now the administration must criminalize anyone who takes it.

The government declared millions of Americans terrorists. The Dragon Slayers are writing checks to these same people.

Everyone is still trying to recover from Tuff's outrageous announcements, trying to untangle the impact and subsequent horrendous consequences to follow.

I need to speak up.

"Listen I get it. This new situation has put more pressure on us. I know it feels like the walls are closing in around us, but we can't give up. FBI agents do not accept defeat. We keep to the tasks at hand."

They nod in unison, and the silence remains. My phone pings, breaking the quiet.

It's a text from Lex.

Hey, can you talk?

In the midst of mayhem, once again I had forgotten about her.

Yes, come to my office.

I try to get there first, hoping to fix my disheveled appearance. But there she stands at my office door, a refreshing sight for my tired eyes. There's an oddity about her aura, a peculiar agitation; she is not her usual self.

"What's going on? I sheepishly ask as I open the door for her.

With a curt sigh and a headshake, she goes ahead and speaks her mind.

"Charlie, I can't work here anymore."

Lex's words don't process right away. She is not a quitter. This is not another one of her off-the-cuff remarks. She is serious.

"What do you mean by done?"

"I mean, this is just way, way too much."

Lex had envisioned her career with the FBI would include tracking down perpetrators and deflecting danger. Now, she is embroiled in a firestorm, one she is not willing to fight.

"Charlie, I will not be a party to imprisoning innocent people. I'm going to resign."

How could she even possibly consider resigning? That familiar voice inside me, sharp and unrelenting, demands I speak up. Demands I fight back. If she walks away from her career, she walks away from us.

Instead, I say nothing. My entire life has been forged by the FBI principles of fidelity, bravery, and integrity. Instilled at an early age by my father and with my career as an agent.

When challenges arise, you do not abandon the ship. Instead, you steady the course. Quitting is never an option, but I can see how this is different, especially for her.

Lex has always deserved a better relationship. She alone understands me like no one else ever will. It's only fair that I offer her the same level of understanding, from her point of view.

I won't argue that she should stay, even though I have a handful of reasons. I want to tell Lex that agents like her are the backbone of the Bureau. That losing her will be a significant setback for the FBI and our relationship.

Most of all, I will not reveal my true feelings, that every time she walks through those doors, her presence becomes everything to me. I can't because it wouldn't be fair to put that on her. Not now. Not after everything that transpired between us.

Instead, I force the words out.

"You have a valid point, Lex. I understand."

"You're not going to say my resigning is a bad idea?"

"No, you shouldn't be compelled to engage in something that goes against your beliefs. I totally understand.

"However, don't think your time as an agent was a waste in any way. You helped save countless numbers of lives."

She looks at me for a second, waiting for the hidden trap-door to open. A flash of skepticism veils her face. Then, she is back to being the Lex I know so well.

"Wow, Charlie, what a relief. I thought you'd be mad. I thought you'd be upset with me, and then things would be awkward with us, and well, things have been so good between us lately; I mean given the time we have…"

Lex's words pick up speed, excitement bubbling to the surface as she starts to ramble. How she wasn't sure what to expect, how she had five different worst-case scenarios playing out in her head. She catches herself, lips pressing together for a second before she laughs.

"You're busy, but Charlie, really, *thank you.* This isn't easy for me. Gotta run."

Watching her leave, I feel guilty for being somewhat relieved. Out of sight, out of mind. I dive headfirst back into my work.

Hours are fleeting, and I have lost track of time. Before me there are stacks of reports, videos, and feeds, none sharing a hint about the Dragon Slayers. Billionaire after billionaire appears on the screen, their faces, their names, their security details, their life stories.

The clock harasses me with its hourly updates: 5 PM, 6 PM, 7 PM, and suddenly it's 10 PM. I don't know how to stop; I am in overdrive, going nowhere fast.

My mind begins to drift as I scroll through picture after picture, a frustrating game of Eye Spy. Why can't I see it?

And then. A blue shield.

Barely visible in the corner of a grainy photo is a logo on a security badge. My subconscious tells me to stop.

Safe Serve.

SAFE.

I start connecting the dots.

SAVE.

Evan Marshall's voice echoes in me.

"They just kept saying, save something. When they got save something, they felt they would get even more."

My eyes sharpen, fatigue replaced by a surge of urgency.

Save something. Safe something. Safe Serve.

This could be it. We've been looking for the wrong word all along.

I rabidly attack my keyboard. Safe Serve isn't just any ordinary private military firm; it's much smaller, but made up entirely of ex-military operatives. That reputation has earned them a high concentration of billionaire clients.

A pulsating, wavelike feeling of energy streams through my body. Marcus Bloodso is the President, and Safe Serve has a satellite office ten minutes away from us.

E-mail commands need to be sent.

Graham: Get your gear. Meet out front. Heading to Safe Serve's office.

Carter: Need everything you can find on Safe Serve. Personnel, clients, finances.

Tactical Team: Target location—MGRS 18SUJ23307645. Move ASAP.

I grab my gear and take a moment to visualize the mission before heading out the door.

Time to turn up the heat.

CHAPTER 23

A DESPERATE GAMBLE

"In order to rally people, governments need enemies… if they do not have a real enemy, they will invent one in order to mobilize us."

- THICH NHAT HANH

THE MOMENT GRAHAM sees me, he can sense that something is brewing.

"What is it, Charlie?"

"I think it's Safe Serve."

"Are you sure?"

"It's just a hunch. They're a smaller PMC, but proportionally, they serve more billionaire clients than anyone else. If they know where the missing billionaires are, then we actually could have a shot at a successful rescue.

"Tactical team is set. They'll arrive in twenty to twenty-five minutes to get there. Five-minute drive for us."

"Charlie, a rescue would be huge. But we might be outnumbered."

"Graham, if we pull this off, we'll be the first to rescue

someone kidnapped by the Dragon Slayers. And after Tuff's new bill? We don't have time to wait. BlackSteel could lock everything down by tomorrow.

"Do you really believe we can't hold them off until our backup arrives? We need to find something, and it's now or never."

We climb into a waiting SUV. Five minutes. That's all we have before we find out if this is our big breakthrough or just another setback.

Pressing down on the accelerator, I speed through the empty streets. Graham is silent, his eyes darting between the road and his phone as he tracks the tactical team's ETA.

We don't speak, as there is nothing more to be said. We're all in. We're moving fast.

I dial Carter.

"Boss, I hope this pans out. I'm digging deep into Safe Serve now. Personnel, clients, everything I can get."

"Perfect. We're almost at their HQ. Talk later."

I end the call as Graham's fingers drum against the console.

"Charlie, what if no one is there?"

"Then we kick in the door and see what's on the other side. Warrants are no longer needed. You heard Tuff. It's either Black Steel or us doing this job."

Ahead, Safe Serve headquarters comes into view. It's late, but the lights are still on.

Graham catches his breath.

"Could just be an overnight cleaning crew in there. Doesn't seem like they have many cars parked here."

I drive around the back. Then we see them. Safe Serve employees in full regalia, loading unmarked vans. No third-party movers, no moving company. Just them, quickly moving around as if they're trying to disappear before anyone catches a glimpse.

As we get out of the vehicle, the staff stop, look straight at us, and then go back to work as if we are invisible.

I step closer, my badge ready in my hand.

"FBI Deputy Director Grayson, and this is Special Agent Cross."

Graham remains steadfast by my side.

"What's going on here, guys?" he yells.

One of them stiffens, gripping the edge of a crate a little too tightly.

"Uh, just relocating some gear," he weakly responds. "Supply issues and such."

"Yeah," another joins in. "Freeing up some storage."

A man steps forward from the dock, unruffled and composed. His Safe Serve uniform is well-pressed and more tailored than the others, signaling authority.

"Good evening, I'm Lieutenant Aaron Shaw. How can I assist? "

Graham doesn't shift, but I can feel his tactical senses on high alert.

"FBI. We're on patrol. Saw the men moving around, thought it best to check it out. But since you're here, we do have a few questions."

The man offers a polite smile and extends his hand.

"Of course. No trouble at all. I appreciate you watching out for us. Given our line of work, you never know. The Dragon Slayers have made it clear we're walking targets.

"We can chat inside."

As he turns, he gives a subtle nod to the two workers near him, a brief, imperceptible signal. They hesitate for a fraction of a second before falling into step behind him.

Something is off. I glance toward Graham, and his look confirms my suspicions.

We're surrounded, but it's only a few more minutes until backup arrives. Our strategy now is to slow things down.

Shaw takes the lead. We're in the middle. Two employees fall in behind us, boxing in the doorway.

He continues to keep things light, addressing us as if we are there for a fireside chat.

"Long day for you two, I'm guessing. You'd be surprised how much of my job is logistics these days. Moving parts, moving people. Never a dull moment, so I can only imagine what it's like on your end."

He welcomes us into his office as though we are old friends, keeping things light and informal.

Shaw gestures toward two chairs in front of his desk, then takes a seat, leaning back with ease. The two men stand by the door, close enough to make their presence known.

"Those Dragon Slayers are something else, aren't they? Never encountered anything like them. It's been utter chaos on our side."

"Tell me about it," I say, keeping my demeanor friendly.

"So, Grayson and Cross. What can I do for you?"

"We've been touching base with some of the private security firms, routine check-ins, same as we're doing with Safe Serve.

"Since we're here, just wondering if we could ask you a few questions about some of your clients. Take it off our to-do list.

"We've been working on missing persons cases, which include some billionaires. Maybe you, or someone higher up, perhaps Marcus Bloodso, could help us look into this?"

Shaw lets out a quiet, almost imperceptible chuckle.

"Oh, you want to speak with the head honcho himself. This matter must be pretty significant."

"Lieutenant, we just need to make sure we pursue every lead

and cover any loose ends, so we're setting up similar calls across the board."

"Loose ends, huh? Hope you're not suspicious of us."

"We have several suspects. It would be to your advantage if we could eliminate Safe Serve from the list. It would be just a quick meeting at FBI headquarters."

"So, are you asking me in? Or is this an order?"

Graham stirs next to me, his words as flat as his expression.

"Depends on how you want to do it."

Shaw observes him for a moment before letting out a gentle laugh, shaking his head as though this is all some huge misunderstanding.

"The last thing we need is trouble with the FBI. Well, I suppose I have no choice then."

For a moment, his eyes wander as if he is turning something over one last time. But that's all it takes to convey his message.

The two Safe Serve guards act in a flash, grabbing Graham and forcing him onto the ground.

Two against one, both men larger than Graham, pinning him down with brute force. He grunts, straining muscles, but they have the leverage.

I jump up instantly, but Shaw intercepts me. His stance is relaxed and controlled. There is no hurry in his movement, no tension. He is bigger and stronger and thinks he is in full control.

My entire life, I've embraced that I would be smaller in stature compared to my male counterparts. Weaker. Maybe even slower. But there is one thing I've always relied on.

They will underestimate me.

I let my body go limp and hold up my hands in a surrendering gesture. My voice trembles just enough, shoulders curling inward as if bracing for the inevitable.

"Wait… please don't."

Shaw wickedly smiles. The kind a man gets when he feels that victory is undeniable.

That's when I know I have him.

I spin and lunge, my actions fast and deliberate. My hand crashes into his throat, not to kill but forceful enough to stun him, sending him backward, struggling for air. Instinctively, he raises his hands to regain control, but I'm already closing in on him.

Shaw charges at me, staggered but confident, still believing that brute force will overtake me. As he goes for a takedown, I turn, using his momentum to my advantage. His weight propels him forward, and I skillfully hook his arm and twist my body into the throw.

His feet leave the ground as he crashes into the floor, his spine hitting the thick tile with a jarring, pained thud. The impact sends his breath exploding out of him in a ragged gasp.

Without hesitation, I drop down on Shaw and drive my knee into his ribs, pinning him in position as I jerk his arm back at a vicious angle. He tries to struggle against me, to turn loose, but I grip tight.

I recognize the instant he realizes he cannot escape. Panic draws over him as his fingers desperately claw in the empty air, but it's no use. My hands are already moving, cuffing him without thinking, pure instinct taking over.

The sudden turn takes the other two Safe Serve guards by surprise. Their heads jerk around to face us. That moment of hesitation is all Graham requires.

He rams his elbow deep and hard into the ribs of the man holding him down, the force punishing and deep. In one fluid motion, he quickly throws a right hook that smashes the other guard back into the wall.

Now free, Graham carries the kind of fury that only vengeance can quench.

The first man is still reacting to the blow as Graham pushes the advantage, reaching out and grasping the front of the guard's shirt. He tugs him downwards, right into a vicious knee to his gut.

The man grunts, doubling over. Graham flips him effortlessly and smashes him face-first onto the desk, the impact cracking through the room.

It's brutally smooth, decades of combat instinct distilled into a single motion. I've trained for this and drilled it a thousand times, but there's a difference between knowing the steps and owning the moment.

Graham spots the other guard and rushes forward with savage strength, pinning him against the wall while launching a flurry of heavy blows to his victim's face. A good left hook has the man stumbling, but Graham shows no sign of stopping. He throws the man into a filing cabinet, his fists nonstop, swearing as he catches the guard with another punch to his jaw.

Watching him, it's impossible to ignore the sheer force and control he carries beneath the surface, power and skill wrapped in absolute precision.

He growls, his adrenaline-filled voice tight with anger.

"You fucking idiots."

The first guard foggily tries to stand, but Graham delivers a quick kick, sending him crashing back down.

His comm crackles to life.

"Tactical team on-site."

Shaw's breathing is ragged, eyes unfocused, the bluster broken.

"Well, looks like you did have a choice," Grahams says heatedly. "Let's get these dumbasses back to HQ."

The tactical team swoops in, taking Shaw and his men away with smooth, professional efficiency. There is no struggle from the Safe Serve employees. Graham and I had already beaten it out of them.

My concern quickly switches to Shaw. He is too composed for the circumstances that he finds himself in. We got him, but will that lead us anywhere?

The lieutenant smiles cunningly as he passes by me and is loaded with his men into an armored vehicle. He knows the game is shifting, and it may not be in his favor.

Graham and I head towards our SUV, minds racing with what comes next. A debrief, an interrogation, and sorting out what Safe Serve has actually been up to. We're halfway across the lot when a wild movement attracts my attention.

A kid. Short and skinny, probably not even older than eleven. He's squatting in front of our SUV, stuffing something on the windshield. As soon as he spots me, his body stiffens, and he takes off.

I sprint after him and yell.

"Hey! Stop!"

He doesn't look back. He's fast, but my adrenaline makes me faster.

Graham threads the lot with accuracy, intuitively calculating the angle and positioning himself for the interception. The boy barely has time to swing his leg over the bike before Graham is upon him, grabbing his collar and roughly pushing him against the side of a van.

The child gasps, thrashing, but Graham keeps him pinned.

"What the hell do you think you're doing?"

My eyes lock on his terrified face. He's a kid, so young. His black hair is mussed from the struggle. He is scared but defiant.

"I… I was only supposed to leave the note there," he stammers, trembling with fear. "That's all! That's all they told me to do!"

I step in.

"Who?"

The kid's Adam's apple bobs as he swallows hard, eyes filling with tears.

"The Dragon Slayers. They told me that if I placed that note on your car, they would give me a hundred thousand."

What the fuck. I exchange a look with Graham. A hundred grand.

I turn to the child again.

"And you didn't think that sounded a bit suspicious?"

"I didn't care! My sister. She needs surgery. We can't pay for it. But with the Dragon Slayers' money? We can."

I scan him, searching for fear, but it isn't pure fear that I find. It's defiance, sharpened by conviction, the kind that only comes from believing in something greater than himself. Poor kid doesn't grasp the full weight of what he's doing.

Graham tightens his grip on him.

"You know this is terrorism, don't you? Do you have any idea what happens if we take you in?"

The boy raises his chin.

"I don't care. They've paid us already. My sister will live. So go ahead, lock me up. I don't care."

Graham and I don't speak.

If we bring this kid in, his life will be over.

"Listen, punk," Graham growls. "I could have fucking killed you just now. In fact, I can still kill you, and nobody would care cause you're a terrorist now. Do you understand?"

The boy doesn't answer. He just stares, panting.

Graham shoves him once more.

"Do you fucking understand me?"

The kid nods, tears streaming down his face.

Graham's face inches closer to the boy.

"You do anything else for the Dragon Slayers, and somebody else finds out about it, instead of us, they won't just bring you down. They'll bring your sister down. Your whole family down. You get it?"

The kid shakes his head frantically, gasping.

"I understand. I understand."

Graham releases his grip, shoving him away forcefully.

"Get the hell out of here!"

The boy trips, picks himself up and flees without looking back. We watch as he disappears into the darkness.

I force myself to take a breath.

"Jesus. They gave him a hundred thousand. For just a note."

I walk towards the SUV and tug the note off the windshield. I smooth it out, recognizing the Dragon Slayers' seal. My hands shake as I read it out loud.

Charlotte Grayson,

We are not your enemy here.

We are closer than you think.

The Dragon Slayers

Rage coils through me, sharp and unrelenting.

We are not the same.

These fucking monsters don't know a damn thing about me.

CHAPTER 24

SMOKE AND TARGETS

"No society can surely be flourishing and happy, of which the far greater part of the members are poor and miserable."

-ADAM SMITH

THE RIDE BACK is steeped in silence. The low murmur of the engine hums through space, tranquilizing our nerves. Graham stares out the window, his expression rigid, his fingers opening and closing as he tries to wrangle mixed emotions from the Safe Serve confrontation.

I keep my eyes on the road as my thoughts drift beyond the stretch of pavement ahead. I can't help but think about that poor kid. He had no clue how close he came to getting mixed up in a reality where there was no point of return.

Graham watches me pondering the same insufferable outcome.

"Charlie, if BlackSteel comes to power, someone like that kid, well, that little shit would be screwed. Life imprisonment if he's lucky."

"I know. That's precisely why we have to stop The Dragon Slayers before it's too late."

"At least we may finally have something, right?"

"Hopefully. Just not sure how it all fits together. It could turn out to be an important key to this case."

Graham shifts in his seat, flexing a strained muscle, then lets out a low, amused chuckle.

"Charlie, let's get one thing straight about what happened back there. I could have handled all three of them; I just thought I'd give you a chance to practice some of your combat skills."

I let out a quick laugh, tapping the gas a little harder.

"Graham, you sure had them right where you wanted them."

"Yeah, yeah. But no, seriously, Charlie, you proved yourself in the field tonight. I'm impressed, to say the least. You can handle your shit."

"Thanks, but let's be honest. You're the reason we came out of there in one piece. Even though we were outnumbered, you handled them. Well, more like demolished them."

"Deputy Director, if that's the story you wanna go with, I won't complain."

The dash screen lights up with a call from Carter.

"Got anything?" I fire off.

Carter's voice resonates through the car.

"Boss, you were right. Safe Serve is super sketchy."

"What did you find?"

"It's dirty as hell. I'm tracking a bunch of suspicious VPN traffic from Safe Serve's low-level guys. Thankfully, their security protocol is fucking incompetent, so they're dropping electronic breadcrumbs everywhere."

"Perfect. We've got the upper hand now, but we still need Bloodso and, more importantly, the billionaires that were taken."

"I've got names. There are three major figures. One of them

stands out: Thaddeus Montclair III. Net worth? A staggering $200 billion. He had a history with Safe Serve, but whether they were still actively protecting him when he went missing hasn't been confirmed.

"If we find Montclair, I know this op will break wide open."

"Roger that. Carter, we're pulling into HQ now. Will head right over to you."

The second my headlights sweep across the parking lot, I know something is wrong. There are more cars than usual. A lot more.

I slow down, taking in the sight of streamlined, armored transport vehicles flanking the entrance. Each one bears the BlackSteel logo.

Graham lets out a low whistle.

"Well, fuck me. Charlie, what is all this shit?"

"I have no idea, but whatever this is, it's not good."

As we enter the Bureau, I spot them.

Jackson Kane waits in the middle of the entrance. As usual, he is impeccably dressed in a sharp black suit that marks him above the law. His cowboy hat makes him look like an actor from a spaghetti Western movie.

Kane is a man well-versed in the warfare of the boardroom. He has the skillset to combine corporate strategy with military discipline, creating an unnerving whole that is more than the sum of its parts.

He moves forward, his grin broadening as he tips his hat and holds out his hand.

"Deputy Director Charlotte Grayson, Agent Graham Cross, it's a pleasure to finally meet both of you in person. I'm very pleased to hear that we will be working with you and the FBI."

His handshake is firm and deliberate, meant to convey mastery. I extend my hand, matching the intensity of his grip.

"Mr. Kane. Pleasure."

"Let me introduce you to Commander Reddick. He has been instrumental in developing BlackSteel into what it is today."

Encased in ballistic armor, Reddick resembles a metallic beast far more than a man. Heavy plates give him a hulking presence. He stands like a monument, every inch designed to intimidate. His bald head and sharp black eyes complete the picture; a man carved from discipline and rage.

Reddick straightens, laced with restrained aggression.

"It's an honor to finally bring order to what the FBI has been incapable of containing."

Kane nods with approval.

"Reddick here's one of the best we've got, perfect for this Dragon Slayer situation. He will be overseeing our integration of your bureau."

"Integration?"

"Come on now, Deputy Director. With the Protection of Freedom Act in effect, it's quite clear who's in charge here. Your full cooperation is appreciated, not just for my sake, but for Commander Reddick's and the numerous BlackSteel Agents that will be transitioned into the FBI."

In the private sector, Kane is a tyrant who has never had to clarify himself. He built BlackSteel by swallowing up smaller PMCs, consolidating forces until no one could match his reach. For Kane, this transition is simply one more hostile takeover.

He clasps his hand on my shoulder as if we are old pals.

"I've spoken with your boss, Director Cartwright. He's fully on board. I know I can count on you and your team as well. I'm expecting great things from you.

"One more thing. Reddick will be relaying your orders from now on."

I maintain a firm stance as Kane walks away. Reddick quickly steps forward.

He speaks to us in a condescending tone.

"Deputy Director Grayson. Agent Cross. I need you both to start working harder. Much harder. You'll soon learn that BlackSteel operates on a much more efficient schedule than our government.

"We are quicker, smarter, and we don't waste valuable time or money.

"And let me be clear, any delays, any inefficiencies, any failure to assist with this transition will be recorded and appropriately acted on.

"In times like these, internal obstacles are more than just inconveniences. They verge on willful neglect. And under the new Executive Orders, not opposing the Dragon Slayers is as condemning as aiding them."

Yet again, more confirmation that any insubordination will be labeled terrorism. I meet his gaze and remain neutral.

Reddick's eyes narrow by a fraction, watching intently for any sign of pushback, but he sees none.

He steps back, inclining his head quizzically.

"Deputy Director, what's your latest status report? What exactly have you and your team accomplished since this Dragon Slayer fiasco started?"

"Commander, we've just arrested three operatives from Safe Serve. We suspect that they might have turned over billionaires under their watch to the Dragon Slayers."

Reddick barely reacts. If anything, there's a flicker of satisfaction, as though we just confirmed something he already knew.

"Interesting. We'll commence our own interrogations in the morning when our staff is fully up and running. Remember, we expect a smooth transition."

"Of course, Commander. Glad you're taking the lead on this. My team and I will assist you in any way we can."

I can feel Graham's burning hot eyes on me, but he offers no comment.

Reddick gives us both a sidelong look.

"Good. Dismissed."

We turn, heading for the exit, leaving the impression that we will submit to any new orders that come our way.

The moment we're outside, Graham grabs my arm.

"What the fuck was that? Are you just going to hand everything over to them on a silver platter?"

"Of course not. I won't hand over our only lead for Reddick to mishandle or suppress evidence. We're going to interrogate those Safe Serve employees. We need answers, and we need them now.

"Starting tomorrow, the FBI will change into what, I don't know. Which is exactly why we can't afford to wait around."

"You're right, Charlie, let's question them while we have a chance."

BlackSteel's presence is everywhere, bearing down on us. Unfamiliar operative faces fill our headquarters like they already own the place. We head to our offices, casually walking to avoid any suspicion, as their watchful gazes press against our backs.

A pair of agents stand near the stairwell, they speak softly, but I hear the tail end of a sentence:

"They're booting out entire FBI teams. This is just a blatant purge."

As we reach Carter's office, I push open the door without knocking. I find him slowly spinning in his chair, chewing on a pen, deep in thought.

"Geez, you both look rough. Were you two fighting again?"

"Minor run-in with some thugs," I reply casually.

"Well, I've got twenty BlackSteel goons arriving tomorrow. Apparently, they want me to train them and keep working cases."

"Yeah, Carter, it's a mess. I'll do whatever I can to make it less painful for you and your team."

He gives me one of his familiar smirks, trying to camouflage his concerns.

Reaching into my pocket, I pull out three phones, setting them down in front of him with a quiet tap against the desk.

Carter rolls his neck, sitting up to take stock of what I've just laid out. He picks up one of the phones, turning it thoughtfully between his fingers.

"Okay, burner phones. Dime a dozen," he quips.

"These are from the Safe Serve guys we've arrested. This one belongs to Shaw, the man in charge. He's the important one; the other two are his subordinates. What can you get us?"

"Oh, I can get you plenty. And get this. We'll be unlocking hidden backdoors in their operating system that they don't even know exist."

"How soon?"

"You want fast, or you want useful?"

Graham steps next to Carter, arms folded.

"Enough with the theatrics, Diaz. Just fucking do it."

Carter mutters something under his breath but grins as he starts to screen mirror the phone.

"Give me a few minutes, and I'll at least let you know where this thing's been."

Lines of data stream by on the screens, extracting location pings and last logins. Threads that could provide us with the answers we desperately need.

I give Carter's shoulder a hasty pat.

"Your talent means a lot, Carter. Keep us posted."

"You'll know about it as soon as I do, boss."

Graham hastily heads to the door.

"Alright, let's see what we can get out of them. The underlings most likely don't know a thing. Let's go speak with Shaw."

As we walk down the corridor, our thoughts are occupied by what is about to take place.

Graham composes himself before entering the interview room.

"You think Shaw's gonna break?"

"Your guess is as good as mine. Everyone's got something, and we'll take anything."

We sit at the end of the worn table as I skim through Shaw's file. He has a great resume: ex- Army officer, several deployments, POW for twelve months. He endured harsh living conditions and rough treatment, yet he made it out alive.

It's obvious that with his background experience, Shaw has a leadership role. As CEO, Marcus Bloodso grew Safe Serve into more than a security agency. He created the company to give a second chance to soldiers the system left behind.

That means three things: Shaw is disciplined, loyal, and dedicated to his fellow Vets. Odds are that he's not the exception; he's the blueprint for how Safe Serve operates. It's going to be a long shot to get them to break ranks.

He enters with a guard who escorts him to a seat, hands bound in front, his attitude nonchalant. His gaze meets mine with a knowing reassurance that suggests he has endured harsher treatment than this interrogation will ever be.

Shaw gives a measured, thoughtful dip of his head to us, courteous but inscrutable.

I sit opposite him, placing his file in front of him.

"You've had quite a career, Lieutenant Shaw."

He responds smoothly.

"All for service and duty."

"Numerous awards, leadership positions and distinguished honors. Also, a survivor of captivity as a POW."

The lieutenant doesn't acknowledge my comments. He is set in stone.

I shut the file and meet his gaze.

"What would motivate a soldier like you to associate with the Dragon Slayers? They're terrorists. Don't you love your country?"

"Terrorists? You and your partner attacked us because you thought we were terrorists?"

Graham swiftly corrects him.

"Attacked you? We defended ourselves."

"It felt like an attack on my men and me. I guess that's for the lawyers to settle."

I keep my response to his legal threat neutral.

"Lieutenant, we both know you and your boys aren't going to be bringing in lawyers. That's why you attacked us in the first place. Let's cut the bullshit.

"Safe Serve is a very interesting firm. Extremely veteran-centric. Marcus Bloodso made sure it safeguarded people the government discards after duty.

"Honestly, that's very respectable."

Shaw lightens up just a bit. There's a faint squaring of his shoulders, a twinkle in his eyes, a flash of pride.

"Deputy Director, we are here to help our brothers and sisters in arms in any way we can. I believe you will find this ethos permeates every aspect of Safe Serve. We look after our own, and we never leave anyone behind."

"Listen Shaw, BlackSteel plans to take complete control of the FBI. We won't be in charge anymore, we won't be able to help you."

I watch my words sink in, waiting to see what will surface.

"You're the only one standing between your country, your team and countless innocent civilians. BlackSteel won't be asking questions."

Shaw's eyes widen slightly, a realization of what's approaching. He controls his emotions and leans back in his chair.

"When I first got to the POW camp," he says, his voice unyielding, "they starved me for three weeks. I'm still here. I think I can handle it."

"Maybe you can, but can your men and their families?

"You do care about all of them, don't you? Safe Serve is a haven for veterans who want to rebuild their lives. Bloodso built something that gave vets like you a new sense of purpose.

"That's noble. Refusing to cooperate with us is not, and it puts lives in jeopardy."

He doesn't answer.

"It's simple. Give us Montclair. Tell us where he is. We get a billionaire, this goes up the chain, and you and your men are in a much better position.

"Show us where your allegiance lies."

Shaw slowly, very deliberately, straightens up, shoulders squared as if he's back in uniform.

Then he speaks a simple declaration.

"Lieutenant Aaron Shaw. United States Army. Service number 342-71-981."

Name, rank, serial number. The traditional POW answer.

"Sorry, Deputy Director, but I'm not going to make this easy for you."

"Then we're done here."

I signal to the guard to escort him out of the room. Graham and I just sit there watching him walk away. I failed to execute.

"Well, Charlie, you can't say that didn't go as we expected."

I don't have a chance to reply as my phone vibrates.

Text from Carter: *Get back here STAT. I got something.*

"Graham, we have to step to it and get to Carter's office. He may have a breakthrough."

He jumps up, and we rush down the corridor hoping he has unearthed something we can use.

As we enter his office, Carter diverts his attention from his screens to us.

"I've been routing everything through those burner phones you gave me. It did take some digging, but I've uncovered something very interesting.

"Shaw and his other two dudes spent most of their time together; no surprise there. Seems like they're a team, so their phones routinely pinged from the same locations.

"Here's where it gets interesting. Three times, just three, those phones pinged in tandem with another phone. Each time, it was a different number, and these three numbers all have a lot more activity recorded. Calls, movements, encrypted messages. It certainly stands out."

I perk up, scanning the logs.

"You believe one of those numbers is Bloodso?"

"I'm not certain, but if I had to place a wager? One of these three meetings was with him. Just need to figure out which one."

Graham studies the screen.

"Carter, where were these meetings?"

"Three locations: Baltimore, Tysons Corner, and, oddly, in the middle of the Shenandoah. Can't determine which location and who was there. So, if we pursue the incorrect one, we squander our time."

I consider the different angles. Then, it falls into place. A means of cutting through the confusion and reaching a definite answer.

I can't help but make an imitation of Carter's smirk.

Graham immediately catches it.

"Charlie, what are you thinking?"

"We'll tell them each a different location and see how each Safe Serve employee reacts."

"Misdirection."

"Exactly. Each one gets a different address. We watch how they react alone, then watch how they react when their narratives don't match."

Carter pushes back from his desk, fascinated.

"That could work. Pretty smart of you, boss."

Graham is thinking fast.

"Okay. So, who gets which location?"

I turn to Carter.

"Which do you think is most probable?"

He takes a moment to process the choices before responding.

"Baltimore and Tysons are the most plausible. There's enough digital chatter to sustain both. As for the Shenandoah one? It doesn't make a whole lot of sense, but the fact that there was a high-traffic burner there at some point makes me leery about excluding it altogether."

"Alright then. We can skip Shaw and Shenandoah for now. He would likely give us the same reaction for all three locations, anyway.

"We offer one site to each of his men. Let's see who offers us something back first."

Carter grins.

"Clever. I'll monitor things on my side."

I give Carter a quick thumbs up and step outside. Time to set the trap.

Sitting in the observation room, I review the files of the other Safe Serve men that we arrested. Ryan Davis and Johnathon Sanders, both have military backgrounds. They might not be at Shaw's level of military expertise, but they are well-trained.

Baltimore. Tysons Corner. Shenandoah. I'm not looking for a full confession; what I'm looking for is a solo reaction, something to tip the balance in favor of the actual meeting spot.

I decide to interrogate Davis first. He glances up as I enter; his stance is relaxed, almost slouching. No instant tension. He anticipates the usual push-and-pull of questioning, but I don't play that game.

Taking a seat across from him I push his file across the table.

"You were with Marcus Bloodso in Baltimore. We know that. Just give us the number, and you're out of here."

"What? I. What the hell? I don't have any number!"

His exasperation tumbles out, unguarded and unfiltered. There is no attempt on his part to control a reply; it's sheer confusion.

I don't respond. I simply observe. Let Davis stew in silence; let his own words sink in. His mouth opens as if he is going to protest, to fight back.

Before he says anything, I get up and head toward the door.

"Alright, Davis. Guess you're useless, then. Graham, let's go."

The Baltimore location hasn't fallen entirely, but now its chances are low. Davis's reaction had the sort of exasperation that comes from being totally outside the loop.

We move into the next room. Sanders straightens up when I come in, his fingers flexing on the surface of the table. He's already bracing himself.

I sit, same movement, same contained confidence, and open a file in front of him.

"You were with Marcus Bloodso at Tysons Corner. We know that. Just give us the number, and you're out of here."

Sander tenses. His breath catches, his fingers curl, and he

diverts his eyes away from me. He hesitates just a second or two, but it's there.

I press in a bit more, gentle but unyielding.

"We're not asking whether you were there; we know you were. What we're asking for is the number. Don't play dumb."

He tries to conceal a gulp.

"I don't have it. Believe me, if I had it, I'd give it to you, but I don't."

That's the slip. They need to clarify, to convince me. Davis didn't do that. He just seemed annoyed. Sanders cares. That makes Tysons Corner the strongest location so far.

My face emotionless, pretending not to care.

"Alright then. You don't have the number; you don't have anything for me," I say, drawing my chair back and heading towards the door.

"Wait."

I stop, but I don't look back.

"Do you have the number?"

Silence.

"No," he finally responds.

I walk away. That's all I needed.

In the observation room, I watch as they bring all three men together. Graham is beside me, watching their reactions as the live feed goes on.

Davis is upset but not nervous. Sanders is a mess, twitching, glancing at Shaw for direction. Shaw is calm and composed, watching everything.

Then Sanders breaks. He heads straight for Shaw, who pulls him in close, voices too low for us to pick up anything. It's a contained damage control maneuver you make when something is slipping away from you.

I stare at the three of them and then look at Graham.

"It's Tysons. It has to be. Now, we just need Shaw to confirm it."

My reaction is sudden as I speak to a guard.

"Get Shaw prepped. We're on our way."

Shaw's eyes rise the moment I enter his holding cell, but there is no hint of surprise in them. He was expecting me. I stride in confidently; the three files clutched in my hand.

I purposely drop them in front of him, allowing the weight of the files to make a loud thud.

Shaw says nothing, doesn't even flinch, just sits there and blankly stares with the same quiet calmness. He knows the game, and he plays his role with artful precision.

I push the chair out and sit.

"Lieutenant, I want to remind you again just how bad things are going to get for you and your men tomorrow when Black-Steel takes power."

His face is expressionless; he shifts his posture as if some part of him acknowledges the seriousness of what I have just said.

"Give us one confirmation, just one, and we're set. This will allow us to focus our resources, act quickly, and reach the Dragon Slayers.

"But if we can't make any progress here. Once BlackSteel is in control, you and your team will disappear forever."

He breathes slowly, his gaze holding mine. I push the files closer to him systematically, opening each one in turn, each move calculated.

Graham edges forward, waiting for a visible reaction.

"We have three locations where we believe you were with Bloodso," I state. "All we need from you is to confirm which one.

"Shaw, we'll get to the bottom of this one way or another. But if you assist us now, it will be very advantageous for you and your team.

"I need you to verify this. Baltimore. That's where you met up with Bloodso, isn't it?"

Shaw leans back, drawing a deep breath. His eyes remain fixed on mine, probing and assessing. And then, after an awkward silence, he emits a low laugh.

"Well, I suppose you've got us, Deputy Director. I know when I've met my match. Look's like it's over now.

"You're right. We met in Baltimore. I wasn't part of the conversation. I was just there, taking the big man around with my crew. Happy?"

"Shaw, that's all I needed to hear."

"So, does this have any implications for me and my men?"

"Have to check your intel first. Need to confirm that you weren't at Tysons chatting with Bloodso there instead."

His expression does not shift, but his eyes do the talking.

"Because that means," I say, rising to leave, "your men would be in far worse trouble than they are now. Graham, let's move."

I leave Shaw behind and slam the door shut without looking back.

There's no time to waste.

We need to get Marcus Bloodso.

CHAPTER 25

UNDER SIEGE

"Overgrown wealth is as dangerous as overgrown military power."

- GEORGE WASHINGTON

HEADING DOWN THE corridor, I am certain that we have got precisely what we needed. I reach for my phone to text Carter.

It's Tysons Corner. Start extracting intel.

Graham looks at me, smoothing his mustache with just the faintest trace of a smile.

"Shaw's going to regret this when he realizes what just happened."

"Maybe. Let's just hope the number he gave us isn't a diversion. It's time we caught a break."

We backtrack to Carter. He looks up at us as I drop into the chair opposite him.

"Well, Carter, what's next?"

"We have the number. That's a good start. But…"

"But what?"

"It hasn't been active for the past two days."

"Where was it last used?"

Carter taps a few keys, enlarging a specific location on the map.

"Right here. We have a unit canvassing the area, but nothing yet."

"You're saying that this number may never become active again?"

"Yeah, boss. But if it does happen, we can pretty much bet it's Bloodso."

I drop my head, fighting the growing feeling that this might be in vain.

"All this effort, all this work, for a mere possibility."

Graham shrugs it off.

"Hell, it's better than nothing. And considering how buttoned-up these guys are, this could be a good lead. We focus on the number as being Bloodso and see what turns up."

I don't know if I should laugh or scream.

It's not the answer I wanted to hear. It's not the magic moment that's going to crack this op wide open. But it's something. A substantial clue that can take us to Marcus Bloodso. And for the time being, it's enough to propel us forward.

Graham and I head our separate ways, dragging ourselves toward our offices.

The burner phone can ring at any time, and if we miss it, Bloodso will be gone from our grasp. This unspeakable thought keeps me awake. My mind yearns for motion, my body pleads for rest, but I choose not to suffer in the oppressive stillness here.

Craving fresh air, I head for the outdoors, passing by the bullpen where a few agents toil through the early morning hours. They glance up, their eyes fatigued, their bodies resigned enough that they don't even register my presence.

Outside, an icy breeze slaps my face awake. Floodlights illuminate HQ's exterior as workers erect giant banners with BlackSteel's logo. Their conquest unravels before me, the aftermath being a total absorption of the FBI.

What I am witnessing becomes nauseating, so I head back inside.

In a zombie-like state, I walk back to Carter's office, a path that is too well-worn. I see the same landscape of screens highlighting his cluttered desk as he analyzes data while struggling to keep pace.

Resting my hand on the back of Carter's chair causes him to flinch and knock over a stack of empty cans near him.

"Jesus Christ, Charlie! Ever hear of knocking?"

"Anything?" I ask without offering an apology.

"I've got four of my best techies on this, literally staring at the screen for when the number blips. They're wearing pagers in their pockets, which will activate at the first whiff of action. I instructed them that if I uncover anything before they do, they're fired."

"Quite the leadership philosophy you have there," I sarcastically reply, but Carter is not amused.

"Count 'em. Four people on this full-time, about five grand a day in taxpayer money just to wait for this screen to change."

He's right, and we both know it, so I change the subject.

"Carter, just wait until BlackSteel's shareholders gut our budgets. It's nothing new for this administration to slash and burn, although I thought we'd be safe given the strong-arm impression Tuff likes."

"Actually, I'm pretty worried, boss. Seriously. There are a lot of bad things unfolding around here."

"Like what?"

"The BlackSteel information I'm receiving is draconian. These assholes are about to impose another wave of crackdowns.

"And what could be even worse? Guess who's going to get their grubby hands on it all? The Department of Unified Monitoring Branch."

This is unsettling news: a Schmutt-led fever dream promising trillions in savings has been dismantling the government from the inside ever since it was launched. A billionaire-backed experiment, marketed as simple tech support to improve efficiency and eliminate fraud. It's the same reckless mindset that tech startups apply to rationalize their destructive projects for profit.

The move fast and break things mantra may be acceptable when you're launching an app no one really needs. But when applied to our government? It ruins lives, both for the people working within these agencies and the citizens they serve.

It's already happened in some of the poorest regions of the world, where smaller departments were quickly strong-armed, accused of fraud, and buried in the legal system. Foreign aid was left to rot in warehouses while children died waiting for help that never came.

And the worst part? The world's richest man parades it all as noble, as if gutting these programs is an act of patriotism, as if helping others directly hurts us.

Schmutt seems to always get it wrong. Time after time, the data results have proven them wrong, yet they blame media manipulation.

He is swinging a wrecking ball, and his minions are his demolition crew. Their work is not meant to be accurate or transparent. Their work is to rip the copper wire off a functioning government and bask in the triumph of selling it for pennies on the dollar.

They scream about saving taxpayers' money while taking billions in subsidies each year.

"Just when I think Alan Schmutt's incompetence has reached its peak, now we're babysitting his teenage interns," I lament.

"Yeah, but they don't know anything. They're just clueless. What worries me is Sorakin Tech. Their grip is getting tighter."

"What do you mean?"

Carter pulls his eyes from the screen.

"Schmutt's one thing. He's an absolute moron, but Sorin? He's actually smart. Sorakin has been infiltrating our systems for years, with one contract here and one integration there. Hell, it even worked very well.

"But now? It's all being connected. They've quietly made themselves inseparable from the entire U.S. government. Law enforcement, federal databases, transportation, and defense. It's all running on Sorakin infrastructure, whether we like it or not.

"And boss, that's not even the worst part."

He leans in slightly.

"Everything they've been testing, those drones, those four-legged canine robots, the tactical prototypes, they've been slowly getting better in controlled environments. And now, with this crisis? They've got their excuse. A reason to roll it all out under the banner of public safety."

He pauses, and for the first time, there's fear in his words.

"Sorin is no fool. That's what makes this terrifying. He knows exactly what he's doing."

"It's happening. People are lining up to take advantage of this crisis. Some are in it for the money and contracts. But others…

"They're after something bigger. Something harder to stop. They're capitalizing on the moment to shape what comes next."

BlackSteel is closing in, stirring their pot with an army of clueless thugs. Now, Sorakin's control is spreading right alongside them, tightening the noose without anyone asking any questions.

We need to move quickly before the whole system locks, and once it does, we won't be the ones holding the keys.

I study the map; eyes fixed on the most recent ping from Marcus Bloodso's burner.

"We've got a week. Maybe two, tops. After that, who knows what the FBI will look like.

"We have to bring down Bloodso, rescue some billionaires, and dismantle the Dragon Slayers before BlackSteel steamrolls the Bureau."

Carter lets out a dry, unimpressed breath sarcastically asking.

"Yeah. Easy. Think we can get this wrapped up before lunch?"

"But seriously… what if we don't find them? At the rate this is going, we're running out of time, and soon, we won't even have a shot."

I honestly have no clue.

"I don't know, but we'll find out soon enough. For now, just keep me informed. Not just on the burner phone. On how they're rolling things out as well."

Carter avoids eye contact and doesn't speak. Instead, he returns to the task at hand.

Walking out of his office, the severity of this op becomes unfathomable, creeping into my inner core. A private corporation controlling national security. BlackSteel unleashing its power, cracking down on extremists as well as American citizens.

It's one goddamn ping. That's all it would take to put an end to this madness. The objective is clear, but without a location, it will remain out of our reach.

My body mercifully begs me for sleep, and as much as I want to stay awake, I relentlessly concede. Tomorrow will be a long, tumultuous day, and if I'm worn out, I'll be worthless.

The dorm is somehow a welcome sight as I drag myself to the nearest cot. My eyes close, and I collapse into unconsciousness.

A myriad of sounds and movements awakens me.

My initial worry is the burner. Did it ping? There are no alerts. No texts. No activity at all. Clearly, something else is transpiring.

Disheveled and groggy, I crawl out of my cot. Stuffing my untamed hair under an FBI cap, I pass through hallways that resonate with a heightened sense of unwelcome urgency. Agents hustle forward with an unfamiliar, strained edge. BlackSteel personnel intermingle among them, hushed in conversation.

It's happening. The handover is in progress.

Rushing to the auditorium, I enter to find it filled with confused agents. A pair of doe-eyed Schmutt trainees stand against the walls, notebooks in hand, as if it's their first lecture in college.

I scan the room, observing the divide: FBI personnel are serious, subdued, and anxious; BlackSteel are imposing, exuding energy and confidence.

Jackson Kane is the first to ascend the stage, his face brimming with certainty, carved that way by tempered boardrooms and battlefields. He tips his signature cowboy hat and then holds his hands out as if he is the Messiah.

Kane clears his throat.

"Today marks the dawn of a new age of private and public cooperation. We will be better together, a united front. One bea-u-ti-ful entity, just as the Lord Almighty intended."

His speech is polished and smooth, filled with a sense of progress and inevitability. He holds the whip, corralling us, hoping to avoid a stampede.

"This is the way it must be. A system unshackled from the restraints of outdated bureaucracy, moving forward with the dynamism and innovation of contemporary operations. This is an opportunity, a reaffirmation of intelligence and investigation combined. This is BlackSteel's ultimate model, America's ultimate model."

He markets it convincingly. Were I not wiser, I could be persuaded to believe him.

Kane shifts gears.

"To implement this change, there will be two co-leaders, Director Bill Cartwright and Commander Reddick."

Bill steps ahead, adjusting his tie with a strategic expression. His voice is composed and warm, with a hint of familiarity.

"Naturally, this is a radical change, but our mission remains the same. The threat the Dragon Slayers represent has increased beyond the capacity of traditional methods. This unification provides us with greater resources to combat this terrorist group.

"Think of this partnership as an upgrade. We'll have more resources, more growth, and more opportunities to build stability."

Bill sticks with his diplomatic terminology, avoiding confrontation. He doesn't call it a takeover. Instead, he maintains his professional tone, and steps back.

Commander Reddick takes the podium, and the room fills with a focused intensity, unobtrusive yet undeniable.

"Let's not waste any time," Reddick says, his orders crisp and clear. "Things are going to be different around here, starting now.

"BlackSteel functions on four principles. Speed, efficiency, commitment, ruthlessness. The FBI has not been able to neutralize the Dragon Slayer threat. That's why we're here. And let me make one thing clear: failure will not be tolerated."

He takes a step back as if to give everyone breathing space.

"Any slowness, delays, or hesitation will be recorded. If you don't want to move faster, work more, think quicker, then the exit is in the back. Leave now, because if you stay and slow us down, you'll pay an even worse price.

"A silent liar is someone who doesn't believe in a mission but stays and obeys orders while passively resisting, failing when action is needed. You can think that neutrality protects you, but doubt is rot. It infects. It kills."

A wave of silence crashes over the room.

Reddick roars.

"We are at war! In this war, defiance is the enemy. Any form of resistance at all is terrorism!"

BlackSteel has tightened the noose on the FBI. I catch a glimpse of Bill. He looks down at his hands, defeated.

Our agents appear dejected, sharing uncomfortable looks with their colleagues.

The BlackSteel operatives? They are smiling, laughing, and enjoying the show. They know this is a forceful occupation.

Reddick gives one last command.

"You're all dismissed."

The repercussions of the meeting are a bitter pill to swallow. FBI staff move through the corridors, their faces tight, shoulders hunched. I don't have to eavesdrop on their discussions; we are all thinking the same thing. The bureau they signed up to serve, the agency their careers have been founded on, is at BlackSteel's mercy.

The vibe the other operatives emanate as they exit the briefing is annoyingly enthusiastic. They stride with purpose, heads up, and arrogant smiles. They're the victors in their element.

Schmutt's trainees stand stiffly outside the door, clutching their notepads, feigning comprehension of what they have just witnessed.

I continue walking and then halt mid-stride as I hear Graham's agitated voice.

"Hell no, we're not doing that!"

His words cut through the corridors, razor-sharp.

Seeking him out, I find him in a corner. He's glaring down at a BlackSteel operative, who is staring up at him unimpressed.

"This is part of the op, Agent Cross," the BlackSteel agent remarks with a matter-of-fact attitude. This is what you will be doing."

Graham tightens his jaw.

"I'm not sending my people out there to round up civilians."

The operative doesn't bat an eye.

"All tactical units will be used."

"Yeah? Not mine."

"Cross, that's not your decision to make."

"Listen, punk. It is my decision. My team doesn't kick down doors because someone clicked on a link."

"You're wrong. This is about containing threats before they escalate."

Graham laughs bitterly.

"Sure. Threats. You're talking about some poor guy whose only fault was that he read the wrong story. This is bullshit. You know it's bullshit."

"Enough, Cross. You want to keep debating this? Let's see what Commander Reddick says about your insubordination."

I urgently intervene.

"Guys, what's going on?"

The BlackSteel agent straightens a bit.

"I'm briefing Agent Cross on operational adjustments, and you are?"

"Deputy Director Grayson. Obviously, there's a misunderstanding here. Agent Cross is already allocated to special operations. Director Cartwright authorized it personally. Sorry for any confusion."

The operative pauses, his lips opening as if to protest. He's perplexed. That's good.

Graham shoots the man a dirty look before I grab his arm, pulling him away before this escalates into a fistfight.

I scold him as we turn a corner.

"Graham, you can't do that."

"Who the hell says I can't?"

"Listen to me. BlackSteel agents will take notice of this. You have to stay under the radar."

"Let me get reported. If they think I'm going to start breaking down doors and dragging people out of their fucking houses? Then I'm done.

"Charlie, I know you understand me. But I'm not getting my men killed for this fucking takeover, and I'm damn sure that I will never give the order to kill civilians."

There's nothing I can say that will change his mind.

"Graham, all we can do is be prepared. We wait for the ping."

"And if we don't receive it?"

"We stand by. It will come. Now, head back to your office and cool down."

Morning evaporates into evening. It doesn't matter, as there has been no progress on our end.

HQ grows emptier, desks cleared, as FBI agents leave in a steady trickle. Some furtively pack up, heads down, defeated. Others walk out with purpose, their decisions to resign spurred on by the morning events.

Lex had anticipated this. She left before BlackSteel could even begin to tighten its grip on the Bureau. She heeded the warning signs and acted on her instincts. Now, watching the exodus of my colleagues, I can't help but think they, too, are doing the right thing.

But that's not my path; for now, I will stay.

Those of us who choose to remain are not villains. We are the ones who have committed our lives to service, to duty; not out of blind obedience, but because we refuse to abandon who and what we were sworn to protect.

The tragedy is that the system may eventually break us. It will wear us down, inch by inch, day by day, until doing the right thing looks indistinguishable from following orders.

My phone rings, piercing my pessimism.

It's Carter.

"We got it. We got a fucking ping.

"Holy shit. We've just received another ping. And it's far away."

Carter goes silent as he crunches the information in real-time.

"Wait a minute; it's a plane. Must be. Running coordinates. Checking flight plans."

"Carter, how sure are you that they're airborne?"

"This speed? This distance? Only option."

His energy is infectious, and I find myself absorbed in it.

"Hold on a sec... I've got it. Heading to a small airfield in the Odessa-Midland area.

"Less than two hours until they land. Getting the Black Hawks prepped now. ETA an hour, you'll be there first."

"Roger that. I'm getting Graham."

Everything else has suddenly become irrelevant: the Black-Steel coup, the shifts in power, the slow dismantling of our agency. This is no time for politics or the possibility that everything will simply crumble.

What is transpiring now is the meaning of my life. The action, the chase, the pursuit. The moment when hesitation vanishes, and instinct takes hold. My boots strike the tile as I race through the halls.

The weight I have been carrying has dissipated, replaced by one unwavering focus.

"Graham!" I yell, racing towards him.

"We have a location.

"Load up."

CHAPTER 26

FINAL DESCENT

"Experience demands that man is the only animal which devours his own kind, for I can apply no milder term to the general prey of the rich on the poor."

-THOMAS JEFFERSON

WE SPRINT TO the hangers, tactical gear clinging to my frame; its weight is snug in the familiar grooves on my hips. Graham moves alongside me, his rifle in a cross-body sling, prepped for action. His men follow behind in close order.

The Black Hawk helicopters' sleek bodies beam against the floodlights. Blades turn lazily, ruffling the still night air, making their presence known.

Discipline has cleared my mind; nothing irrelevant dare enter my thoughts. Only the mental picture of how we will engage with complete control.

Strapping down as the cabin door shuts, the rotors burst into life, lifting us from the concrete and into the night. HQ falls away behind us, a cluster of impersonal lights swallowed up by the darkness.

Graham adjusts his headset, his eyes darting to me.

"Okay, what's the plan."

"Land and establish situational awareness. Secure the perimeter. Safe Serve security will probably be armed, so we follow protocol and de-escalate the situation."

Graham leans in, surveying the layout.

"Two teams. We set up breach locations, and as soon as their plane stops, we roll up on them."

"Local police will set up roadblocks," I confirm. "If anyone tries to make a run for it, they'll be caught."

"Charlie, if there are Dragon Slayers aboard?"

"Then we put them down, just like any other threat."

Our plan is clean, leaving no room for errors. The key is the element of surprise before anyone on that plane realizes what's happening.

The radio crackles, and Carter's voice breaks in.

"Boss, got something. It's 100% Bloodso."

"How do you know?"

"CCTV from the private terminal before departure. It's him. No doubt."

Graham grins.

"Well shit, something's finally going right."

We've scored a solid lead.

An actual target. This thought brings me the most satisfaction I have had in a very long time.

As if on cue, the helicopter lurches, a shockwave rippling through the cabin. The pilot's voice crackles over the comms.

"Be advised. Headwinds approaching. It's going to be a bumpy ride."

I peer out the window. The desert below is an endless expanse of vacant black, intermittently punctuated by distant industrial lights. The air currents begin to pull harder, tilting the Black Hawk before the pilot levels us out.

The noise from the rotors deepens, struggling against increasing turbulence. As we approach the airstrip, the helicopter's floodlights reveal sand swirls in erratic patterns.

The pilot flattens out the dive, voice curt.

"Brace for landing."

I set my shoulders, steadying myself. Graham tightens his hold on his rifle, his voice firm but restrained.

"Let's finish this."

The skids hit the landing pad as the second helicopter touches down behind us.

As we step out onto the tarmac, the night air greets us. Floodlights surrounding the airstrip cast long, serrated shadows that stretch into a sandy ocean of darkness. The helicopters' engines whine down, their blades still slashing through the air in slow, ponderous arcs.

Graham and his team flow like shadows, blending seamlessly with the night as they take up their positions. This is our final moment of peace before all hell breaks loose.

A man wearing a frayed windbreaker stands in front of the terminal. His face is worn with apathy.

I move in, flashing my badge in front of him. He isn't fazed by it and just stares blankly at me.

"Alright, lady, just tell me what you need. Bring 'em in like normal?"

"That's right. Let's stick to the routine. When the plane touches down, we'll take over."

He rubs his finger across the stubble on his chin before answering.

"Suit yourself. Just don't ignite a damn war on my runway."

"No promises," Graham mutters.

I ignore his remark and speak directly to the operations manager.

"That won't be your concern. If cleanup is needed, the FBI will handle it. But we don't expect any damage."

He doesn't argue, but his eyes flick with the dull skepticism of someone who's heard it all before. Without another word, he turns away and trudges toward the control tower. Whatever's coming, he's clearly decided it's not worth any effort on his part.

Graham veers off toward the local cops, their forces at the runway's edge. I trail behind, moving at a steady clip, my brain rehearsing our strategies.

The lead police officer is middle-aged and sports a thick mustache; his expression conveys that he is not in the mood for any nonsense, especially tonight.

"We require two of your SUVs," Graham states. "We need them for the breach."

He jerks a thumb toward two unmarked vehicles near the fence.

"Take 'em. Keys are in 'em. Just return 'em in one piece."

Graham's squad takes up positions, spreading out with rifles at the ready. The police stand along the perimeter, sealing off any means of escape. The SUVs crouch like beasts at the edge of the field, ready to strike.

"Lock in," Graham commands.

Then we see it.

A faint glimmer in the sky, easy to mistake for a star, until it blinks, just barely, revealing itself as light in motion.

It's the plane.

"Visual on target." I call out,

It's moving towards us, closing the gap as we prepare to engage. The approach lights dance across the clouds, signaling a slow, methodical drop.

The night holds its breath with us as the plane begins its final descent.

Graham and I throw ourselves inside one of the SUV's, doors slamming shut in unison. The interior is thick with urgency, radios crackling, boots shifting.

"You have rear flank onboarding," Graham says, his voice clipped.

"Roger that."

The engine snarls to life as Graham grips the wheel and hits the gas, thrusting us forward. Tires screech in defiance, headlights slice through the dark as we race down the runway towards the descending plane. I clutch the door handle, bracing myself as Graham accelerates faster, while the backup unit tries to match his speed.

We close in fast. The aircraft's landing gear touches down with a deafening shriek of rubber on the pavement. The engines howl, reversing thrust, its body shuddering from the friction. The runway lights streak past in a blur, illuminating the fuselage for split seconds before plunging it back into the abyss.

I brace as Graham yanks the wheel, cutting hard to the left. The convoy splits, our SUVs fanning out to box the plane in before it can taxi too far. The lead vehicle swings wide, forcing the aircraft to slow even further.

Someone in the cockpit flashes the landing lights twice in quick succession, acknowledgment or a warning?

Doesn't matter. We're here now.

The wheels squeal against the tarmac as the plane lurches to a stop. Wasting no time, I shove open the SUV door, hitting the pavement hard as we bolt toward the plane.

I unsling my rifle, the metal cool and familiar in my hands.

Graham starts barking orders.

"Flank the plane. Nobody gets off until we confirm who's inside."

A chorus of acknowledgments follows as the team spreads out, boots drumming against the ground in near-perfect synchrony. The plane is unnaturally still against the backdrop of the commotion outside it. The cargo hold stays shut, and there is no movement from the main cabin.

Whoever is inside is watching and waiting.

The wind kicks up, carrying the scent of burned rubber and jet fuel, whipping through the open spaces between us. The SUV's idle behind me, headlights carving harsh white lines along the aircraft's belly.

I signal my position with a sharp tap to my comms.

"Rear flank secured."

Graham moves first, stepping toward the stairs leading up to the cabin door. The steel groans under his weight, the sound cutting through the night. I shift my grip, adjusting the stock of my rifle against my shoulder.

"Breach on my mark," Graham orders.

My grip tightens, every muscle locking into place.

This is it. The silence that surrounds the aircraft is oppressive.

For one moment, time stands still. Then, I hear, "Breach in three, two—mark!"

The flashbang detonates, churning tumultuously in a blaze of light and sound. A shockwave tears through the closed space, vibrating the overhead compartments. A deafening roar overpowers all other sounds. The cabin erupts with a fierce brilliance, shadows evaporating across the walls like disoriented specters.

Graham takes point, rifle held high. I step up from the rear flank, my sights scouring the aisle in a methodical sweep. A dense, bitter scent fills the cabin as urgent voices ring out above the chaos.

"Clear left!"

"Clear right!"

Shadows flicker. Something shifts. I adjust my finger, moving it onto the trigger, ready to fire. A frantic figure stumbles into view, moving erratically. Fast and wild, potentially hostile. I swing my rifle into position, center mass locked in. The dim light catches a flash of red on their uniform.

A flight attendant, no weapon, no threat.

"Get down!" Graham shouts.

The woman falls to her knees, trembling, her eyes bulging in fear.

I lower my rifle, keeping my position locked, my voice steady.

"It's okay. You're safe."

The plane is empty of passengers; there is no sign of Bloodso.

Graham and I exchange a puzzled look, the tension between us escalating. The team searches the rest of the rows, but there is nothing. Then we catch sight of it. An abandoned phone on a side chair table, dark but not invisible.

"Charlie, think they just flew the phone here as a decoy?"

"Doubt it. Carter had visuals, Marcus Bloodso was on board."

Something isn't right.

We move forward cautiously. The cockpit door hangs open, light spilling into the hallway in stark, stuttering angles. The pilots are seated inside, their hands raised, eyes darting back and forth between each other in silent alarm.

Graham gets straight to the point.

"Where's Marcus Bloodso? Don't play dumb. We tracked him here on this plane. Where is he?"

The pilot hesitates; shoulders stiff. He sends his co-pilot a meaningful look.

The co-pilot stirs uncomfortably, his eyes darting toward the cabin flight attendant.

Our patience is wearing thin. We need answers now.

I move in closer to them.

"You're assisting a terrorist. Do you have any idea what that entails? Detention centers. Indeterminate sentencing. Is Bloodso really worth the price of your freedom?"

The co-pilot swallows hard, his hands twitching at his sides. The flight attendant is the first to crack under the pressure of my words.

"He jumped!" she exclaims, voice trembling. "He had a parachute, and he jumped five minutes ago!"

In one excruciating moment, her words dash our mission.

Without hesitation. I connect with Carter.

"Carter, we need a visual. Bloodso jumped during the descent. Locate his drop zone; it can't be far from here."

"Copy that. Redirecting drones. Stand by."

I leap down the boarding stairs two at a time, with Graham close behind. The wind has whipped up a wall that I burst through as the familiar rush of adrenaline engulfs me.

Carter's voice cuts through the haze.

"Got something. Landing zone sighted, five kilometers southeast. SUV departing the scene, moving south. Incoming coordinates. Depart now. You can catch him."

I start signaling, raising my hand toward the circling helicopters, and turning on my comms.

"Get those Black Hawks on the ground now. Pursuit requested."

The response crackles through my earpiece.

"Roger that, inbound for pickup."

Engines scream as the helicopters break formation, banking hard before dropping fast. The downwash sends loose gravel whipping around. As the first one touches down, the second hovers just behind.

I turn, scanning the team.

"Graham, take that one. I'll board the other."

"Oscar Mike," he calls back.

We sprint for our respective helicopters, and once inside, I strap in, securing my rifle and syncing my comms. This is it. We're not letting Marcus Bloodso escape.

The rotors roar to life, dust and debris scattering as we lift off in pursuit, spiraling upward into the darkness of the unknown.

Bloodso is out there.

And we are on the hunt.

CHAPTER 27

FIRE IN THE SKY

*"The rich man… is always sold to the
institution which makes him rich."*

-HENRY DAVID THOREAU

THE HELICOPTERS SPLIT the night sky, steel predators prowling over a wasteland of desert and industrial decay. Below, rusted pipes and skeletal ruins stretch into darkness, jagged remnants of gone-by industries.

Searchlights carve through the shifting gloom as gusts of wind push and pull against the Black Hawk, making it hard to keep steady. The cat-and-mouse chase has begun.

Graham's words come through the comm.

"They've got to be here. Keep scanning."

Before I can reply, air currents slam against the fuselage, forcing the pilot to compensate. The chopper lurches, the sudden shift sending my stomach into freefall before leveling out again. I grit my teeth. The wind has become an unpredictable force, making this volatile chase even more dangerous.

Then, a glint of metal. A black shadow moving quickly against the dust-streaked terrain.

The spotlight jerks, catching the target mid-flight as it bounces over uneven ground.

"Grayson, there! SUV at two o'clock, move!"

The Black Hawks react instantly, dropping altitude as the turbulence slams us harder, causing the entire frame to shudder. Searchlights struggle to illuminate the SUV as it continues to tear through the industrial wasteland.

I brace myself against the doorframe as the pilot fights to maintain control. The helicopter bucks, adjusting to another sudden gust.

This isn't good.

The vehicle is heading toward a scrapyard stacked high with collapsed scaffolding and skeletal beams. It's a twisted metal graveyard, treacherous for even the most skilled drivers to navigate safely.

Carter is sharp over the comms.

"Looks like they're heading for the mines. If they get inside, we lose them. ETA. Five minutes."

The vehicle's driver is unpredictable but not completely reckless. They're threading through the open ground now, but they'll have to commit to a route very soon.

"Charlie, we don't have a clean angle from up here, the wind is too strong. If we want a real chance, we have to drop in low to line up the shot."

My order is decisive.

"One Black Hawk stays high for visual; the other drops low to line up the shot. We only have a few chances, so make it count."

"Copy that. We'll go first."

The moment he descends, the storm fights back, dragging

his helicopter sideways before the pilot corrects it. The SUV swerves violently, tires skidding across loose dirt as it tries to dodge the spotlight. It jerks toward a collapsed building, barely squeezing through the skeletal remains of a rusted frame.

Graham's frustration is apparent.

"Too rough. Visual obscured."

The SUV bursts free from the ruins, its back tires spitting loose gravel as it skids wildly onto open ground. The gusts continue to barrage the helicopters, turning the chase into a battle against the elements.

My pilot fights to hold steady, the chopper rocking under each brutal gust. The spotlight bounces across the dirt trail, catching the vehicle in its beam for a split second, enough to make the driver hesitate.

Stepping into the cabin doorframe, I take aim. The crosshairs mark the rear tires, my grip solid. But the wind is unforgiving.

It's too far. Too unstable.

My finger reluctantly moves off the trigger.

"No shot."

The SUV jerks, veering left and dropping into a shallow gully. A wall of dust erupts in its wake, obscuring my view.

"Damn it," I mouth to myself.

Graham's voice comes in, tight with urgency.

"We're not losing him. Dive, I'm taking the shot."

His helicopter dips into the chase, cutting low, rotors roaring. The vehicle lurches over uneven ground, swerving wildly to avoid a crumbling section of pavement. Graham leans out, steady, despite the air currents ripping through the cabin.

CRACK. CRACK. CRACK.

Bullets spark against the rocks, pinging off rusted debris. The SUV swerves, and the driver reacts instinctively, but they don't crash.

They careen onto a winding dirt road, throwing up a fresh cloud of dust. The mining complex looms ahead, its dark silhouettes of rusted machinery frozen in time. A labyrinth of tunnels for them to escape into.

"Stay with him," Graham commands.

His pilot pulls hard into a turn, the wind pushing back with brutal force. The Black Hawk shudders, tilting dangerously close to the ground before leveling out. Graham fires again, each shot a calculated risk.

CRACK. CRACK. CRACK

Sparks fly from the SUV's frame as bullets ricochet off the armored plating near the wheel well. The driver doesn't swerve. He's clearly a professional, and his life depends on reaching that mine.

Graham's pilot bellows, straining to hold control.

"I have to pull up."

The Black Hawk wobbles as turbulence fights against it, the engines groaning under the effort.

Carter shouts, his countdown a ticking time bomb.

"Two minutes!"

Sweat trickles down my spine as the wind howls through the open cabin. My rifle feels heavier, an anchor against havoc, as I fight to steady my grip.

Graham blasts through the comms.

"Clearing coming up!"

I press my back against the doorframe, bracing against the turbulence.

My chopper banks forward, plunging in a steep dive, forcing the harness to dig into my shoulders. The wind has become a brutal enemy, trying to rip me from my hold. I grip the rifle tighter, the ice-cold steel penetrating my gloves, grounding me as the storm rages.

Graham is filled with urgency as he echoes in my comms.

"Charlie, this might be our last chance!"

The spotlight beam struggles to keep the SUV in its sight as it bucks and weaves like a wounded animal, debris flying as it barrels through the landscape. My heart pounds in rhythm with the blades overhead, my breath steady, forcing focus through the chaos.

Carter barks out a warning.

"ETA. One minute. If they get in, they're gone for good."

Sixty seconds.

The rotors wail, struggling against the storm, the entire frame vibrating beneath me. The cabin tilts, dropping into position, giving me a window.

Graham's voice bursts through the comms.

"Charlie, take the shot!"

Suddenly the world feels suspended in a breathless lull as the wind subsides.

Everything around me fades, as if the storm itself is holding its breath. The SUV bursts into the clearing, a perfect target bathed in stark white light.

Instinct takes over before I even realize it. My body moves on its own, and I bring up the rifle, scope locked on the back tires.

These shots are important; I cannot fail. Everything funnels into this, and I know there is no room for a mistake.

I squeeze the trigger.

CRACK. CRACK. CRACK.

The shots miss, kicking up dirt just shy of the mark.

But they speak to something deeper than thought. My mind is instantly silenced, no longer part of the equation. My body knows what to do.

Compensate. Re-zero. Fire again.

CRACK. CRACK. CRACK.

Direct hit. The driver-side tire explodes in a shower of shredded rubber and steel, the SUV jerking violently.

Adjust. Lock in. Breathe.

CRACK. CRACK. CRACK.

The front tire explodes, shards flying as the SUV fishtails out of control. The driver tries to re-correct, but it's no use as the vehicle goes off the road, slamming sideways into a shallow ditch. Debris and dust churn into the air, boiling wildly under the spotlight of the chopper.

A shout tears from my throat, raw and triumphant.

"Fuck yeah!"

"Hell of a shot, Grayson!" Graham bursts with approval.

The storm roars back, the wind slamming into us again, dust swallowing the wreckage. But it's too late for them to escape now.

The helicopter banks sharply, lurching upward as the pilot veers away from the looming mining complex that's carved deep into the jagged mountain slope.

"Circling back for visual," The pilot calls out.

I lower the rifle, my hands trembling as reality sinks in. Two tires, two perfect shots.

The Black Hawk swoops lower, lining up for another pass. The SUV sits in the ditch, smoke curling from its battered frame. Shadows flicker inside, erratic, and frantic.

"Let's bring these birds down," Graham says, with satisfaction.

The helicopters land a hundred yards away. Agents hit the ground running towards the wreckage of the SUV. Its front end is crushed from the collision, flashlights revealing a blood-spattered dashboard. The driver is ominously motionless.

"Driver's dead," an agent calls out.

I look over at the passenger side. The occupant's head is against the door, and my attention is immediately drawn to a black and gold mask covered in blood.

Signaling for agents to move to the rear of the SUV, I yell out.

"Check the back!"

Graham gets there first, wrenching the door open to find Marcus Bloodso. He's pale and sweating as he fights to sit up, his body moving sluggishly from the impact of the wreck.

One of the agents carefully opens the other passenger door. The Dragon Slayer springs to life, violently kicking the door wide open. The agent falls back, sprawling onto the ground.

"Gun!" somebody yells as the Dragon Slayer draws a pistol.

I'm upon him before he has a chance to fire. My shoulder smashes into his chest, and he's pushed back as the bullet hits the dirt. My hands close around his wrist, wrenching it until the gun falls to the ground. I kick it into the darkness.

The Dragon Slayer doesn't hesitate. He's fast and disciplined. His body shifts into a combat stance like it's second nature. I go to counter a sudden lunge, but he adjusts mid-motion, gaining leverage on me.

In a flash, I'm slammed onto my back. His weight crashes down, and before I can recover, a blade glints in his hand. The knife comes out fast, aimed low and brutal.

"Get the fuck off her."

Graham's rifle slams into the back of the Dragon Slayer's head with a sickening, hollow crack. The sound of the blow reverberates around us.

The second the Dragon Slayer drops, two agents grab him, one retrieving the knife, the other locking on cuffs.

"Enemy secure!" someone shouts.

Lying on the ground, I try to regroup as my lungs burn. A few feet from me is the gun I kicked away.

Graham kneels beside me, rifle lowered, eyes steady.

"You good?"

"Yeah," I gasp. "Thanks for the save."

"The thanks go to you, Charlie. You're the reason we caught 'em. Locking that shot in stopped them cold."

Graham glances toward one of his men.

"And you saved one of mine. That's no small thing."

His voice carries something different, something more personal.

"You lived up to the Grayson name tonight, that's for damn sure, Charlie."

"Duty calls," I reply, trying to sound casual, but coming from Graham, it means more than the standard praise.

Our focus returns to the wreckage. Bloodso reclines in the back seat, motionless, except for the faint rise and fall of his chest. Agents swarm the car, examining and documenting the scene, meticulously gathering evidence.

A gust of wind cuts through the night, carrying the scent of smoke and gasoline.

Bloodso is alive... at least for now.

CHAPTER 28

A CALCULATED RISK

*"When rich people fight wars with one
another, poor people are the ones to die."*

-Jean-Paul Sartre

THE WRECKAGE CONTINUES to smolder, twisted metal
hissing as it cools against the desert air. Helicopter blades still
spin, kicking up fragments of dust and debris. Now comes the
part that matters, the part where we make this mission count.

Marcus Bloodso stands with the help of two operatives, his
suit torn, face streaked with dirt and blood.

His eyes are measured and calculating. I can see the gears
turning in his head, crafting the story he's going to tell, the
defense he's going to mount.

"I was kidnapped," he says, voice steady. "For fuck's sake,
you idiots don't understand, they took me! We were protecting
billionaires. That made me a target."

He struggles to get loose; his movements are sharp but
oddly restrained. Something about it feels planned, not frantic, but just enough to pass for an actual struggle.

I don't react, crossing my arms.

"Save it, Bloodso. You and your Safe Serve team have been working with the Dragon Slayers. Best thing you can do now is drop the act."

His lips tighten, but his expression doesn't crack. He lets out a condescending sigh as if we're too naive to grasp what's at play.

"It's all bullshit. You think you have something, but you don't. My lawyer will have this entire mess cleared up in a matter of hours."

Graham corrects him.

"Too bad you don't get lawyers where you're going."

A slight shift in Bloodso's eyes reveals he is aware of his dilemma.

He knows he's not just coming with us; he's going to Black-Steel. Not to a holding cell made exclusively for the wealthy, where a high-priced legal team can swoop in and pull him out with a shady backroom deal.

Bloodso will be disappearing into a system where his money and connections doesn't mean a damn thing.

"Then I guess we might have a few things to discuss."

Graham smirks.

"Nice to see you're capable of reason."

We move Bloodso toward the helicopter, where agents are securing his restraints. He climbs in without saying a word, settling in like a man taking an inconvenient flight.

I step back, letting them lock him down. My gaze shifts to the other aircraft, where the Dragon Slayer is being loaded. He's semi-conscious, slumped forward, partially aware of his surroundings.

Graham follows my gaze.

"You think that Dragon Slayer will talk?"

"If he does, it'll be exactly what they want him to say."

"Yeah. Figured. Bloodso is our key player if we can keep him in our possession.

"Charlie, taking him to BlackSteel, well, we both know what that means. They'll take Bloodso into custody before we can even get a word out of him."

"Then we need to move fast. Let's go."

We climb into the helicopter as the blades churn back to life, the ground disappearing beneath us. For now, we have Marcus Bloodso. The question is, how long before someone takes him away?

The thrill of the chase has waned, leaving us with the possibility of what comes next. Bloodso is secure in the other helicopter, contemplating his own fate.

Graham shifts slightly beside me, checking the straps on his harness.

"Alright, Charlie. How we playing this?"

"We make BlackSteel think the Dragon Slayer is the real prize. We need them to think Bloodso isn't important, that he was kidnapped and exploited by them. The second we land, Reddick and his people are going to come sniffing around for the biggest scalp they can get.

"Our aim is to pretend that the Dragon Slayer is top priority, so they fall for it and take him off our hands. Meanwhile, we keep Bloodso close. Work him without anyone else breathing down our necks."

Graham mulls it over.

"Think they'll take the bait?"

"BlackSteel wants something they can parade around. A real Dragon Slayer? That's way too tempting for them to pass up."

"Okay, it's all we got. Just don't want to get caught up in any crossfire."

"Graham, I know, but we have to try something."

I reach for my radio, tuning to Carter's line. It clicks open, his voice coming in sharp through the comms.

"Boss, still breathing? That's a good sign."

"Still alive for now, Carter. We got Bloodso. He's intact. We're bringing him in."

"Hell yeah. You want me digging up anything specific on him?"

"Not yet. We still need locations for Thaddeus Montclair and the other missing billionaires. I want to know the second anything new pops up."

"Understood. And, uh… not to rain on your parade, but you know that BlackSteel is going to want their piece of him?"

"We're planning for that."

"Good. Because if you don't keep Bloodso on a short leash, he's going to disappear into the abyss, and you'll never hear from him again."

"Unfortunately, that's exactly what we're trying to avoid."

"Alright. I know Graham and you will make it happen."

I close the channel and immediately dial the next number.

Bill picks up on the second ring.

"Charlie, tell me you have something good."

"Bill, we got one, a real Dragon Slayer. Checks out across multiple points of intelligence."

He lets out a sharp laugh.

"Jesus. You finally caught one alive?"

"We did. BlackSteel will be excited to parade him around and brag about their big catch. They needed a headline. Now they've got one."

"And Bloodso?"

"Looks like Bloodso was kidnapped. Some new information came to light after the takedown. It's possible he was forced into all of this."

Bill pauses before letting out a reassuring chuckle.

"Not bad, Charlie. Not bad at all. I'll let BlackSteel know. We'll be ready for you when you land."

The line clicks off.

Graham reclines back, a small smile forming.

"You're unbelievable, you know that?"

"I prefer strategic. Let's hope it works."

He stares out the window for a moment as his expression changes.

"Charlie, how did Bloodso know to jump? We had him cornered. No way out. Then suddenly he's making a desperate leap like someone tipped him off."

The thought's been eating at me too, but I push it down.

"Could be anyone, Graham. With the sums the Dragon Slayers have, they can buy information from anywhere. Hell, they might just be paying people to track all our movements."

He turns back to me, eyes sharp.

"What do you think about Carter?"

The question hits hard, as it's something I hadn't even considered.

"Carter? He's the one finding all our intel. Our lifeline on this whole thing."

Graham studies me for a beat.

"Alright. But I don't like how the Dragon Slayers always seem to know what we're doing. Makes me wonder who the hell we can trust."

Silence settles between us. Both of us thinking about betrayal and just how deep this thing goes.

We keep our thoughts to ourselves, as the city comes into view, the bright lights of headquarters growing closer. I tighten the harness, a bit too snug in an attempt to calm my nerves.

The helicopters descend as the first light of dawn stretches across the city skyline. Regrettably, we will be returning to an ever-changing environment rather than our familiar FBI home base.

The parking lot is lined with BlackSteel tactical vehicles, their personnel standing in formation along the perimeter. Their company name is now carved into the stone where the Bureau's distinguished heritage used to stand on its own.

Graham's expression darkens, lips pressing into a thin line. "Looks like they've been busy."

As we land, BlackSteel operatives swarm the helipad and at the front of the pack is Commander Reddick. He is waiting like a vulture, ready to feast on a fresh carcass.

They move in fast. Not for us, for their prize possession, the Dragon Slayer.

Reddick storms forward. His presence is overwhelming as his BlackSteel team fans out behind him like a personal firing squad. He doesn't acknowledge Graham or me. His eyes are locked on our prisoner.

As they pull the Dragon Slayer out of the aircraft, he sneers.

"Look at you. Not so tough now, you pathetic, treacherous waste. Did you really think you could beat us?"

The Dragon Slayer doesn't react. Doesn't flinch. He just stares at Reddick, unreadable.

Reddick steps closer, his lip curling. He wants a reaction, but he doesn't get one.

I watch the tension coil through his stance, the way his fingers flex as if he's imagining breaking the man's jaw with his fist. Reddick forces himself to relax, shifting his attention to me instead.

"Ah, Deputy Director. I heard you brought in another accomplice of theirs. Safe Serve's CEO, correct?"

"Commander, after further intel review, it looks like the Safe

Serve angle was just a decoy. The Dragon Slayers wanted us to think Marcus Bloodso was the key player.

"We've pieced together the data, and we're confident that this Dragon Slayer was the real mastermind. He coordinated it all and had leverage on Bloodso and his Safe Serve team."

Reddick stiffens. For a second, I think he's going to press the issue.

He cuts me off with a raised hand.

"No need to justify your intelligence failures to me, Grayson. We'll take it from here."

Reddick turns away from me without another word, his full attention snapping back to the Dragon Slayer. He took the bait.

One problem down. One bigger problem still to go.

Marcus Bloodso. He's standing just outside the helicopter, hands restrained, expression unreadable. He doesn't look at the BlackSteel chaos unfolding; he's looking directly at me.

I lock eyes with him.

"Bloodso, you're coming with us. We're going to have a conversation. Lots of people's lives depend on it, including yours."

He exhales slowly, tilting his head.

"I still demand my lawyer," Bloodso says gruffly.

"That's non-negotiable."

"We'll see about that."

His confidence is unshakable. He believes he is in complete control of his precarious situation.

Two agents have been waiting patiently for Bloodso.

"Take him inside," I tell them.

Beside me, Graham mutters under his breath.

"If one more dumbass terrorist asks for a lawyer like this is some corporate embezzlement case, I swear to God, I'm gonna lose it."

I give him a weak smile, allowing myself to decompress from

the mission. Reddick and his goons are fully occupied with the Dragon Slayer. My ploy worked, at least for now.

The sun is creeping up over the city skyline, bleeding light into the edges of the sky, but inside headquarters, it feels like the dead of night.

Marcus Bloodso is wheeled into the medical wing. The staff robotically get to work, moving with the efficiency that comes from dealing with a countless number of high-value detainees.

"How long?" I ask, watching the doctor check his vitals.

"Thirty, maybe forty-five minutes," she replies. "We'll patch him up, should be ready for interrogation soon."

Perfect. One step, one problem at a time. Bloodso isn't going anywhere, at least not yet.

Graham and I step outside the room into an unrecognizable hallway. The grasp of BlackSteel's presence has crept into the soul of the FBI building, pressing into the walls, making the place feel like a foreign adversary.

I stretch my legs, forcing the tightness from standing too long. We survived this op in one piece, but our mission is far from over.

Footsteps echo down the corridor, quick, deliberate. I turn just as Maya appears, moving fast, her face drawn tight with a mix of disbelief and frustration.

"Charlie, Graham, good, you're back," she says, slightly out of breath. "We've got a problem."

"What is it?" I ask, wary.

She doesn't answer. Instead, she steps aside and points toward the front window.

"Better if you see it for yourself."

Graham lifts the shades, revealing unexpected mayhem outside.

News vans. Cameras. Microphones. A whole slew of press is

mingling outside HQ. Standing in front of a sea of reporters is the center of attention, a man claiming the audience as his own.

Attorney Miles Archer.

I've never dealt with him personally, but I'd have to be living under a rock not to know who he is.

The go-to name for the ultra-wealthy, the scandal-plagued, and mainly anyone with a big enough wallet to afford his retainer.

Archer fights cases in court while simultaneously shaping them in the court of public opinion, blending legal defense, PR strategy, and media control into one seamless game, and from what I've seen, he plays it better than anyone.

I spit my words out.

"Un-fucking believable. Marcus Bloodso's lawyer is Miles Archer?"

"They're broadcasting live," Maya says, flipping her phone around so we can see the feed.

"Archer's accusing the administration of illegally detaining someone who was kidnapped by the Dragon Slayers. That they're holding a man who is a victim, not a suspect."

"Charlie, we need to move," Graham fumes. "If BlackSteel gets there first, they'll start cracking heads and hand the media the viral footage they crave."

We move fast, but it's not fast enough.

By the time we reach the front entrance, it's already too late. BlackSteel Agents are moving with precision, cutting through the press like a saw. Reporters shout out questions, camera shutters click, live feeds roll, but none of it slows Reddick's men.

They shove reporters back, knocking cameras sideways, forcing the crews to retreat step by step. A cameraman stumbles as a BlackSteel agent rips his rig away, smashing it against the pavement.

Miles Archer remains composed, unfazed by what is transpiring around him.

He stands perfectly still, hands in his pockets, with an amused look on his face as if he has orchestrated this whole thing. Indeed, Archer has been here before, played this game, and won, so he knows exactly how it works.

Reddick plows through the last of the crowd as if they don't exist. He walks straight to Archer, eyes locked on him. The authority he emits makes men either fall in line or brace for impact.

"You're trespassing," Reddick says, voice low, stance intimidating.

Archer could not care less about his rage, completely unshaken.

"Sidewalks are public property."

Reddick's mouth pulls into a crooked smile, and it isn't friendly. It borders on amusement but tilts dangerously close to cruelty.

"Cute. You really think any of that matters here on my property?"

Archer doesn't budge.

"Touch me, and I'll bury you in legal hell."

"Legal system? Think you're a smart ass? We are in the midst of war; things are different now."

Reddick pokes his finger firmly into Archer's chest, daring him to react.

Archer's smile says it all.

"You keep telling yourself that, tough guy. I am just here to see my client. You know, the whole Bill of Rights thing.

"Wait, maybe you don't know. You seem pretty stupid. Want me to explain it using small words for you?"

Reddick refuses to take the bait, instead replying through gritted teeth.

"This is your last chance, you ambulance chaser. Unless you want to talk with me alone inside a jail cell."

His threat fails to land as Archer doesn't push back. He reaches for his phone, tapping out a quick message.

"Perfect. Deny my client's rights. This is just another offense to add to the long list of illegal injustices I'll be hitting Black-Steel and you with. Obstruction of justice is no joke. Hope your lawyers are better than your thugs."

Archer turns on his heel and walks away victorious.

Either Bloodso messaged Archer before he jumped, or the Dragon Slayers did so after the fact. At this juncture, it means a lot more attention will be focused on Bloodso.

Reddick, frustrated at what just transpired, turns his attention to me.

"Deputy Director, you said Bloodso was a nobody. Funny, but that's a hell of a legal team for a nobody."

"It's all Archer. You know how lawyers are. He'd defend a baboon if it got him screen time."

Reddick stares at me for a beat, eyes narrowing, scanning me for cracks. He's trying to uncover my deception, seeking out a lie.

I offer him nothing to grab onto, and he moves on.

"Well, while you deal with this circus, I've got more important work to do. It's time to crack that Dragon Slayer wide open."

Reddick walks away as if it's just another day at the beach for him. For us, it's nothing but, with time running out as we face a mountain of work. This case can't slip away knowing that Bloodso has all the answers.

And the Dragon Slayer?

One more card for BlackSteel and the administration to play.

CHAPTER 29

A DEAL WITH THE DAMNED

"Everyone can enjoy a life of luxurious leisure if the machine-produced wealth is shared, or most people can end up miserably poor if the machine-owners successfully lobby against wealth distribution."

-STEPHEN HAWKING

AS I WALK back into headquarters, the BlackSteel changes are impossible to ignore.

Empty desks, once occupied by friendly colleagues, are simply collecting dust. FBI agents are abandoning their careers to avoid becoming a footnote in a private military buyout.

Lex's cubicle has the greatest impact on me. She made the right choice, wise enough to embrace the freedom to appreciate the good things in life.

Her workspace had a life of its own. Decorations for every possible holiday, multiple candy bowls for anyone passing by her signature 'Best Secret Agent Ever' mug.

Now, it's a void waiting for someone else. Perhaps Black-Steel won't bother filling her role at all. Their focus has shifted, with less interest in oversight and more emphasis on boots on the ground. Protocols and process compliance no longer carry the same weight, especially when restructuring staff to meet a more force-heavy agenda.

A voice rings out.

"Deputy Director Grayson!"

I turn to face a BlackSteel agent, unrecognizable, but these days, that's to be expected.

"Marcus Bloodso is ready in the interrogation room."

I look over to Graham, who's been trailing half a step behind me. Without another word to the BlackSteel agent, we head to the last chance we have for a lead in the case.

Inside the interrogation room, Bloodso is already seated, his hands cuffed in front of him. A few bandage marks where the med team patched him up, thankfully it was nothing serious. He appears detached but arrogant. His posture says it all: he doesn't plan to be here long.

He looks up and scolds me.

"Where's Miles at?"

I shut down his request immediately.

"We both know that's not happening. That ship has sailed. There is no due process here, not with BlackSteel in charge."

Bloodso pauses, carefully considering his next words, but there is no resistance behind his expression. There is nothing for him to fight for.

"I understand. There's no jury for me. Not anymore."

Everything is out now. Just a man who saw what the world was, tried to play the game and lost.

Pulling a folder from the stack beside me, I flip it open. His military record is extensive, filled with numerous commendations, medals, and accolades. His service spanned decades. Photos clipped to the pages show him younger, standing beside soldiers whose names are scattered throughout these files. Some dead, others forgotten.

"Safe Serve," I say, reviewing another section. "All ex-military. But not just any ex-military, right?"

Bloodso shifts uncomfortably in his chair, his expression darkening.

"They're the rejected ones. The used-up ones. Sure, some were dishonorably discharged; hell, maybe they did snap under pressure. It happens all the time. But why don't they get an existence after duty? Why aren't they given a second chance after everything they've been through?"

He straightens slightly, a flicker of pride surfacing despite the restraints around his wrists.

"That's why I started Safe Serve. It wasn't just about work. It was about giving these forgotten soldiers something. A place where vets could do some good again. Maybe even bring a sense of some normalcy to their lives."

Graham's response is sympathetic.

"That's pretty noble of you, Bloodso. One battle can completely change a man."

"Noble huh? Look where it got me."

His expression hardens again.

I continue, dragging my finger across a highlighted line.

"You built Safe Serve for veterans who slipped through the cracks. And you used your own money to do it."

He gives me nothing. Just sits there, deliberately at ease.

"That's why I'm struggling with this, Bloodso. Nothing adds up. A guy like you, dedicated to helping veterans, running a company built on hope for the future. Why the hell are you caught up in this mess?"

He lets out a slow breath, his eyes glaring at me.

"I'll tell you why, because it was the best shot to take for all the brave men and women who've given everything and were still left behind. What the Dragon Slayers were offering? That kind of money? The good we could've done with it…"

He leans forward, his voice more balanced.

"The opportunity to turn billionaires over to the Dragon Slayers fell right into our laps. A twist of fate. And yeah, I took it. I'd take it again, too, even if the odds were still the same that I'd end up here."

Bloodso looks down, his gaze intense, filled with the memories of every person he couldn't save. They surround him now in this room, silent, unforgiving, grief-stricken souls.

His voice is full of remorse.

"Fuck, for once, we had a shot at something real. Not a medal with a folded flag."

He's a man who truly believes in what he is doing. Fueled by his passion, the desire for change and the burdens he carries make everything conceivably real. Twisted, maybe, but real.

A bitter laugh escapes him.

"But it's more than that. Deep down, I know the billionaires are the reason for all of it. Every war. Every goddamn conflict we fought in.

"Their fortunes grow while good men and women die believing they are fighting for their country's freedom. And it's sickening when they come back home, damaged and defeated. They return with scars, visible and invisible, and all we give them is a cold shoulder and then add them to a backlog of paperwork."

Bloodso raises the volume of his voice, his anger accelerating.

"I spent my life watching the system chew up people like me and my team, feeding us into the grinder so they could buy another yacht, another private island.

"So, I figured, hell, if that's the game, why not flip the board and help the Dragon Slayers? Take back what those billionaires have stolen."

He pauses, savoring the moment, quiet, deliberate, and far too satisfied for someone in his situation.

"And then you fucking shoot out my tires."

"That's what happens when you work with terrorists," I say flatly. "And I don't think you should find any of this amusing."

Then, for the first time in the entire conversation, he smiles. It's not the bitter kind, it's more devious.

"Well, there is one thing I still have," he says slyly.

Bloodso lets the silence sit. He's not rushing this. He knows he has leverage, and he wants to see us squirm or beg.

"I know where they're keeping Thaddeus Montclair III. Or at least, I know the last place they were holding him."

There it is, exactly what we needed to hear.

Montclair is one of the wealthiest of those that were kidnapped. We find him, then we have a good shot at finding the other missing billionaires. It's imperative we locate him before the Dragon Slayers decide he's no longer worth keeping alive.

Bloodso examines us carefully. He's not trying to sell this, only watching our reactions before continuing.

"Now, those Dragon Slayers said they planned on keeping their hostages there for a while. These aren't quick jobs. They squeeze as much as possible out of their targets. Money, assets, you name it, they'll get it.

"I got no clue if he's still alive, no clue if they've already moved him, or if they have been tipped off that I am here.

"But I can give you that address."

Graham asks the billion-dollar question.

"What's the catch?"

Bloodso folds his hands before speaking again.

"You make sure that it's just me that goes down for this. I don't want any of my people to suffer for my actions.

"My team had no idea what they were signing up for; I made sure of that. They weren't part of the planning, they weren't part of the calls, and they sure as hell weren't sitting in at any meetings.

"This was me. All me. And I want to hear from you two that it's only going to be me when the hammer falls. That you make sure it is known that I forced them into this, that I kept them in the dark."

"That's an honorable thing to do, but that's not really up to us," Graham truthfully replies. "Given the current state of the country, I don't think we can guarantee a damn thing."

"Damn straight. I know you can't make any promises. And I can't give you a definite answer on whether Montclair and the Dragon Slayers are still at the location.

"What I'm asking is that, as someone who's served for a higher purpose, you'll do your best and show me exactly what that looks like. If I think this will help my team, you'll have your address."

Graham narrows his eyes as he pressures Bloodso.

"How about we just turn you over to BlackSteel? I'm sure their enhanced interrogation techniques will get that address out of you real quick."

Bloodso doesn't blink. Doesn't smile. He holds Graham's stare steady and unshaken. His voice is calm when he finally speaks.

"I like your spunk, kid, but trust me, torture is no way to make me talk. You have no clue what others have done to try to break me. It won't fucking work, and you won't get your man.

"Ball is in your court. Time is ticking."

It's glaringly obvious that Bloodso isn't going to fold without his demands being fulfilled. He's already accepted his fate, and that makes him damn near impossible to break.

"Fine," I say, pushing away from the table. "We'll see what we can do."

Not waiting for a response, I motion for Graham to follow me out of the room, leaving Bloodso alone with his convictions.

Graham speaks his mind.

"Shit, Charlie, that's a big ask for us to forge records. What's your take?"

I do the only thing I can think of; I call a lifeline.

Carter.

We step inside his office, shutting the door behind us. He spins his chair around, Rubik's cube in his hand, apparently taking a mental health break.

"Hey, guys. Graham, did you yank some teeth and get Bloodso to spill his guts?"

"Not quite," I reply.

"Oh, one of these conversations? Hmmmm, guess I need to come to the rescue again."

"Carter, Bloodso has the address of the holding site for Thaddeus Montclair III. So, yes, we need your help and fast."

"No problemo. A quick Google search, and my job here is done."

"It's not that easy."

"Of course it isn't. What's the catch?"

"Bloodso won't give us the address unless we can make sure his team doesn't get flagged. He wants Safe Serve out of it. No tracking, no blacklists, no one getting rounded up."

"Ouch. That's... yeah. That's tough. I mean, not just difficult, like, actually impossible."

Graham quickly agrees with him.

"Thought so."

"Don't want to be a downer, but what you're asking is literally a huge contradiction of how intelligence works. Every framework in place is designed to do exactly the opposite of that. You don't just erase names from the records.

"Everything that comes through gets tracked, flagged, stored. If someone sneezes in the wrong direction, it gets logged somewhere. The idea of just making a group disappear?

"Bummer. It's not gonna happen with the FBI's platform."

Graham lets out a deep groan.

"So, in other words, we're screwed."

Carter gives us one of his classic smirks.

"Oh, absolutely, totally boned. Unless of course we use the new system."

I'm not amused by him dragging us along.

"What new system?"

Carter rubs the bridge of his nose, relishing his next words.

"Oh, you guys are gonna love this. BlackSteel is playing with the big boys now. They're scrapping their legacy networks and migrating everything over to Sorakin's platform, the same one we're using.

"But here's the kicker: Alan Schmutt and his lackeys are the ones helping them set it up."

He gives me a look that says it all.

"It's a tech debacle. Massive breaches. Schmutt's people can't even lock down admin access properly. I mean, if someone knew where to look? They'd have everything."

"Carter, how bad is it?"

"It's a blank canvas. Obviously, if someone's already watching a detail and it suddenly vanishes, sure, that raises flags. But small changes? Quiet edits? Names here and there? No one would notice. Not with the mess they created."

I don't hesitate.

"Then you pin it all on Bloodso. Revise every record you need to. Scrub his team completely. Make it clean. That's an order, Carter."

His fingers respond at once, typing something too fast to be tracked. The seriousness of the implications of my order is not even on his radar. Carter is all in.

"Making history on the fly," he mutters under his breath.

"Everything needs to appear as if Bloodso was in charge. No loose ends for BlackSteel."

Carter doesn't stop typing and doesn't look up, but I know his smirk is the biggest it's ever been.

"You know, boss, they always say history gets rewritten by the winners. I just never thought I'd be the one writing it."

"Carter. Please, now is not the time for your jokes."

"Just saying, it's kind of fun in a deeply unethical way."

"Let us know when it's done."

"Give me five. You'll have a fresh version of the truth ready for Bloodso."

Graham looks at me.

"And after that?"

"We find Thaddeus Montclair III and bring him back alive."

CHAPTER 30

SIGNED AND SEALED

"The causes which destroyed the ancient republics
were numerous; but in Rome, one principal
cause was the vast inequality of fortunes."

- NOAH WEBSTER

BACK IN MY office, I know exactly what I have to write, but I hesitate anyway. The words are molded in my mind, a careful arrangement of truth and manipulation. Measured and precise, the way it needs to be framed for maximum results.

Nothing more, nothing less.

Marcus Bloodso takes full responsibility. Safe Serve is cleared of wrongdoing. His men were unknowingly coerced and misled, following orders without being aware of their boss's grand but illegal scheme.

Behind it all, the Dragon Slayers had been manipulating Bloodso from the start, exploiting his ambition and ego to gain leverage, twisting his operation into a tool for their ends.

I continue typing, fingers moving with muscle memory, not pausing to think about the severity of my actions. This is how the world works now. The truth is that whatever you can put on paper, whatever you can justify, and whatever survives long enough is considered a fact.

It's not about what's real. It's about what sticks.

The deeper I delve into the report, the more I begin to think about the ramifications. Even if I do everything correctly, even if I structure this perfectly, there's no guarantee that BlackSteel won't hunt down the rest of Safe Serve's staff.

The new regime controlling us doesn't make deals. Black-Steel takes. It erases. It devours whoever it wants, whenever it wants. Bloodso can sign this, I can sign off on it, and Carter can bury the evidence.

However, if someone gets suspicious about Safe Serve, who knows how deep they will delve?

Still, I have to try. Setting this in motion and stabilizing the situation may slow down BlackSteels' purge, keeping this debacle from escalating into a situation far worse.

Maybe it keeps me from watching the FBI transformed into a skeleton of its former glory. The Bureau I had dedicated my life to is quickly becoming a privatized monster.

A ping from my terminal pulls me from my dark thoughts. It's Carter.

"Boss, check what I just sent you. Safe Serve dossier all wrapped up, nice and clean."

I open the file, scanning through it for key highlights.

Marcus Bloodso: coercion of team members confirmed.

Safe Serve operatives unknowingly participated in activities linked to the Dragon Slayers.

No operational knowledge of any future schemes.

Dragon Slayers worked directly with only Marcus Bloodso.

The dossier will be finalized with his statement, a confession that will require his signature. I keep it simple, direct, and all-inclusive.

I, Marcus Bloodso, take full responsibility for Safe Serve's past and present acts and omissions. I knowingly and intentionally withheld critical information from my team that could inflict irreparable harm on them. I misrepresented operations that I solely created to be implemented by my Safe Serve staff. My team acted under my directives without full awareness of my intentions for a broader mission. I acknowledge that the consequences of these actions are my sole liability.

Printing it out, I don't give it a second thought. Maybe Bloodso will sign it without balking. This document with his signature is our final recourse; there are no other options.

Finished, I head toward Graham's station.

"So, what's the approach here?" he asks as I hand him the document folder.

"We go in and lay it all out for him. No tricks, Bloodso is a straight shooter. If we prove to him that we've put in our best effort to save his men, I know he'll sign the doc."

Graham stops, considering the scenario.

"I get that soldier-to-soldier vibe on Bloodso too. He's not the type to play mind games. If we show him that our offer is legit, he'll take it.

"Charlie, there's another issue. My squad has been commandeered for another mission. So, when we hit that Dragon Slayer location, it will be with another strike force.

"Trust me, they'll do just fine."

"Who's on it?" I ask suspiciously.

Graham smirks.

"That would be just you and me. These days, you can't trust anyone else."

It's a bold move on his part, just the two of us, but it's the only way we stay ahead of BlackSteel.

We move fast, get there first, assess the scene, and hopefully find Montclair. If we hit any resistance, we set BlackSteel up for a head-on crash into the Dragon Slayers.

"Graham, I'm good to go. Wherever Bloodso sends us, we'll move as quickly as we can."

We head to the interrogation room where Marcus Bloodso has been waiting, confident in our decisions and more than ready to put our plan into action.

Suddenly, a gruff voice stops us in our tracks.

"Grayson."

I turn, bracing myself before I face him.

Commander Reddick surges toward me, his expression unreadable, his tone filled with effortless condescension.

"That damn Dragon Slayer of yours doesn't speak English. Are you sure he's the prime suspect here?"

"Doesn't speak English? That's bullshit. During his apprehension, he wouldn't shut up.

"It has to be a ruse, Commander. If you'd like, I could spend some time with him. I have extensive interrogation experience and speak a few languages…"

He cuts me off, unwilling to even entertain the idea.

"Enough, Grayson. You'll leave this lying bastard to me."

"Of course, whatever you think is best."

Reddick folds his hands, his voice cool and deliberate.

"I just wanted to let you know that your leads are continuing to disappoint ."

His words are designed to hit; to remind me that in his eyes, I'm already on thin ice. It's clear that no matter what I accomplish, it'll never be enough for Reddick. I refuse to give him the reaction he seeks.

"Is that all, Commander?"

Reddick's eyes search for my weaknesses, waiting for me to flinch. I will not give him the satisfaction.

"Dismissed," he barks as he turns and walks off, his posture rigid, his presence suffocating even after he's gone.

BlackSteel's leadership has absolute power, yet it is still not enough. They press their boots down just a little harder to make sure there's no question about who's in control.

The overcompensation of it all is pathetic. However, that makes it much easier for me and my remaining team to stay under the radar. Any individual who craves that much power becomes predictable.

A little deference here, a little praise there, keeps men like Reddick satisfied.

The question is, for how long?

Every day, the FBI becomes more like a private army.

And how long before they start paying attention to me? Before they decide I don't fit into their new order?

Before I am deemed a traitor.

That word is chiseled in my soul. An ugly, sharp-edge cutting word that I try to push away. Yet, it remains.

Overthinking the situation, I remind myself that what I'm doing is not wrong. I'm keeping everything from spiraling into something worse.

There's no room for further personal justification, yet I know that this internal dialog will remain with me.

Graham and I enter the interrogation room and place the document in front of Bloodso as if it is a rare manuscript. He glances at it, then up at me, then back down, flipping the pages slowly. This man is in no rush.

"So, this is what I did, huh?"

"This is what you did," I say evenly.

He lets out a sigh of defeat, the barest hint of sadness tugging at the corners of his mouth.

"This is all, just a signed statement of my guilt?"

I slide a file across the table.

"That and this."

Bloodso flips through the second set of documents. His facial expression begins to shift. The details he is reading are airtight: transaction logs, call histories, and intelligence reports that all point to one inevitable conclusion.

Marcus Bloodso acted alone. Safe Serve operatives were misled. They followed orders under false pretenses, unaware of the larger scheme.

He continues to take his time, flipping back and forth between pages, his fingers pressing hard against the paper's edges.

"This is clear evidence against you. As you can see, it corroborates the ongoing efforts that you, under false pretenses, completely deceived your entire team and the Safe Serve corporation.

"This is all your fault, Mr. Bloodso."

He chuckles, a dry, tired sound, then tosses the file onto the table like it's nothing.

"You know, I couldn't give a damn about the Dragon Slayers. I couldn't give a damn about you and the FBI.

"But I'll tell you what I do care about. My crew. They didn't do anything wrong. They just exist in a system that was built to chew them up and spit them out.

"So, if this helps in any way to make sure they don't get thrown into the fire with me, it's worth it."

Graham's patience is wearing thin.

"Then sign it. And give us the address."

Bloodso doesn't move. He just watches us for a moment, his

eyes unreadable, his expression settled into something quiet and resigned.

I push him.

"Agent Cross is right. Every second counts. And the quicker you cooperate, the better chance you have of this working for all of us."

"You gotta pen?"

I slide one over, and without hesitation, he presses it to the paper, signing his name in firm, deliberate strokes. He caps the pen, sets it down, and looks up.

"Two hours west. Fairchild Manor, off Route 16. Private estate, tucked behind the property's airstrip. High walls, cameras everywhere, security crawling all over the place. That's where they were keeping them."

I don't waste a second. My comm is in my hand.

"Carter. AO. Two hours west. Fairchild Manor, off Route 16. Confirm."

"Roger that. Checking the fastest route. Air transport."

Graham speaks quickly as we bolt from the room.

"Charlie, what's the play?"

"We tell BlackSteel we broke new intel as we lift off. We tell them that we're only securing the perimeter first before their arrival. That should delay them long enough for us to get in before they arrive on the scene. If the Dragon Slayers are there, then we will wait for BlackSteel reinforcements."

"That might be tricky. Dispatch logs, flight tracking, someone's gonna notice a sudden deployment."

"Graham, I know. Let's hope that the logistics department hasn't figured out who they're reporting to. We have to move fast before they catch on."

We grab gear from the armory, our boots leaving a trail of sound as we move toward the helipad.

There's no certainties anymore, no guarantees. If this is a setup, if the Dragon Slayers are already gone, if BlackSteel is quick-sighted, then this entire operation crumbles, and so do we.

This might be our last shot. Not just to save a kidnapped billionaire. Not just to clean up someone else's mess. We need something that changes the entire game.

If we fail, everything collapses with us.

CHAPTER 31

INTO THE DRAGON'S DEN

"Where justice is denied... where poverty is enforced...
neither persons nor property will be safe."

-Frederick Douglass

THE SILENCE OF the building is broken by the pounding of our boots, as Graham and I race to the tarmac. Outside, a helicopter stands by, its blades spinning in anticipation of our arrival.

I raise my hand to my earpiece.

"Carter, we need all assets available."

"Roger that. Fifteen minutes and the complete layout for Fairchild Manor is yours."

We force our way through the heavy doors and out into the cool night air. The rotors of the Black Hawk glisten under the floodlights as they turn in slow, mesmerizing arcs.

The pilot stands outside the cockpit, holding a tablet, his eyes staring us down as we approach. I feel a lump form in my throat as we meet up with him.

"Deputy Director Grayson, Agent Cross. There's no approval for your mission in the system."

It's here. The chokehold of BlackSteel's control tightening on the Bureau, bearing down on our every movement. If I allow this to stall, we're finished.

I quickly respond.

"We've just received orders to follow up STAT on critical intel for a Dragon Slayer stronghold. We need to move now to confirm this information. If we don't act right now, you'll be the reason this op is aborted."

I move closer to the pilot, my voice steadfast.

"And you certainly don't want to be reported to Director Cartwright and Commander Reddick for insubordination."

He shuffles his feet as he scans the tablet, desperately hoping to find something he missed. Still undecided.

I press harder.

"We need to go. Now."

His eyes move back and forth between his tablet and us. Then without saying a word, he climbs into the cockpit and powers up the engine.

Graham and I haul ourselves aboard, strapping in as the earth below fades away. We're airborne. For now, we are untouchable.

I text a message to Bill and Reddick

Bloodso just gave us intel on a location for the Dragon Slayers and hostages. He said they were moving their captives. We're en route now.

Graham looks at me.

"Charlie, there's no going back from this."

"It's a decision that had to be made. I take full responsibility."

Graham doesn't have a chance to reply as my earpiece crackles again.

Commander Reddick.

"Grayson. What the hell do you mean Bloodso broke? You said he was a low-value target."

"That's what we figured too, Commander. He gave a location. Could be a hoax and probably is.

However, there is a small chance that they have kidnapped billionaires there. We're responding as per protocol."

"What the fuck? Why wasn't I informed first? Why are you two heading out there without backup?"

"Bloodso said they were on the move. If the Dragon Slayers hear we have that intel, they won't stay put. Quick action is required. We can't let them get away."

There is a long silence over the line. When Reddick speaks, his voice is deadly serious.

"This is an order. You do not set foot anywhere in the target location. You secure the perimeter and wait for my team to handle this. Do you understand me?"

"Copy that."

The connection drops.

Graham looks at me and whispers,

"That guy really needs a victory."

"It's more than just Reddick. BlackSteel, Tuff, and Sorin need to rescue a billionaire. That's their win.

"And if we find them and their hostages first, we take that win away from them."

That's what a private entity does. Forget duty, or prevention, or stopping the next attack before it happens. It's all about the credit, the optics, the control, all to ensure more profits for their shareholders.

My earpiece crackles once more.

Bill.

"Charlie, what the hell are you doing?"

"Reddick is overreacting. We caught a break, and we're moving on it."

Bill lets out an excruciatingly long sigh.

"Charlie, you don't get it. You shouldn't have done this. Things have changed. For your own sake, you'd better find something."

He's right. If this leads to nothing, I have given BlackSteel the perfect reason to pull me the second we get back to HQ.

"I know Bill, but we're going to find something."

"Charlie, I hope you do."

The line goes dead.

I let my hand fall from my earpiece, surveying the endless black ahead, beating down the dark thought I may be wrong. The BlackSteel power struggle is accelerating at a much faster pace.

"We're close to being removed from the case permanently."

Graham reaches out and puts his hand on my shoulder.

"We'll make this count, Charlie."

The Black Hawk continues to pierce through the darkness as we draw nearer to Fairchild Manor. Below us, the landscape sprawls out, a pocket of extreme affluence nestled in the heart of nowhere.

The estate is a world of its own. Winding stone paths meander through neglected gardens, with vast terraces reaching up into the tree canopy.

Moonlight glints off high wrought-iron gates adorned with ornate swirls forged to flaunt the wealth of the owners. Past the entrance, the massive estate looms motionless, and immortal. Once a refuge for people who never had to want for anything, built and sustained by people who needed everything.

Carter's voice comes in tense through my earpiece.

"Charlie, got a bad feeling about this. I'm getting nothing.

Either this facility is empty, or the Dragon Slayers have invested a lot into blocking any signals."

"Copy that. Looks deserted from here. We're going in, slowly."

The pilot, increasingly uncomfortable, cuts into the speaker.

"I won't be touching down in the middle of a Dragon Slayer den. Too damn risky."

"Fine. Drop us down and stand by for extraction if needed."

"Roger that."

Graham and I are moving as soon as the Black Hawk touches ground. We sync with controlled urgency, rifles down, eyes scanning every potential point of cover. Rotor wash sends dust and dry leaves spinning outward across the aged cobblestone courtyard, projecting a visual warning for anyone to see us.

The Manor's gates are slightly ajar, revealing an eerie quiet of the dense woods surrounding the property. Our path is lit only by the soft glow of the moon as it seeps through the twisted branches overhead. Every step we take is an invitation for a sniper's bullet to tear through the night.

My shoulders are rigid, my hand firm on my gun as I survey every ivy-covered alcove and arch that could conceal danger.

Nothing.

No moving shadows inside the Manor. No signs of trouble, and yet my intuition begs to differ.

Graham paces a few steps ahead, poised for action, waiting for an unseen presence to strike out at him.

The grand hand-carved wooden front doors stand partially open, beckoning us to enter.

I look across at Graham, who has positioned himself on one side of the door, poised, awaiting my signal. The wind howls through the trees, causing the iron gates behind us to groan, but inside, it is completely silent.

I take a deep breath and give the signal.

We make our way into the entrance hall, meticulously covering all angles with sharp, practiced movements. Inside, the two-story foyer echoes our footsteps, its vastness unfurling in every direction.

White sheets, now stained with the yellow of time, shroud the furniture. An ornate chandelier, crystals dull from neglect, catches the wayward beams from our flashlights. Tiny bits of refracted light play along the walls. The air is stagnant with the putrid smell of neglect and decay.

Graham tries the nearest light switch. Nothing.

I continue a sweep of the area, my flashlight beam revealing mold-covered books stacked everywhere, as particles of dust swirl around me. It appears as if nothing has been disturbed here in a long time.

Bloodso might have sent us on a dead-end hunt.

Still, something doesn't feel right.

Graham points to a stretch of vacant corridor ahead. We head in that direction, brushing past portraits of long-deceased men and women immortalized in tarnished, gold-gilded frames. All of this was designed to stand forever, constructed for a legacy that would never end.

Every room we strategically enter is the same, full of remnants of an opulent life lived, yet devoid of the things that matter.

We enter a large chamber that feels different from the others, every detail tugging at my awareness.

The spaces we had searched were in a natural disarray of chaos, a sign that nothing had been touched by human hands for a long time.

But this room?

It's still decrepit, but the arrangement isn't right. Sheet-covered furniture is pressed squarely against the walls, leaving the center open… immaculately, impossibly clear.

Graham slows alongside me, raising his rifle up, as his position locks in.

"Something's off," he says.

Then we hear it.

Click.

An unexpected sound.

I spin around as floodlights hit us. There is no time to react.

A shockwave of white light explodes blindingly bright. My eyes shielded by my visor, struggle to adjust. My body's fight-or-flight response short-circuits while my arms lift my gun. The sheer force of the lighting immobilizes us, freeze-framing our bodies into a rigid position.

Next, a voice.

Absolute and commanding.

"Drop your weapons, or you're dead."

The words boomerang around the room, echoing off the high ceilings. Speakers. The voice is sharp, clear, unnaturally controlled, coming from no one direction.

Graham's head is down to avoid the painfully intense light. We both hold tight to our rifles, unwilling to obey their commands.

"Put down your guns now. This is your last chance to live."

Despite being invisible, their presence can't be mistaken. They are observing us intently, as if we are living mannequins in a window display.

A silent communication ripples between Graham and me. We have no option.

With deliberate ease, we set our weapons on the floor. The moment our rifles touch the ground, they're on us.

Hands clamp on my arms, yanking me ahead with a force

that is not hurried, one that has been practiced and perfected over years of experience. There is no need to struggle; there is no chance to fight back. The decision made to enter alone has come back to bite us.

Graham does what comes naturally to him. His body contorts tight, muscles stretched taut as he tries to struggle free. Two men have him by the arms, as another one moves in, striking a hard, well-aimed blow at his stomach.

He gasps sharply, his body bucking forward, his hands involuntarily reaching out from the impact, precisely what they had intended.

The instant his resolve wavers, they thrust him into a chair.

Two men push me down onto a cold, metal chair, my wrists wrenched behind me as plastic cuffs bite into my skin. No need to resist as there are no other options at hand.

The floodlights dim, enough for my eyes to adjust. The flashes of bright light spots slowly rescind, allowing for a first look at our captors.

I blink several times.

Black and gold.

Dragon Slayers flank the perimeter of the room, weapons at their sides but not lifted as they stand at attention.

The deadly predicament we are in is all because of me. The relentless drive to successfully complete every mission, to never fail, to prove I'm capable of the role and my name.

It's been this way my entire life. The unending desire to validate my worth.

That desire now has us strapped to chairs, at the mercy of the Dragon Slayers. It wouldn't hurt as much if I hadn't sucked Graham into this mess.

I am crushed by my failure. Ready to accept my fate.

Then I hear a loud sound that shatters my thoughts.

Thud.

Thud.

Thud.

The sound of a giant shaking the earth with every step.

It can be no other.

Lancelot.

He is a Goliath, a force of nature clad in brilliant black-and-gold armor, his mere presence smothering. He moves methodically, each step deliberate and slow, his ominous size implying that even without the armor, he is indestructible.

Six-seven, maybe six-eight. Easily over 350 pounds of muscle. The powerful warlord of the Dragon Slayers.

Lancelot stands before us like a king surveying the battlefield after victory.

We are at his mercy.

CHAPTER 32

THE DISEASE OF GREED

*"In a good society, the rich would be
ashamed of their wealth...."*

-Oscar Wilde

LANCELOT STANDS THERE, observing us in silence.

Unwavering and absolute, devoid of the restless movement most men have upon entering a room, making no superfluous gesture.

Bound, we have only our thoughts as he stands over us. Waiting.

The plastic ties dig painfully into my wrists, and my arms ache from the unnatural position. Yet, I compel myself to be motionless, my breath steady despite the chaotic thoughts shredding their way through my brain in every direction.

My mind races as I try to predict the inevitable.

Will he execute us right here?

Maybe Lancelot will use us as leverage, parade us in front of a camera, or, worse, trade us like we're commodities, bargaining chips in a war that will have no end.

What is his plan? What the hell does he want?

And then Lancelot speaks.

"Deputy Director Grayson. Agent Cross. We've been expecting you."

His deep voice is filled with measured self-assurance. Lancelot knows that he alone will determine our fate.

"How?" I say, the word tumbling out more sharply than I intend, but I don't care.

Lancelot's mask shifts slightly towards me.

"We have our ways."

He speaks without inflection, making his point a fact that we need to accept. The Dragon Slayers have compensated countless of their followers, so it would make sense they would have infiltrated our Bureau or BlackSteel as well.

Lancelot looks at Graham and then back at me.

"Both of you have outstanding service records."

The shift is so unexpected, so abrupt, that for a moment, I question whether I heard him correctly.

"You have served your nation, having offered your lives in conflict, for what you thought was just."

I still have no idea what his intentions are; I don't know whether this is the dawn of a decision or the ominous specter of an execution.

And then his tone hardens, imperceptibly shifting the dynamic of the moment.

"But the nation you struggled for has been corrupted. The disease of greed created the billionaire class, who viciously stole it."

The words slip under my skin like a knife being pressed close to my neck.

The wealthy elite did take over. I know it. I've seen it. I've spent my entire career watching the boundaries between corporate and government power dissolve, watching agencies like mine being warped into attack dogs for the nation's richest individuals, and watching policies shift to serve those with money at the expense of those without.

I know he's not wrong. And yet, that is the most terrible thing about it.

Then, with the same steadiness and unshakeable confidence, he discloses the portion of the greatest importance.

"That is why you're still breathing."

Graham and I don't flinch at what he just said. We were never the targets.

If the Dragon Slayers didn't hold themselves to their self-imposed standard, if their rage had extended beyond the architects of the system to people who simply operated within it, would I be here now? Where would Graham be?

The line the Dragon Slayers drew kept us on one side, but if they'd chosen differently, we could've just as easily been bodies in their wake.

Lancelot doesn't wait for a response from us; he simply turns around and leaves.

No threats or actions. Not even a single word.

His departure alters our mood, switching from suffocating tension to unexpected relief. We are still alive, at least for the time being. The invisible hand that had squeezed Graham and me so tightly when we were first captured has loosened as we take our first real breath.

Another Dragon Slayer steps forward. He is lean and tall, projecting a calm stance; his build is not quite as formidable as that of Lancelot's. Still, this man is an undeniable presence, the kind that needs no dramatic show to dominate a room.

His black and gold mask differs from the others, sleeker

and less severe in its lines. It displays a refinement that neither screams intimidation nor ignores attention.

He stops next to me, close enough to catch his scent. When he speaks, his voice is deep and calm, with no cruelty or hostility in it, only an expression of serene confidence.

"Deputy Director Grayson. Agent Cross. Nothing for you two to worry about. As the big man said, we're not here to hurt you."

He moves behind me, and I steady myself for a blow to the back of my head. Instead, he gently places a set of metal cuffs on my wrists and cuts the old ones off.

The metal is cold yet smooth, tight but not cruel.

The Dragon Slayer does the same for Graham, who, as expected, fights against the restraints. Our captor's reaction is one of amusement rather than anger.

"Hey now, no need for that. Trust me, the last thing I want is to fight you.

"Those cuffs I just put on you two will trigger open in a few minutes. Enough time for us to disappear, so no need to waste any more of your time."

This doesn't make sense. Why go through the trouble? Why not vanish and let BlackSteel agents find us all tied up? Undoubtedly, they would take great pleasure in seeing us gagged and bound.

"Why the fuck are you doing this?" I blurt out.

"Well, if we left you wrapped up for BlackSteel, like a present under a Christmas tree, they'd be asking questions. This way, you simply tell them we weren't here. It's less trouble for everyone, but especially for you two."

I process mental notes of his voice, his speech, his stance, and his walk. This man strolls through the trenches of war as if it is a walk in the park.

"Oh, almost forgot. We left you both a gift of sorts. Let's just say some necessary endings had to take place. Better hurry and find it before BlackSteel shows up."

He quickly turns, and the other Dragon Slayers in military formation march behind him into darkness.

Graham is enraged. His voice is bitter, rough, and angry, implicating both of us for the circumstances we are facing. This is a side of Graham I have never seen before.

"Jesus Christ, Charlie. How fucking stupid!

"I swear, I can't believe we tried this. All our field training, all our experience, every tactical lesson drummed into us, and we walk right into this mess like a couple of fresh recruits."

Graham shakes his head, the motion is quick and agitated.

"We should be fucking dead. Honestly? That might have been the better option instead of being toyed with, fuck, this is so pathetic."

He pauses, his jaw working as something darker crosses his face.

"And how the hell did they know we were coming? They were expecting us, Charlie. Those were his exact fucking words."

I will not debate with him. Graham is right, except that I own this. Should have known better should have seen it coming, should have just waited for backup. It doesn't matter now.

"Graham, I'm sorry. Trust me, I know. Under normal circumstances, do you really believe I would have taken this chance?

"We would have gathered intelligence. We would have followed the protocols to the letter.

"This is no routine mission. Tuff and his administration are methodically dismantling the country from the inside out. The FBI is now their personal strike force. We are their scapegoats.

"So yeah, I took the chance, and you took it too. We knew this could happen, and it did."

Graham's eyes narrow, the anger shifting into something colder.

"But they shouldn't have known we were coming. Someone told them, Charlie. Someone on the inside."

His voice gets more heated, angrier.

"It has to be Carter. They have all the intel, and he's the fucking intel guy, dammit!"

"Graham, the operation became clear to a lot more people once we took off. Could it be Carter? Sure. But honestly, why even help get us here? He could've just led us down a wrong lead."

Graham seems to be having an internal debate as his anger deflates slightly.

"Yeah, that's possible." Graham's anger starts to subside. "But I don't fucking trust him. Or anyone at this point."

He releases a bitter laugh, one with no humor in it. He looks up at the ceiling as though seeking an answer that might be written there.

"I don't know about you, Charlie, but I've never felt this goddamn humiliated in my entire life."

Before I can respond, we hear metallic clicks signaling our freedom.

The cuffs are open.

I roll my hands and wrists; a dull pain lingers from the metal cuffs. The tightness is gone, and circulation is restored.

Graham shakes his hands loose, massaging the impressions that are left on skin.

"Well, you heard him. Let's find whatever the hell he's talking about."

I rise slowly to my feet, checking my balance before rolling my shoulders back and drawing a slow, deep breath. Our equipment is untouched, right where we dropped it.

The Dragon Slayers were not worried about us following them.

I insert my earpiece, changing over to my secure line.

"Carter. Come in. Situation under control."

"Jesus, boss, why the radio silence?"

"We can talk about it later, but we're safe for now."

"Well, shit. Alright, but just so you know, BlackSteel is coming in with full force."

I disconnect Carter before he can push for more information. My hands are shaking as I connect to Bill.

"Bill. No Dragon Slayers. Estate deserted. Will do one more sweep for evidence."

"Charlie, Commander Reddick arrives in less than fifteen minutes. Graham and you follow his commands. This is a direct order."

I am helpless to oppose, at least not without repercussions.

Bill disconnects me before I can say anything else.

"Fifteen minutes," Graham repeats. " Let's make them count."

We divide our search, scouring each area swiftly and cautiously, pushing open doors that lead one after the other to vacant rooms. Our actions become a rhythmic pattern of open, check, clear, move on.

Nothing.

A dining room large enough to accommodate a party of thirty waits in anticipation of a meal that will never be served.

Nothing.

A sitting room filled with valuable antiques covered in white sheets waits to be warmed by an ash-filled fireplace. The scent of aged wood permeates the air.

Still nothing.

We go on, room by room, until we reach the top floor.

Upstairs, the cobwebbed hallways are more intimidating, the

ceiling towering, the doors bigger and heavier. This is a lavish display of wealth, a reminder of who was the master of the house.

But it's not the gaudiness of the rooms that catches my attention, it's the graffiti.

Thick, bold letters were painted directly onto the ornate wallpaper, their vivid red hue contrasting sharply like a fresh wound.

The Disease of G—

I stretch out my flashlight, my grip automatically tightening around it. Graham follows the beam's motion and peers in the same direction.

We move forward, my gaze tracking the words as they fade towards the huge double doors at the end of the hall. The air here is charged differently; hairs stand up on the back of my neck as my heartbeat quickens.

Graham steps forward and pushes the doors open.

In front of us, a library room stretches out, huge and daunting, a witness to the owner's power and wealth. Books that have probably never been opened line shelves, while floor-to-ceiling windows are dressed in musty velvet drapes.

A once stunning chandelier hangs from the ceiling, reflecting craftsmanship, history and prestige. This room was a sanctuary of intellectual power.

The grandeur barely registers; all I care about is the rest of the message.

THE DISEASE OF GREED HAS CONSEQUENCES.

The letters are enormous, sprayed on the towering walls in dripping blood-red paint.

And below those words, in the center of the room, tied to a chair, head down, motionless.

Thaddeus Montclair III.

For a moment, he seems to be a wax figure. His hands rest

elegantly on the arms of the chair, his posture uncannily straight, but he's still breathing.

Suddenly, the scent of blood engulfs me.

It's fresh. It's here. But it's not from him, too much even for one body.

I step forward before I can think, my flashlight casting each side, scanning the room. The moment my beam hits them, I feel my stomach drop.

Montclair's family.

His wife. His two children.

Tied to chairs beside him. All dead.

I break off, choking for oxygen, my voice snagging in my throat as I try to absorb the nightmare scene before me. They were left exactly as they died, still tied to chairs. Each body sits upright, facing forward, a grotesque freeze-frame of their final moments.

Graham steps behind me, his breath catching as he takes in the view.

He lets out a primal rage.

"Those fucking monsters!"

I can't bring myself to look at him. My gaze stays on Montclair, who sits locked in whatever pain they have left him to endure.

In front of him is a polished golden tray with a small black box placed on it. This must be the Dragon Slayers' present to us.

I carefully open the box to find a thumb drive inside.

My hand twitches by my sidearm, despite knowing that there is no enemy to battle. Instead, I am left with the suffocating shock of what we have just experienced.

The realization dawns on me that we were never here to stop the Dragon Slayers.

We were here to bear witness.

CHAPTER 33

THE COST OF ACTION

"Greed is a bottomless pit which exhausts the person in an endless effort to satisfy the need without ever reaching satisfaction."

-ERICH FROMM

THADDEUS MONTCLAIR III hardly stirs as I remove the gag from his mouth. His head twitches, and for a fleeting instant, his breath hitches. It's a strangled, uneven inhale that seems to indicate his lungs have momentarily lost their way.

He starts gasping, greedily pulling in the air, his eyes wide and frantic as they flit between Graham and me.

"They... they... killed my family," he stutters.

The words stumble out of him, his throat straining to make it clear that it is not a question.

I look over at Graham, kneeling, tugging at the ropes that hold Montclair's arms in place. There's no consoling response for the massacre here. There's nothing to say that can make it okay or make it anything other than what it is.

Doing my best to keep myself composed, I try to comfort him.

"We're here to help you."

Montclair isn't listening. He blinks tightly, his eyes unfocused, his body trembling with something deeper than shock, perhaps rage, or the final remnants of whatever fight he has left.

"Those bastards killed my family," he repeats, and this time, there is something more than pain in the words. This time, there is anger.

"They said they would kill them if I didn't surrender my money. I was never going to let those terrorists get their hands on the wealth I've created."

His voice cracks on the last word as his anger rises.

Graham and I are speechless. We're still stunned at the scene before us, as well as the implication behind it all. The Dragon Slayers had given Montclair what should have been an easy choice for so many, and yet he still chose his money. And now his wife and children are dead as a result.

I feel the weight of the USB that I had slipped into my pocket. There was no hesitation when I'd grabbed it from the table. It's not going to BlackSteel before we see what's on it.

This isn't the moment for uncertainty. I catch Graham's eye, and a silent communication passes between us. We have Montclair, a win that might buy us some more time.

There is no need to rush as we guide him through the never-ending halls, past the grand staircases, past the untapped wealth that adorns every nook. The Dragon Slayers are gone, there is no fear of an ambush, and backup is almost here.

Then, in a flash, the world explodes.

The impact is deafening. Doors splinter inwards as armored transport vehicles crash inside, causing the Manor to tremble.

Marble shatters, shards of debris fly through the air as the din of machinery envelops everything.

Two flashbangs detonate on the floor. Blinding light. My senses are overwhelmed as I instinctively shield Montclair from the explosion. It sends us crashing to one side.

Sound becomes a searing, needle-like ringing, and my vision melts into a static blur. I close my eyes tight in anticipation of the shockwave as Montclair's body stiffens with fear and panic.

Graham finds me and covers his body over mine, his movements automatic.

BlackSteel bursts in like a demolition team, guns held high, shouting orders, their movements brutal and precise. Hands grab me, pulling me away from Montclair and slamming me down onto the marble floor.

"We're FBI!" I yell, struggling against their hold, but it doesn't matter.

They don't care. Graham is pulled away and shoved down hard, his knees slamming into the floor as they pin him down. Montclair is forcefully grabbed, but he does not struggle. He simply lets them lead him along like a specter in his own body, oblivious to the destruction around him.

The knee wedged between my shoulder blades is heavy and unforgiving. I can feel the vibrations of a slow, measured set of footsteps coming towards me.

It's Reddick, acting like a director on a film set, ecstatic with the destruction his men have produced.

Graham and I remain pinned to the ground as the commander steps next to us.

He turns towards his men who are holding us down.

"Let 'em up," he snaps.

The knee on my back disappears. I push myself up, gasping, keenly feeling the ache in my muscles from being pressed against the floor. Graham rises to his feet, rubbing his wrists, his face deadpan.

"Grayson. Cross. I gave you an order. Perimeter only," he shouts. "So why am I looking at you inside this shithole?"

"Commander, it looked abandoned," I say, brushing dust from my palms. "No guards, no movement. We were pulling back when we heard a suspicious noise coming from inside. We went in."

Reddick's eyes land on Montclair, propped up between two agents like a broken puppet. His brow furrows as the pieces connect.

"So, this is him?"

Reddick addresses me louder.

"Grayson, we'll discuss your insubordination when we're back at base."

Reddick turns his attention back to Montclair, studying what's left of this billionaire elite.

Montclair, dazed and unfocused, struggles to speak.

"They... killed my family. Fucking dragons... murdered them... all of them..."

Reddick sneers.

"What the hell is he mumbling about?"

"Commander, his family is upstairs. Library room. They were murdered."

Something shifts behind Reddick's eyes. Not shock or sympathy. Just calculation. The story writes itself: Dragon Slayers executing a billionaire's family in cold blood. He can already see the headlines and the next round of contracts.

"Casualties upstairs. Library room, sweep the rest of this place. Take anything of value. Anything we can't move, we'll bring in a scrapping crew to strip it clean."

"By law, this property is now in the custody of BlackSteel. Might as well get something for our time and effort."

He faces Montclair, with disgust.

"You call yourself a man? Couldn't even protect your own blood. Take him out of my sight."

Reddick then turns his full focus back on me.

"And you, Deputy Director, the only thing you found was some dead bodies?"

"Yes sir, that's all we found."

I maintain a straight face, the USB sitting in my pocket, its pressure against my skin reassuring, it's our last lifeline.

Reddick barely registers the response; he turns away with a wave of his hand towards his agents.

"Get these two cleaned up and out of here."

Outside, there is a dramatic show of defensive forces. Black-Steel SUVs, sleek and armored, line the drive like a private military parade. But it's not the vehicles that turn my stomach, it's what's moving around them.

Sorakin drones hover in fluid formations overhead, each one AI-enabled and untethered. There are no drone pilots, no oversight, just synced programming and a shared tactical feed. The UAVs orbit the convoy, surveillance vultures, communicating silently with the ground units.

And then there are the dogs.

I've read the files, *C.E.R.B.E.R.U.S.,* officially. *Combat-Enabled Robotic Breach & Enforcement Response Unit System.*

The teams call them Metal Mutts. Cold doglike machines with rifles mounted along their spines, they move with terrifying precision, programmed with algorithms specifically constructed for target elimination and fire control.

The Mutts have been in the pipeline for years, repeatedly stalled by one sticking point: the kill chain authorization.

No one wanted to be the first to approve autonomous engagement. But here they are, fully deployed, rifles locked and loaded, coated in BlackSteel's signature colors, the corporate logo stamped on steel flanks. They went live. And no one blinked.

We're escorted into one of the SUVs, the door slamming shut behind us with finality. No need for me to look back.

The movement of the SUV tries to lull me to sleep. I resist, but it snags the fringes of my consciousness, pulling me under. The instant my muscles release their vigilance, I slip deeper into the seat and drift off into a fragmented slumber.

I don't dream. I don't dissolve into something soft and peaceful. It's just a black, heavy void, dense, complete, and it lasts until the SUV stops. The sudden shift in speed pulls me back up like a hook embedded in my side.

My eyelids slowly open, the world returning in broken jagged bits. Graham is beside me, head tilted in silent repose. Ahead, FBI Headquarters is lit up like a monument to dominance. Floodlights blaze logos skyward, massive red banners hang from the facade; every inch designed to draw the eye and declare authority.

I need to acknowledge what it's become. I will just start calling it BlackSteel's HQ. No sense in pretending otherwise. It's clear, the FBI I knew is no more.

Graham and I step out and are greeted by a medical team. We undergo a routine exam before we are given the all-clear to return to duty.

I notice Reddick chatting amiably with Jackson Kane. The scene is not surprising. The billionaire architect of BlackSteel's rise stands there savoring another lucrative business deal to fill his coffers.

Kane is wearing one of his trademark cowboy hats, this one

matching another bespoke suit. It is a personification of effortless authority.

His voice rings out forcefully as he grasps Reddick's hand.

"Commander. Absolutely amazing job getting Thaddeus Montclair out alive."

Reddick's response is smooth, self-assured.

"Yes, sir. We executed perfectly. And our intelligence and interrogation of Marcus Bloodso clearly marked him as a traitor. He was compromised by the Dragon Slayers and forced to use his position at Safe Serve to mislead his team."

I let Reddick's words go right over my head. Naturally, he would spin this into one of his false legends of victory. This isn't a mission to uncover the next link in the Dragon Slayers' chain or to end the escalation of turmoil unfolding. That's not what's important to BlackSteel or him.

What actually matters is boosting their share price up, buffing their image, and ensuring their investors that BlackSteel is the only invincible behemoth that can safeguard America.

Kane continues, loud and full of manufactured pride.

"The President is personally coming here. We have a photo op that Americans must see. We will show them that BlackSteel and President Tuff are the guardians of freedom."

I turn to make my way into the building, done with this circus, ready to disappear inside.

And then I spot him.

Alexander Sorin.

He is standing behind the others, detached from the noise and congratulations. It's the first time I've seen him in person. A visionary, ruthless technocrat who believes the key to true power lies not in wealth but in control of the most advanced AI systems in existence.

When our eyes meet, something shifts. Not alarm or challenge. Recognition. He knows exactly who I am.

Sorin steps forward from the fringe, anticipating our introduction.

His voice is mellow-toned, a press release come to life.

"Deputy Director, Agent Cross. I want to introduce myself and personally give my thanks for what you and your entire team have done.

"As you know, Sorakin Technologies was born from the defense sector. And it remains at the heart of our mission to ensure that the Western values we hold so dearly are protected. I hope you'll see this transition process, and our systems, not as a replacement, but as enhancements. Improvements to your operations."

Graham's posture tightens, his eyes reacting with displeasure. His response is reluctant.

"Thanks."

I chime in just enough to sound neutral.

"Mr. Sorin, we appreciate that. Your tech advancements are always very impressive."

Sorin smiles graciously, full of self-satisfaction.

"Well, you're the true heroes here. We're not quite at the point where our machines and AI can do everything... not yet. Moving forward, if you two need anything at all, we will be happy to assist. My company's number one goal is working on the integration of our systems with BlackSteel and your Bureau."

I force a fake, appreciative smile.

"Thank you, Mr. Sorin. We look forward to working with you."

He gives a slight nod and steps away, disappearing back into the crowd as though he was just passing through.

Sorin isn't here for optics. He's here to ensure his platform is fully operational within BlackSteel.

Any gaps we could have used to slip through? They're likely sealed now.

Graham and I cut through the polished hallways of Black-Steel's fortress, the sound of boots and drones still echoing behind us. Whatever theater is still playing outside, it doesn't matter anymore. There's only one thing on my mind.

What's on the USB?

We head straight for Carter's office, the last place BlackSteel hasn't laid claim to yet, at least for now.

Carter jokes when he sees the bruises on our faces.

"You two look like you went through some serious shit. So, boss, what the hell happened?"

"It was a trap. The Dragon Slayers knew we were coming, and they apprehended us."

"Wait. What?"

Graham's demeanor turns hard.

"They knew we were coming, Carter. And they seem to know a lot of things."

He leans forward aggressively, his eyes locked on Carter.

"Cut the bullshit, Diaz. Are you fucking working for the Dragon Slayers?"

Carter reacts in panic and shock, his eyes darting back and forth between Graham and me.

"What? No! Why would... that would be suicide for me for so many reasons. Fuck..."

Graham's accusation shocks me. I try to intervene.

"Graham, please..."

But he keeps going, rapidly getting louder.

"They've been one step ahead of us this whole time! And you'd be the best person for them to get to!"

"Yeah, cause they're fucking smart!"

Carter shoots back, then looks desperately at me.

"Please, Charlie, you have to believe me. You've seen what happens to people who even get accused of that."

I step in.

"Listen, Graham. I have full faith in Carter and his efforts. I'm just as frustrated as you are, but without Carter, we would have never come close to the Dragon Slayers. We need him if we are going to catch them."

Graham looks at me for a long moment, then nods reluctantly.

"Okay, fine. I'll trust you on this, Charlie."

He turns back to Carter with a hard glare.

Carter shifts uncomfortably.

"Well... thanks, I guess. But how the hell did you survive?"

My voice reveals my disbelief.

"Apparently, they have stricter rules of engagement than BlackSteel, or it's just another tactic of theirs to fuck with us."

"Boss, that doesn't make any sense. Shit, we're technically a part of BlackSteel, which makes you both Dragon Slayers targets."

"Carter, they don't care about the Bureau. They don't care about us. Their interest lies only with their mission."

I thrust my hand into my pocket, extracting the USB and place it on Carter's desk.

"In fact, they even left us a gift, at least according to one of them."

My thought shifts to that Dragon Slayer. The way he spoke, calm, composed, poised for victory. It all still feels unreal.

Carter's pupils dilate as he holds the USB in his outstretched hand.

"Boss, you two haven't told anyone else here?"

"Not before we see what it is first, then we'll decide what to do with it."

"Okay, let's see what we got here."

He grabs a second laptop and plugs in the USB. The screen flashes before stabilizing into clarity.

Thaddeus Montclair III appears in the frame, the same way we found him. Restrained in the chair, hands tied, mouth gagged.

His face is twisted in knots of anger, his eyes seething with defiance.

The timestamp in the corner is recent, taken less than 48 hours ago.

We hear someone speaking off-screen.

"It's quite straightforward, Thaddeus. Or should I address you as Master Montclair, the Third?"

A Dragon Slayer comes into view, clad in black and gold.

"Just sign over your assets and provide us with your account information. That's all we need. We're not asking you to endure hardship. We're not asking you to become destitute. We're asking you to finally redeem yourself and your actions against humanity.

"You can still live your life as you please. You'll be protected. Your family will be protected. You can still have all the monetary things that you think bring you happiness and pleasure."

Montclair doesn't look afraid. If anything, his eyes register disgust.

The gag covering his mouth is removed so he can respond.

His first reaction is to spit at the Dragon Slayer.

"How dare you? Do you know who I am? I deserve to keep what is mine. My family worked for this money for centuries, in blood and sacrifice.

"And you morons think you can take it from me? You're a pathetic bunch of losers."

The Dragon Slayer leans forward, considering Montclair's response, then lets out a remorseful sigh.

"Okay, okay. We tried to help you. We've given you several chances. Can't say we weren't fair."

He slowly moves out of view.

Then comes the sound.

Thud. Thud. Thud.

Heavy boots reverberate against the floor, every step intentional.

Lancelot slowly comes into view.

At first, just the edges of his black-and-gold armor and his looming size. He advances with the same meticulous caution that defines him; each step is deliberate, each movement freighted with purpose.

When he finally stops, his voice is steady, unshaken, final.

"Thaddeus Montclair. This is your final chance to prove that the disease of greed does not plague you. Surrender your money now or suffer the consequences."

His nostrils flare as he squirms to break free.

"Over my dead body!"

"Watch closely. You will now witness the effect your greed has on others."

He backs away from Montclair.

My pulse slows as I stifle a scream.

I know what's coming next.

The camera pans, revealing them. Montclair's wife and his children. Tied to their chairs. Motionless, but alive.

Lancelot approaches, unflustered, his gun drawn.

The children break first. Their hysterical wails resound

around the room, high and raw, overlapping in a storm of shrieks that claw at the air.

One kicks against the chair, fighting against the restraints, while the other sobs so violently it comes out as choking gasps.

Montclair's wife bucks violently too, her own voice cracking into a primal howl.

"No! Please! PLEASE, THADDEUS, GIVE THEM THE—"

The gunshot cuts her off. Her skull jerks back unnaturally, and she collapses, her body twitching once before sagging against the restraints, slumping over.

The children's cries surge into hysteria, a pitch so piercing it almost drowns out Montclair's ragged begging.

Another shot rings out, causing one of the screams to cut out mid-note.

The surviving child's shriek doubles in pitch, until the next flash of the muzzle.

Montclair is screaming, thrashing so hard his chair rattles.

Lancelot turns to face him.

"Witness the cost of your greed."

The screen cuts into darkness.

Carter's face is ghost white. He tries to catch his breath as he covers his eyes.

"What the fuck?" he squeaks out.

Graham is full of rage.

"Those goddam, mother-fuckin' bastards. Tell me they aren't terrorists now!"

I cannot speak, and I don't want to. The Dragon Slayers left this behind. Left it for us to witness.

Carter's head shakes in disbelief.

"Why… why would they do this?"

Graham's voice cracks.

"Don't know, kid. Worst thing I've seen in a while, and I've seen some nasty shit. Now what do we do?"

"Guys, we do nothing," I state.

"Boss, why not?"

"This video needs to be kept under wraps. If not, it will get exploited. Propaganda for both sides. Spin it however they please."

Carter is still dazed from what he has seen and can only give a weak thumbs up.

Graham's face remains twisted in revulsion.

The door to Carter's office suddenly barges open.

Commander Reddick stands there and shouts.

"What are you all doing in here?"

Carter snaps back in his chair as Graham and I automatically stand at attention.

My response is firm.

"Just doing a quick debrief. Reviewing intel."

Reddicks's body bristles with suspicion.

"Sure, sure. Grayson, you need to come with me. Meeting with Cartwright and Kane."

I look at Carter, then Graham. Their expressions say it all.

Reddick heads out into the hallway as I trail behind.

We walk in silence. Reddick's steps are swift as if he is trying to see if I can keep pace with him. He is asserting control; situations like this are what he truly relishes.

The door to Bill's office is wide open. Kane is there, and he tips his hat to acknowledge our arrival. Bill is behind his desk, face inscrutable, his posture too rigid.

As we enter, Bill offers us a seat as Kane wryly smiles.

"Now, Ms. Grayson," Kane begins, silky and well-rehearsed, "On behalf of all of us here, I'd like to express our gratitude for your years of devoted service to the FBI. Everything that you have done has been wonderful, simply wonderful.

"As you are fully aware, circumstances have changed with our recent merger with the Bureau. New positions and processes are needed to aptly suit our private enterprise.

"Director Cartwright and Commander Reddick will brief you on the details, but once more, thank you, Grayson. Sincerely."

He stands up, straightens his suit coat, pats Bill on the back, nods at Reddick, and walks out. His job is done. The classic CEO routine: shake a hand, flash a smile, deliver a hollow thank-you, then vanish before anything real has to be faced.

My calmness is surprising, but then I knew this day was fast approaching. I had held on to the slight hope that somehow, I'd figure out a way to avoid it.

Reddick is savoring the moment.

"Grayson. You're no longer deputy director. Based on your recent insubordination, you've been re-assigned as a GS-9 Analyst. Until the time you can prove yourself to BlackSteel, you will remain in that position. Understand that we are a completely different system than the FBI."

I knew this was a possibility, knew it from the second we stepped out of that manor. Hearing it spoken out loud, knocks the wind out of me. My eyes flick from Reddick to Bill, searching for a spark of hope. Instead, Bill looks away. And that reveals everything.

"I was only doing what's best for the nation and this mission," I say, trying to steady my voice. "We've made great progress on the Dragon Slayer case... more than anyone else. You know that for a fact."

Reddick snaps back.

"If you had, Grayson, we wouldn't be having this conversation. Clearly, you've failed."

I open my mouth again, pushing past the sting.

"We can still…"

"Charlie. Enough," Bill snaps. "This is the best option for everyone here. Trust me."

He looks directly at me as he speaks. The message in his eyes is clear: don't push it.

Bill must have taken the hit for me, framing my actions in the softest light he could. He must have twisted the narrative because with the wrong spin, what I did wouldn't just be insubordination.

It could be treason.

My apology is quick.

"I understand, I do. And I'm sorry. I wish I could have apprehended the Dragon Slayers. I wasn't able to. So… yes. I understand."

I don't say it to Reddick. My attention is focused only on Bill. He's the only one in this room who ever gave a damn about what we were trying to accomplish with this op. The only one who knows the price I now must pay… my career.

And maybe that's why it stings so damn much.

I swallow the rest, my pride, my anger, all of it. There is one thing that is painfully clear, my options are limited. I can stay or I can go.

Bill gently speaks.

"I'm sorry, Charlie, this is the way it is. We're proud of everything you've done, but your reassignment means you're off the Dragon Slayers lead operation."

I remain sitting straight up, my tone steady.

"Understood, sir."

Reddick responds harshly.

"Good. You'll report to me. Same goes for Graham, Carter, and the rest of your team."

Everything within me wishes to rise, pound my fists on the desk, say fuck you to Reddick and tell Bill to grow a goddamn spine. But I know it's pointless.

Bill is stuck in a no-win situation.

I can walk away. What will that do?

There is no exit strategy.

The same drive that has sustained me from the start is depleted.

For the first time, I wonder if anything I've done was ever worth it.

And then I think of my father.

Would he have understood the choices I've made?

Or would he be disappointed in what I've become?

I'll never know.

And that's the part that could haunt me the most.

CHAPTER 34

WHEN THIS IS ALL OVER

"The day the power of love overrules the love of power; the world will know peace."

-GANDHI

I CLOSE THE door firmly behind me, severing the conversation between Bill and Reddick as they continue to negotiate on transitions. My pace is slow, each step bearing an invisible load.

Even though I am crumbling inside, I must stand tall and keep my composure. I head to the one place and the two people who can bring me some solace.

The moment I walk in, both of their eyes meet mine. They already know.

"It's official," I declare solemnly. " We're all off the case."

Graham sighs.

"Yeah. Figured."

Carter rubs his eyes.

"I mean, what can you expect from those idiots."

"Sorry, this is all my fault," I say emphatically.

Graham's eyebrow rises as he tilts his head forward.

"Seriously?"

Carter laughs.

"Boss, what the hell do you have to apologize for?"

I shift my posture, running my hand through my hair.

"I did everything I could. It just wasn't enough."

Graham blinks at me as though I've uttered something absurd.

"Charlie, stop with the pity shit." Graham commands. "You acted because it was necessary. You didn't let anyone down."

Carter arches forward.

"Yeah, seriously. If it weren't for you, we'd have nothing. Less than nothing. You got us solid intel."

"Guys, it wasn't enough."

Graham shifts in place, eager to speak his mind.

"No, Charlie. This op was never meant to be. Not due to you, but because of them. It was a lost cause from the beginning."

Carter holds his arms straight up over his head, groaning.

"Well, at least now maybe you'll finally get some decent sleep."

I give him a look.

"That's what you're thinking about right now?"

"What I'm saying is, you pretty much worked double time, trying to break the case and break down doors at the same time. At least Graham and I can get some rest here and there."

Graham smirks as he changes his position.

"That's right. I do require my beauty sleep to look good when I'm busting in skulls."

"You two are the worst, but you're right."

"Well, I know where I'm heading, and it's not some shitty

dorm bunk," Graham replies. "I have a king-size bed with my name on it waiting for me."

Carter tilts his head slightly, regarding me with a prolonged gaze.

"Well, boss, I know what you ought to do."

"Oh, really, and that would be?"

"Go see Lex and relax."

I pause. Not because I don't want to, but because it's exactly what I should do. My head is still in mission mode, circling the Dragon Slayers even after I was tossed off the case.

Carter settles back in his chair, his eyes on me.

"For real, go unwind for once. There's nothing you can do here. Not tonight."

Graham agrees.

"It's fine. We're fine. Get a break from this shithole."

A tired smile pulls at my lips before I laugh quietly.

"Okay. And guys, thanks again."

It's cold outside, but I don't shiver. It is soothing to my body full of aches and pain. My breath frosts in the air as I reach for my phone.

The same old messages from me to Lex pop up.

Hey, just checking in. I'm fine.

Hey, I'm fine.

Hey, things are going well. Don't worry!

Sent at odd hours and out of context. Sent so Lex wouldn't worry.

Her answers are always prompt and full of energy, care, and comfort.

Okay, perfect!!! I was nervous!!!

Good to know! Keep me updated!

I know you are busy, but you've been on my mind <3.

I stare at the screen, scrolling backward, examining the pattern and its cadence. Lex is open, warm, offering a space where I can belong. And me? Holding my words close, my check-ins are basic. Enough to keep her from worrying. Not enough to let her in.

Why does that amazing woman put up with me?

I justify my way of living as a necessity, but it is more than that. I crave it. My work has been my drug of choice. The world is crumbling, and I feel like it needs me to hold everything together.

What is Lex's reasoning for putting up with me? For tolerating my choices that directly affect her?

Deep down, I know why; she is crazy about me. She sees the parts of me worth holding onto, worth loving, and that should mean everything. The worst part? I know I don't deserve her.

The thought lingers, but I quickly shift my focus.

Maybe I didn't deserve her before, but that doesn't mean I can't be better now, not just for her but for both of us. I press the call button without hesitation. I can't wait to hear her voice.

Lex answers on the first ring.

"Charlie? Are you alright? What happened?"

She knows I usually don't call, so I get straight to the point.

"I was taken off the case, Lex."

There is a pause, a minute too long of silence before I hear her sigh.

"Fuck, Charlie, I'm so sorry. You have to be upset about this, but I find it... well, I find it to be... absolutely amazing."

"Amazing?"

"Yes! It's a great thing, Charlie. It's a really great thing!"

"I'm lost, Lex. I don't know what to do..."

Lex replies enthusiastically.

"Well, for starters, you should come over."

She has read my mind yet again. And she's right. That's exactly what I want right now.

"Yeah. That's what I was thinking. I just want to see you."

Lex whispers.

"Charlie, I've missed you so much."

The feelings stirring inside me are warmer, stronger, and dedicated.

Her words settle before I reply.

"I've missed you too."

The drive to her place is a rare moment of tranquility. For once, I am not hurried. There is no sense of urgency, no nagging crisis waiting on the horizon, just a familiar expanse of road beckoning me to her.

Pulling into her driveway, I see her waiting outside, shivering in the cold. A mischievous grin spreads across her face as she wraps her arms around me.

I sink into Lex, wallowing in her warmth, allowing myself to melt into her, into us. Lex's hold is firm, as though she understands the magnitude of my need for her right now.

Her lips lightly touch mine, slow and tender. Her fingers brush gently down my cheek as she whispers to me.

"Hot bath. Bottle of wine. Warm meal. Then sleep. That's an order."

There is no argument from me. I follow her like a lost puppy and collapse on the couch. There is nothing left in me.

The bath Lex has prepared is soothing against my bruised skin. The lights are off, and the glow of scented candles dance on the surface of the water.

I close my eyes and try to erase the image of Montclair's murdered family from my mind. Sinking deeper into the water, I dissolve every memory from that mission and all the turmoil that followed.

For now, I am suspended in an intimate cocoon of peace as my problems wash away.

The bathroom is dark and filled with steam as I reach for a towel. Instead, I am startled by Lex standing there holding one for me. The moment our gazes meet, I see that look on her face, the playful smile pulling at the corner of her mouth.

I know that look. And I want it too.

Lex leads me to her bed and gently kisses each bruise she finds on my body. There is no sense of urgency, nothing pressing, just the gentle brush of lips across skin, the weight of Lex in my arms, and the hitch of her breath as I shift against her.

My mind is finally free of distractions. No threats are waiting for me at dawn's break.

Just this. Just her. As easily as our bodies do, I let myself get lost in each sensation, holding nothing back without needing to know what follows.

And when it's over, when we finally collapse onto tangled sheets, I know this is not the end; it's the beginning.

Lex traces slow, distracted circles on my arm, her fingertips feather-light, grounding. The warmth of her body molded against mine reminds me of how easily we fit together.

She rolls over and sits up on one elbow, staring at me.

"Well, Ms. Grayson," she laughs softly. "What's your next mission?"

"Lex, I don't know. I really don't know."

"So, take tomorrow off. Call in sick."

"That's a great way to start my first day as an analyst."

"You know you should quit."

"And do what?"

"Private security? Consulting? Charlie, you could do just about anything. Hell, we could travel the world as street performers."

"Can't sing, dance or play a guitar, we'd starve."

She smiles, gently brushing a strand of hair away from my face.

"Okay, maybe not, but you could write a hell of a book."

"Right. That's my next big plan. I'll be a writer. Fiction or nonfiction?"

"Both. And I'd read it."

"You'd have to. I'd make you edit it."

She giggles, warm and easy, and then inclines her head, giving way to something softer.

"Okay, how about a vacation? You do know what those are, right? Costa Rica, Pura Vida. "

A vacation. The very idea is so foreign. I don't say yes, I don't say no. Instead, I hold her tighter, as she rests her forehead on my chest, allowing fatigue to overtake me.

There is but one thought that enters my mind as I fall into a peaceful slumber.

I still owe her so much more.

CHAPTER 35

DECLARATION OF POWER

"Power tends to corrupt, and absolute power corrupts absolutely."

-Lord Acton

I WAKE UP slowly, basking in the afterglow of our night together. Not just physically, it goes deeper, settling into my spirit in a way that I have not felt in a very long time. Next to me, Lex is curled up, her breathing slow and rhythmic, her arm flung lazily across my hip.

My body feels lighter, my muscles limp, and my head is clear from the fog of exhaustion.

The early morning light peeks through the curtains, coaxing me to get up, but I don't want to.

Lex stirs, letting out a sweet sigh, her voice heavy with the reminisce of sleep, wrapping her arms around me.

"Morning, cutie. I'm making you breakfast."

I chuckle.

"You cook now?"

Lex shrugs, playful.

"I embrace life with a learner's mentality."

She leaps out of bed and heads for the kitchen. I decide to enjoy the moment a bit longer, listening to the chorus of cabinets opening and closing, eggs cracking, and the gentle sound of the coffee machine sputtering to life.

This is the feeling of happiness, the things I've always pushed aside for my mission and career.

My phone starts pinging, and I grab another pillow, covering my head to block out whoever is trying to reach me. The buzzing is relentless, so I surrender and reach for it.

When I see Maya's name, my stomach tightens immediately.

Hey Charlie. First, I don't want you to feel obligated to do anything here because we're no longer working on the case.

But I thought you would want to know.

The Montclair footage has apparently been leaked. The administration is creating a big scene about it.

I sit up, choking, repeatedly reading Maya's text, hoping this isn't true. Rushing to the TV, I see Lex in the kitchen, singing to herself, oblivious to the storm brewing in my mind and the outside world.

She looks up, her brow furrowing.

"Charlie, what's the matter?"

I'm silent, grabbing the remote and turning the TV channel to SLY News.

A live news conference appears, registering a shock wave of unease through my body. Thaddeus Montclair III stands at the podium, his face carefully composed for the cameras, looking paler than I remember; his features are a perfect mix of shock and sorrow. Commander Reddick is positioned to his right, eyes fixed, ready to obey any order given to him.

The Montclair video is paused behind them, unnecessary now; everyone has already viewed it.

Tuff steps forward, his expression somber, head bowed slightly.

"Today, we witnessed a tragedy," he begins, voice low. "Innocent lives lost. Families destroyed. It is a dark, dark day for our nation. Very sad. Terrible."

He pauses for a second.

"But we cannot, and I mean cannot, afford to sit around feeling bad while these terrorists plot their next attack. We have to be strong. Stronger than ever. That's why, effective immediately, I am declaring a new national state of emergency. A big one. The biggest. Full authority to eliminate the Dragon Slayers and their anarchist threats."

He leans into the microphone.

"This emergency declaration will allow us to bypass all the broken bureaucracy, and believe me, it's very broken, that has let enemies of this country hide behind red tape. Red tape everywhere. It's a disaster. We're authorizing immediate detention or deportation of individuals who endanger national stability. No trials, no appeals. None. We're creating emergency tribunals that will deliver swift, uncompromising justice outside the traditional legal system. Outside. Because the system doesn't work anymore.

"We will not wait for more lives to be lost!" His voice rises, fist slamming down on the podium. "We will not, we will not let fear spread another inch! Not on my watch! Not happening!"

The moment his fist hits the podium, firework pyrotechnics explode from the front of the stage. Red, white, and blue bursts shake the room. The doors at the back burst open, and Jackson Kane strides in, flanked by BlackSteel guards in full tactical gear, marching in formation to the rhythm of the explosions.

The crowd goes wild.

That's it. That's the end of any grief they actually felt for those children. They never saw them as anything other than a tool they could use. The theme changes from mourning to spectacle in the span of a fist hitting wood.

Kane removes his black cowboy hat with a flourish, holding it over his heart as he approaches the podium. His face is a mix of solemnity and spite, a predator wearing the mask of a patriot.

"These monsters!" he bellows, pointing his finger directly at the camera.

"Look what they've done. Look at what they will do to you and your loved ones. This isn't about money. This is about terror."

He slams his hat down on the podium.

"But let me tell you something. We have the power now. We have the control now. And we will destroy them."

The crowd roars. Kane feeds off it, his voice rising to match their fervor.

"BlackSteel will protect this great country of ours. We will hunt them down. We will root them out. And when we find them," he pauses, letting the tension build, "there will be no mercy."

The cameras pan over Tuff's passionate supporters, who erupt in cheers as if they've just been promised eternal salvation. Behind Kane, the others come into view: Sorin, Laskey, Victor, and Dr. Hart clustered together, stone-faced and watching.

The only thing that registers for me is the part no one is willing to say out loud.

This is a hostile redefinition of what it means to be a citizen. Under this emergency action, anyone can be imprisoned or deported without a hearing, without charges, without legal counsel. The right to due process, gone with a single televised signature.

Habeas corpus, a foundation of our Constitution, seems to be the next victim of this authoritarian power grab.

My fingers clutch the remote, my heart pulsating in my ears.

I barely register Lex moving beside me until her hand lightly touches my arm.

Her tone is soft but firm, pulling me back to her.

"Charlie."

I keep my gaze on the screen.

"Lex, this is going to get so much worse. They're going to use this as a pretext to go full authoritarian."

She fixes her gaze on me, intensity simmering behind her eyes.

"You don't have to do anything about it."

She's right, but we both know that might not be enough to stop me from wanting to.

The administration has everything they need in Montclair's video to succeed with a hostile takeover. That's why I tried my best to keep it confidential and not something for them to exploit.

But it's out now, and I am positive that the Dragon Slayers are behind the leak.

The video is forcing the administration's reaction. Leaving them to show their hand to the world, revealing exactly who they are.

Lex hasn't moved. I feel her suspicion and frustration before she even speaks.

Her tone grave.

"Charlie."

"Lex, I have to go in."

"Charlie, please."

"I just need to know what's going on. I need to know if there's anything I can do, if I can delay this, prevent it, or…"

"Goddamn it, Charlie! You can't stop this."

"I know that. But if they're about to institute new controls, if they're about to lock down tighter, I'd prefer to be on the inside of that."

Lex glares at me, incredulous.

"Inside? Inside BlackSteel? Charlie, do you even hear yourself?"

I remain silent, devoid of a suitable reply.

She moves in closer, her voice a gentle whisper with an undercurrent of urgency.

"I think you shouldn't get tangled back up in this mess. Forget all of this and really move on."

"Lex, if I just walk away right after being demoted, it will be a red flag. I need to step up and present myself as something more than an analyst carrying out routine tasks.

"I promise you, Lex, this is temporary. Plus, they're already intensifying their efforts on those leaving."

My hand rubs the back of my neck as I try to unravel my thoughts.

Lex's face conveys her utter disbelief.

"I'm not going to stand in your way. But if you're going back in, then I'm setting the rules for this relationship."

"Rules?"

"Charlie, three months max. If things don't change, then you have to leave."

"Lex, be reasonable. You know what this means to me…"

She cuts in fast, sharp.

"I do. More than anyone. That's why you're lucky I'm letting you have more than two weeks' notice. The FBI we swore to serve is gone. And staying now? That's not loyalty, Charlie. That's lunacy."

Lex stomps her foot forcefully, her eyes on me with the same intense stare.

"See that? That's my foot. It's down, Charlie."

A startled laugh escapes me despite everything.

"Okay, okay, I can see you mean business."

She scowls, arms still folded, chin lifted.

"That's right. Three months and you're quitting. Subject closed."

My expression hardens, but I say nothing. There is something about her refusal to back down, her ability to fiercely fight for me, for us.

I relent because, as much as I don't want to admit it, she's right.

"Alright, alright. I get it."

Lex's eyes narrow.

"No active ops either. You're to remain at a desk until you're out."

"I'll be careful," I say, raising my hands in a surrendering motion, aware that my idea of careful differs from hers.

She examines me for a moment, weighing if she should believe me, and then, with a gentle sigh, she moves in closer.

"Good. That's my girl."

Lex draws her hands over my hips, pulling me close so that my forehead rests for a moment on hers. I tilt her chin up and kiss her slowly, deeply, purposely. It is an anchor, my pledge to her.

"You better text me," she whispers.

"I'll do more than that, I'll call."

Lex pushes me back playfully.

"Now I know you're full of shit, but if you want to get there in time, you better come grab breakfast."

Her meal is delicious, better than I deserve, with everything I continue to put her through. Finishing the last bites, I get ready in a rush, pulling myself together just enough to face what's coming.

When I reach HQ, I expect to see my nameplate removed from the door, but it's still there.

Deputy Director Grayson.

The title no longer applies, and apparently, nobody has had the time to take it down yet. Guess I'll just set up here until they remember that I exist.

I head to Carter's office, knocking gently before pushing his door open.

"Wow, you look like a new you, boss."

"It's called sleep."

"Good. You deserve it."

I close the door quietly behind me.

"So, do you have any idea what's coming?"

"Yeah, it's not good."

Carter adjusts himself forward in his seat.

"The administration is launching a heavy campaign today on SLY News, a straight PR onslaught. They're going to go into the whole 'Dragon Slayers kill kids' thing, really pound it in."

"Which I suppose, is a valid argument. The real issue is the other whispers I'm picking up on."

"What kind of whispers?"

Carter taps his fingers on the surface of his desk, a wave of apprehension crossing his face.

"They're gearing up for a complete crackdown after this new order. Something big is coming."

He leans back, frustration creeping into his tone.

"What's worse is I'm being shut out. The new system they've been implementing is deploying quickly. Many of my old channels are going dark.

"There were places I could look in before, track movement, and follow resource deployment, and now? Nothing. It's as if somebody's pulled a goddamn blackout curtain across sections of the intelligence grid."

"How much access do you have?"

His fingers start drumming against the arm of his chair.

"I still have my sources, but boss, this is different. BlackSteel is using Sorakin Tech to compartmentalize information, even from individuals who used to have full access. Bad, bad omen.

"Sorin is up to something, and he doesn't want anyone outside his inner circle to see it coming. Have to admit, though, the dude's platform is the real deal. It's what happens when you throw unlimited money at the smartest people alive and let them do their thing without any red tape."

If they're cutting off access to people like Carter, then they're moving toward total control.

"Anything we can do?" I ask.

Carter frowns.

"I'm stumped. Guess we just hope for the best."

His words land heavy, pressing down with an undeniable finality. He's right. We're stuck watching it all unfold. I make my way back to my office, the weight of our conversation pressing down on me like a storm about to break.

Only a few steps down the hallway, I bump into a frazzled but well-rested Graham.

"Charlie. Do you know what's going on?"

Graham is rarely this worked up unless there's a good reason for it. I look suspiciously around us to make sure we are alone.

"I just spoke with Carter," I whisper. "He doesn't have any insight, just a feeling that something big is coming."

"Reddick ordered me to get my men ready. No details or target. Just be prepared."

Reddick is not a man who messes around. If he orders

Graham to get his team ready without providing him with any information, then the mission is already underway.

"Charlie, this is a major play. You must have something on the Dragon Slayers? Damn it, I thought Carter could dig up something else."

"He has been completely shut out. And remember, I'm just an analyst now."

"I think BlackSteel, the administration, they've uncovered something. That's why they're mobilizing."

Maybe BlackSteel has uncovered a lead, or maybe they've pinpointed a location, a key player, something significant enough to justify action. It's possible that the crackdown goes beyond mere public narrative.

"So, what do we do?" Graham's words are edged with defeat.

"Nothing, we can't do anything about it now."

He doesn't fight it, but he doesn't like it either.

It's as if we're trapped inside a burning house, watching the flames creep steadily towards us.

The way out is clear, but we find ourselves paralyzed.

CHAPTER 36

THE RIGHT TO OBEY

"Sic semper tyrannis."

-Marcus Junius Brutus

I MAKE MY way back to my office, even though there is nothing for me to do.

My clearance has not yet been revoked, but I have not been assigned anything either. If they are trying to make me feel useless, they are succeeding.

With little else to keep me occupied, I soak up the available information in the news, status reports, and the atmosphere of public opinion. If I am stranded here, at least I can track how the world is evolving.

Polls show that public sentiment against billionaires has gone up dramatically. They're not mourning Thaddeus Montclair's loss at all; it's exactly the opposite reaction the administration was hoping for.

I read through the comment threads, watching the flood of real-time responses pour in.

Thaddeus Montclair III literally couldn't handle having $999 million, so he let his family die. WTF is wrong with him???

Dragon Slayers are right. Greed is an illness. That guy could've easily been richer than 99.999% of the world's population, yet it was not enough for him.

Billionaires are accountable for deaths every day over money. Given the decision between wealth and people's lives, they always choose money. And we're supposed to be surprised he chose it over his family? They're the actual monsters here.

Of course, he did that. Billionaires are terrible people. We all know this by now, right?

I recline, observing the numbers rise, thousands of likes, shares, retweets. The administration is desperate to trumpet the billionaire-as-victim angle, but it's not catching on.

The rage is no longer directed at the Dragon Slayers. It's directed at the system that created them in the first place.

The news headlines tell the same story.

Millions in Federal Charity Funds Frozen as Crackdown on 'Terrorism' Widens

State Governments Must Look After Themselves as Federal Funds are Relocated to Freedom Zones.

Public Outcry as BlackSteel Increases Private Policing Contracts

Rather than inspiring fear of the Dragon Slayers, Tuff's regime has emerged as the greater evil. The harder they push, the more resilient the resistance of the people grows. Protests are being stirred up, not for the Dragon Slayers, but to demand genuine change.

More interview clips offer confirmation.

We don't approve of what they did, but we can't dismiss why it happened.

The billionaire class is out of control, and people are desperate. We need reforms, not retaliation.

Reviewing the latest poll figures, I see Tuff's approval ratings are at a historic low. As the election gets closer, if these trends persist, he stands in serious danger.

It's unappealing, but I turn on SLY News, anyway. The Montclair video will obviously be the hot topic, and I need to see how they're spinning it.

The screen flickers to life, and there he is, Rocker Callahan. Trademark red bowtie accenting his overly starched shirt. Hair dramatically styled, too perfect to be real.

Callahan leans forward on the desk, ready to deliver his sermon.

"I can barely believe I'm saying this, but here we are," his tone solemn but insincere.

"Children are being murdered in America. And not just any children. Good children. The kind of young men and women who were destined to shape this country's future.

"We're not talking about street kids raised by a pack of wolves. We're not talking about anchor babies or children of undocumented immigrants who sneak into our country and drain our culture."

He pounds his desk to garner full attention.

"No! These were well-mannered, respectful, true American children."

Callahan's voice tightens.

"These precious children stand for the values we built this nation on. They are not out there causing trouble. They are attending prep schools. Practicing violin. Learning leadership.

"They know the proper way to shake a hand. They know how to say sir and ma'am. These are the kind of kids who grow up to run companies, create jobs, maybe even sit in this chair one day."

His expression is sorrowful, as if he is giving a eulogy, but it's only a performance. There's no true sadness in his eyes. Just satisfaction. Just the self-importance of a man who knows exactly how much airtime he gets and how many people still believe in him.

"The Dragon Slayers are exploiting every loophole we've got," he says, tapping his pen against his desk. "Because of outdated constitutional delays, they're using the laws of this country as weapons against the very people who built it."

He leans in closer.

"And don't fool yourself into thinking it ends with the billionaires. No, no, no. That's just the beginning. If they can claim a billion is too much, what makes you think they'll stop there? Sooner or later, a million will be too much. Then, a hundred thousand. Then ten. Then five."

Callahan throws his hands up into the air.

"Maybe next, it's having a car. Or a home. Or wearing a shirt with the wrong logo. Don't you see? They're not trying to balance the system. They're trying to erase it. Trying to erase us, trying to erase you."

He pauses for dramatic effect, then continues.

"First, they come for the billionaires. The true heroes among us. The innovators. The protectors. The job creators. And next? They come for whomever's left. The easier targets. The quieter ones. The ones who still dare to stand in the way of their destruction.

"And that's why we can't wait. That's why we must act now."

He smooths his bowtie, proud of himself. Every word scripted. Every pause well-rehearsed.

"The legal system is broken. We all know it. It was built for a simpler time. But thanks to Sorakin Technologies, BlackSteel, and the brilliance of our country's top innovators, we don't have to keep waiting.

"We can act. Swiftly. Precisely. Permanently."

His voice becomes subdued but remains firm.

"And that's what this new emergency order does. It allows us to remove threats before they fester. Before they poison more minds."

He spreads his arms as if he's wrapping the country in a warm embrace.

"Because this isn't about class. It's about character. These purebred American kids are the best. And now they're gone. And if you don't care about that, maybe you were never really part of this great country to begin with."

The segment ends. SLY News rolls straight into another talking head who's already parroting the same lines.

True American children.

What I have just heard is beyond perplexing.

Callahan's words echo louder than the rest. So, the other children don't matter? The ones who never get a fair chance because they don't have the right last name or were not born into wealth?

The only people who cry for those disadvantaged children are their families. Parents buried in grief and bills are left to suffer alone in silence.

I flip the channel again and land on a live panel. A serious, even-toned moderator sits between Attorneys Miles Archer and Eugene Lasky. For once, it's not a shouting match. Instead, it is a somewhat civil conversation, which makes it feel worse.

Archer seems composed, but there's heat behind his voice.

"Let me make something perfectly clear. This order doesn't protect anyone's freedom. It destroys it. You don't even have to be remotely involved with the Dragon Slayers for the government to show up at your door.

"Someone points a finger and says you're part of them, and

boom, you're gone. Shipped off to whatever facility they want, in whatever country they choose.

"That is not justice. That is not the law. And it sure as hell is not American. They are taking the legal system away from us, piece by piece, and dressing it up as patriotism. It's disgusting."

The moderator nods, turning evenly to Lasky.

"Mr. Lasky, your response?"

Lasky adjusts his cufflink.

"Oh, of course, Archer, who is a highly paid defense attorney, is upset. Let's all take a moment to have a pity party for the guy who's made millions exploiting the loopholes of a broken system.

"Mr. Archer here is very passionate. But what he's really upset about is that we're finally closing the gates on people like him, people who've spent their careers twisting the law to protect criminals and block justice."

He turns slightly toward the camera.

"And let's be honest. With how much sympathy he's shown for that terrorist organization lately, it's reasonable to say he sounds a little like a Dragon Slayer. Now, I'm not making accusations, of course, but there are questions being asked about your motives in serious legal circles."

Miles cuts in, sharp and steady.

"You see, folks? Right there. Right on cue. Just that accusation alone... after this new order. They'll be able to detain me, lock me up, and ship me off to whatever offshore site they want.

"And that's the issue. That's the danger. And I get it, I really do. They'll say these people are terrorists. They'll say they're monsters. Fine. Then prove it. Use the system. Use the courts. Use the Constitution. That's what it's there for.

"Because if they can take one person without evidence, they

can take anyone. And if you don't care about that now, you will when they come for you or your loved ones."

Lasky chuckles.

"Please. The only thing we're trying to lock up is chaos. And if you don't support this, maybe it's time to ask what side you're really on. Because in America, we stand for law and order."

The moderator concludes the interview with a cordial thank you to both guests. No theatrical fireworks. Just two visions of the country sitting side by side, trying to authenticate that their talking points are equally valid.

I mute the TV.

The terrifying part is that we're debating whether the Constitution should still apply. And people are nodding along like this is normal.

A loud, deliberate knock at my door breaks my news information overload. I lift my gaze as the door bursts open.

Reddick stands there smirking, as if he has just caught me in some transgression.

His eyes dart towards my nameplate on the door.

"Grayson, don't get too comfortable in here."

"Nobody told me where to go, Commander."

He laughs, his presence permeating the room like a bad odor that refuses to leave.

"Don't worry, Grayson. We'll have you in the pen where you belong in no time."

"Looking forward to it, sir."

His grin widens as though he has just shared a joke with me that he will relish for years to come.

"All-hands meeting. Assembly hall. Now."

He does not wait for me to respond. Instead, he turns and walks away, confident that I will jump up and tag along.

Whatever this is, it carries immense weight, and I am not in any hurry to find out what it is.

The corridors are filled with individuals, bodies crowding through in whispering waves towards the direction of the hall. Faces masked with concern and confusion, while others are unmistakably grim. Pushing through the crowd of people, I see the subtle shifts and undercurrents around me.

BlackSteel security is imposing. Guards patrolling each hallway crossing observe the crowd as if we're cattle going to slaughter. They're searching for negative reactions.

The auditorium smells like sterilized metal and fresh paint, but it's the silence that unnerves me most. Every inch of this place is polished, prepped, and militarized. Rows of chairs stretch out in tight formation, lined with BlackSteel agents, analysts, and whatever's left of the Bureau's spine.

Even the Sorakin drones are different, sleeker, darker, more aggressive in posture. The mutt patrols are in tactical formation, marching down every aisle. Mounted rifles are locked in place as targeting systems glow faintly beneath red-tinted lenses.

Jackson Kane steps onto the stage in a tailored black suit with blood-red accents stitched into the lapels and down the seams. His cowboy hat mirrors his clothes, giving him the appearance of a country singer on a fascist propaganda tour. His smile flashes with perfect confidence as the overhead lights catch the silver pin on his chest: the emblem of BlackSteel.

"Thank you all for being here today," he says smoothly, voice amplified across the room. "As you've seen, the Dragon Slayer menace was something the government failed to contain. Their weakness cost lives, peace, and stability. But that failure ends with us."

He starts to pace the edge of the stage, slow and deliberate.

"It is now up to BlackSteel, up to each and every one of you, to preserve this patriotic nation we all love. And to do so, we will use every tool at our disposal."

Everyone listens. Rigid, alert, afraid to be the first one to react incorrectly.

Kane spreads his arms, entitlement never leaving his face.

"With the new authority granted, we are no longer bound by slow, outdated procedures. We are streamlining everything efficiently, permanently. This is what emergency orders were made for. To ensure that when it counts, we act fast, we act smart, and we act without apology."

He turns slightly, gesturing behind him.

"Commander Reddick. Mr. Sorin. Gentlemen."

Alexander Sorin glides onto the stage as if he's floating. Simple white t-shirt, disheveled silver hair, and an expression so odd it barely registers as human.

The screen behind him lights up with graphs and wireframe diagrams, production metrics, rollout charts, drone schematics.

"Thank you, Jackson," Sorin replies. "And thank you to the staff here for embracing the transition to Sorakin systems. You've adapted quickly, and we appreciate your teamwork and compliance.

"I'm pleased to announce that our C.E.R.B.E.R.U.S. combat platforms and suppression drones have scaled up production to over ten thousand units per month. And that's only the beginning."

Sorin continues, tapping a small controller in his hand. The screen behind him displays a glowing neural net, red dots pinpointing cities, suburbs, even neighborhoods. A heat map of guilt.

"Thanks to our predictive learning model, we no longer need to rely on manual clearance or subjective oversight. The net compiles behavioral history, biometric data, spending patterns, online posts, affiliations. Once the criteria are met, the system renders a verdict automatically."

Sorin manages a polite smile.

"If the subject is deemed a security threat, a BlackSteel unit with Sorakin drones is dispatched. Immediate containment. No delay. No legal review. Continental Containment receives the transfer directly.

"By removing the human element, we've achieved what democracy never could, perfect administration."

Sorin steps aside with quiet grace, as Reddick stomps forward, a battering ram in human form.

He doesn't bother using the mic.

"They wanted a war," he says gruffly, talking to his squads of enforcers huddled along the front rows. Well, now they're gonna get one."

There's no showmanship or euphemisms. Only rage.

"They thought they could flood the system and stop us. Let 'em try. With Sorkin bots, we're building a force that can't be outnumbered anymore."

I catch the unrestrained firebrand look in his eyes.

"From here forward, we hit harder. Faster. Anyone with even a hint of association to those Dragon Slayers or any other anti-administration group will be singled out. It doesn't matter who they are or even if they served or retired with honors. If they're a risk, they're gone.

"Military, contractors, public officials, we're reviewing every record. Every connection. There are rumors of something new out there, a new movement. Whatever it is, whoever it is, we shut it down. We don't let them organize. We don't let them breathe."

He looks to his team, dead center.

"We will make them submit and obey!"

A ripple moves through the hall like cold air.

Reddick nods, more than satisfied.

"Briefing over."

No one claps. There's nothing to celebrate. Everyone carefully starts to stand as if they're trying not to set off a landmine.

I stay seated a moment longer, watching as Kane flashes another easy smile and steps back into the shadows. Sorin vanishes behind a parting curtain of security. Reddick's already barking orders to his men before he's even off the stage.

Looking around the room, I can see it on their faces. Most understand exactly what this means.

BlackSteel, along with whatever is left of the FBI and other agencies, will now be used to round up and deport anyone Tuff and his administration deem to be the slightest opposition.

This country was built on the right to challenge power.

Now, challenging it in any way makes you a target.

CHAPTER 37

THE ROGUE REGIME

"We cannot ignore the fact that much of the world is ruled by governments that do not reflect the will or interests of their people."

-RONALD REAGAN

THE ROOM IS shrouded in suffocating silence. No one whispers, just a void of those who know that whatever they say may doom them.

Carter is the first to shatter the silence around us, speaking softly enough for our small group to hear his voice.

"That was fucking insane."

Graham doesn't hide his frustration at all.

"This is bullshit."

Carter throws a glance around.

"Can they actually do this? Just… change the entire legal system?"

Maya wraps her arms around herself, an anxious expression on her face.

"I mean, I suppose they just did."

She's right. The reality is we knew this day was coming. Perhaps not in these precise words or at this exact moment, but this was always the administration's predestined objective.

I look around the room, noting that FBI agents and analysts are still seated, some murmuring amongst themselves, others gazing at the empty podium where Reddick's warning was unfurled. There is no doubt in my mind that many of them can't process what is transpiring.

This is now a war on dissent.

Maya inclines in, her voice hushed with concern.

"So… what do we do?"

That's the real question, isn't it?

Quitting means being replaced by individuals who will be eager to carry out these orders. Staying means becoming a part of this authoritarian regime.

Graham's mind is already made up.

"This is only going to get worse. We need to get out before it does."

"Graham, we have to choose the lesser of two evils." I reply, "BlackSteel won't hesitate to swap us out for people who won't think twice about pulling the trigger."

Carter cocks his head to the side, his reply dissonant.

"So, we stay. Play along."

His tone makes me uncomfortable. It's one of shame and vulnerability, but perhaps he is right.

"For now, we stay and do as instructed. We need to be on alert and look out for each other."

"I second that." Maya replies.

Graham is full of skepticism.

"Bad idea, people."

"So is running," I state firmly.

"Alright Charlie. But if things go down the shitter, don't tell me that I didn't warn all of you."

"Guys, I promise. We'll get out before that day comes."

Returning to my office, I find a figure in front of my door. It's a maintenance worker unscrewing my name plate.

I pause for half a second, long enough to watch the last screw come loose, long enough to absorb the permanence of it.

He looks up at me.

"Sorry, been so gosh darn busy taking all these things down."

Another voice rings out. A Blacksteel agent waves vaguely toward the analyst section as if he's directing me to a new parking space.

"Oh, yeah. Reddick told me you're in the pen now. Your office stuff is in a box on the floor somewhere over there."

I accept it without a fight.

"Right. The pen."

He doesn't say anything else. Doesn't need to. He knows I am irrelevant.

I slip past him and make my way to the open-floor analyst section. A box on a table has my last name scribbled on it in thick red letters.

The room is packed, desks jammed into tight rows, classified databases easily visible on unguarded screens. An annoying, persistent buzz of conversation and equipment mingles in the air.

There is no structure here, just misplaced FBI agents crushed between an unsettling number of BlackSteel operatives.

I settle into a hard mesh office chair, my view enabling me to observe other employees pretending to look busy. It's easy to spot the BlackSteel personnel, new faces fumbling through procedures they clearly don't understand.

Their fingers move slowly over their keyboards, eyes staring blankly at the screens, a telling sign that they don't know the first thing about what it takes to work here.

They are quasi-analysts, just another arm of the government crackdown. Warm, obedient bodies ordered to flag whatever or whoever they see fit without understanding the full consequences of their actions.

I unpack the few items that were thrown into my box. My desk name plate is gone, and so is almost everything else.

No time to dwell on things lost, it's just stuff. I fire up my laptop, waiting for something, anything to appear.

A notification appears on my screen.

My first assignment. I open up the file.

Identifying possible terrorist sympathizers.

I scroll through the parameters.

Liking a post related to the Dragon Slayers.

Sharing a video discussing their ideology.

Following an account that has engaged with pro-Dragon Slayer content.

Sending or receiving any money to an account that is linked to the Dragon Slayers.

It's a declaration of Dragon Slayer direct offences. There is to be no engagement with them in any way, shape or form. Senseless encounters that now bear the burden of suspicion.

I breathe out slowly, my fingers poised on my mouse as I scroll down. The list goes on, longer than it should be. And it just keeps growing.

Another notification comes in.

Carter: Boss, I need to see you. Head on over.

Without asking if I need permission to leave, I push away from my desk, my chair squeaking in defiance.

The brass plate on his door still bears his name, Carter Diaz,

Cyber Operations. Entering his office, I shut the door quietly behind me. He doesn't speak, just points to his split monitors.

Lancelot and Guinevere are on the screen.

"Our two friends have posted additional videos," he says.

"Carter, why am I not surprised? Of course, they would."

Whatever these videos contain is only going to make things even worse.

He pushes files off a chair, pulling it up next to him for me to sit. Then hits a button that makes Lancelot come to life.

There he stands in the same poorly lit room, his signature black-and-gold mask, as always, the focal point of attention. His voice bites with the power to make everyone who listens captive.

This corrupt administration is showing its true colors.

Confronted with overwhelming pressure from the people,

*with millions calling for the billionaire class
to be divested from its grip on society,*

they were at a crossroads.

*They could have listened. They could have
done their job to represent the people.*

But as always, they succumbed to their masters.

*They chose to leave the masses behind in
an effort to save their wealth.*

Now, in their desperation, they have committed the unthinkable.

He waits before speaking again, a momentary flash of calculated control.

They've torn down democracy.

*Centuries of striving, revolutions, and blood-
shed all destroyed in a moment.*

Not in the name of security. Not in the interest of stability.
But fueled by greed.
In their quest to protect their billionaire masters,
they've stripped away your freedoms, erased
your right to defend yourself,
and shattered the legal foundations this country was built on.

Lancelot's tone darkens, each word sharper, laced with quiet threats.

This is no longer just a war on billionaires,
it has become a battle against the system that empowers them.
It is a battle with the machine that removes your choices from you,
that insists your voice no longer has any value.
That machine only requires that you be pres-
ent to further their agenda.

There is a pungent silence.

Lancelot wants every word to sink in, deep. He is reaching out not only to his loyalists but to the entire world. Then he bends forward, voice cutting sharp.

The Dragon Slayers will not fight alone.
We will stand with any force, any move-
ment, any group willing to commit
to restoring real democracy and returning this country to its people.
This government has forfeited its legitimacy.
It no longer represents the public; it defends power, not freedom.
And now is the time for action.

They are desperate.

They tighten their grip not from strength but fear.

With every law they pass, every right they strip away,

they reveal just how little control they have left.

But we will not back down.

We will strike until they understand

that the world will not allow them to
enslave the future of humanity.

Lancelot speaks with conviction, his statements foreboding warnings.

And then, he releases the truth that makes him more dangerous, more frightening than any government smear campaign.

We are not good people. We don't pretend to be heroes.

We are monsters, but sometimes, monsters are necessary.

Sometimes, only those willing to embrace the dark-
ness can tear down those who thrive in it,

who hide behind a rigged system designed to protect them.

Our purpose is defined, our mission is clear,

and we will not stop until the corrup-
tion they built is nothing but ash.

A lengthy silence. Then, at last, he speaks with finality.

This is not the end. This is the beginning.

The screen fades to black.
Carter doesn't try to hide his disbelief.

"Boss, he's making a real move to overthrow the government."

My response is impulsive.

"Do you think it could even work?"

Carter delays his reply, clearly considering the seriousness of my question.

"No clue. We both know that some people in the military, the government, and law enforcement are disillusioned. If the Dragon Slayers can organize them, if they can turn this into something bigger, they might actually have the means to pull off a coup."

He has very valid points, it's something I've been considering as well.

"Carter, if you had told me before that this was the Dragon Slayers plan all along, I would have said they're dead on arrival.

"The Dragon Slayers have done more than just survive. They've thrived, and more importantly, the public is now embracing them."

Carter makes a sly grin.

"Ready for the second act? The lovely Miss Guinevere is up next."

I lift an eyebrow.

"Lovely?"

He shrugs, smiling.

"What? She's got a certain charm."

A small laugh escapes me.

"If you have a crush, you can tell me."

Carter doesn't miss a beat.

"Right, you know liking the Dragon Slayers makes you a terrorist. What do you think having a crush on one does?"

"Probably lands you in the deepest, darkest BlackSteel pit."

Carter chuckles half-heartedly as he reaches out to his screen, making some adjustments.

"Okay. Let's hear what she has to say."

With a touch of a key, Guinevere appears.

The contrast is immediate. Where Lancelot emanates raw power, she is poised, elegant, contained.

The room behind her is softly lit as warm shadows embrace her fine features. She sits casually, her face a mask of calm amusement, as if she's addressing an old friend.

Guinevere knowingly tilts her head, smiling.

Good tidings, Resistance!

As I'm sure many of you have seen,

a video was recently released by the administration.

They are going to great lengths to ensure that their video

makes its way into every home, every screen,
and every corner of this nation.

They want you to view it, over and over.

They want you to see that we are truly monsters.

She raises her hands a little, a subtle movement as if she is framing the narrative in the present.

You saw Lancelot stand over Thaddeus Mont-
clair III and deliver an ultimatum.

It was actually an easy choice.

He could give up his billions, his empire.

He still would have hundreds of mil-
lions left and his family would live.

But he chose greed.

Guinivere bows her head as if paying respects to Montclair's murdered family.

That's the challenge we have.

*If your own flesh and blood, your own
family, can't surpass your greed,*

then what hope do your neighbors have? Your workers?

The rest of the world?

If their wealth means more to them than their wife and children,

what do you think they believe your worth is?

Her tone remains steady, but beneath its surface it's caustic, intended to wound.

This isn't some horrific, unusual occurrence.

This isn't something out of the ordinary.

This is who they are.

Guinevere's pause is perfectly timed.

So yes, we did it.

We killed the Montclair family. Mother and children.

Innocent lives lost to greed.

We never claimed we were good people.

We never claimed we were righteous.

We are no heroes.

We're not here to be moral examples.

We are here to question and destroy this broken system.

Guinevere frowns, lips curling downward.

But you want to discuss outrage?

Okay, let's do that.

Because the way this administration is acting,

the single death of a child is something
that can never be allowed, right?

The screen flickers, revealing a number beside her. It is a genuine statistic, a grim death toll.

30,000 children each year die in the US
from issues related to poverty.

5 million die each year globally.

The numbers are damning.
Guinevere lets out a long sigh.

Every single day, children starve.

Every single day, they are denied medi-
cal care, shelter, and clean water.

Every single day, they die, because of men
like Thaddeus Montclair III.

Because of their greed.

Because of the billionaires who inflate prices,

slash wages, tear apart social programs,

cut benefits, all in the name of accumulating ever-greater profits.

Her fingers extend a little, her posture unchanged, her expression unwavering.

When parents of a child are laid off in the
interest of shareholders' profits,

when families are left homeless as rents skyrocket out of their reach,

when a mother must make the painful choice
to feed her child or keep the lights on.

Who do you think is responsible?

Guinevere's voice is flavored with something dark.

The government needs you to mourn one family.

But where is their indignation for the millions?

Where is their grief for the starving? For the homeless?

For the kids who die before they even get a shot at life?

She stares deeper into the screen, burning her words into everyone's souls.

They don't care.

They view kids as tools to be used when
they can advance their agenda.

But we know. We see the truth. We know their fears.

And we know that this fear is growing.

They are desperate. They are panicked. And soon?

Guinevere dusts off her hands, signaling her speech is coming to an end.

We will finish them off.

Good tidings, Resistance.

Carter and I are wedged in place, still trying to process her statements.

He speaks first.

"Jesus, the worst part is it's hard to argue with what she's saying."

"She's right about everything," I groan. "The fake outrage. The convenience of anger. The denial of any responsibility."

"Yeah, boss. That's what makes her so damn dangerous."

"Carter, she's more than dangerous because now people are really listening."

I glance down at my watch. Time's up.

"Sorry, Carter, wish I could stay longer, but I don't want anyone to start looking for me."

As I walk out of his office, my head spins with the totality of everything we just saw. My pace is slow enough so that by the time I reach the pen, I have managed to bury it all deep inside me.

This analyst work is brainless for me. I scan flagged names, checking off the obvious ones, allowing others to filter through.

Then a message comes in with no warning. Donovan Pierce.

Meet me at Mathers. 25 minutes. It's important.

I stare at it, then fire back.

Donovan, I'm not Deputy Director anymore. I can connect you with someone else.

Three dots flash immediately as he responds.

Titles don't mean shit. Meet me.

Part of me just wants to delete the message and forget about him, but something about the timing and the tone tells me this isn't one of his games.

I decide to take my lunch break and go.

The place is a run-down outdoor joint tucked behind a building that's probably half-abandoned.

Chain-link fence on uneven concrete with umbrellas faded by the sun.

When I get there, he's already seated with two empty glasses and another drink half gone. Cigarette in one hand, lighter still between his fingers.

He doesn't look up.

"Donovan."

He exhales smoke through his nose and gestures to the chair across from him.

"Thanks for coming kid."

I sit, cautiously.

"Not sure what I can offer you anymore. Like I said, I was kicked off the Dragon Slayer case."

He waves a hand.

"You still know things. I need insight."

"Insight? Into what?"

He glances at me for the first time. His eyes are bloodshot, but sharp.

"I'll be blunt, Charlie. Are you with BlackSteel and the administration or not?"

My spine stiffens. I study his face, trying to read what this is. A trap? A loyalty test? Is he wired?

"Donovan, the administration's in charge. And with Black-Steel's... involvement, there've been changes. But I still believe in the FBI. I believe in the law."

He knocks back the rest of his drink and lets out a raspy laugh.

"Christ. You're like the Virgin Mary."

"Cut the shit Donovan, I'm tired of your washed-up, self-pitying crap. Why am I here?"

He leans back, flicks his cigarette onto the concrete, and lights another before answering.

"Simone was fired this morning."

I blink.

"What?"

He takes a long drag.

"Yup."

"She pushed back. Told them no. Whatever they're trying to pull, she wasn't going to be part of it. So, they replaced her. Not officially, of course. She'll get a bullshit press release about early retirement."

I sit with that. The weight of it.

"What about you?"

His look becomes serious.

"That's the problem. They're asking questions I have the answers to, but they're the kind of questions I don't like.

"Not how do we find terrorists. It's the real ugly shit, how to control population zones, how to make people disappear. Stuff you don't ask unless you're planning a regime change."

His hand trembles slightly as he brings the cigarette to his lips.

"I'm a piece of shit, I know this, hell I have come to embrace it at times. Someone has to be if you want to get anything done, and I figured that's why I am here in the first place. The problem is, I don't do this shit here to Americans and it sounds like that's what this administration wants now."

I stare at him, as I recall the files Carter dug up on this man sitting across from me now.

"Why are you telling me this? With everything going on, this could be considered treason, and you know it."

Donovan exhales smoke through his nose, eyes drifting upward like he's watching the sky crack. Then his expression shifts in the most brutal way.

"I'm telling you because I don't give a fuck anymore. They want to lock me up? Let 'em. I'm dying anyway. Stage four. Lungs. Shocker, right?"

He lifts the cigarette like a toast.

"Doctor says I've got maybe a year if I stop smoking and play nice, but fuck that. So yeah, I figured why not finally try to do one good fucking thing in my life before I punch out.

"Might not be redemption. But at least it's not silence. Plus, you remind me of myself. Back when I still believed in work. Before I gave away the last parts of my humanity."

He finishes the last sip of his drink, stands up slowly, and tosses a few bills on the table. Then he looks at me one last time.

"If I get anything real, I'll find you. If not… maybe this is it for us. Good luck, kid."

He walks off without waiting for a response.

I sit there in silence, the smell of smoke still hanging in the air, watching a ghost walk away in daylight.

If Donovan Pierce is spooked, if he's finally drawing lines, then this is worse than I ever imagined.

With Simone gone, the agencies are being swallowed whole. Every part of the machine I thought I knew is being consumed piece by piece, until there's nothing left but a new system of control.

Before, I might have pressed him for more or tried to help, but I'm past that now. I won't throw myself into the fire for nothing.

So, I leave it where it is, letting the thought fade, and turn myself back toward the work that still waits for me.

Mask back on as I settle back into the pen. No one's paying any attention to me. At least not yet.

The hours drag on, but I don't care. I perform the actions, reminding myself that this is all temporary. A character I'm pretending to be. A game I'm playing. Waiting for the epiphany of what comes next.

One thing is certain now. Lex is constant.

That is more than enough to get me through the rest of the day.

I shut down my screen, push my chair back, and step away from the madness.

Whatever happens next, I know that she will always be there for me.

CHAPTER 38

PAPER DRAGONS

"It is not the man who has too little, but the man who craves more, that is poor."

-SENECA

THE CITY FADES into a blur of headlights and street signs, my hands resting on the steering wheel as I escape BlackSteel HQ.

Wake up, go to work, and then see Lex. It's a rhythm developing, one I am quickly becoming fond of and willing to navigate.

There's still a part of me screaming inside, I should be more involved with everything happening at work. BlackSteel clawing for more power, the Dragon Slayers expanding their influence, the slow erosion of our democratic society, but none of it is in the car with me right now.

I'm simply on my way to her.

Arriving at Lex's place, I make my way inside, no need to knock. Her door is always open for me. The aroma inside is warm and welcoming as I step into her kitchen.

Lex greets me with a kiss and, without saying a word, goes back to putting the finishing touches on what will be another appetizing meal.

Her dinners are a real luxury after eating takeout food and snack machine offerings. Pure necessity without any enjoyment. She is teaching me to learn to embrace the simple things in life.

After dinner and dishes, Lex and I curl up on the couch with a bottle of wine, carelessly channel surfing, paying little attention to the usual late-night shows.

My attention is caught by a live timer ticking away in the corner, but what stops me in my tracks is Alan Schmutt's face on the screen.

"What the hell is this?" I blurt out.

"Oh, yeah. Charlie, forget about this shit. It's just Schmutt doing some kind of live event. Another 'billionaires are our saviors' campaign. Only this one is a rally to help Tuff's re-election."

She turns to me, curiosity in her eyes.

"You really wanna watch this?"

The screen holds my attention longer than it should, and I finally admit it.

"In spite of how much I despise Schmutt, I have to say seeing him make an ass of himself is really one of my guilty pleasures."

Lex starts laughing.

"Okay, okay. I won't judge you too hard."

She puts the remote down and snuggles in beside me.

As the counter on the TV hits zero, the screen fades. Dramatic orchestra music blasts out, the kind played in a B-rated movie when the hero saves the day. The picture comes alive with cameras panning a half-empty arena.

The footage cuts to black. For a moment, there's nothing, and then white text fades in, solemn and slow, creating a strong visual impact.

PROTECT OUR JOBS!

The scene shifts to a stark, industrial warehouse. Billionaire Jeb Brazen stands on one side of a conveyor belt, carefully handing a package to an overworked factory employee. Brazen turns to the camera with a wide, empty smile and gives a thumbs up, another corporate smoke and mirrors act.

The frame fades, and another white text message appears.

PROTECT OUR FAMILIES!

The screen shifts to children outside, laughing, running, and working together to solve puzzles. Then, the image softly fades. A dull white overhead glow replaces the sunlight.

The same children now sit perfectly still in sleek white chairs, each wearing a VR headset. Their hands twitch gently, mimicking motions.

The camera glides past them, slowly and gracefully, only to reveal billionaire Zach Mucker seated at the center. He turns to the lens, smiles with practiced warmth, and lifts a thumbs up like he's given them a world better than reality.

The video fades to black again as a different set of words appear.

PROTECT OUR VALUES!

A peaceful protest moves through a tree-lined plaza full of families, students, and signs waving in the breeze. Billionaire Edward Voros stands near the walkway, calm and smiling. He hands a small protest sign to a young girl who proudly holds it high as she joins the march.

It reads: *CAPITALISM IS AMERICAN!*

The screen abruptly turns black, holding viewers in limbo as they await the next scene.

Then they appear.

Billionaires seated against plain backdrops, perfectly centered to talk directly to their audience.

Each takes a turn to speak, words spliced in perfect rhythm.

We've created millions of jobs...

...invested in the future...

...taken risks no one else would dare to...

...sacrificed our personal life, family, everything...

...all to make the world a better place for you.

...and now we're under attack for it.

Finally, it shifts to Alan Schmutt in the same black-and-white staged room. He's too close to the lens, eyes wide, posture stiff like he's holding back a rant.

I'm not gonna let them tear this apart. Not our companies, not this country, not the future of humanity. You hear me? I won't let them destroy everything we've built.

The crowd in the arena erupts in cheers.

That's when it hits me, not the propaganda or the polished editing or even the arrogance of it all. I remember when some of these people used to hate each other. Political rivals. Opposing industries. Public feuds so messy they trended for weeks.

But now?

Now they stand together. They're unified not by belief or morality or even necessity... just fear. Fear of losing the one thing they all still have: power.

I wonder if it's always been this way. If all the rest of us were just noise to distract from the fact that the people at the top never truly fight each other because deep down, they know they're on the same side.

And that's not the end, not for Schmutt.

Massive screens flash a golden filter of Alan Schmutt pictures, each image fading into the next: him shaking hands with world leaders, overseeing space launches, standing on a cliffside staring at the horizon like a prophet.

His name is stretched across them in bold, blinding golden letters.

THE SMARTEST AND RICHEST MAN IN HISTORY

THE HERO THE WORLD NEEDS. THE GEN-
ERATIONAL GENIUS OF OUR TIME.

Lex groans beside me.

"I'm literally going to die from cringe, Charlie."

"Just wait; it will get worse."

The slideshow continues, the music building as new words materialize over a slow-motion clip of Schmutt dramatically removing his sunglasses in a bomber jacket.

HE SAVED THE WORLD WITH INNOVATION.

NOW, HE'S SAVING HUMANITY BY TAKING
US WHERE NO MAN HAS GONE.

The cameras try to project the illusion of a full house, strategically broadcasting only the most rabid of his supporters. The ones screaming, waving signs, and losing their minds.

An announcer's voice echoes through the speakers.

"Please welcome... the savior of innovation, the protector of wealth, the most brilliant mind in human history... Alan Schmutt!"

Lights explode across the stage in synchronized bursts. The massive digital screens behind the podium flash between slogans:

WEALTH IS STRENGTH.

BILLIONAIRES BUILT AMERICA.

PROTECT INNOVATION. DEFEND PROSPERITY.

Not a single American flag is displayed. Instead, there is a sea of BlackSteel's red-and-black banners adorning the arena.

Every entrance and visible corner is guarded by BlackSteel security. They are fully armored, weapons visible, standing at rigid attention as if it is a military occupation, not a rally.

The music hits its climax; anticipation is at its peak. The crowd's herd mentality is unhinged, chanting Schmutt's name. The screens behind the stage go dark for just a second, stoking the adulation.

And then, nothing. A murmur ripples through the audience. People search the arena with confused faces.

Schmutt finally steps onto the stage, tightly gripping his youngest daughter like a human shield. He's had children with multiple partners, but none of them speak fondly of him. As they grow older, they distance themselves publicly. All the billions in the world can't buy their love or even their respect. To them, he's just a rich stranger who was never there in any meaningful way.

"I don't get how anyone could ever sleep with that loser. Even if you gave me a billion dollars, I wouldn't," Lex says amusingly.

His daughter is scrawny, pale, no older than four and is struggling to wiggle free. She's the one who was given an algebraic formula for a name, one she will probably change as soon as possible.

Schmutt hoists the girl up, positioning him in front of his own chest like a barrier. His grip is firm; fingers tense around the child's sides as if keeping a buffer between himself and the crowd. He doesn't wave. He doesn't bask in the applause. Instead, he lingers, eyes darting across the arena, his expression stretched a little too tight beneath the forced bravado.

He continues to move at a snail's pace across the stage floor, still forcing his daughter to be a human barricade. BlackSteel guards flank him on both sides, walking in sync, a full security escort for a man acting like he's entering a warzone.

The stage itself is massive, but the center podium is encased in plexiglass, so thick it must be bulletproof to a high caliber. It gleams under the overhead lights, giving off the unsettling image of a human display case.

Schmutt barely breathes until he's inside. Then, the second he reaches the podium, he shoves his kid away like he's discarding a used prop.

"Go, go, get out of here," he snaps at his daughter, waving her off.

She hesitates, confused, her small hands gripping Schmutt's pant leg, eyes pleading for a reassuring hug.

Schmutt's voice turns sharp, frustration bleeding through.

"Not now, I said leave! You listen? Shoo! Get!"

The words echo through the open mic for the entire arena and viewers at home to hear. Two assistants rush forward, ushering the child backstage. Schmutt straightens his cap and clears his throat sharply, gripping the podium as if he's about to get hit by a tornado.

His voice booms over the speakers:

"We are not afraid of the Dragon Slayers!"

The crowd explodes into cheers.

Lex lets out a disbelieving laugh.

"Yeah, he looks really fearless."

I take a big gulp of wine, fortifying myself for whatever is about to come out of his mouth.

Schmutt clears his throat with a raspy "ahem" before speaking into the mic.

"So, uh, yeah. Just because I wasn't born in this country doesn't mean my opinions don't matter."

The attendees are confused. A half-cheer goes up. Some people clap; others aren't sure what to do. A few just keep waving their "BILLIONAIRES BUILT AMERICA" banners.

Schmutt shrugs, like he's confirmed a great truth.

"In fact, if you think about it, I have the most money; I should have the most opinions."

The crowd hesitates, trying to decide where he is going with this.

"It only makes sense! Like, I don't get why people don't see this. Like money equals intelligence. If you don't have money, then you don't have enough knowledge, and more knowledge means more power.

"And power is great!"

He is already moving on, like a manic person rambling alone at night.

"Look, guys, isn't it obvious why all the billionaires support our side?"

Lex sarcastically asks out loud.

"Is it cause the other side is actively trying to remove them from existence?"

Schmutt continues, his voice ramping up.

"I mean… think about it. If we're so successful and so smart, why would we all agree on the same thing unless it was actually correct? People, this isn't rocket science, and I know! I build rockets!"

He laughs, a forced, mechanical laugh at a joke he's told a hundred times. Then stops, waiting for a reaction. The arena goes pin-drop silent. A few loyalists keep waving their banners, but most just stare, waiting for Schmutt to give them something easier to process.

This is Alan Schmutt in his purest form, a man who bought a comedy club just so he could force the world to sit through his set. Desperate for applause. Addicted to the sound of validation. So starved for attention, he bought entire empires just to center himself in the spotlight.

He throws his hands up.

"Like, come on, that's just common sense."

The crowd cheers, probably relieved they were finally given clear instructions to do so.

Schmutt grins.

"The other side, I don't know, man, they just seem dumb."

Another weird pause.

Lex sighs.

"This man's entire argument is "billionaires are smart because they're billionaires."

Schmutt continues to ramble.

"Like, seriously. Have you ever noticed that? How the people against us are just, I don't know, low IQ?"

There it is. A few awkward laughs ripple through the stadium, but someone in the front row takes the bait, shouting, "Yeah!"

Schmutt immediately points at them as if they've made a breakthrough discovery.

"Exactly! Exactly!" He claps his hands, nodding rapidly. "We need people with big ideas, not small brains.

"Take the Department of Unified Monitoring Bureau, for example. Remember when I first created it? Everyone panicked, acting like I was going to break things. Well, guess what? Billionaire geniuses move fast and break things. That's how progress works!"

Schmutt lets out a theatrical chuckle, shaking his head.

"Sure, some people suffered because of it. A few lives got, what's the word? Disrupted. But hey, that's the price of innovation. A sacrifice we were all willing to make."

He leans in toward the crowd, eyes sparkling.

"And look what we got in return: massive tax cuts for the 1%! So, really, who's complaining, not me or anyone I know…"

Another random cheer rises, dull and scattered, more reflex than enthusiasm.

Schmutt starts to panic. The pace of his delivery becomes forced as he stumbles through his off-the-cuff speech. Beads of sweat appear on his face.

The massive screen behind him flashes three new words.

INNOVATION. SECURITY. PROSPERITY.

Schmutt turns to look at them and then back at the crowd again. It's clear he has no idea what he's supposed to say next. He lowers his head in what seems to be an attempt to read notes.

Then he yells out the words the crowd has been waiting for.

"But you know who's not dumb? Our great President Tuff!"

His supporters explode into loud cheers.

"TUFF! TUFF! TUFF!"

Schmutt straightens, smiling wildly.

"Yeah, yeah! I love Tuff too! Great guy, great guy."

I close my eyes for a second, forcing myself to process what I am seeing. This is an actual rally to support billionaires.

Schmutt keeps it rolling.

"When our beloved President first came to me, I had so many ideas. So many. The best ideas, really."

He pauses, then lights up as if he's just remembered that he's a genius.

"And you know what the first thing he said to me was?"

The crowd hushes, hanging on his words.

Schmutt leans forward, milking it.

"He said Alan, how much money can you give me?'"

Lex bolts upright with surprise

"Wow Charlie, he just admitted he's nothing but a pay pig for Tuff."

A weird tension starts to spread through the arena. Schmutt doesn't seem to notice. He spreads his arms, laughing.

"And you see? That's leadership! Our President understands that money moves things."

The crowd cheers again, uncertain of what, but at least he is gaining momentum.

Schmutt doubles down.

"We get things done."

He's moving his hands frantically, whipping up energy, a sorcerer casting impotent spells.

"I mean, think about it! If it weren't for money, I wouldn't be talking to all of you right now! And if I weren't here, would we even be having this conversation?"

The camera cuts to the audience. People are dumbfounded. It's clear they don't know how to respond. Some are heading for the exits.

Schmutt shakes his hands triumphantly.

"Money equals good. Billionaires have money. That means billionaires are good. Money plus billionaires equals good things!"

I swirl the last sip of wine in my glass, watching him with a level of horrified fascination. His few loyal fans are still waving their *BILLIONAIRES BUILT AMERICA* banners, masking the manufactured fervor.

BlackSteel armed guards stoke the feeling that we are watching a militarized display instead of a political rally.

Schmutt wipes his forehead dramatically, then lets out a heavy sigh into the mic.

"Wow. Wow, guys. This... this is amazing."

The remaining crowd cheers louder, feeding his ego like oxygen to a flame.

Schmutt exits his plastic cage and starts pacing again on the stage. He places a hand over his heart in deep reflection.

"You know, I just… I feel like, for the first time… I belong with all of you, that I can really be myself."

The audience erupts, eating up every ounce of his self-aggrandizing bullshit.

Schmutt stops in the center of the stage, his chest puffed out, signifying that he's about to say something historic.

And then he throws his right arm straight out, palm down.

"I GIVE MY HEART TO YOU!"

Lex sits up too fast, spilling her wine.

"What the fuck was that?"

My brain stalls, refusing to process what I just saw.

"Oh my God… you have to be kidding me."

We watch in shock as the crowd obediently cheers. Some automatically. Some hesitantly. Some just caught in the blind enthusiasm of the moment. Only a few people in the front rows look visibly uncomfortable.

Schmutt, completely oblivious, turns around and does it again.

"I GIVE MY HEART TO YOU!"

Another full salute; there's no question about it now.

This time, the crowd's reaction is less enthusiastic. The cameras break away as the cheering falters. Hands freeze mid-clap.

A cameraman zooms in on an elderly billionaire in the VIP section nervously observing the change in atmosphere. Another shows a couple of BlackSteel security guards exchanging uneasy glances.

"He did it twice." Lex gasps. "What the fuck is wrong with that guy."

Schmutt is still beaming. His hands are shaking, not from fear, but from sheer dumbass enthusiasm. Maybe it's the moment, maybe it's the drugs, but right now, he's riding a wave of pure euphoria.

"Ha! Ha! This is amazing! You get me! I love you all!"

His arms flail wildly as he laughs, completely blind to the fact that half the room is now watching with a different kind of tension.

Then, like some kind of deranged child, he suddenly jumps about four inches off the ground. Throwing his arms up, forming a Y, as he lands with a heavy thud, his grin is wider than ever. The arena is full of confusion, the kind where everyone is collectively processing.

Lex stares at the screen.

"What the fuck is he doing?"

I don't have an answer.

Schmutt, standing dead center on the stage, eyes wild, throws his arms up again in a Y-shape.

"Y! Y! Y! Haha! Yeah!"

I watch in stunned disbelief as he continues to barely jump off the ground, each time to form the logo of his failing social media platform.

The camera crew cuts back to the audience, revealing a stark reality. The energy is shifting as they look awkwardly at each other with the realization that they are now part of something very, very bad.

CEOs who were honored guests are visibly uncomfortable. Even BlackSteel staff cannot camouflage their apprehension.

Lex turns expressionless, her tone dry.

"Okay, you win, Charlie. That was definitely entertaining, but for all the wrong reasons."

"More like gift-wrapped propaganda for the Dragon Slayers."

"Well, good thing they're not your problem anymore. Right?"

"Yeah, you're right. The Dragon Slayers aren't my mess to clean up anymore."

"That's my girl. The only serious problem you'll have is if you keep hogging the bed and stealing the blankets."

Before I can respond, Lex pounces, tackling me onto the couch, mock wrestling me into submission. She grins down at me, her expression softening into something warm, something so wonderfully familiar.

I laugh, shoving back playfully.

She pulls me closer, and in an instant, Schmutt and the rest of the world fade away.

The night is easy, effortless. A blur of laughter, teasing and warmth.

By the time morning drifts in through the curtains, we're tangled up, half-asleep, half-awake, caught in that perfect in-between.

This is my new normal. My new story. And I crave it more and more.

We move through the familiar rhythm of getting ready. Lex pulls on an oversized hoodie, me in a half-hearted search for clean clothes as I scroll through my phone. I'm not expecting much, just the usual news cycle of chaos.

Then a familiar figure emerges.

Guinevere.

She's responding to Schmutt's rally. A clipped headline, a flood of engagement and a new video.

I hold up my phone for Lex to see.

"Looks like the Dragon Slayers fired back after last night."

Lex tugs her hair into a loose ponytail and immediately perks up.

"Oh, we're watching that. You know I love her videos."

I hit play, and she appears.

Guinevere is poised as ever, the glow of the camera catching the smooth contours of her mask. The lighting is soft and deliberate, casting just enough shadow to make her presence feel larger than life.

In her hand, a delicate origami paper dragon shifts between her fingers, folded with careful precision.

Good tidings, Resistance.

Her voice is warm, almost playful. She lifts the small paper dragon higher, tilting her head like she's admiring it. Then, with a soft, amused laugh, she turns her gaze back to the camera.

Amazing. I haven't seen a rally quite like that since the 1930s."

Guinevere flicks the dragon between her fingers, rolling it lightly.

Yes, it's truly amazing.
That some people might still stand behind this man, Schmutt,
even when he is literally embracing an ideology
that goes against everything this nation claims as sacred.
Fascinating, isn't it?
That just because he is wealthy, people will defend him.
That people will still look at him after that and say,
Yes, this man is good. This man is smart.
This man deserves the power that comes with unlimited wealth.

Guinevere shifts the origami dragon to her other hand, her voice carrying a hint of calculated coldness.

Yet again, this is the issue we face, isn't it?

Billionaires have spent decades perfecting their greatest PR trick,

*convincing the world that wealth is synony-
mous with virtue and intelligence.*

*That they cannot be wrong. That they cannot
be evil. That they cannot be fools.*

After all, look at how successful they are. Look at how rich they are.

The paper dragon tilts in her hand.

But we know better, don't we?

Guinivere pauses, letting her words sink in. She holds the dragon up between her fingers, her voice turning serious.

Alan Schmutt was never a threat to us. Oh no, not that clown.

*Because for all of his fortune, all of his power,
all of his so-called brilliance...*

She rolls the dragon between her fingers, letting it crinkle softly,

It's all just paper.

Lex is entranced beside me. The energy between us shifts. Once again, Guinevere has captured her audience.

She slowly holds up the dragon.

And the funny thing about paper?

Guinivere pulls out a lighter. Flicks it open with a soft click and holds the flame just beneath it.

All you need is just a little fire…

Her voice is barely above a whisper, letting the flame waver. Then, it touches the tip, and the paper dragon instantly ignites. The flame races across the delicate folds, devouring it in seconds, turning it into smoldering black ash.

Guinevere watches calmly, unmoved at the dragons' demise. The last embers crumble to the floor.

She looks back at the camera.

And poof. All gone. So, here's what we're going to do.

For those of you who don't know, Alan Sch-mutt's wealth isn't what it seems.

See, Alan has a secret. He hasn't actually built anything.

Not a single thing. He doesn't innovate. He doesn't create.

All he does is take, take, take.

Guinevere's voice is smooth as silk.

Schmutt built his fortune by the hostile takeover of companies.

Companies that were already great.

Companies that already had brilliant engi-neers, talented workers, and real innovators.

And what did he do? He gutted them.

Took their labor, took their ideas, took every-thing that made them valuable,

and used all those companies as his personal piggy bank.

She leans closer as if telling a bedtime tale.

> *The problem with Alan's fortune? It's not real.*
>
> *Alan doesn't have any actual money; he borrows against his companies' stock.*
>
> *All his wealth is inflated; overvalued shares that exist because of banks and his billionaire comrades are all in on the 'big' lie.*
>
> *He never sells them because if he did, he'd have to pay taxes like the rest of us.*

Guinevere lowers her head as if speaking to a child.

> *Instead, Schmutt takes out loans against them. Loans from his friends.*
>
> *Loans that let him spend endlessly while keeping the illusion of his wealth intact.*

She lets that settle before continuing.

> *And then, we have Schmuttler Motors.*
>
> *What do they do? They sell cars.*
>
> *That's it. They're not reinventing AI. They're not unlocking autonomous driving.*
>
> *They're making cars.*

Guinivere lightly taps her finger on her chin.

And yet, somehow the company is worth over a trillion dollars, directly paying him more money than all their profits combined. To be fair, at first, Schmuttler Motors made great vehicles.

Here's the thing: they weren't his designs.

They were the original founder's designs.
The creative talent before him.

And once Schmutt started sticking his hands in it?

Once he decided he wanted to play inventor?

She turns her head from side to side.

It's been a decade of sheer nonsense for the companies he hijacked.

Broken promises. Announcements of nonex-
istent technology. Fake prototypes.

Selling software for two decades with promises that
it's only a year away before you can use it.

Truly the definition of vaporware. And
yet, the stock kept climbing.

Because markets aren't real.

Guinevere snaps her fingers.

The stock market is a rigged system.

A system that billionaires designed to convince you they're gods.

A system where perception matters more than reality.

Where a company worth maybe ten, fifteen bil-
lion dollars gets valued at over a trillion

because billionaires and their minions are
very good at preserving illusions.

It's all that matters… for them.

She smiles, but it holds no comfort.

And Alan? I know you're watching.

It's time we show everyone what your fortune really looks like.

Starting now, all Schmuttler employ-
ees will have two options with us.

She pauses, weighted, intentional.

Option One. We will immediately buy you out.

Four times your annual salary. No strings attached.

All you have to do is never go back.

Option Two. You stay at Schmuttler.

And depending on what you can do for the Resis-
tance, you might make even more.

The severity of what Option Two implies alarms me.

Now, I know some of you might already own a Schmutler vehicle.

Maybe you bought it before you knew that.

Alan Schmutt was a raging, crazy fascist.

It happens.

Well, it hasn't before, but I guess it happened here.

She shrugs with amusement.

Like to get rid of your Schmuttler? We'll buy it back.

Ten thousand dollars over the sticker price. And you know why?

So, we can rip them apart and recycle for scrap.

If you choose not to take us up on this offer within a week, well...

Guinevere pauses, taking another look at her paper dragon ashes.

Then it's open season.
From that point forward,
anytime you destroy a Schmuttler vehicle,
we will pay you double its value.

She claps her hands lightly. Her tone becomes soft like she's comforting a child.

Now, Alan, I know when you see this,
you might be having a little bit of a panic attack.
Well, actually, maybe not.
You may be so dosed up on one of your drug cocktails
That you won't even comprehend what's going on around you.

Guinevere leans forward again. The camera tightens, drawing the focus directly on her mask.

I know you think this won't work, Alan.
That's only because your greed has rotted
whatever remnant of intelligence you once had.

She lets that simmer. Then, her voice drops to a razor's edge.

But now you're done. It's over. You're finished.

Her final words are a death sentence.

This will be your legacy now, and human-
ity will be better as soon as you are gone.

The screen abruptly cuts to black.

I stare at the empty space where Guinevere dropped her bombshell.

Lex breaks my trance.

"I mean… I know she's a terrorist and everything… but I think Guinevere is kinda cute."

"Jesus, Lex. Seriously?"

"I bet she's lots of fun, you know, like a blast to go out with? I'm a big fan of hers."

A laugh escapes me before I can stop it.

"I'm sure she'd be a lot more fun than Lancelot."

Lex pretends to swoon.

"Ooooh. Right. You met the knight in shining armor."

I already know where this is going. I give her a flat look, waiting for it.

She pretends to swing a sword, her grin widening.

"So, how was he?"

"Lex. I thought I was going to die."

"Sorry, I shouldn't have brought that up."

"It's fine; I'm just glad I'm here. With you."

As we continue through the morning, the only downside is the thought of heading to Blacksteel. It's painful, but it's a steady routine: punch in, punch out. No surprises, no late-night emergencies.

This week, however, has been anything but routine. Watching Alan Schmutt's downfall has been nothing short of entertaining. Guinevere's video made a profound impact, with the market reacting instantly and brutally.

On Monday, Schmuttlers' stock was down 40%, with Schmutt's platform Y on the verge of collapse.

He's been spiraling, ranting about market manipulation, calling in every favor he has to get analysts to slap inflated price targets on his stock. But no one's buying it.

Schmutt floods Y with all-caps rants, demanding the SEC

step in, threatening lawsuits, insisting short sellers will be jailed as terrorists.

Tuesday, another 50% vanishes. His analyst friends go on TV, scrambling to pump the stock, raising price targets with no basis in reality. The market doesn't care.

The Dragon Slayers have spoken.

In an even more pathetic attempt, Schmutt asks the President for a PR stunt. Tuff tells Americans there will be a huge tax incentive if they buy a "Smurffler." Apparently, the President thinks that's the brand name.

On Wednesday, another 40% of Schmuttler stock is wiped out. Panic sets in. Shareholders start jumping ship. Institutional investors dump their holdings. Schmutt swears that "everything is fine."

Thursday, the final blow. News breaks that Schmuttler Motors is in chaos; staffing shortages have completely grid locked production. No new cars. No supply chain. Nothing.

The market doesn't hesitate. The stock craters another 60%.

And then, social media erupts.

Finally, free of this hellhole working for Schmuttler. Best day of my life.

Schmuttler was literally the worst. I'm so happy to be out.

Someone PLEASE buy Schmuttler back from this cringe loser and make it a company again.

LMAO Schmuttler's worth like $1 now. I'll buy at 25 cents, maybe.

For real tho, if Schmutt wasn't running it, I'd buy one.

Friday morning is the kill shot. The market opens, and Schmuttler is worth $0.64 per share. One week ago, it was $445.

And now? Nothing.

Everything Schmutt built, his loans, his collateralized stock, his entire fortune, liquidated overnight.

The richest man in the world?

Now, the poorest man in history, thanks to all his leveraged debts.

As simple as that, another dragon goes up in flames without even firing a bullet.

CHAPTER 39

ASHES OF AUTHORITY

"Greed is a bottomless pit which exhausts the person in an endless effort to satisfy the need without ever reaching satisfaction."

-ERICH FROMM

ALAN SCHMUTT HAS gone missing; nobody seems to care, and the world continues to spin without him.

For a couple of days, the media worked to turn his downfall into a martyr's tale, a tragic fall from greatness, a stark warning of the dangers of unrestrained populism. These days, attention spans are short, and people lose interest quickly, so it was no great surprise when all the viral stories about him also vanished.

Schmutt's empire dismantling was swift, picked apart by the same banks that nourished it for decades. His assets were gutted and repurposed. Y becomes Chipper again. Schmutler Motors brings in a new CEO, wiping the board clean.

The startups, once tethered to his orbit like space debris, remove any trace of him. He has become obsolete code. The assembly lines whir, the supply chains chug along, and nothing skips a beat.

Schmutt was never holding anything together. Life goes on without him.

For me, it's been two months of the same quiet ritual. Each morning, I arrive with my bag on my shoulder, neutral expression, badge ready, mouth shut. The only real bliss I have is the time with Lex, every day a reminder of how incredible it is to be with her again.

But everything around us only continues to deteriorate, though now at a slower pace. The country is locked in a grinding stalemate between collapse and control.

Since the emergency orders and the Protection of Freedom Act passed, everything's shifted. A few clicks, a few cold directives, and you're gone. Scooped up and rerouted to Continental Containment, where your life is a file waiting to be erased.

And yes, some individuals crossed lines. Property damage. Sabotage. Vandalism. The Dragon Slayers have not been subtle. They've been pumping money into the cracks of society, empowering anyone willing to stir chaos.

Desperate people do desperate things. But a spray-painted wall or destruction of property shouldn't result in permanent disappearance. This is America's new reality: absolute, unrelenting erasure.

Most never saw their demise coming. A warehouse worker who shared a video. A retired Marine who sent twenty bucks to a group later flagged for sympathizing with the Resistance.

Outside the Freedom Zone walls, the pushback is growing. Protests have exploded; riots have increased. What started as sporadic marches have evolved into a nationwide roar. Millions in the streets wave their homemade signs.

The only people defending these crackdowns are billionaire spokespeople and their paid media puppets.

Everyone else? They're either marching, hiding, or holding their breath.

The administration refuses to blink. They don't care that half of the country is crumbling. Their attention is solely on one thing: the billionaire Freedom Zones. Cities with clean streets, full shelves and, most important, lethal protection. Their entire mission revolves around protecting that fantasy.

Everything outside the Freedom Zone gates is background noise, like the rest of us are just props in someone else's world.

When questioned, they just blame the Dragon Slayers.

"It's not our fault the roads are failing, the schools are closing, the power grids are unstable. That's what happens when terrorists hijack a nation."

Meanwhile, the actual work is carried out by strangers who refuse to give up.

A church in Ohio that manages to keep its food pantry stocked. A community center in rural Georgia that keeps the lights on when the county budget vanished. School districts that were supposed to shut down somehow found the funding to keep paying teachers.

At first, everyone assumed it was Dragon Slayer money, another anonymous payment flow, pumping quiet chaos into the cracks of a crumbling system. They fund the desperate because desperation is combustible.

What is transpiring now feels different. Less revolutionary. More… restorative.

Slowly but surely, voices are rising from within the very system that let this mess happen. Former military officers. Retired intelligence agents. Politicians, some long gone, others still sitting behind desks with a flag on the wall, finally speaking out.

There are no manifestos or threats. Just affirmative statements and quiet condemnation of the crackdowns, the disappearances, the puppet laws dressed up as patriotism.

Many of those who spoke out vanished. Scooped up like the rest. In the mix, a name began to slowly emerge.

The Union Guard.

There's no formal structure or visible hierarchy, but the name alone carries substantial weight and hope. For many, it's become shorthand for what might finally put a stop to all the madness.

BlackSteel doesn't acknowledge the Union Guard publicly. Neither does Tuff or his administration. They don't like the shape that's starting to form.

My arrival today at work is greeted by an atmospheric switch. BlackSteel HQ always has tight security; the more control, the better. But something is askew this morning.

The presence of guards has increased, but it's not just the numbers. Their usual scattered patrols are gone, replaced by coordinated units that move with purpose.

Something's brewing. But I won't be the one to find out. Nor do I care.

I head towards the pen, but before I enter, I hear a familiar voice.

"Charlie."

Maya is standing beside her workstation, arms crossed, fingers idly drumming against her sleeve.

She seems exhausted, worn down and frayed.

"Hey, Maya. It's been a while."

"Charlie, are you free? I have like a small favor to ask."

"It depends. What's the favor?"

"Just look over some reports, it might help keep me sane."

A Sorakin mutt creeps past the pen, sleek and silent, sensors scanning, stalking for disobedient prey. Another trails close behind it, assuring that nothing has been missed.

I catch Maya watching them the same way I am, unsettled and disgusted.

"Okay, any place we can sit without being spied on?"

She smiles in appreciation and points to an empty desk in the back of her work area.

"Charlie, I'm not really sure if BlackSteel knows I exist. I don't even know who to report to after they took you off the Dragon Slayer case."

"What are you talking about?"

"I still haven't been reassigned, and it's been almost two months. I feel like I've fallen through the cracks.

"Asking anyone is out of the question. If they realize I'm not needed, they'll let me go. I'd rather not throw away my entire career so early."

Maya's right. What they don't know won't hurt them or her. As long as she's getting a paycheck, she can simply remain invisible.

"I'd stay under the radar if I were you. Now what about that favor?" I ask.

"I finished this briefing I've been working on, but now I have no one even to send it to. I have no clue what to do with it. But I just, well, I'd feel better if you looked at it."

"Maya, I'm not surprised, they have no clue how to use their best assets. Let's see what you've got there."

Her energy changes, and the enthusiastic Maya returns. She opens a file for me to read.

"The Union Guard, it's expanding and fast."

Not surprising to hear. When you strip people of their rights, they look for another way to fight.

Maya keeps scrolling, flipping through feeds, encrypted chatter, and financial transactions.

"The Union Guard has support networks in almost every major city now. Full-scale infrastructure, funding sources we can't track. It's all moving through blockchain. Whole decentralized networks that BlackSteel can't take down. They lost their chance to contain it months ago."

Maya swipes to another feed, her fingers moving faster, more frantic.

"And it's not just the funding, Charlie. It's how BlackSteel is retaliating."

She presses play on a video.

A man is being dragged out of his home, screaming.

"We voted for Tuff! What are you doing? We voted for you!"

Another clip shows a woman sobbing, clutching at the arms of a BlackSteel operative as they drag her son away.

"What are you doing to my baby?! He's only fourteen! He's just a kid!"

The clip that follows shows drones swooping in low, recorded demands ring out in metallic bursts:

"Stop resisting. Stop resisting."

Sorakin mutts follow, realigning rifles strapped on their backs, their targeting systems locked with mechanical precision. No warning or hesitation, just cold enforcement. One by one, people are pulled from buildings, hands raised, hauled away without explanation.

I've seen worse. Far worse. But this isn't a warzone. This isn't some foreign operation. This is home.

Maya looks up at me, her voice barely above a whisper.

"Charlie, I don't see it getting better. I don't even know what better looks like anymore."

"What's your plan?"

"I was hoping things would get better. But now, I don't know. Maybe I do need to start thinking about an entirely different career."

Maya sternly looks at me.

"What about you?"

There's no point dragging it out, Lex already made up my mind for me.

"I'm giving it one more month, if even that."

Maya rubs the back of her neck, apparently not surprised by my answer.

"Gosh, I can't believe you're leaving. Thanks again, though, for your time. I know it's not a big deal in the grand scheme of things, but just talking it through helps. And Charlie, good luck."

Maya forces a half-smile, her eyes consumed with exhaustion, her brain refusing to shut down. She is held together only by routine, a paycheck and a shred of belief that what she's doing still matters.

I get it. I do. A few months ago, I was in the exact same place, clawing for purpose in all this chaos.

But now? I've mellowed out. At least, that's what I keep trying to convince myself.

Maya gathers her things, leaving me alone in the dimly lit office space, my fingers drumming against my knee. My mind shifts to something else, something that's been stuck in my head and refuses to budge.

It's Bill. Aside from a bit of small talk here and there, we haven't really spoken since my demotion.

I've been evading him for not standing up more for the FBI and me.

Things have changed so rapidly, and BlackSteel is arming up to march into something irreversible. My gut instinct is to speak directly to Bill about my concerns. After all, he was my mentor at the Bureau, and we went through a lot together.

Heading to his office, I lock tight the conflicting emotions flooding me. Bill's door is open, so I enter without knocking. He doesn't notice me at first, his attention buried in reports that seem to crush him.

"Hey, Bill. Have a second for me?"

His voice doesn't reveal any surprise to see me.

"Charlie. I'm a little busy."

I start to back off.

"Okay, Sorry, I…"

Bill stops me before I can finish.

"No, no. Come on in, Charlie. Have a seat. What's on your mind?"

I hesitate, then sit down, struggling to find the appropriate words.

"Just wanted to check in about everything that's been happening around here."

Bill releases a long sigh. He's been expecting this conversation.

"Charlie, it's a lot more than I think any of us expected.

"There's a line we walk in times like these. Orders need to be executed, and in war, things happen. It's chaotic. Messy. The only thing we can hope for is for it to end sooner rather than later."

It's disappointing to hear that Bill believes in the merger and BlackSteel's mission instead of the FBI's. It's unfathomable that this is what he has become: another company sycophant.

"I understand that. But Bill, a lot of these things are escalating. How far is too far?"

"What do you mean?"

"I mean, is there a point where we've crossed a line? No accountability or oversight?"

Bill's face tightens with annoyance and disbelief.

"Charlie, what part of we're trying to save this nation don't you understand?"

"Save it from what? Itself?"

Bill glares at me as if I'm an adversary.

"Goddamn it, Charlie! Why couldn't you just follow orders?"

The rage in Bill's voice startles me. He feels like a complete stranger. I open my mouth, but he stops me, continuing to blast out his words.

"I don't understand how we have such issues. We're under so much stress, and good people like you go rogue and don't follow orders. For Christ's sake, how hard is it?"

My stomach twists into knots.

"Bill, I'm sorry."

"Don't sorry me. The fucking shit I have to deal with from everyone here and now you."

Bill's eyes lock onto mine as he lands the final blow.

"You know who always followed orders? Your father."

My blood runs cold as Bill continues his rampage.

"Your father never questioned anything. He'd be out there leading the charge. He'd understand what was necessary. And now? Now, any little pushback is treated like some moral crisis when it's just basic fucking discipline.

"Your father would be so ashamed of you, Charlie."

My heart is pierced as I gasp for air.

This isn't Bill. This isn't my mentor, the man who guided me through my career, the man who looked after me for so many years.

The only thing I can do, the only thing that makes sense, is to leave his presence.

So, without saying anything, I turn and head towards his office door.

"Charlie, stop. Wait."

He lets out a sharp breath, the anger draining from his face almost as fast as it came. Regret settles in, but it's too late. I close the door behind me and shut him out of my life.

Without hesitation, I head for Lex's place instead of returning to work.

She is sprawled out on the couch, one arm draped over the back, deep in relaxation.

The second I step inside, her eyes flick open, scanning me the way only she can, cutting straight through whatever mask I've tried to put on.

"That bad, huh?" Lex asks, already knowing the answer.

"I need a stiff drink."

"Charlie, I can't believe you've been able to put up with this crap for two months now."

"Yeah, I know. Me and my work brain."

"I swear I'm going to have to get you a little hamster wheel or something. Keep you occupied when you finally leave."

I chuckle. It's easy, normal, a stark contrast to the tension I wade through every day. And there is no doubt she is irresistible.

Lex's expression shifts, a glint of hesitation in her eyes, a pause in her rhythm.

"Hey, before I forget, I got something weird in the mail today."

I raise an eyebrow.

"Weird, how?"

She picks up an envelope from the table and tosses it to me.

"I don't know if it's junk mail or what, but I figured you should see it before it gets recycled."

The name on it surprises me.

The Union Guard.

Without hesitation, I rip open the envelope. The language is formal, direct, and with bold fonts ensuring the contents appear urgent.

Dear Alexa Thompson,

We are contacting you as someone who has served in an agency dedicated to the security of this nation. The time has come for those of us who once stood for order and democracy to unite again.

Our mission is simple: to restore the legitimacy of the U.S. government. We are trying to reestablish the legal rights of citizens.

We do not call for violence. We call on the people to stand up and reclaim their voice.

Attached, you will find instructions for secure communication. Should you choose to engage, know that your identity will remain protected.

I flip the page over, scanning the bottom. The instructions are familiar. A VPN, a backchannel, a way in.

Lex watches me closely.

"Well, what do you think? Dragon Slayers? BlackSteel? A scam?"

I should analyze this, look for the angle, the play, the real power behind it.

Instead, I toss the letter aside.

"Honestly, Lex? I couldn't care less about this."

"Oh my God, Charlotte Grayson doesn't give a fuck. About time!"

"More like I'm done. I'm past done. Bill chewed my ass out today."

"What?"

"He chastised me for not following orders and implied that I was an embarrassment to my father's legacy."

"Hope you told him to go fuck himself."

"Lex."

"Don't Lex me, Charlie. I'm serious. Bill doesn't get to say that shit to you. What the hell?"

"It wasn't the normal Bill. It was stress. BlackSteel. Everything,"

Lex rolls her eyes.

"That doesn't make it okay. He was your mentor! Him, of all people, to say that shit."

"I know. But if I didn't have you, Lex, I'd probably still be working toward a position just like his."

She watches me for a long moment; the frustration melting into something softer, something quieter. I meet her gaze, my voice steady.

"Thank you for listening... for understanding."

"Of course, Charlie... you're so cute. Let's get you something to drink."

Liquor, food, Lex, just enough to blur the sharp edges of the day. The hours slip by before I even notice.

It's late when my phone vibrates on the bedside table. Something's off. Late-night calls stopped weeks ago. No one needs me anymore.

It's Carter. I debate whether I should take the call.

I relent and answer.

"Carter, what's up?"

His voice is distraught.

"They took Graham!"

"Calm down. What do you mean they took him?"

"Boss, they detained him. He was on an op, and they said he refused orders, but I think they're cracking down. They're targeting people. I could be next!"

"Carter. Listen to me."

He is hyperventilating and doesn't stop stammering.

"I'm at my apartment. Grabbing my stuff. Gotta get out of here."

"Stop and think for a second. We don't even know if you're marked, but if you disappear without a trace, that's how you'll get flagged for sure."

"What the fuck! You want me to sit here and wait for BlackSteel to kick down my door?"

"No, you come over here. I'm at Lex's. Let's at least talk through it before you do something irrational."

The sound of a suitcase zipper can be heard in the background.

"Yeah. Yeah, okay. That'll help. On my way."

The call leaves me rattled as I nudge Lex awake.

"Lex, I'm sorry. There's a big problem. It's Graham and Carter."

Lex sits up, rubbing her eyes awake.

"You know I'm a good eavesdropper. It's the spy part of me. Give me a sec, and I'll make coffee."

Once again, Lex gets it… she always does.

But Carter's warnings echo in my head.

If he sounds that worried, I should be, too.

CHAPTER 40

A NAME ON A LIST

"It is said that no one truly knows a nation until one has been inside its jails."

-NELSON MANDELA

CARTER BANGS ON Lex's door, rushing inside before it's fully open, breathing in ragged gulps as his hands shake at his sides.

He skips any sort of greeting.

"Charlie, I'm telling you, this is fucking bad."

"It's okay; you just need to sit. Lex is getting you some coffee. What's going on?"

Carter is unraveling, his body trembling.

"I've been monitoring BlackSteel's systems; something big is about to happen. The mass incarceration and deportation network is live. BlackSteel's muscle, Sorakin's tech, and Continental's camps. This shit is all happening on a mass scale."

"Who's the target?"

"Ex-FBI, ex-military, anyone who isn't one hundred percent on board and loyal to them or who might stand a chance of pushing back."

"Carter, that's a pretty wide net they're casting."

"Yeah, well, it's closing in. I noticed random things: background checks reopened, internal audits on staff. Individuals who had already been cleared. Then Graham's name got pulled, and he vanished into the system."

Carter scrolls through his phone, his thumbs unable to keep up.

"I ran through the list of detention centers, and there he was, Graham Cross."

"That's all it says?"

"Detained. That's it."

Lex comes in with mugs of freshly brewed coffee. She gives one to Carter, his hands still shaking as he grasps it too tightly.

She looks at him with a mix of concern and suspicion.

"So what?" she cross-examines him. "You think you're next?"

"I don't know. Maybe. I've done plenty of questionable stuff, sure, but it's more about who could be a threat rather than who's actually done anything. And let's be real, I'm not exactly the model BlackSteel lackey. I'm sure I'm on a list somewhere."

"But you haven't been marked yet? What about me?"

He shakes his head again, but this time, it's stiff, tense.

"No boss. Not technically. Not yet."

Lex leans to one side, frowning.

"Charlie, it has to be Bill. He's keeping you guys covered."

I watch Carter closely. He's afraid, and for good reason. Graham might have gotten himself into a mess. Sending him to a detention center shows how things are different now, and if Bill is keeping us safe, it can only last as long as he has the power to do so.

"Okay, better to be safe. Let's get you out of here."

Lex's eyebrow goes up.

"Wait, shouldn't we just leave too, Charlie? I mean, if they're targeting people, maybe don't go to the damn office?"

"There's no way around it Lex, just disappearing would raise flags. It's a bad idea for me to just take off with no warning. I need to go to HQ, let them know I'm done for good. Make sure it doesn't look like I'm running."

Carter, exasperated, knows that there are no other viable options. This isn't about being heroic, it's about not being stupid.

"I don't like it either, but it's all we got." he states. "It's the smart play, relaxed, no sudden moves. We don't want to call attention to ourselves."

Lex studies me for a beat, clearly weighing the risks. Then, she gives a reluctant nod.

"Alright, fine, but I don't like it one bit."

Carter is still agitated; his mind is already pivoting to the next step.

"Okay. I'll go back to my place, pack up the rest of my stuff, and then get a motel, somewhere remote."

"Good. Just let me know when you're settled."

"Yeah. Thanks, boss. I mean it."

"Carter, we've got each other's backs, no matter what."

"Right," he says, level-headed.

Lex watches the exchange, her tone landing between sarcasm and surrender.

"Jesus. Can you two just be done with this drama for good?"

"That's the plan."

The unease remains as the energy in the room becomes more focused. Carter has a way out. I have my exit planned. There will be no sudden moves by either of us.

Carter slings his bag onto his shoulder, shifting his stance indecisively. His fingers play with the straps to release his tension.

"Alright. I'm heading out."

"It's going to be okay. We're going to be safe. Just let me know when you're settled."

"Yeah. Will do. Thanks again."

Lex watches Carter from the kitchen, her arms crossed, back braced against the counter, her eyes following him like a hawk. Once he is out the door and the latch clicks, she speaks her mind.

"God, I hope this isn't the last time we see him."

There is no appropriate response. Instead, I hug her and forlornly head to the bedroom. It's not just Graham's absence or Carter leaving; it's the sense that everything is in flux. The walls are closing in on me.

I can't sleep. Staring at the ceiling, my body sinks into the bed but never settles, as my mind keeps racing. Every time I nod off, some vague thought jolts me awake.

When the alarm finally goes off, I can barely manage to climb out of bed. Splashing cold water on my face doesn't help, so I head into the kitchen for a caffeine fix.

Lex is already up, coffee in hand, eyes glued to the TV. A broadcaster rambles in the background, suddenly interrupted by a breaking news alert. It's a special update from the President without network branding.

Tuff appears, seated stiffly behind a small desk, optics to make him look larger than life. The American flag droops behind him, a poor attempt to distract from the cold concrete background.

His voice is measured.

"My fellow Americans. We are facing adversity during this critical time in history. A time where everything this nation has cherished, our freedom, our equality, our free markets, is under attack. And not by a foreign power. No. This threat comes from within… it is homegrown.

"These radicals. These Dragon Slayers. They are not here to build; they are here to destroy. They hide like cowards behind masks, slogans, and violence. They call themselves liberators. And if you think life would be better under them or their Union Guard allies, you are part of the problem.

"This is not a movement. This is not political dissent. This is outright war."

Lex shifts next to me, neither of us willing to speak.

"As your esteemed leader, I will fight this war. I will not surrender our power. I will not hand over the United States to cowards, criminals, or conspirators."

Tuff leans forward, his eyes cemented to the camera.

"That said, I have made the ultimate sacrifice to suspend all elections until the threats posed by the Dragon Slayers and the Union Guard are eliminated."

Lex catches her breath.

"Oh my god. This can't be real."

Tuff continues with his autocratic speech.

"We cannot risk turning this country over to another administration that would corrupt it from within. That would destroy the very values we hold near and dear.

"Sorakin Tech and BlackSteel will now commence a coordinated operation to remove those working against our government. That includes enemies within, individuals who have embedded themselves into our institutions, our systems, our communities in an attempt to overthrow our government.

"We have tracked them. We have identified them. And now, with our advancements in automation and robotics, we have the capability to act aggressively on behalf of the nation.

"Over the next week, these individuals will be purged from our system and brought to justice."

Tuff straightens his posture.

"There is no need to worry. If you support America, if you support me, you will be safe.

"I am the protector. Only I can save you.

"And I will."

With that, the President disappears from the screen.

Lex watches the blank screen, trying to comprehend the full consequences of what she heard. She turns toward me, her voice cracking with fear.

"Charlie, this is it. They're going to start cracking down on anyone who can fight back.

"You can't go to HQ. Not now."

"Lex, this is exactly why I have to show up for work. If they're actively looking for traitors, it makes even more sense to be there. Running now would only make it worse."

Her expression doesn't shift, but I know she's already cycling through every worst-case scenario.

"Charlie, if you think that's what's best… I'll trust you. But I want you to know that I've got a terrible feeling about this. I mean it."

"I know, I don't like it either. I'll be safe, I promise."

Lex steps forward and pulls me into a hug. The kind of embrace that says everything she's too afraid to say out loud.

Heading outside, the fresh air does nothing to ease my tension. The sidewalk feels longer than usual, the silence louder. Keys in hand, I go to open my car door, and then I notice it.

A letter is stuck under my windshield flaps in the wind. At first glance, it appears to be nothing more than an advertising flyer. I visually sweep the lot. No cars creeping by. No strangers loitering. Nothing out of the ordinary.

My car is where I left it, untouched, except for that.

The letter flutters again, soft against the glass. Innocent on the surface.

Wiggling it free from the wiper, two words stand out.

Union Guard.

I inhale slowly as I open it, glancing around once more as I direct my eyes to the bold, typed letters.

It's the same message as the one Lex received. A call to action disguised as an invitation. A call to the people who once maintained the stability of the government to re-commence their work.

My speculation is within reason. Not because I'm considering it, but because I have no clue what this entails.

Words whisper inside me.

This doesn't matter. None of this matters.

I have no stake in this anymore, whether it's for the Dragon Slayers, the Union Guard, or BlackSteel's oppressive grip on the nation. I am finished being drawn into other people's conflicts, tired of weighing the ethics of different sides, and weary of questioning who is the lesser evil instead of who is actually righteous.

Folding the paper back into the letter carefully, I tuck it into my dashboard, and then slam my car door shut.

As I start to drive, I can't shake the thought of BlackSteel lists. This crackdown is not about finding who the best people are, it's about finding who's the most obedient. That's why the BlackSteel screenings are now making the targets grow. That's what Graham's detention is. It's not who's best at the job, it's who can be trusted.

Great teams aren't afraid to argue. They say you're wrong, they push hard, and then they come back to the table stronger. Aligned. Focused.

This is the exact opposite.

This is all about eliminating any friction. It is about deleting anyone or anything who upsets the illusion of efficiency.

For now, I need to make sure I play the part and give them no reason to see me as a risk.

Make them think I'm just like the rest of them.

The lobby is packed when I arrive. BlackSteel operatives with Sorakin drones move with precise intent. Security stationed in their usual places. Commander Reddick stands by the far door, talking with two of his soldiers. If anyone can make my entrance more complicated, it would be him.

I move closer, my strides purposeful, my expression effortless. When I am within reach, he sees me, measuring my presence before I say a single word.

"Commander Reddick. I want to let you know that after seeing the operation firsthand, it's amazing how efficient BlackSteel really is. So much better than when it was just the FBI."

He doesn't hide his skepticism.

"What are you getting at, Grayson?"

"The pace. The clarity of the mission. The way decisions lead to positive outcomes. It's not something I'm used to, coming from the public sector. Everything used to move intentionally slow. Over managed. Here, it's sharp, quick, and regulated."

Reddick eyes me, unconvinced.

"Well Grayson, most people flounder when they switch sides. Public sector types usually crumble under real pressure."

"Commander, I can see how they would. But that's what makes this such a rare opportunity for someone like me to learn from a place that runs like a well-oiled machine."

He scoffs, waving a hand.

"You don't have to butter me up, Grayson. You're just grateful to still be on the payroll."

"I'm grateful to learn. And for the reminder that there's a higher standard."

"Hmph. Guess the time in the pen has been good for you. Glad to know that even someone like you can still be saved by BlackSteel ethics."

"Thank you, Commander. That means a lot."

I turn and walk away with a smile on my face.

Funny how little it takes. A compliment here. A little deference there. Men, like Reddick, aren't difficult to win over. You just have to let them think they're converting you.

That's the real trick.

One down and one to go. I head toward Bill's office, pleased with my performance for Reddick. Our interaction had gone well. It made me small, agreeable, and non-threatening.

Now, Bill.

I pause before going in. Not out of fear or discomfort. I don't know which version of Bill I'm about to get.

His door is open, but still, I stop to softly knock.

He looks up from his desk, his expression guarded but not hostile. He looks tired, with dark bags under his puffy eyes, his posture stooped from the burden of stress.

"Hey, Bill. I just wanted to say I'm sorry. For yesterday."

"I'm sorry too, Charlie. I didn't handle it the way I should have."

"It hasn't been easy for either of us. No excuses. I just wanted you to hear it from me, that I appreciate everything. The trust. The opportunities. You gave me more than most bosses ever would have."

His expression loosens, the edge finally giving way. Bullseye.

"There are choices we make in this job," Bill says sincerely. "Some of them feel wrong at the moment. Sometimes, even long after. But you make them anyway because the alternative or hesitation is worse. That's what leadership is, execution of what others don't want to see or do."

No time to argue with him. I've heard it before from generals, handlers, directors. The rationale doesn't change. Only the consequences. I give him what he needs to hear right now.

"Bill, you can always count on me. That's why I came here. I wanted you to know that."

Those words hit him hard. I watch the shift happen internally. He softens and recalibrates.

"Thanks, Charlie. It means a lot to hear that from you."

There's nothing else to say. I leave his office and head down the hall as the truth starts catching up to the lie. Will I ever actually tell Bill to his face that I'm not coming back?

Or will I let that version of me, the loyal one, be the last thing he remembers?

I no sooner get back to my desk when an all-hands-on-deck screeches over the intercom. It's a sharp interruption, irritating like fingernails scratching a chalkboard. We constantly have these drills, but this time the announcer's voice sounds urgent.

Colleagues in the pen gather their belongings like zombies and head out the doors. At the assembly hall, BlackSteel's presence has doubled. Operatives in full military gear patrol the area, busily sweeping the crowd as we enter. The room is packed with more security guards than regular staff members.

Reddick makes his way on stage, his stance stiff.

"It has been confirmed that The Union Guard is targeting current and former operatives. This is no longer speculation. They are trying to infiltrate BlackSteel. Working to tear us apart from the inside out."

The room remains quiet as if this is old news.

"This marks our transition to a new phase. As of today, we have compiled a list of final targets for detention. It consists of former operatives, analysts, and individuals with verified links to previous intelligence organizations. These targets have skills that could be leveraged by the Union Guard against us, people from agencies and the military who know how the system works.

"These individuals have been deemed terrorists. They have engaged in defection and disloyalty. You are all mandated to contribute to processing the names."

His decree means additional arrests. More living corpses packed into the bowels of Continental Containment. BlackSteel's relentless, ever-growing machine is becoming an unstoppable force.

Reddick smiles wickedly.

"Everyone back to work. Dismissed."

After Carter's late-night visit, the uneasiness inside me surges. His name better not be on that damn list.

My computer can't boot up fast enough. The names are listed in alphabetical order. No Diaz, Carter. Relief. Scrolling through more names, I recognize some as agents I briefly worked with on cases.

My eyes keep moving, taking in the names, the charges, the notes appended. I do my best not to react to what I am reading.

Then I see it.

Thompson, Alexa, Immediate Detainment.

Everything gets fuzzy. This must be an error. I can't reason what I'm seeing.

Lex. Flagged for detainment.

My vision blurs as a creeping electric panic spreads up my spine.

What the fuck do I do?

I can't just sit here. I have to go… now.

Logic sets in. If I move too fast, if I leave without a reason,

I'll be flagged and added to the crackdown. If I stay, they'll get Lex.

My decision takes seconds; I must risk it and try to save her. I'll excuse myself and leave through the side exit.

I pretend to head to the restroom, veer left, and slip into a quieter hallway. Thankfully, no one is there. I step through the side door and into the open air, lungs tightening as I reach my car.

Driving fast, traffic barely registers. The city blurs past me, blocks vanishing in seconds. My mind races, playing out all scenarios. One thing is certain: I have to get there before anyone else does.

One block away. I make a turn, and my heart sinks.

At the end of the street, there is a parked van with two people standing in front.

BlackSteel.

Then I catch sight of her.

Lex.

Handcuffed, being shoved toward the van.

She is fighting, thrashing against their grip, shouting, but I can't hear what she's saying. Her voice is drowned out by all the commotion.

I can only watch as the doors slam shut, and the van pulls away, disappearing into heavy traffic. Another name crossed off BlackSteel's list.

If only I had been here earlier.

But what was I supposed to do? Stop them? Get apprehended, too? What would that have achieved?

My mind scrambles for a plan, a course of action.

I need Carter.

I can barely manage the words as I hear his voice.

"They took Lex."

"Oh fuck, what happened?"

"What should I do?"

"Shit, Charlie, you're not going to like this, but you need to go back to HQ. Return to work. Complete the rest of the day."

"Carter, are you crazy! Return to work? After this? You want me to go back and act like nothing happened?"

"It's all I can think of right now. If BlackSteel catches a whiff that you're going to try and rescue Lex, you'll end up next to her in jail. Keep your shit together. We'll meet after work."

I try to respond, but nothing fits. Nothing feels right.

"Carter, I…"

"Boss, you gotta trust me. I've got burner phones. Cash. Car. All untraceable. I'll text you the location."

Carter's right. I have no other option.

My body won't stop trembling. I rest my forehead on the steering wheel.

A thought springs into my mind.

The Union Guard letter.

Doubt engulfs me, and I am unsure what next steps to take.

But one thing I know.

I will do whatever it takes to get Lex back.

CHAPTER 41

NO OPTIONS LEFT

"For the love of money is the root of all evil."

— 1 TIMOTHY 6:10

HEADING BACK TO HQ, I anxiously keep looking between the road ahead and the rearview mirror. My mind replays Lex's abduction, how fast it unfolded and how powerless I was to stop it.

I chastise myself for having no options to rescue her.

Carter is right. Returning now to BlackSteel is my only viable option. I brace myself for what is to come next.

My return, just like my departure, goes unnoticed. The morning announcement has left staff in a state of acceptance or denial. Everyone has chosen a side. Some employees look satisfied; they've been waiting for this day. Others sit rigid and quiet, staring past their screens, nervous that they will be accused of being a BlackSteel foe.

"They were on that list," someone mutters as I pass.

"About time," another replies. "President Tuff's finally taking the appropriate action. Those traitors had it coming."

I lock down my expression, forcing it into something blank and forgettable. Keep moving. One foot in front of the other.

As I step into the BlackSteel pen, a recognizable voice shouts above the background noise.

"Running a bit late, aren't we?"

I freeze in my tracks.

It's Victor Hargrove, with his polished shoes propped up on my desktop. He's grinning like the Chesire Cat.

"Victor. Just left for a break, I wanted to make sure I locked my doors. Crime is way up."

He gives a questioning look, brushing imaginary lint off his expensive suit jacket.

"How careless. Memory issues at such a young age? Makes me wonder how you were ever promoted."

"Victor, what are you doing here?"

He gives a tight shrug.

"Waiting for Jackson Kane. We've got a meeting, an important one, but that's not something you'd be privy to now. Tell me, Grayson, are you at least productive down here?"

He obviously doesn't care, so I lie through my teeth.

"I'll be honest with you. I was wrong. About all of it. I didn't see the big picture before. Should've supported the merger from the beginning. BlackSteel is the most efficient system I've seen in my entire career. Decisions get made.

"Privatization, consolidation, and the shift in how we approach intelligence is exactly what this country needed."

Victor appears pleased instead of skeptical. That took little convincing on my part.

"Well," he slowly lets the words drip out, "of course you were wrong. Glad you're man enough to admit it. I'll let Commander Reddick know that you're ready to fall in line. Maybe it will get you out of the pen someday."

He removes his feet off my desk, stands up a bit unbalanced and says no more. He leaves without incident. Performance over. My relief is immeasurable.

I force myself to sit and get back to work.

My screen flickers with the next file, another flagged name rolling into sight. Former FBI agent retired five years ago. No public disagreement. No apparent connection to the Dragon Slayers.

Lex continues to haunt me. Her face appears everywhere as the hours drag by painfully slow. I start packing all of my belongings as the clock inches closer to the end of the workday.

Alone in my car, I wait for Carter's text. A few minutes later, it appears.

Passenger side glove box. White sedan, four blocks north, plate ends in 2L9. Keys inside. Pops' Motel #3.

No response needed. I drive a few blocks, and park on a side street far enough to remain forgettable. No one watches me walk the rest of the way. I'm just a woman getting into a beat-up white car with sun, faded paint and dusty floor mats.

Surprisingly, it starts on the first try. The motel isn't far, but every block feels dramatically extended. There are too many unknowns. Too many things that can go wrong.

Pop's Motel is in need of a major facelift. Rusted cars are sporadically parked, not a soul in sight. The door to room three is unlocked. I cautiously push it open.

The room is dim, lit only by the flicker of a muted TV and the static blue glow of disconnected monitors. The stale air is thick with the smell of cold fries and leftovers, but what stops me in my tracks isn't the unseen or the unheard.

It's Carter.

He's not at his keyboard. He's just sitting in the corner chair, elbows on his knees, hands hanging uselessly like he doesn't know what to do with them. I've never seen him this solemn.

I slowly approach him, unsure of his state of mind.

"Carter? Is everything okay?"

His eyes lift to meet mine, face hollow and wrecked.

"It's my sister."

The words barely leave his lips.

"I just found out... she's missing."

He swallows, jaw clenched tight.

"I think they took her, Charlie. I think BlackSteel got her."

It has to be serious, as he didn't call me boss. I put my hand on his shoulder, his shirt damp with sweat.

"It's bad," he mutters. "It's really bad. It's happening."

Carter reaches for the remote and turns the volume up.

The screen flashes with breaking news.

The anchor's words burst through the speakers, controlled but laced with panic.

"We've never seen anything like this. Major cities are reporting mass detentions across multiple districts. Currently, the administration has not released any official numbers."

Carter doesn't move. I sit down next to him as the screen cuts to raw footage, no transitions, no filters, just mass chaos.

A cell phone video shows a door splintering under the weight of a battering ram. Screams echo from inside as masked Black-Steel agents invade the home.

Another clip captures street footage of Sorakin drones flying low in between buildings, their mechanical demands blaring.

"Do not resist. You have been flagged for detainment. Comply immediately."

One drone hovers midair, projecting a spotlight as BlackSteel operatives charge forward. A man tries to run, but a Sorakin mutt bolts after him. The robotic canine releases a robust hiss as it launches a weighted net.

The man crashes to the pavement, his legs and torso entangled in the heavy mesh. The mutt digs in, dragging him like trash toward a waiting truck.

Another scene appears on the screen, a street corner in a small downtown area. Crowds are shouting at one of their local police officers, who is aiding a BlackSteel op in cuffing a middle-aged man.

"Don't do that, you pig!" someone yells. "He didn't do anything!"

More outcries of protest.

"Stop! Come on, you know him! What are you doing?"

A nun pushes forward from the crowd, grabbing the officer by the arm.

"Officer, you go to my church," she cries, eyes wide and filled with tears. "How can you do this? How can you do this to one of your own citizens?"

The cop avoids looking at her.

A cutaway shot projects a group of teenagers outside a holding site, standing behind barricades, waving makeshift signs. FREE LEO! LET LEO GO! BRING LEO BACK!

An adolescent girl, fighting back tears, shouts at a security officer.

"He didn't do anything! He just posted online! He just graduated from high school!"

Another boy beside her pounds his fist on the fence.

"You can't just take someone for that! He's a kid!"

The camera shakes as guards move in to disperse them. Another officer lifts a restrained teenager toward a hovering drone. It scans his face with a soft chirp.

"Suspect acquired. Immediate detention."

The officer nods like he's ordering lunch and throws him into the back of a van.

The footage keeps rolling. A woman in a bathrobe is yanked from her home as she screams for her child. Drones circle overhead, steely voices shouting out in the same metallic bursts.

"You are in violation of national security protocol. Compliance is mandatory."

I don't realize how hard I'm gripping the edge of the table until my knuckles ache. I've seen regime collapse overseas. But this? This is home.

The footage fades, replaced by the familiar red and black frame of SLY News. The tone shifts dramatically, like a veil being lifted. A polished anchor with a perfect veneer smile faces the camera, calm and clear.

"It's never easy to govern during times of unrest. But the President made it clear, this is what our great nation needs."

Victor Hargrove appears next, seated comfortably in a sleek studio. His attire reeks of arrogant perfection.

"We tried to be fair, but we were called fascists for defending law and order. Well, now these wannabe terrorists understand, actions have consequences.

"If you aid the Dragon Slayers, if you sympathize with their cause, you are a threat to the United States of America. And threats are neutralized."

The screen shifts again. Jackson Kane's face appears, feigning legitimate concern.

"Nobody wants this. But sometimes, to protect the body, you must cut away the infection. That's just governance. You think President Tuff enjoys this? Of course not. But look at what they've forced him to do."

President Tuff flashes onto the screen. It's a prerecorded message with him seated behind a desk. A single American flag is draped behind him. His eyes are dull, devoid of any human emotion.

"For too long, we let the loudest voices pretend they were the majority. Not anymore. You want to support terrorists? Fine. But now you have seen the price that has to be paid for insubordination. We are not negotiating with radicals. We are eliminating them."

He glares into the lens.

"Let this be your wake-up call."

The screen cuts to black.

Carter and I are stunned into silence. The images we have just seen are branded in our minds.

My next words to him are choked with shock.

"My God. It's actually happening.

"I can't believe it.

"I can't believe this is how we fall. Not with war, not with bombs... just... this. Turning on each other. All because the people at the top are scared."

Carter doesn't answer right away. He remains slouched in the chair again, arms still limp, his face suddenly aging.

"Yeah," he says quietly. "But honestly... this is just how it works."

"What do you mean?"

"It's the cycle. Empires rise, rot, collapse. Something new crawls out of the ashes and swears it'll be better. Rinse and repeat. It all starts over again.

"France, Russia, Britain. The Ottomans. Doesn't matter what anyone calls it, democracy, communism, monarchy, it's all just a machine to funnel power to the few. And eventually, that balance breaks."

His tone is subdued, but there's no peace in it.

"I thought maybe we'd finally broken the pattern. That we'd

built something solid enough to hold. But here we are. Drones in the sky. Friends and families disappearing.

"Shit, I don't know, maybe I was naïve. Maybe we all were. Thinking we'd gotten past something like this."

I look at him, unmoving. Not from fear. From recognition.

Carter has a valid point.

Perhaps we can't escape historical recurrences. Each repeat cycle just becomes louder, faster, and deadlier. Knowing the pattern doesn't make it easier to live through. It doesn't bring Lex, Graham, or Carter's sister back. And it certainly doesn't stop the detainments.

Theory means nothing without action.

"Carter, are you able to see anything inside BlackSteel?"

He shakes his head no and keeps working.

I take a step closer.

"Nothing?"

He looks up at me, face is deathly pale.

"Charlie, I've been working nonstop. I even burned access points I've been holding onto for years. BlackSteel has flipped the switch on me. I'm locked out."

"Fuck. Lex is in there somewhere. She has to be."

"Yeah boss. Not giving up. It's not just encryptions and firewalls now. It's Sorakin Tech, truly next-level stuff."

"Carter, I thought you of all people would find a way in."

"Me too, but I've never seen anything like this."

Neither of us says what we're both thinking.

If Lex isn't found soon, I might never see her again.

Carter shifts uncomfortably in his chair.

"What about the Union Guard?"

I look at him sharply.

"Did you get a letter too?"

He runs a hand through his hair before answering.

"Yeah, I destroyed it. But maybe we should reach out to them. They're the only ones with the resources to hit a detention site from the outside in. If we offer our services, maybe they can help us get Graham and Lex free."

I feel my stomach drop. The idea of contacting what amounts to a terrorist militia makes my skin crawl.

"Carter, that's insane. We'd be crossing a line we can't come back from."

"Boss, look around. The lines are already gone. They took Graham. They took Lex. They took my sister. What line is left to cross?"

There is urgency when he speaks.

"We don't have the luxury of time. We're not going to rescue them by just sitting here, hoping for a lucky break. This is our only shot."

"Carter, do you hear yourself? Contacting a terrorist militia?"

"Yeah, I do. And I also hear BlackSteel's drones outside every night. I see the detention vans rolling through neighborhoods. You want to stick to protocol while more people disappear forever?"

His words strike hard. I look at the muted TV screen, still showing footage of the mass detentions.

"Carter..."

"Boss, we do this, or we do nothing. Those are our options."

"This could be a death sentence Carter."

"Maybe. But what's the alternative? Let them rot in some BlackSteel hole?"

The weight of it settles on me, the decision crystallizing. He's right, and we both know it.

His fingers drum an impatient beat against the side of his laptop.

"Carter, I have the letter they sent me."

"Shit, boss, we're serious. Okay. But if we're doing this, we're not doing it here. Last thing I want is them pinging this location."

I scoop up my bag as he closes his laptop.

"Carter, where are we headed?"

"Somewhere less traceable. I've got another car parked a few blocks away. We'll leave the one you drove here. You got everything out of it, right?"

I give him a thumbs up, quietly impressed. It's smart of Carter to keep our tracks covered like this, even if it feels like we're one step from vanishing ourselves.

We wait until dusk before leaving the motel, heading for Carter's latest ride. It's a battered SUV, the sort of car you would buy at an auto auction, for parts. The engine sputters and then bellows to life, a dark, endless road lies ahead of us.

Carter is focused on driving with dull headlights, while I look out the window revisiting Lex's abduction. I need to mentally stop beating myself up over my failure to keep her safe.

I break my mental torment with a question for him.

"Hey Carter, why did you join the FBI?"

He lets out a short breath, almost a laugh.

"I kind of had to. Got caught hacking into a few off-limits systems. Mainly a satellite or two, when I was only fifteen. Thought I was slick until they showed up at my door asking for me by name.

"Thankfully, we struck a deal. Sure, I was basically on eternal probation. Lucky for me, the FBI saw what I could do, and I jumped at the opportunity to avoid prison for the next twenty years."

He leans back, eyes distant for a moment.

"But I'm glad it worked out the way it did. Honestly, my

brain is just wired to keep working on something all the time. And doing something that makes a difference in people's lives? That keeps me sane. There's no way I could ever be one of those tech bros pushing dopamine buttons and pretending it's innovation."

"Why not? Think about all the money and fame you could have."

"Those losers think they're God's gift to mankind. They slap together some app that ruins lives and makes people miserable, calling it disruptive innovation. Acting like they're saving the planet when really, they're raking in billions. Then they have the nerve to ask themselves why the rest of us are suffering. That's not the world I signed up to be a part of.

"I do what I do for the challenge and to make people's lives better. Not fame, not fortune."

He looks at me.

"And sometimes you meet some interesting people along the way."

"Interesting? I hope that includes me."

"Oh, you're more than interesting. You're the main event. The one who is going to get me killed or make my life a lot more entertaining. I'm still trying to decide which outcome is more likely."

Carter pulls into a vacant lot. The air is peaceful, the surroundings too quiet, making the night feel strangely soothing.

Doubt flashes across his face.

"Alright, you ready boss?"

Without hesitation, I open the Union Guard letter, grab my phone and read the instructions out loud.

Sign on to the VPN.

Type in the encrypted number.

Instantly, the call connects.

"Charlie. We're glad you called."

No ringing or delay. Just a direct link. Someone has been waiting for this, which makes me wonder if we're being watched right now. His voice jolts something loose in me. It's familiar, but I can't place it, like something on the tip of my tongue.

"I want to know what this is all about."

His reply is precise; every word sharpened for effect.

"Our current government has abandoned its citizens. What we seek is restoration. Real representation. To do that, we're bringing together those with the experience and conviction to make it happen."

"And you think that's me?"

His words are full of conviction.

"We don't think it, we know it. Your record. Your recent actions. All clear statements."

My mind jumps back to Lex and Graham, alone and trapped in a system built to make people disappear.

"Please, I need your help. People I know were taken by BlackSteel. I need to get them out!"

"Charlie, we have the means. But before we take any action, we need something from you."

"What kind of something?"

"You'll hear that in person. Sending a location to this number. Come alone. We'll discuss what comes next."

The line goes dead before I can ask anything else.

"So? What the hell did he say?"

"He knew my name. They've been watching us. Asked for a face-to-face meeting."

"Then you should do it. If there's even the faintest chance they can help us, you have to take it."

I shake my head.

"Carter, we don't know who or what this is. Union Guard,

Dragon Slayers, BlackSteel setting traps. I could disappear just like Lex and Graham."

"I know boss, I get it. Believe me, I don't like the idea of you walking into something like this alone. But I do think this is the only thing we can do."

I stare out the windshield for a long moment, weighing it all.

"You're right," I finally say. "Even if this does backfire, the thought of not doing everything I could would haunt me more."

My phone vibrates with a message. It's the location. Just coordinates that put us about forty minutes outside the city limits, by an unfamiliar rural access road. A perfect place for a meeting or an ambush.

We drive back to the motel in silence. Carter pulls up next to the car we left there. Before I can open the door, he turns to me.

"Hey. You've got this, okay? And if something happens, if you go missing, I'll do everything I can to find you. I swear."

"Thanks, Carter. I mean that. For everything."

"Oh, and boss," he smirks. "Take care of that ride."

I slide into the car and start the engine. There's no point in second-guessing it now. I've made my choice. I follow the route on my phone, driving straight into the unknown.

As I pull into the destination given to me, I check the dashboard clock: 9:47 p.m. Three minutes.

Exiting the car, I take a breath of fresh air and try to compose myself. The clearing is empty, with nothing but dust, gravel, and some scattered trees. My footsteps crunch underneath me as darkness recedes into infinity.

Two minutes. My heart beats faster, my nerves unhinged.

What am I doing? What if this is a trap? What if Blacksteel is lurking, waiting to make me vanish forever?

Then there's the other possibility, insidious and unrelenting.

What if the voice on the phone was not telling the truth?

What if this is a Union Guard or Dragon Slayer setup? What if they're done playing games with me?

I need to banish my paranoia. If the Dragon Slayers wanted me dead, they would have killed me at the Manor.

At 9:49 p.m., headlights emerge on the far road. My breath hitches as the darkness is lit up, the low growl of a powerful engine shattering the stillness.

I check my watch once more: 9:50pm. Naturally, whoever it is would be on time.

A dark-colored van rolls into view, high-beam headlights aimed straight at me. I instinctively shield my eyes, but the light doesn't move. It stays locked on me like a hunter's spotlight on a trapped deer.

The engine cuts out. Doors open, heavy, and slow. I can't see anything beyond the glare, only silhouettes moving toward me with practiced coordination.

One of them speaks, firm and impersonal.

"Turn around. Hands above your head."

I hesitate.

"You asked me here to talk. Is this really necessary?"

There's no reply. I do what they demand, lifting my hands, and try not to flinch at the sound of footsteps moving closer. Gravel shifts behind me, fast and sharp.

"Why do it like this? I'm not here to fight."

Before I can react, a hood is yanked over my head, and I am plunged into darkness. I fight back, but they are stronger. My wrists are yanked behind me, zip ties biting into my flesh.

My struggle is muffled beneath the hood.

"What are you doing? We're here to talk!"

No one replies, their grip unshaken as they drag me into the van. My boots scrape along the ground as I struggle to no avail.

The van door groans open, and I feel the cold metal edge as

they push me inside. The hard surface bites into me as they strap me in place.

Doors slam shut, the sound ringing through the tight space like a gun blast. Then, with a thunderous roar, the engine kicks into life, and the van lurches forward, pitching me off balance.

Bound and blindfolded.

I am at their mercy.

CHAPTER 42

NO TURNING BACK

"If you want a picture of the future, imagine a
boot stamping on a human face—forever."

- GEORGE ORWELL

THE PAIN IN my body is rising from the van's constant jerking, the cold metal floor unforgiving beneath me. My focus now is on tracking the passage of time by listening to the vibration of the tires and the mechanical purr of the engine.

It's difficult to concentrate on any sensory clues as my mind is scattered with frantic thoughts. It must be them, the Dragon Slayers. The timing, the precision, it all adds up.

The van stops abruptly, jerking me forward. The engine shuts off as front doors creak open, followed by the sound of boots scuffing in the gravel. A flood of light and fresh air enters through the hood, as the doors behind me open wide. Firm hands grasp my arms lifting me up and leading me away.

I strain to hear muffled voices, scrapes from shoes on pavement and the groan of a heavy door opening in front of me.

Inside, it's warm, the scent of lemon wood polish and fireplace ember inter-fused together.

My captors lead me through a series of twists and turns. I stumble once, but steady hands correct me, readjusting my balance.

We reach their destination as they guide me to a stiff wood chair, heat radiating against my back. My heart pounds in my chest, as I sit, bound, blindfolded; helplessly waiting for their next move.

The hood that blinded me is carefully removed. Light assails my eyes, and I blink rapidly to adjust my vision.

The room I'm in is lavish, tall ceilings, dark wood paneling, with a fireplace burning brightly in one corner. My chair is in the middle of the room with people standing around me like sentinels, wearing black and gold masks. The Dragon Slayer insignia adorned on their tactical gear.

A wave of relief washes over me. It's not BlackSteel, yet there is no guarantee of my fate. The Dragon Slayers were not my executioners last time, but it doesn't mean it will be a similar outcome this time around.

The mask is familiar, as is the way he stands, unfazed, self-assured. The voice on the phone.

It's the same man from the ambush at Fairchild Manor.

"Well, well, well, Charlotte Grayson. We meet again."

I meet his gaze.

"You certainly went through a lot of trouble getting me here. Now what?"

He looks at me for a moment, his head tilted. The others are still, their masks revealing nothing of their thoughts. The silence is heavy, deliberate.

"Patience," he says, dripping with an air of authority. "You'll know soon enough."

I fight against the zip ties; the plastic cutting into my flesh. My eyes scan the room before coming to rest on him once more. He seems far too relaxed, far too self-assured for a man who has just abducted me.

"Do you actually need to keep me bound like this? I came of my own accord."

"Precautions, Charlie. You understand. It's not often an agency higher up like you strolls into our clutches."

His tone carries a hint of amusement, as though he's explaining something that's painstakingly obvious.

"For all we know, this could still be a trap."

"If this is a trap, would I be sitting here tied up in the middle of nowhere? I'm just saying you're not providing me with much of an incentive to cooperate here."

A low chuckle escapes him.

"Fair point. You've got guts, Grayson. I'll give you that. Perhaps I have been rude. Let's start over."

Before I can answer, he grabs his belt. My muscles react as he draws out a knife, but he doesn't look to strike, merely steps forward and cuts through the zip ties with a neat, efficient motion. The plastic cracks, and I release a breath, massaging my wrists, skin chafed from the restraints.

"Better?" he asks, standing up straight.

"Marginally," I reply, rolling stiff shoulders.

The Dragon Slayer raises his hands to his mask and, in a graceful move, takes it off. His face is sharper than I imagined, high cheekbones, strong jaw, and dark eyes that pin me with quiet intensity. There's a gentleness to him, the way his gaze stays in place longer than it should, a hint of kindness.

Not to be mistaken, his body structure makes it clear he's dangerous. Muscles carved by years of combat, a frame built for endurance and violence.

"You can call me Tristan."

"Is Tristan your actual name, or just an alias?"

"Code name. But at this point, that is all I am."

"Okay, Tristan. Why am I here?"

"We're trying to stop the world from collapsing, Charlie."

"Really, with everything you Dragon Slayers have already done? It seems that you're trying to make it collapse."

"You have a fair point. But rest assured, we're also doing our best to right the wrong. Honestly?

We never expected to go this far. In the beginning, it was all about disruption, breaking the system, making people forego their ignorance and see their blindness."

Tristan's face darkens.

"But the way citizens got behind us, the way the money started rolling in, it exceeded our expectations."

He exhales, the kind that comes before a trigger pull.

"We thought we'd get caught. We were ready to die at any point. The system doesn't let people like us win, not for long."

Tristan shifts his stance, standing a little taller.

"We didn't make it this far on our own. It was ordinary people who did. The masses snowballing our plan until it became unstoppable. And the administration's response?

"They only fueled the fire. They're the ones that made us inevitable."

"So, Tristan, what's next? You've got momentum, popular support and god knows how much money. What's the Dragon Slayers' end game?

"We wanted all of it, definitely, but it's the classic case of a dog catching the car they're chasing."

"Not exactly reassuring, given the state of America."

"Charlie, you're not mistaken. We thought breaking the system would make room for something better, something righteous, something that can actually last. But the administration's response changed everything.

"The crackdowns… they're not just brutal anymore. They're efficient and automated. Sorakin Tech's AI has given them a force multiplier we didn't anticipate this soon."

He pauses.

"We're not just facing soldiers who follow orders for a paycheck, even when they know deep down it's wrong. Now we're up against emotionless machines that don't blink, hesitate, or wrestle with morality. They execute."

Tristan lowers his tone.

"If we're not careful, what we've done could hand the oligarchs everything they need to make their power permanent."

"So now you're attempting to keep it together?"

"Exactly. We're in touch with the Union Guard, military officers, political allies, and business leaders who've distanced themselves from the billionaire class. We have verbal guarantees, promises to stand down when the time arrives.

"Right now, they're not actively assisting. But they're listening. That's why we need individuals like you, who can fill in the blanks. Those who can rebuild."

"Rebuild how? Are the Dragon Slayers planning to dictate the next government?

His expression turns stern.

"No. That's not our task. We're building a foundation to hold free elections. No kings or dictators. A free choice."

I search his face for any hint of deception.

"You actually believe that can happen?"

"I must. It's the only way it's going to work."

"You want me to be a collaborator?"

Tristan's eyes tighten.

"That's half of it. We'd like you to continue what you've been doing after everything falls into place. You came close to catching us. That kind of talent is worth holding onto."

I look at him quizzically.

"And the other half?"

"That's the tricky part, Charlie. We need you for something bigger. Our next mission is to break out the ones being swallowed up by these crackdowns. If we free enough of them, we can rally the support we need to finally push the regime out.

"The real problem now is Sorakin. Their tech is locking these facilities down tighter than ever."

"What's your plan?" I demand.

He reaches into his jacket, pulls out a USB drive, and holds it up high.

"This."

"Another USB? Let me guess. You want me to plug this one into BlackSteel's network."

"Right answer. You can help us access everything, facility locations, prisoner manifests, security levels. But more than that, this gets us into Sorakin's systems. Their infrastructure is tied directly into BlackSteel's backbone. If we can breach it through this access point, we'll have a chance to disable their platforms, drones, surveillance, AI targeting. The whole shebang.

"We can't afford guesswork and need total precision to hit every site at once. If BlackSteel senses a breach, they'll start executing the detainees before we even get close.

"If we pull this off, we can take down Sorakin long enough to strike. It'll show the regime isn't untouchable and will ignite a firestorm. People will believe it's possible, and that's all the Union Guard needs to make their move."

I feel light-headed. It's reckless. It's suicidal. There is no other alternative.

"I'm in. But I want something in exchange as well."

"Alexa Thompson and Graham Cross, right? Saving them hinges on you, Grayson. Secure access for us so we can get to your friends and free them along with a lot of other innocent people.

"You need to move quickly. The longer we wait, the better chances BlackSteel will have to clean house. And if they do…"

"Tristan, I understand what you're saying. I'll take care of it. But let's be clear. I'm only doing this for Lex and Graham. Don't think it's more than that. The Dragon Slayers' actions, your actions, they're horrific. You've caused nothing but destruction and pain."

There's no retreat in him. He stays steady, locked in.

"You're not wrong. I've been surrounded by war my entire life. I used to tell myself that it had meaning, that the killing was for a purpose."

Tristan stops, his words hitting a nerve deep inside him.

"Eventually, I realized none of it mattered. I'm just another cog, keeping it running smoothly. Yes, I've done terrible things. We all have. The Dragon Slayers aren't heroes. We're what happens when a system built to destroy finally turns on its creators.

"But after this? After all we've accomplished? I will stand proud. Call me a monster and I won't deny it. The world is a different place now. The people in power? They're afraid. And they should be.

"Even if we don't succeed, the world will never be the same. Those in control will always be waiting for the next uprising. They'll never rest easy again."

There is truth in Tristan's words. This moment of vulnerability replaced by the familiar confidence he wears like a shield.

"Now, let's get you back to your car," he commands.

Tristan gestures to two masked operatives standing at either side of the room. One of them is holding the same black hood I had placed on me during my abduction.

"Seriously?" I deadpan. "Again?"

Tristan's words are tinged with amusement.

"Precautions, Charlie."

The hood is placed back over my head, engulfing me in darkness. I can feel Tristan beside me, his hand firm on my back, ensuring my safe passage to the van. He helps me inside as I settle against the metal floor. It's still uncomfortable, but this time, I'm not afraid of what's ahead. The doors close behind us, leaving me alone with my thoughts.

The drive back seems endless until the van brakes sharply, throwing me forward. The door groans open as the cold night air rushes across my face. Dragon Slayers help me out, removing the hood as one of them hands me the USB.

"Get moving, Grayson. Make sure you finish the job."

I turn to face him, but the doors close before I can even utter a word. The tires screech as the van speeds off, leaving me alone beneath the star-marked sky.

The clunker that Carter gave me takes several attempts to start. When it finally does, I head back to the motel in great haste. The USB drive concealed in my pocket presses against my skin, a constant reminder that I am at the point of no return.

By the time I rap my knuckles against the motel room door, I am physically and mentally depleted. He cracks open the door, and I see that he is mirroring my exhaustion.

"Charlie, thank god," he says, shaking his head in incredulity. "To be honest, I didn't think you'd return."

I arch an eyebrow.

"And you just let me go with them? You didn't even try to stop me?"

"What was I supposed to do? Tackle you? You'd break my arm and throw me on the ground and then walk out anyway."

"Good point."

I retrieve the USB from my pocket and slide it to him.

"It was the Dragon Slayers, and they're asking me to plug this into the BlackSteel systems to get to Sorakin."

"You're kidding? That's insane. Even for you."

"That's the job. Get all the intel on the detainees and cripple Sorakin."

He rubs his hands together.

"Alright, let's see what they're sending you off with."

Carter fires up a laptop and inserts the device. Rows of code flicker across the monitor as he begins to scroll through the files.

"Well?" I ask impatiently.

His eyes stay locked on the code.

"Boss, here's the deal. If you insert this, it'll try to auto-execute, but that's a gamble. Sorakin's endpoint security can block autorun, sandbox the process, and flag the signature.

"But if you're logged in and run it, then it's a whole different story. Because now it's operating inside a trusted session. With elevated access, permissions, Sorakin can't stop that."

"So, what are the odds of it working if I just plug it in?" I ask, dreading his answer.

"Honestly? Ten percent. Tops, and that's the generous version. If you try it without being logged in, there's a good chance Sorakin flags it on the spot."

"Okay then. What are the odds if I'm already logged in?"

Carter's words flow right out.

"One hundred percent success. As long as it's the right machine, with admin-level access. That's the key. If you've got that, the system won't question a thing."

"And I'm guessing I don't have that authorization clearance."

Carter reclines back in his chair, a devilish grin on his face.

"In the pen? Not even close. But you know who does?"

"Bill… fuck you're telling me that I have to access Bill's computer?"

"Exactly. Tough, but doable. And you're in luck. Got something that'll help."

Carter waves a piece of paper in the air.

"Bill's password. Assuming he hasn't changed it."

"Christ, you have Bill's password?"

"I snatched as many passwords as I could get my hands on before I walked out. Figured they'd come in handy."

I stare at him in disbelief.

Carter clears his throat theatrically.

"Let's see, for Director Cartwright, it's *CorvetteLover4545!*"

"You're kidding."

"Nope, I guess Bill loves cars. You just need to figure out how to get into his computer without him noticing."

A few weeks ago, I would have balked at this whole thing, not even taking the time to consider it. The idea of betraying the Bureau, of placing a backdoor into a system I once swore to defend, would have been unthinkable.

Treason. That is what this is. That is what they will label it.

The new normal is that the FBI doesn't exist anymore. Tuff and his administration gutted it and allowed BlackSteel to fill the void. The true betrayal did not begin with me. It began when those in power determined that billionaires were more vital to safeguard than the nation itself.

But none of that matters now.

They have Lex, and I am going to get her back.

CHAPTER 43

BREAKING TIES

"It is the duty of the patriot to protect his country from its government."

-THOMAS PAINE

IT'S EARLY MORNING when I leave. My feet feel like lead as I head towards the car. There is no way for me to deny what I am about to do. It's treason. But then again, it's not the FBI anymore. And this sure as hell isn't the United States I signed up to defend.

If this were a year ago, I wouldn't have even entertained the thought. Now? I've jumped over the line. And if it means getting Lex back by pulling her out of whatever hell BlackSteel buried her in, I'd forsake every accolade and honor I've ever earned.

First stop, the pharmacy. Entering the store, I hurry to the OTC aisle for digestive aids. Ex-Lax. One box will do. I take it and walk directly to self-checkout and then continue my drive to work.

At the entrance of headquarters, Reddick's voice cuts through the air like a whip, shouting at employees to get a move on.

I muster a respectful smile as I walk past him.

"Good morning, Commander Reddick. I saw your proposal for redirecting resources. It's a great reallocation for our efforts."

Reddick replaces his scowl with one of surprise.

"Glad somebody around here has some common sense. More people need to appreciate my strategic genius."

God, I hate that bastard.

Pretending to head to the pen, I sneak a peek at Bill in his office, flipping through a file.

Ex-military, he balances his life and work with daily routines. Exactly at 8:45 a.m., without fail, he gets up and heads to the break room for his second cup of coffee. Like clockwork.

Today, his ritual will come in handy.

At 8:43, I knock on Bill's open door. He looks up, surprised to see me.

"Good morning, Bill. I'm going to get coffee. Do you want me to bring you a cup?"

He looks at his empty coffee mug and hands it to me.

"Sure, Charlie. Black, two sugars. Thanks."

In the break room, I fill his mug with coffee, add a pinch of sugar, and retrieve the Ex-Lax from my bag. My hands tremble as I break off a few pieces, drop them into the steaming coffee and stir until the laxative is completely dissolved.

Here we go.

"Hope I didn't make it too sweet," I say setting the mug on his desk.

"Thanks, Charlie, for saving me a trip."

Staying out of sight in the corridor, I watch him take his first sip. He doesn't grimace at the taste.

It will take a while for the Ex-lax to work, hopefully sooner rather than later. I can barely make out Bill's office from the Pen, but I'm focused, watching through the glass as he shifts around inside.

Around two o'clock, I see him.

Bill hustling past, hands pressed to his stomach, posture hunched just enough to give him away.

Leaving my desk I say to no one in particular.

"I'm gonna grab something to eat."

Nonchalantly, I head to his office, enter and close the door behind me. His laptop is open, so I enter his password.

My hands shake as I type it in: *CorvetteLover4545!*

Invalid password.

Fuck.

Do I try to insert the USB and hope it works?

If Bill catches me hovering over his laptop, it's over. He'll know something's off. I pause, weighing the risk. No, I need to be logged in first. That's the only way this will work. I have to try again.

Maybe I entered it incorrectly. My pulse hammers as I try again, slower this time.

CorvetteLover4545!

Invalid password.

My fingers tighten into fists. Bill must have changed it. If he did, there's no way I'm getting in without a few more tries before being locked out.

I grit my teeth, my mind racing through contingencies. Do I just risk it? The second I insert the thumb drive, who knows how many alarms it'll set off.

Then I notice it.

The tiny, glowing light on the keyboard. Caps lock.

A sharp exhale leaves my lips, half-relief, half-frustration. I switch it off and try again, forcing my hands to stay steady.

CorvetteLover4545!

The screen wakes up, then unlocks.

Relief washes over me, but it's fleeting. I insert the USB and the computer pings softly. A message pops up: Do you want to run this program?

My fingers hesitate over the trackpad. This is treason. I won't just lose my job, I'll disappear. And so will Lex. I don't think twice and click on yes.

The progress bar pops up and my stomach drops. Carter didn't mention this part. I freeze for a second, watching it slowly crawl forward. Every little noise, the running computer, clock ticking, footsteps in the hall, is earsplitting. I look at the door, my heart pounding. 43%. Each second feels like an eternity.

A shadow crosses by the door frame, and I hold my breath. I twist a strand of my hair in an effort to remain calm as the shadow moves on.

At 75%, the doorknob clicks. I dash toward the shelf next to Bill's desk. My eyes land on a framed photo, Bill and my dad from decades ago, smiling together. I grab it just as the door creaks open.

Bill walks in, a look of confusion on his face.

"Charlie? What the hell are you doing here?"

I turn, holding the photo tightly, mustering a sheepish grin.

"Sorry, Bill. I don't know what came over me, but this photo of you and my dad, I've always liked it. I saw it earlier this morning. And well. It's just been so hard lately."

Bill's face softens as his confusion gives way.

"Ah, that was a great day. Charlie, your dad was one of the best, if not the best."

I continue to study the photo.

"I've been thinking about him a lot, with all that's going on. What do you think my father would say about all this? About me?"

Bill smiles warmly.

"He would be very proud of you."

Internally, I'm screaming for the loading bar to finish. My head is reeling. Speak, Bill. Just a little longer.

"Bill, I keep feeling that I've let him down. No matter how bad things got, he always had a solution. What do you think he'd do in a situation like mine?"

"Your father was a special guy. He had a remarkable way of cutting through the bull and seeing the big picture. I think he'd tell you to trust yourself, Charlie."

I nod as my eyes wander to the laptop. 94%. So close now.

Bill's stomach starts to growl ferociously . His face tightens in response, and he winces a bit.

"Uh, hold that thought. I need to…"

He truncates himself mid-sentence, already moving toward the door.

The moment he's gone, I rush behind his desk. The screen flashes the message: Program installed successfully.

My hands tremble as I yank the USB free and tuck it safely in my pocket. I tug my shirt straight and calm my nerves. You did it. Now, get out.

The thumb drive in my pocket feels like a ticking time bomb as I enter the hallway.

My heart races, but I pace myself, my steps measured. I take in my surroundings, looking for a spot, somewhere to get rid of it.

The women's bathroom.

I check the stalls to make sure no one else is in there. It's empty. Perfect. I crush the thumb drive with my boot and flush it down the toilet. I scrub my hands as if I have blood on them.

Back in the pen, paranoia overwhelms me, and I feel sick to

my stomach. I sit perfectly still, pretending to read reports, while a maelstrom of what-ifs spins in my head.

What if they tracked it through the system? What if Bill suspects something is wrong? What if there is security footage of me logging onto his laptop?

Every time a BlackSteel agent walks by my gut clenches.

"Grayson."

Reddick jerks me out of my uneasiness. He is a few feet away, face impassive.

"Grayson, come with me."

My blood freezes. This is it, they know. My legs wobble as I stand and follow Reddick. My mind beseeching me to run.

What's my story? What can I say? Will the Dragon Slayers keep their word even if I'm caught?

He walks in front of me, guiding me into a small conference room. My heart races as I enter and see wide-eyed faces staring at me.

Interns. A group of them, barely old enough to buy beer, stand in a group looking as hopeless as I do.

Reddick points at them.

"You're going to train these analysts."

"Train them? On what?"

"Analysis. We're shorthanded. These are the best we could get."

I gaze at the group of wannabe agents. They look like they've been plucked from the street. One of them is scribbling in a notebook. Another is obnoxiously chewing gum.

"Commander, do any of them have experience?"

"No, but they're here. Put them to work."

The absurdity of it all hits me like a wave. BlackSteel, the great, feared organization, is scraping the bottom of the barrel.

I clap my hands together to get everyone's attention.

"I'm Analyst Charlotte Grayson. We have rules here. Rule number one, no doodling."

The young man gives me a sharp look before awkwardly shutting his notebook.

"Rule number two. No chewing gum."

The intern blows a bubble, pops it, and then spits the gum into the garbage bin.

These little shits. Well, if Reddick said to put them to work, I certainly have brainless tasks for them. Hours and hours of it.

I continue to anxiously look at my watch while reviewing the basics of analysis with the interns.

Finally, it's time to clock out. I gather my belongings to head to Carter at the motel. The whole day has been a case of walking on eggshells, waiting for something to blow.

But nothing did. Either I managed to pull it off or it was a complete failure.

I drive to the lot where Carter had parked the swap car and transfer my gear. Inside, I squeeze the steering wheel tight.

Was that the last time I'd ever walk through HQ's doors? Has to be. There is no going back from my treasonous actions. Installing the Dragon Slayers' virus was an overstepping of boundaries. The ultimate betrayal.

The motel looms before me, depressing and impersonal. I drive into the parking lot, shut off the engine and try to compose myself. My heartbeat hasn't slowed down.

As I open the door, I see Carter. He's sprawled on the couch, one arm tossed over his head, but as I come in, he sits up, grinning.

"You know I am looking forward to the day when you leaving doesn't make me wonder if you're dead or not."

I collapse into the chair opposite him, my head dropping back. The ceiling is a blurry haze as I close my eyes, the adrenaline coursing under my skin, tightening its grip rather than easing.

"Yeah, well, considering how things stand, I wouldn't hold your breath, Carter."

"So, this is it? They got us to carry out one of the most important cyber sabotage missions in history, and now we just sit around waiting?

"I mean, I have been thinking, what if the Dragon Slayers are done with us?"

"Then we're deadlocked until one side wins out. And if it's Blacksteel…"

Carter squirms.

"Then we're traitors, boss, well likely very dead traitors. Or the other side wins, and the nation collapses. Not exactly ideal choices."

"No, they're not."

Carter grabs the remote and turns on the TV, lowering the volume.

"Might as well watch how bad it is out there."

The news feed isn't supposed to shock me anymore. I've seen mass detainments. Drone strikes. Children dragged out of homes. But this? This is different.

A line of soldiers stands rigid on a highway overpass. One of them drops his rifle. Another follows, tossing his helmet into the back of a transport truck. A third just shakes his head and walks away. A tank hatch opens, and the armor crew inside willingly climb out in reckless abandonment.

"In cities struck by BlackSteel's crackdowns, riots are subsiding as local governments regain control. Police units have resumed patrols, and community leaders are urging solidarity."

The clip shifts to a general in full dress uniform, speaking into a cluster of microphones outside a federal building.

"These are not lawful orders, we will not act as enforcers for private corporations. Not now. Not ever."

The feed keeps rolling.

State governors hold rushed press conferences, their statements steady and determined.

"BlackSteel has no jurisdiction here, and we will not permit the use of Sorakin platforms for detention in our cities."

Another chimes in.

"The administration has abandoned vast sections of this country. We are filling the gap ourselves, without them."

The camera cuts away, citizens hosing down graffiti, sweeping broken glass off the fronts of stores. A mayor at a podium, surrounded by officials, speaks boldly.

"We rebuild together. We will not wait for someone else to do it for us. To our local residents, please, the billionaires are not in our communities anymore, stop trashing businesses, cars and homes."

The video switches to looming walls, vigilant guards, and concrete bastion towers behind steel barricades.

The reporter continues his broadcast.

"Meanwhile, the Freedom Zones remain in lockdown, with supplies being routinely dropped off to their compounds. The U.S. government insists it still has command of the nation."

Carter scoffs.

"Withdrawing from the majority of the nation hardly suggests command."

The next segment continues with pictures of vacant government buildings, deserted federal offices, the husk of a nation wiped out.

The anchor grows more incisive.

"The administration's latest actions seem exclusively aimed

at preserving the fortified zones, resulting in much of the country being devoid of federal supervision, supplies and support."

"They're running out of people," I whisper. "And resources, as well."

"That's the outcome, boss, when you're no longer the wealthiest in the room."

The chaos is unraveling in every direction, but for the first time, BlackSteel doesn't look invincible. The fissures are there. The question is who will be left standing when it all comes crashing down.

The burner phone buzzes. I pick it up.

It's Tristan.

"Good work, Charlie. Next step. Pick up tomorrow. Diaz and you. 10 a.m. Be packed and ready."

The line goes dead.

My expression lets Carter know that I have another request.

"Well boss, let me have it."

"They want you to come too."

Carter's eyes widen, confusion replacing fear.

"Wait what? What do you mean they want me?"

"Look. I don't think we have a choice here Carter."

"We? I'm not talking about we? I'm talking about me."

My plea is sincere.

"Carter, if the Dragon Slayers want us, it's because they need us to free Lex and Graham. They need your tech-savvy skills. They're gearing up for war. This could be our only chance to save scores of lives."

"Damn it. This isn't what I signed up for."

"I know, but we're already in the thick of it. Do you think BlackSteel will care if we were forced to assist the Dragon Slayers?"

"Shit. Fine. Whatever. They better at least give me one of those masks."

The burner phone buzzes again. It's an address. I hold it up for Carter to see. He leans in, squinting.

"A mall? That's where they want us to meet?"

"Apparently. Tomorrow. Ten a.m."

We exchange a look. No words, just a quiet agreement settling between us.

Carter walks over to the small sofa and settles down on it.

"Guess I get the couch again. Not going to get much sleep anyway."

I will not protest, giving him a weak smile as I settle into bed. The worn bed sheets are musty, in need of a good washing, but right now, they feel wonderful. I close my eyes, and everything ceases to exist.

It's not restful sleep, but it's the kind I can't fight. I toss and turn, nightmares fractured, my body bracing for dawn.

Sunlight finally starts cutting through the motel window. I rub my eyes and check the time. Two hours before we need to move out.

The bathroom door clicks open, and Carter steps out in fresh clothes with a towel over his shoulders.

"Morning. Ready to hang out with some terrorists at the mall?"

"Carter, you coming along means a lot for Lex, Graham and especially for me."

He gives me a look, half teasing, half sincere.

"Boss, don't get all sentimental on me. I've been thinking about it, and somehow, this might be the best plan we've got. Which says a lot about how shit the rest are."

"Fair enough. I'm grabbing a quick shower, then we'll head out."

He gives me a mock salute.

"I'll be packed in ten."

The lukewarm water trickles out of the showerhead. It's a small comfort, but I relish it. Could be days before I get another one. Might as well enjoy it while I can.

Dressing quickly, I step out of the bathroom to find Carter ready to go. He has two large gear bags and a suitcase at his feet. Most likely, they contain all his worldly belongings. We head out together, walking toward the car, our fate unknown.

As we leave the parking lot, Carter starts to fidget.

"What do you suppose this is about? And what did Tristan mean by my skills?

"Carter, you're a master of tech and network analysis, a valuable commodity. Any side would want to have you."

"Yeah, sure whatever, I guess. But last time you were zip-tied with a hood over your head. Doesn't sound like a fun interview process."

Carter smirks as he runs his fingers through his wavy black hair.

My response to him is direct.

"The Dragon Slayers didn't hurt me, and they're not going to hurt you. I promise."

"You say that, but I'm getting a bad feeling."

He's not wrong. This meetup seems off the mark.

As we pull into the car park, it's nearly full. The mall is crowded, even though most stores have only just reopened after the chaos of the riots finally subsided. Customers bustle in and out, some already loading shopping bags into cars. None of this suggests a secret meeting.

We step out of the car as Carter looks around the lot, his eyes darting back and forth.

"So, we just wait here and an unmarked van swings by and collects us?"

I ignore his comment, instead focusing my attention on our surroundings.

A man approaches. No armor, no mask, normal clothes, blending right in.

I recognize him at once.

"Tristan."

He grins, extending his hand.

"Charlie. Good to see you again. Mr. Diaz, glad you could join us."

Carter hesitates, then extends his hand.

"Uh, yeah. So, no van kidnapping?"

Tristan chuckles, shaking his head.

"Nope. Just me this time, sorry to disappoint. You'd be amazed how easy it is to blend in without the masks and armor."

"Yeah. The masks do sort of scream terrorist."

"Exactly, but they're just symbols and well, bulletproof. They look scary, sure, but the real power is what happens when they come off. How you can blend right back in without them.

"Right now, I'm just an ordinary guy doing some shopping. Hell, there could be Dragon Slayers walking right past you in broad daylight, and you'd never know."

He gestures to a parked sedan, black, gold trim and dark tinted windows.

Carter mutters under his breath.

"So, no zip ties and hoods?"

Tristan glances over his shoulder, breaking a smile.

"Nope, unless you're into that stuff."

I stifle a laugh getting into the front passenger seat, as Carter slides into the back. He immediately starts drumming his fingers on my headrest. I grab his hand and squeeze it tight. Message received as he slumps back into his seat.

The atmosphere in the car feels like we are out for a Sunday drive. No one speaks; we are preoccupied with what lies ahead for us. The road narrows, lined with dense trees that cast their shadows across the car.

As we move further along the secluded route, a tall, fenced gate comes into view. A man in uniform stands out front, and Tristan speaks briefly with him. The gate buzzes open, and we drive inside.

Rounding a curve, an estate unfolds before us. It's massive, surrounded by immaculately manicured lawns, radiating an eerie tranquility. Security cameras turn to follow our progress, blinking red lights emitting an odd reassurance.

Carter moves his face closer to the window.

"Well, this is quite the setup."

The vehicle pulls up to the front entrance, and I half expect to see maids and butlers coming out to greet us. Tristan exits the SUV, stretching casually as if this was just another normal pit stop.

"Okay. We're here. Everybody out."

He leads us to the entrance, as the doors automatically open before us. Inside is a space both luxurious and militarized. The interior gleams with polished surfaces and high-end imported furniture. Tactical gear is strewn across tables; revealing what this place is; a top-notch military command center.

Individuals walk through the halls with quiet intent, some in partial armor, masks secured to their belts, others in civilian clothes.

Carter nudges me and fixes his eyes in the direction of a group of people gathered around a raised stage. I follow his gaze and freeze.

At the center of the stage is Guinevere, recording one of her infamous videos.

"Good tidings, Resistance."

Her voice is steady, measured, with the sort of charisma that makes it clear why she's a force to be reckoned with.

Carter whistles low.

"Wow. This feels like I'm seeing a movie star."

Tristan laughs but continues walking.

"A lot of people are fans of Guinevere. Let's just say she's very popular right now."

Carter blinks.

"Yeah. No kidding."

We walk through a maze of hallways, the murmur of discussions gradually receding as we proceed further into the castle. Tristan stops in front of a colossal, aged oak door, engraved with ornate carvings of dragons, iron bands bolted on to fortify its strength. Two masked Slayers guard the door, adding an extra layer of protection for whoever is behind it.

Tristan addresses one of them in a low tone. The guard bows his head and forcefully swings the door open.

Within, the atmosphere immediately shifts. This space is the epicenter of all the Dragon Slayers' operations. Tactical maps and mission strategies are carefully spread out on long tables. Screens light up the room with real-time satellite feeds, encrypted messages, and movement trails. This is where strategy becomes a reality.

At the middle of it all is Lancelot.

Though he does not stir, he fills the room. Black and gold armor, colossal in size, everything about him is designed to inspire.

Tristan steps forward.

"Sir, I have Charlotte Grayson and Carter Diaz, as requested."

Lancelot approaches me, the muted thud of his boots on the floor. When he halts directly in front of me, he puts both of his hands on my shoulders; his grip is firm but not overwhelming.

"Charlotte Grayson," he states, looking down at me. "You have no idea how many lives you've saved with your bravery and how many more you will save. We thank you."

In the videos, Lancelot is nothing but terror, every word calculated to instill fear, every movement designed to dominate.

But here, his tone is steady. Supportive. It's not weakness; it's leadership. The kind of leadership I've seen before. The kind that doesn't need to raise its voice to command loyalty.

Lancelot turns to Carter.

"Carter Diaz. You've been a thorn in our side for a while now. There were too many times that you came very close to uncovering our network. You have my utmost respect."

Carter, clearly surprised, croaks.

"Uh, sorry or thanks. I guess?"

Lancelot steps back.

"It's so heartening to see both of you here, understanding the reality of our mission. But now we shift to the final phase of our operation. We will free this nation and the world from the oppression of billionaires. There is no turning back now."

I catch a glimpse of Carter, my stomach twisting at the expression on his face. It's the same as mine.

This is it, the final act in the play.

CHAPTER 44

A KINGDOM OF ASH AND GOLD

The tree of liberty must be refreshed from time to time with the blood of patriots and tyrants.

-THOMAS JEFFERSON

"I HAVE PREPARATIONS to see to," Lancelot declares. "We'll meet again for a briefing soon. You'll be fully apprised then."

He gestures to Tristan.

"In the meantime, Tristan will give you a tour. Accustom yourself to how we operate."

Lancelot exits, each step resounding long after he's gone.

Tristan snaps his fingers.

"Well, I suppose you're stuck with me. Come along, time for the grand tour."

As we follow him into the hall, Carter leans over.

"Boss, this is a lot to take in. Like, too much."

"I know; it's all so surreal."

We walk through the hallways, passing Dragon Slayer operatives who hardly give us a second thought.

"What did you think of Lancelot?" Tristan asks, looking over his shoulder at us. "A bit intimidating, right?"

Carter innocently shrugs.

"A bit? Yeah, no kidding. The guy's built like a human tank."

"And he knows how to use it, whatever it takes to achieve our goal."

Tristan's face darkens as he slows down his pace.

"Lancelot knows the price of all this. We've done horrible things. We've taken too many lives.

"Some of them… were certainly innocent."

Carter stops in his tracks.

"You just admitted that you've murdered people. How can you live with that?"

Tristan shrugs, indifferent.

"What's the point of pretending otherwise? Lancelot knows that once all of this is finished, the public will need a lot of help.

"That's why he's being so… inviting. He needs people like the both of you to fill the void when we're no longer here."

A jolt of surprise moves through me.

"Not here?"

Tristan stops and faces us.

"We're not here to make something new, Charlie. What we have to do is bring down the old. And as soon as we accomplish that, our mission is done."

He doesn't wait for a reply. Instead, he continues walking, guiding us into a vast control room.

Tristan gestures toward a man in the corner, typing with one hand, holding a sandwich with the other.

"That's Merlin. He's our Carter Diaz."

Pale as printer paper, with long frizzy hair and a beard to match, he looks like he hasn't seen daylight in a very long time.

Carter's eyes narrow.

"That son of a bitch has made my life hell."

Tristan grins.

"You should hear what he says about you. Some ripe four-letter words about some annoying FBI asshole who patches up all his great work."

Carter tries to play it off, but I can sense inside he is full of pride.

Everything Tristan has shown us clearly demonstrates how the Dragon Slayers were able to stay ahead of us. Their operations team here is just as sophisticated as ours, and they have a nearly unlimited sum of money to deploy.

We move on, into the armory. Walls lined with weapons, racks of black-and-gold armor flashing beneath fluorescent lights. Operatives check their gear with clinical efficiency, preparing themselves for battle.

Carter whistles.

"Geez, Tristan, where the hell did you get all this?"

"The military's a bloated machine with more cash than responsibility. Billions get dumped each year into prototypes that never see the light of day. These models get stuck in storage, collecting dust. We simply borrowed a few things."

I nudge him with a look.

"You're stealing military technology?"

"Charlie, you'd be surprised what people accidentally lose when the price is right."

As we exit the armory, the scope of it all sinks in. Lancelot and his Dragon Slayers created something immeasurable, much larger than I ever could have imagined. And now they're prepared to put it all into action. Their revolution.

We're seated in a quiet lounge area, as I continue to absorb it all.

"Tristan, why do your people stick around?" Carter asks. "Big payouts?"

"Nope. If this were only about money, we'd have all high-tailed it after the first successful hit on a dragon."

I lift an eyebrow.

"Why do they stay then?"

He shifts forward, placing his elbows on his knees.

"Once you have a billion dollars, you can go wherever you wish. Do whatever you want. But the ones here? The ones you've seen all over this place?

"They are different from the people we've paid off for intel or support operations. The ones you see here are all damaged, in one way or another.

"We're scraps of the war machine. Governments trained us and turned us into tools. They pulled the strings, and we pulled the triggers. We believed we were fighting for freedom, doing what was right. But we weren't."

Tristan's tone is steady, but there's something hollow in it, something fractured beneath the surface.

"The puppet masters pulling the strings weren't fighting for justice or democracy. They were billionaires fighting to protect their assets, their stranglehold. And when we were no longer useful, they cast us aside."

His gaze darkens, eyes locked onto something distant, something I can't see.

"I was in one village for two and a half years. Two and a half years trying to win hearts and minds. We constructed schools, installed irrigation systems, and worked with the people there. I honestly believed we were making a difference."

Carter is fixated on his story.

"What happened?"

"An attack. A local terrorist cell ambushed troops in the area.

We lost good soldiers. Command retaliated hard, bombed the village. Airstrikes, artillery, drones. They didn't level the village, but they might as well have.

"Innocent villagers got torn apart, and all it did was fuel more violence. Many more ended up dying because of it."

He falls silent for a moment.

"Including Zayd."

"Who's Zayd?" I ask.

"He was a boy in one of the villages. Maybe ten. Maybe younger. The other kids bullied him. He was different in ways they didn't understand, likely somewhere on the spectrum if they had the resources for a diagnosis.

"He asked too many questions, never knew when to stop talking. And for some damn reason, he liked me."

There's no warmth in Tristan's words.

"At first, it made things worse for him. They called him a traitor. A dog for the Americans.

"It took time, but soon the villagers warmed up to us. They liked the work we were doing, the clean water, the stable food supply, the fact that we were keeping extremists away instead of just shooting and leaving like the last guys.

"For a while, things were good. They'd invite us into their homes, bring us food, laugh with us. We weren't just soldiers anymore. We were people."

His expression hardens.

"But after the attack, the locals saw what happened, saw their families buried in rubble, and they wanted revenge. They blamed anyone they saw as siding with us. They saw me as the reason their homes were wiped from the earth. And they saw Zayd as my shadow."

He inhales sharply, his hands clenching into fists.

"They murdered him for it. But what really fucked me up…

I found out that they tortured him, that little boy had been ripped to pieces.

"Something broke in me. I couldn't unsee it. I couldn't pretend that I gave a fuck about right and wrong anymore.

"It wasn't just him that I lost. It was everyone. Every single person who'd shaken my hand, every child who had come running up to me, every damn thing we built. We were supposed to protect them, and instead, we brought them death."

Tristan's body locks, ready to explode.

"I couldn't get the image of what they did out of my head, so I went back. But not for a mission. I went back to make them pay.

"I wasn't alone. Some of the guys felt the same way. We started launching our own raids. No command or oversight, just vengeance. We tracked down the terror cells, burned them out, hunted them in the dark. And yeah, some of them were guilty. Some of them were the ones who planted bombs and pulled triggers."

He pauses, jaw tight, his words thick with pain.

"It all stopped mattering. If we had even a shred of intel that suggested someone was part of that terrorist cell we went in after them. We didn't wait to confirm. We didn't care. The moment we touched ground, everyone there was already dead. Men, sometimes women. Anyone who didn't run fast enough or didn't look scared enough.

"I told myself it was war. That they brought it on themselves. But deep down, I think we just needed someone to bleed for what happened. Anyone. We weren't fighting for anything anymore. We weren't men, we were monsters. Even worse, for a while I got real satisfaction from our actions.

"That's the thing about war. Even if you survive, it changes you. You're never the same."

We're drowning in Tristan's confession. The room feels like it is closing in on us. I glance at Carter, who's watching Tristan, both of their faces lifeless.

Time for me to switch the subject.

"Tristan, how did you become a Dragon Slayer?"

His laugh is bitter.

"I completed my tour, gave up trying to care. After that, I dropped into the world of mercenaries, took missions, kept my head down, and told myself it didn't matter anymore.

"And then I heard about him. Lancelot. He'd experienced the same shit, the same disillusionment, the same anger."

"And you joined him."

"Not at first," Tristan confesses. "I thought it was totally insane, too big, too ambitious. But the more we discussed it, the more it made sense. We couldn't repair the system, but we could break it."

He reclines in his chair.

"That was our intention. We never imagined getting as far as we did. We figured we'd make our point, do a bit of damage, and then they'd discover us and take us out with a drone strike."

"But they didn't," Carter whispers.

Tristan's voice sinks.

"Well, not yet. But now we're here, on the brink of something we never imagined we could have done."

I study him intently, struggling to understand it all. The Dragon Slayers aren't trying to be heroes. They have transformed all their anger, all their pain, into something greater than themselves. Another war, but one on their terms with their values.

Curiosity flashes across Carter's face.

"I have a question. What's up with the Union Guard in all this?"

Tristan's smile returns.

"It's never been just about the Dragon Slayers. All of this, every plan, every asset, even both of you is about making sure the Union Guard can do the hard part. We're breaking the system, but that means there has to be someone to rebuild it.

"We have the easy part. Going in there and showing this administration and the billionaires that they aren't untouchable. However, there needs to be someone left when we're no longer here."

"When the Dragon Slayers are no longer here? You keep saying it as if you're all just going to vanish."

"Don't worry, Charlie. We've got a plan to tie things up. But yeah, we won't be here for long."

Carter's curiosity sharpens.

"You're just going to walk away? After everything?"

"That's why the Union Guard exists. We need people who get it, who know what's at stake and who are willing to pick up the pieces. To make sure everything we did wasn't in vain. More importantly, people without blood on their hands."

Trepidation settles in me.

"It sounds like the Dragon Slayers are planning something extreme. What the hell is it?"

Tristan gazes at me, his expression blank.

"You'll know soon enough. One last hurrah, then we're done."

I attempt to press him for details, but a sharp voice rings through the halls, slicing straight through our tension.

"Assembly in the war room. All personnel report immediately."

Tristan stands up straight.

"And there's your answer. Time to find out what the big man has planned. Follow me."

Carter's unease is a reflection of my own. We quickly follow

Tristan, each step cumbersome with the weight of his confession. Whatever the Dragon Slayers' last operation is, it's going to change the course of history.

Lancelot is in the Command Center, even more imposing, as the Dragon Slayers surround him. There are too many of them to count, as they stand stationary, waiting for him to speak.

His voice is filled with sincerity; his gaze sweeps across the room.

"Before we begin, I want to take a moment to thank every single one of you. Your sacrifices, your dedication, your steadfast belief in our mission, all these things and more, are why we have come this far. Without you, none of this would be possible."

There is a moment of silent reverence.

"You all have lost so much. Friends, comrades, loved ones in this fight. You sacrificed everything for the opportunity to build something better, not only for yourselves but for the world.

"I won't forget it. This great nation will not forget. The world won't forget."

Lancelot's position stiffens.

"We are reaching the culmination of our mission. Everything that we have built has been leading up to this end. And it starts with freeing those taken by this corrupt administration and BlackSteel."

A ripple of tension rolls through the group. This is the beginning of their end.

"These disgusting fortresses of greed have imprisoned important political and military figures. Individuals who will play a significant role in the reconstruction of this nation. We will strike decisively and liberate those imprisoned.

"There will be a battle. There will be bloodshed. But there is no other choice."

I glance at Carter, who appears as uncomfortable as I feel.

Lancelot somberly continues.

"The people who run these prisons will not go down without a fight. With Sorakin's autonomous drones and robotic sentries, these sites are untouchable. Impenetrable fortresses run by non-stop production machines that don't question orders."

His speech escalates in intensity.

"Now, for the first time, retaliation is possible. An operational disruption in their systems will give us the opening we need to hit them where it hurts. We will free the people they've buried.

"We will sacrifice our lives in order to guarantee a brighter future for generations to come. This is it. This moment is the culmination of all our sacrifices and struggles. United as one, we will finish what we started."

A pulse circulates through everyone, its current intense. The shift is almost imperceptible, postures straighter, shoulders squarer, focus sharper.

I stand still, taking it all in. It's the deepest of convictions, the moment when belief transforms into reality.

Carter shifts closer to me.

"Fuck, this just got real."

"Yeah, Carter, it's all in motion now."

The war room buzzes with activity. Operatives hustle between stations, voices blending in with the constant rattle of machinery.

Tristan breaks through the mayhem, motioning for us to follow him.

"You two are with me. Let's move."

He directs us into the tech center, where monitors glow harshly, illuminating rows of analysts typing at keyboards. Amidst this activity, Carter's nemesis, the Wizard, still sits hunched over his desk, banging away with one hand, a cup of coffee in the other.

Tristan halts a few feet away and gestures toward him.

"Merlin, Carter. Carter, Merlin."

Merlin doesn't look up, too engaged with his screens. He takes a sip of his coffee before acknowledging us.

His expression is a mix of curiosity and amusement.

"Carter, huh? The FBI legend. Thought you'd be taller."

Carter puffs his chest out.

"Merlin, thought you'd be shorter."

"Cute kid, maybe that's why it was so easy tricking you with all the secondary tor layers."

Carter claps back.

"The one that kept me chasing my tail for three weeks? Yeah, I recall. I thought it would be something more advanced, coding-wise, so I missed how simple it actually was."

Merlin shrugs, unapologetic.

"Worked, didn't it?"

Tristan sighs, stepping between them.

"Okay, are the two of you going to act like professionals, or do I have to intervene and separate you two?"

Carter rolls his eyes.

"I guess, I'm here to help."

Merlin's smile broadens.

"Same. Hope you can keep up."

"That's better, boys," Tristan says. "Carter, you'll be teaming up with Merlin to leverage the access we've secured into Black-Steel's networks.

"You've got the most experience with their architecture. Think you two can manage that?"

Merlin gives a curt nod.

"We've already built most of the disruption package. With

the right deployment timing, it will scramble Sorakin's coordination layer long enough to create a breach window."

Carter chimes in.

"Merlin, you might want to check how Sorakin handles fallback protocols. Some of their AI builds alternate routes midstream. They designed it to be self-patching. Might screw with your timing."

Merlin raises an eyebrow, like he's already considered it, but not enough to dismiss the point.

"Yeah… sure, kid. You can take a look if you want. I'm sure I have it accounted for, but just to be safe."

Carter gives a small shrug.

"Happy to. Just want to make sure we don't miss anything."

Merlin turns and gestures to Tristan.

"Tristan, a moment alone, please. I need to share with you some details that Lancelot had me look into."

Carter and I step back, as Tristan and Merlin engage in a serious conversation. They both pause for a second and sneak a look at me. I meet their eyes, which makes me slightly paranoid.

Has Merlin uncovered something about me? I banish the thought as I see a faint smile appear on both of their faces.

"Charlie, let's go," Tristans says as he rejoins us. "Carter. Good luck. And it's been a pleasure."

As I walk away, I take a final look back at Carter. He is already yapping away with Merlin, as they dive into their mission.

Tristan guides me back to the armory, which is bursting with kinetic energy. Operatives are in full prep mode, gearing up into tactical suits, methodically checking guns and inserting rounds into magazines.

He takes me to a black-and-gold tactical equipment-lined

wall, each piece sleek and tailored for accuracy. I select a HK416 rifle, comfortable and familiar.

"What's the plan?" I ask as I inspect my new weapon.

"The compound where Lex and Graham are being held isn't one of our high-priority targets. It's not holding as many valuable political or military prisoners as the others. But I made sure that we're hitting it, anyway."

Relief surges through me.

"You're sure?"

"I keep my promises. Lex and Graham matter to you. I understand that. And truthfully? Good people like them are significant to what lies ahead."

I slide my sidearm into its holster.

"Alright. What do I need to do?"

"For starters, Charlie? Don't let me die."

I let out a short, amused laugh.

"I'll do my best."

"Good enough for me. When the time comes, you'll be breaching with my team. Take what else you need from here and report to the staging area."

Outside, everything bustles with military precision. SUVs, vehicles, helicopters, all parked in tactical formation. The sheer extent of this mass of Dragon Slayers catches me by surprise.

I turn to Tristan.

"Is this everyone?"

"Not even close. There are additional teams located closer to the targets."

Vehicles start to slowly roll out, metal phantoms disappearing into the darkness of the night. Everything is done with a sense of deep purpose.

Tristan points toward a blacked-out SUV at the edge of the lot.

"That's us. We're headed to Lex and Graham's location with another crew. About an hour drive."

In the vehicle, we're enveloped in quiet shadows, punctuated by the growl of the engine as we depart from the staging area. Tristan sits across from me; his attention fixed on a tactical map on his tablet. The other Dragon Slayers in the vehicle are expressionless, their faces taunt.

I lean forward and touch his arm.

"Tristan. If Lancelot and the Dragon Slayers succeed, any idea what the future will look like?"

"Charlie, don't you ever give your brain a break?"

"It's a fair question to ask Tristan . You're the one tearing down the system. But what comes after if it's too much to fix?"

He shrugs.

"Then we did everything we could. But I don't waste time planning for failure."

Unsatisfied with his answers, I look out the window, watching the convoy snake down the deserted road, headlights cutting through the night.

An hour later, the convoy slows, veering off the main road and onto a concealed path. Trees encroach on either side, the road narrowing as we near an improvised staging area. The SUV halts, and operatives spring into action, offloading equipment, establishing defenses, and preparing for what lies ahead.

Tristan gets out, stretching his legs.

"Alright, Charlie. Get your tent set up and catch some rest. We hit the ground running before the crack of dawn."

I nod, walking into the cool night air. The camp buzzes with measured urgency, whispered murmurs, the sound of metal on metal, the shuffling of feet. The Dragon Slayers gathered here are painfully aware of the battle about to begin.

Around the perimeter, teams are setting up signal disruptors and camo netting, weaving it between trees and vehicles to mask heat signatures and confuse overhead drones. Every movement is deliberate. Every step draws us closer to battle.

In my tent, the cot that I lie on is stiff and cold. So is my body. So is my mind. The sounds of preparation filter through the thin canvas walls, disrupting my thoughts about Lex and Graham.

Somewhere beyond the confines of this camp, they're waiting for a miracle. Tristan, the Dragon Slayers, and I have to be that miracle.

I roll onto my side, gazing up at the green fabric, rippling in a gentle breeze. Just a few months ago, I could never have imagined that I would be in this predicament. I was hunting the Dragon Slayers, plotting missions to ensure their demise.

They are terrorists. They are a danger that needs to be eliminated.

Now?

They are the only hope I have left.

CHAPTER 45

SHOCK AND AWE

"Let them eat cake."

-MARIE ANTOINETTE

I MAKE MY way out of the tent into the cool morning air. The moon casts everything in a blue haze, making it easy to see. I push through the fatigue and keep walking, letting the distant noises of the camp fill the silence in my mind.

Muffled voices come from various groups around the camp mixed with the familiar sounds of equipment being readied. The smell of wood burning hangs in the air, layering in the crisp night air.

Then, I catch sight of him.

Tristan waits at the perimeter of camp, his tall silhouette rimmed in silver from the moonlight. A cigarette dangles between his lips, the ember glowing bright as he draws in a slow breath. He exhales a puff of smoke coiled tight, unraveling as it spirals into nothingness.

He sees me before I can speak.

"Hey Charlie. Can't sleep?"

"Don't think I can right now."

Tristan motions with his cigarette.

"You smoke?"

"Not under normal circumstances."

Tristan smiles knowingly and offers a cigarette to me.

"Well, this is anything but normal, can't hurt too much?"

I've never liked smoking, but I take one anyway. Tristan extends his lighter to my cigarette. The first drag stings, but it gives my mind something tangible to wrap around.

He taps ash off the end of his.

"Bad habit."

I expel the rest of the smoke.

"Yeah, well. Looks like I'm developing a few of those."

Tristan takes another drag, eyeing me intently.

"So, what's on your mind?"

I don't want to say it, but I'm tired of carrying the burden alone.

"All of this, with all of you. I feel like I'm betraying the Bureau, my country, and my father.

"I spent my whole career chasing people like you. I believed in what I was doing. I believed in the mission. And now, now I'm aiding and abetting Dragon Slayers."

My confession feels raw. I have offered him a piece of myself that I have never revealed before to anyone. Not to Lex, not to Graham, not to Carter and not even to Bill.

Tristan doesn't interrupt. He lets me come clean.

"I know that any government can be corrupt; I've seen it with my own eyes. For this administration, it's not about the people for them. It's about power."

I take another pull, the burn softer than before.

"But all this? Making billionaires give up their wealth or die. It's sheer madness. And yet, here I am."

I named it for what it is. Spoke the undeniable truth out loud.

Tristan shifts his posture, his expression softening with understanding.

"You didn't betray your country, Charlie. You just finally stopped betraying yourself."

He flicks his cigarette, and the embers scatter like fireflies, fading into the night sky.

"It has always been a performance for anyone associated with the government. They wrapped warfare in flags and called it freedom, but it was just leverage. Enough to make obedience a virtue and to convince us to do their dirty work."

Tristan draws closer.

"Look at me, Charlie. You did good things. Don't lose that. You saved lives. You fought hard. You believed in all things righteous, that mattered and still does.

"But you did bad things too. We all did. And not because we are evil. It's because the people feeding us the orders were. They used the idea of goodness like a leash. They talked about duty, justice, sacrifice, values they'd never follow. But they damn knew we would."

Tristan lifts his head toward the sky, stars reflecting in his eyes, his mind miles from here.

"The worst lies aren't shouted. They're built. Layer by layer. On school walls, in recruitment ads, in presidential speeches. They make you feel ashamed for ever questioning it. That's how they win."

Tristan's blunt honesty catches me off guard, his point valid. His words pressing against everything I was raised to believe, everything I used to fight for.

But none of it matters now.

My voice comes out quieter than I expect, but sharper all the same.

"Honestly, I don't care what happens anymore. I just want Lex and Graham back."

Speaking those words makes it true. Gives it conclusion. That's what holds me here.

The cigarette burns low in Tristan's hand as he contemplates what to say next.

"It's a noble thing you're doing for them, so trust me, I get it."

Tristan glances at his cigarette, turning it over in his fingers.

"And for what it's worth, I wouldn't say you're one of us."

My response is not one of anger, but confusion.

"How can you say that? I'm literally about to take part in a full-scale assault with you."

He shakes his head.

"You're here to save Lex and Graham. To get your people out. That's your goal. Ours is bigger, messier, and built to destroy. It just so happens our paths overlap here.

"But don't confuse proximity with purpose. Charlie, you're better than us. You're chasing something personal. We're tearing down the world."

The difference between us hangs there, unsaid but unavoidable. I might not be one of them, but I'm no longer on the outside, either.

For a moment, we just sit there, the night pressing in close. I take one last drag, then snuff the ember out.

Uncertainty appears on Tristan's face. He shifts his feet slowly in the dirt.

"When you set up that access point, we discovered something that's very significant for you to hear. I wasn't sure whether I wanted to tell you this before or after."

"Before or after what?"

"Tomorrow's raid. You know as well as I do that going into any mission requires a clear head. Listening to you just now, I think this could help in some way."

Tristan digs into the side pocket of his vest, extracting a small tablet. The screen's light dances across his face as he scrolls, tapping through encrypted documents. He pauses as if a part of him wants to spare me the pain that he is about to inflict.

"There was some information Lancelot wanted to investigate specifically . He had his reasons."

Tristan blows out another slow plume of smoke, passing me the tablet. My hands shake as I take it and start scrolling through the files.

"As it turns out, his instincts were sound."

Bill Cartwright's name is plastered all over them.

My heart begins to sink.

Memos. Emails. Encrypted messages. Meetings with Bill, Victor, Dr. Hart, Schmutt, Kane, Sorin, and Tuff. Discussions about reorganizing the FBI, transitioning its operations to private contractors like BlackSteel.

As I read faster, my head starts to spin. There's no hesitation in Bill's approval of the takeover, no reluctance or regret. His intentions are blatantly obvious. He personally gives the perfect pitch.

We need a more agile, results-oriented model of intelligence. We become more efficient with more privatization.

Government oversight hinders us. The private sector is the way forward and more lucrative for everyone involved.

Congress won't be able to stop us if we move quickly enough and push this through. The Dragon Slayers are exactly what we need to secure the level of control we've always desired.

It all hits hard, suddenly, undeniably, and exactly where it hurts the most.

Bill Cartwright, my mentor, lied straight to my face. He swore that we needed to fight back against privatization. He swore that Tuff and his administration were unscrupulous.

He, of all people, was leading the charge from the very beginning.

I want to stop, but my mind forces me to continue reading. More correspondence. More lies.

Then, a file pops up, marked Immediate Detention with two names.

Agent Graham Cross. Former agent Alexa Thompson.

Internal security evaluations.

Bill's approval marking them as liabilities, sealing their fates.

"That bastard." I gasp.

Tristan doesn't react. He allows me to process every single detail.

"I thought I knew him. I thought…"

"Sorry, Charlie, it gets worse."

The deeper I delve, the more certain I am that I'm not ready for what's next, But I cannot stop.

A new document. A name at the top.

Operation Silent Aegis

Seeing it knocks the wind out of me. My father's mission, the one that took him from me.

I open the document. The text blurs for a moment, my mind refusing to read the words. I make another attempt to focus.

Classified intelligence indicated that the attack was going to occur, and it turned out to be unquestionably accurate.

Internal memos note a high probability of casualties, and that they should evacuate fully, and relinquish the area.

Private conversations giving the green light as a means to

counterattack and gain more strategic assets. It simply equates to more oil for billionaires.

Bill's recommendations:

James Grayson needs to head up the mission. He is perfectly suited for our needs in this situation. He will remain in combat, ensuring we have a reason for the counterattacks planned. He will become a symbol of courage to be celebrated. Heroes can motivate public support, and we can utilize this to our advantage.

This last file is the finishing blow. My whole world collapses.

The screen fades to black as my grasp fails. My father did not die because of a noble cause. He did not die because he was defending something bigger than himself. He died because Bill Cartwright and others needed a pawn.

A fucking human sacrifice.

A strangled noise escapes my throat. I don't know whether it's a curse or a sob or something in between. My body trembles, my heartbeat ear-splitting.

I don't recognize my own voice.

"He sent my father to fucking die!"

Tristan remains quiet, observing me with the sort of patience of a man who has watched others shatter from the impact of truth they were unprepared for.

I thrust the tablet back at Tristan, unable to bear looking at it any further.

"Bill fucking got him killed."

I'm already moving before I realize it, pacing in jagged circles, my mind spiraling faster than my steps can keep up. I don't know where I'm going, but I need to move, to do something, anything, to keep from falling apart.

Everything, my career, my choices, my loyalty, was built on a lie. A lie I defended and bled for.

My chest tightens, legs wobbling under the weight of it all.

I stagger toward the nearest tree, bracing my hands against the trunk, but it's no use. My knees give out and I drop hard to the ground, landing on my back. I pull myself up into a sitting position against the tree like it's the only thing keeping me from dissolving completely into the earth.

The sob hits before I'm ready. Raw and loud. Then another. And then I can't stop.

I've carried my father's legacy with me for years, like sacred armor. I've honored him in every way I could. I've attempted to live up to him. And now?

Now I face the reality that he was never supposed to make it out of that mission alive.

I grip my hands on my knees, bracing myself against the trembling. The anger follows, hot, bitter, and overwhelming.

Bill Cartwright is the reason my father is dead.

Bill Cartwright is the reason for Lex and Graham's abduction.

Bill Cartwright has been lying to me throughout my entire career.

The white-hot truth sears through me.

The worst part? I don't know what to do with it. I don't know where to put this intense rage.

Catching my breath, the sobs are gone, but the tears keep coming. Then I hear his footsteps, measured and unhurried.

Tristan kneels beside me without a word, not invading my space, not asking anything of me. He doesn't touch me, just holds out a folded handkerchief. I take it with a shaky hand, wiping my face without looking at him, grateful for his gesture.

"This is the way they work, Charlie. There are thousands of Bills in the system, because it's designed to create them."

I raise my head slowly, vision clearing, breath steadier. His words land differently now, less shocking, more like a confession.

"They tell you what matters and what to believe in. Tell you that you're fighting for justice, for freedom until it stops serving them.

"And when individuals like us are no longer useful? When their unethical objectives are fulfilled? They discard us, letting us rot like garbage."

Tristan is merely reemphasizing the cold, hard truth. And for some unknown reason, it's exactly what I need to hear.

"Listen up Charlie," he commands. "It happened to me. It happened to Lancelot. It happened to every single person in this camp.

"A system that devours people, lies to them, and then discards them. That's a system worth breaking."

I stay quiet, my thoughts tangled in a web of confusion. Bill's voice still echoes in my head; every carefully chosen word laced with the kind of betrayal that never fades. I spent years believing him, trusting him, letting his version of the truth shape mine. And all along, he was just another piece of the machine. Another lie I built my life around.

My father died for that machine. For a version of this country that doesn't exist anymore, if it ever did. And I kept chasing his shadow, trying to live up to a man who was sacrificed for an illusion.

The silence around me stretches, heavy with everything I can't make sense of. What does any of this mean? What I'm supposed to do with it?

Tristan doesn't push. He just stands there, steady, and present.

"Charlie, we'll start getting prepped in thirty," he says softly. "I'll leave you be."

He rises without waiting for a response. His footsteps fade behind me as I stay rooted to the earth, staring into the darkness.

I sit by myself, apart from the stirring bodies, the subtle motion of operatives gearing up for the morning to arrive. The ground under me is cool, hard, anchoring. My fingers dig into the dirt, pushing into something solid, something real, something that doesn't change and distort under me.

Everything is completely different now.

I lived my whole life trusting a system that never warranted it, standing on a foundation that was decayed from the inside out. My father's death, Bill's betrayal, the truth spread before me like a corpse on a slab.

There's no avoiding it. No fleeing from it. No burying it under duty and loyalty with the reassuring lie that all I've done has been for good intentions.

But what does any of it change?

The Dragon Slayers are moving like clockwork, adjusting gear, readying weapons, their faces set with quiet determination.

And me?

I close my eyes, exhaling into the cold, letting the thoughts settle, forcing my focus onto the only thing that matters.

Lex is out there. Graham is out there. They are the only important things in my life now.

Not Bill. Not the system. Not the war being fought on both sides.

Just them.

I push away from the ground, shaking the stiffness out of my limbs, allowing the chill to steel my determination. There is no room for doubt. No place for hesitation.

The only important thing is retrieving them.

The team gathers in a clearing. The sky is dark but starting to shift, dawn creeping in at the edges. The trees catch the earliest hints of light, casting long, restless shadows across the ground.

Thirty Dragon Slayers, armed and ready, move with quiet

purpose. I'd expected fewer, based on what Tristan had said about limited numbers. Seeing this many individuals steadies me enough to keep doubt from taking over. Maybe we're not outmatched. Not yet.

Tristan steps forward, spreading a map across an ammo crate.

"Alright, listen up, everyone. Here's the plan."

His finger traces the perimeter of the map, indicating important positions.

"We've got twenty to thirty BlackSteel guards and maybe twenty staff, give or take, inside the prison. It's not going to be easy, but we have a solid plan.

"We're going to hit them with a little shock and awe."

My forehead creases, but I don't say anything. What the hell does he mean by that?

Tristan strides over to a nearby crate, yanks off the blanket covering it, and steps aside.

Inside, dozens of Javelin missile launchers lie tucked neatly into foam cases, each one clearly marked and battle ready.

So, this is what he meant by shock and awe. Not a metaphor. Actual firepower and a hell of a lot of it too.

Enough to light up the sky and hopefully to send every guard in that prison fleeing.

Tristan plants his hand on the edge of the table, eyes scanning the other Dragon Slayers.

"When I receive word that Sorakin's networks are down, that's when we strike. Once it's offline, they lose all their robotics and drone support. That blackout gives us our opening, without it, we're going in blind against machines that don't miss.

"We've got four teams. First, two fire support teams. You'll be positioned throughout the forest around the perimeter, set up with Javelins, light machine guns, and sniper rifles."

He points to the tree line on the map, circling key positions.

"On my signal, you're going to light this place up. I want all four of these guard towers and their gates gone. Missiles, 50-cal rounds, everything. We want it to feel like hell just broke loose on them.

"I'll give my mark, and we all hold fire. That's when we hit the PA system, give them a chance to surrender. Hopefully, we can get as many of them out as possible without a fight."

He taps a route marked along the forest edge.

"Anyone who comes out gets sent to the secure line with fire support team Alpha. They'll be detained and held there until after the mission wraps. Make sure we immediately get any intel and information from them about the prison.

"For the ones who resist, we go in and get them. Two attack teams in SUVs, one striking from the north, the other from the east."

Tristan's expression hardens as he draws a line toward the center.

"The goal is to push in and meet in the middle. Fire support will keep covering us as we breach, and if things go sideways, they're our reinforcements or will cover our retreat.

"Shock and awe first. Clean sweep after."

His eyes find mine.

"Our main targets are Alexa Thompson and Graham Cross. Location unclear. Intel says they are here. Extract them first, then free as many other prisoners as we can.

"This is a critical operation. Everything we've worked for leads to this one mission. Every drop of blood we've spilled, every brother and sister we've lost, this is where we tip the scale.

"We've come too far to fail. Today, we finish what we started. We bring them home."

Tristan closes the map, then looks around one last time.

"Gear up. We roll in fifteen."

He reaches down, picks up his mask, and slides it over his face, the black-and-gold Dragon Slayer emblem catching the first sliver of light from the rising dawn.

In an instant, Tristan transforms into a powerhouse. A Dragon Slayer.

This is who he is. A force you don't want as an opponent in a fight. He is intimidating. It's impossible to look away.

But more than anything, he's inspiring.

Tristan throws his voice into a powerful and commanding. "Oorah!"

And then, rising from the group in chaotic, powerful unison. "Oorah!"

"Hooah!"

"Hooyah!"

It's not rehearsed or polished. But it's unified. Shouts from every corner of service, those who gave up the uniform but never the mission, rising together. They're aligned in purpose, bound by something real. And after hearing that, hearing them, I believe we can win.

The Dragon Slayers scatter, gathering their weapons and checking gear. Their plan is solid, but brazen, a lot could go wrong at any point.

Tristan steps out of the shadows with something cradled under his arm, wrapped in black cloth. He stops in front of me, his expression unreadable, but the way he holds the bundle deliberately pulls me in.

"I've got something for you," he says.

"What's that?"

He doesn't answer. Just unwraps the cloth, folds it back, and reveals what's inside.

The mask catches what little light there is, matte black with a trim of muted gold along the edges. A Dragon Slayer mask.

I stare at it for a second, trying to fit the image into the reality I still haven't fully accepted.

"I thought we agreed I wasn't a Dragon Slayer."

His expression remains steady.

"We did. This isn't about that."

He holds the mask out.

"It's bulletproof."

I run my thumb along the edge.

"Shouldn't there be a ceremony? A nickname? A bonfire and some chanting?"

Tristan laughs, low and short.

"Let's just stay alive and take it from there."

The joke fades quickly as his expression shifts. He glances toward the tree line, the direction of the prison still hidden in the dark.

"Truth is, the ones who've really earned these masks aren't the ones wearing them. They're in that prison. Right now. Waiting for us. Lex. Graham. And others unknown to us. People who stood for justice knowing it could cost them everything.

"It's not about who we are. It's about who I refuse to let die."

My pulse quickens as I raise the mask, align it with my helmet, and press it into place. It snaps in with a clean, quiet click. A perfect fit.

I look up at Tristan, eyes steady behind the mask.

"Let's bring them home."

"Oorah," he whispers.

The two of us are now bound by this pledge.

"All right, Grayson. Time to execute. You're with my team."

I follow Tristan's movements as he hastens to SUVs idling nearby. Six Dragon Slayers stand clustered around the vehicles, geared up, weapons slung, faces masked. They've been through this before, more times than I can imagine. And still, they're here. For each other.

One by one, they look at me and give a symbolic nod. It's not about what I'm wearing. It never was. It's about the fact that I'm here with them.

Willing to risk my life for those who can't fight back. Willing to stand beside them and do whatever needs to be done.

That's what earns their respect. That's what makes me one of them, at least for the time being.

Tristan moves ahead without a word, stepping through the forest until the land opens in front of us.

From where we stand now, we can see it.

The prison sits in the distance, crouched low against the landscape, its shape hard and unnatural against the soft rise of the earth. The sky hasn't turned yet, but the air is shifting, washed in faint bluish green light that shows up right before dawn.

Through the trees, we can see Sorakin drones circling methodically overhead, red lights blinking in slow, deliberate rhythm. On the ground, robotic mutts prowl the perimeter fence, silent, precise, their heads sweeping left to right as if they have picked up our scent.

I watch them move and wonder how this would be possible if we had to go in with the system still active. Fighting through Sorakin's tech head-on would be suicide.

Tristan stands tall, his gaze locked on the prison fortress.

He lifts his comm mic.

"Prepare to engage."

Confirmations are immediate.

"Fireteam Alpha, set."

"Fireteam Bravo, set."

"Strike Team Bravo, set."

Tristan lowers the mic. The surrounding forest is alive in the stillness. The soft rustle of wind through branches. The distant calls of birds waking with the light. It's peaceful in a way that makes what's coming feel even more surreal.

I take a deep breath, which reveals everything, knowing what this moment means. Knowing there's no stopping once it begins.

Tristan remains steadfast. He bears the look of a man who knows he's about to change something forever.

He checks his watch, then looks at me.

"Let's see if Carter and Merlin are as good as they think they are."

He glances back at the screen, lips moving with the numbers.

"Three... two... one..."

In perfect sync, the drones circling overhead cut out mid-flight and drop like stones. The Sorakin mutts on the ground freeze mid-step, heads jerking once before locking solid. Metal puppets whose strings have suddenly been cut.

The blackout has begun. Tristan lifts the comms to his mouth.

"Fireteams. Engage!"

The sky erupts.

Orange streaks rip through the predawn light. Javelins launch with a violent rush, their afterburners blinding as they scream across the open ground. The sound is instant, overwhelming, the roar of fire and propulsion tearing through the air with merciless speed.

A second later, they hit their intended marks. All of them.

Explosions blossom along the prison's edge, one after another, as the rockets slam into their targets with pinpoint accuracy. Fire coils into the sky, debris hurtling outward in every direction.

And then, layered over the thunder of the blasts, comes the full force of the storm.

Tracer rounds streak out from the tree line. White, orange,

and red molten threads blazing across the open stretch with terrifying precision. Light machine guns rattle in synchronized bursts, cutting through the darkness like sawblades. Sniper rounds pop like a distant metronome.

The tranquility felt before is gone. Gone so quickly, it feels like a delusion I made up in my head.

I brace instinctively, my body locking up as the ground shudders beneath my boots. Even with all my years of training, my knees still twitch and my shoulders flinch against the shockwaves.

In front of me, Tristan is motionless.

He stands stoic next to a large tree, the flash of explosions reflected in his mask. Unshaken.

The battlefield blazes in color and fire.

Tristan raises his mic again.

"Hold fire."

Immediately, the chaos stops. The weapons fall silent so fast it feels unnatural. What's left behind is entirely different.

Smoke curls through the treetops, drifting high, forming ash gray clouds. Burned metal. Shattered concrete. Broken earth. The sight, sound, and smell of a battlefield.

The opening strike is complete.

Shock and awe. Tristan wasn't joking.

My hand tightens on my rifle. Now comes the choice.

From the opposite side of the building, a flare cuts upward into the sky, trailing smoke before bursting into a harsh red bloom.

Tristan's voice amplifies through the speakers placed around the compound.

"Attention BlackSteel forces."

He gives it a moment, enough to make them listen.

"Your compound is under siege. You are completely surrounded. Sorakin systems are offline. Your drones and your reinforcements are gone. No one is coming to rescue you.

"Lay down your arms and move to the red flare with your hands on your head. You will not be harmed. I repeat. You will not be harmed."

Tristan projects loud and clear.

"You are not our target. We're here to liberate prisoners being held under a treasonous regime. Don't risk your life defending their lies."

The wind shifts. Fog like smoke drifts low, curling over the grounds. The compound is unnervingly still.

Tristan continues.

"This is your last chance. Drop your weapons. Hands up. Walk to the flare."

For an endless minute, nothing moves. Until a side door creaks open.

A small group emerges, hands raised, steps slow and stiff. They're not just guards. Some wear medic vests, administrative uniforms, and staff who are not trained to fight. They make their way apprehensively across the open ground, toward the flare.

Tristan pauses before speaking again.

"Anyone else in the buildings. This is your final warning. Walk out now, or you'll be treated as hostile targets."

Another door opens. This group is larger, moving quicker, stumbling in their haste. One appears wounded and is being half-carried, half-dragged. The fear of survival has flushed them out. They reach the flare and join the others, huddling together like a herd of cattle.

The numbers grow, eighteen, twenty, maybe more.

Still not enough.

The front gate of the building groans open as a final wave of employees steps outside. More staff than guards. I count twenty-eight, then two more. Thirty in total.

Our wait continues. No one else ventures outside.

Tristan lifts his mic and releases his command.

"Strike Team Bravo, move into position.

"Fire Team Bravo, prep for covering fire on my mark."

He lowers the mic, turns to us, eyes sharp behind the mask. "Let's roll."

The Dragon Slayers fan out in practiced formation, boots pounding against the earth. They load into the two waiting SUVs with smooth, mechanical precision.

Tristan rounds the front of the lead vehicle and throws the door open. He yells as he slides behind the steering wheel.

"Grayson. Shotgun,"

I move fast, yank the door open and jump in, as the engine growls to life. Behind us, another SUV roars, as the rest of the Dragon Slayers pile in.

The final pieces are locked into place.

No more waiting. This is it.

Tristan lifts the mic one last time and shouts.

"Strike Team Bravo, engage. Fire Team Bravo, light 'em up."

The forest erupts once more, muzzles flashing, as tracer rounds scream overhead. The fortified compound is rocked by steady, controlled orange and white bursts of gunfire. Those waiting inside brought this carnage on themselves.

Tristan slams the SUV into gear, tires spitting up dirt as we lurch forward. The other vehicle follows as we charge straight for the prison.

Gunfire intensifies as we draw closer, the SUV bearing the brunt of the impact. We are in a steel beast; custom made for the Dragon Slayers to withstand battle.

Ahead, the thick steel gates are distorted, clinging to their hinges, in marked defiance from the earlier strike. Smoke billows from the guard towers, reduced by the explosions to crumbling chimneys.

Tristan doesn't hesitate.

"Hold on!" he shouts.

He slams on the gas pedal, metal screams, steel bends, and the gates burst inward. The second SUV breaks through right behind us, tires shrieking as it fishtails into place.

At first, there is only the alarms blaring high and grating. Then gunfire. Shots ring from the windows above, scattered, and wild.

Tristan barks into his comms.

"Covering fire, now!"

The air explodes with gunfire from the support teams. The sharp crack of sniper rounds is followed by the deep, punishing roar of heavy machine guns. Lead rains down against the prison windows, hammering glass, metal, and stone, shredding the positions where the guards had been firing.

The building shakes under the assault; tracer fire flashes like lightning against the dark.

Anyone too close to the openings is either torn apart or forced into retreat. The return fire dies down almost instantly, replaced by the groans of those who didn't move fast enough.

Tristan waits for the dust to settle before giving the order.

"Let's go! Covering maneuvers as we advance."

I emerge from the vehicle, rifle up, eyes scanning. My heart thumps against my ribs, my breath constricted in my chest.

Tristan is first to the door, weapon at the ready.

"They're trying to regroup. We can't give them that opportunity."

He gives the orders to the teams, his words swift and efficient.

"Let's go. Sweep the building. Quick and quiet."

The Dragon Slayers don't hesitate.

They fall into place, moving forward with determined accuracy and precision. I follow Tristan, my rifle locked tight in my grip. The courtyard vanishes behind us as we cross the building's threshold.

Inside, the harsh red emergency lights appear to make the ceilings and walls bleed. The corridors are narrow, tighter, squeezing the life out of anyone who dares to enter.

Deep breaths. Remember your training. Move forward.

But concern persists, scratching at the fringes of my determination.

This is real. Anything can happen.

We move in formation, sweeping through the corridor with practiced, precise maneuvering. Each corner is cleared in rhythm, tight, clean movements, rifles up, eyes sharp. I mirror every motion Tristan makes, as we advance deeper into the compound.

Suddenly it breaks.

Gunfire erupts ahead, short bursts, controlled but close.

BlackSteel guards rush out from a side hallway, and our team immediately shifts, taking cover behind doorframes and corners. I automatically do the same, pressing to the wall, weapon ready, adrenaline flooding through me.

For a second, I'm locked into the fight, focused on the danger in front of us.

Instinct cuts in.

Our flank. Cover the flank.

I snap left, pivoting toward a narrow corridor just off our position, as two BlackSteel guards approach, rifles raised, slipping into our blind spot.

I fire.

Two bursts. Fast. Clean.

The bullets resound down the hall, guards dropping before they can shoot back. Their bodies strike the floor with a loud thump.

Tristan looks back, unfazed. He gives me a quick nod and gestures for me to move forward. My legs propel me before I have time to digest what I just did.

They're dead, both of them. Their killing doesn't feel personal. It doesn't feel like anything, at least for now.

We breach the room carefully, weapons up, formation tight. It's an open administrative space, low counters, scattered desks, highlighted in red by the emergency lighting. It feels off, unsettling and quiet.

BlackSteel springs their trap.

Gunfire explodes from behind the counters, brutal and close. Muzzle flashes strobe against the crimson light. Two Dragon Slayers drop, one hit in the shoulder, the other going down with a choked shout.

"Contact front!"

Tristan's reactions are swift, returning fire in short, surgical bursts as he drags one of his wounded men behind cover.

He yells over the comm.

"Two hit. Set the perimeter. Hold 'em back."

The rest of the team fans out, finding cover in the chaos. Bullets rip across the space, ricocheting off desks and walls, a hazy scene of smoke and blood red light.

I duck behind a pillar, scanning for an opening, and then I see it.

A clear gap, low and narrow, leading behind the far side of the counters where the BlackSteel guards are concentrated. They're pinned too, crouched low, focused on the rest of the Dragon Slayers.

Time slows, just for a heartbeat. I know I can end this.

My hand moves to my belt. The flashbang is already there. The pin slides free with a metallic whisper. The weight of the grenade in my palm is smooth and ready.

"Flash out!" I yell.

The flashbang arcs over the counter. I quickly find cover as the room implodes.

A burst of white light erupts; the sound hits a half-second later. In that instant, I see them rising from the smoke, war gods from Greek mythology.

Black and gold armor catches the red light, weapons raised, movements smooth and unshaken. Tristan and the Dragon Slayers, stand tall, masked figures carved by the fire.

They move forward in lockstep, rifles up, muzzle flashes cutting through the haze. Smoke coils around them, as the flare of gunfire erupts into red and white tracers.

Within seconds, it's over.

The red emergency lights keep pulsing. The smoke lingers. The trap they set for us has become their graves.

Tristan's already moving before the last shell casing hits the floor.

He crosses over two wounded Dragon Slayers, crouching beside them, checking their gear and vitals. One of them groans, clutching his side, still conscious. The other gives a knowing nod, blood seeping through his sleeve.

"Clean hits, lucky. You two will live another day."

He stands and gestures.

"Move 'em. Find a secure room, close it down, hold position. Keep them safe."

Two men lift the injured, carefully moving them to a side hallway without a word.

Tristan turns to me.

"Good shit, Charlie. Perfect toss, you broke that entire line."

He doesn't give me a chance to answer; instead, he quickly switches to comms.

Lifting his mic, he asks with urgency.

"Fireteam Alpha, any of the guards or admin give up the gate controls yet?"

A brief pause crackles over the comms before the reply comes through.

"Yes sir. One of the admin staff cracked. We've got full access codes ready for use."

Tristan's eyes narrow as he steps toward the control panel beside the reinforced door.

"Copy that."

He pulls up the interface, punches in the code without hesitation, and waits for the system to respond.

A metallic clunk echoes through the compound. Then another. And another.

Somewhere deep inside the fortress, cell blocks begin to unlock.

Tristan turns to us.

"All right," he barks. "It's showtime."

Prisoners start to emerge slowly, uncertain and unsteady on their feet. They appear gaunt and beaten. Others are slumped in their cells, too weak and scared to stir.

Tristan commands his team.

"Eliminate the remaining targets first. Waste no time."

We spread out, searching each cell.

"Come on," I whisper to myself. "Where are you two?"

A man is slumped against the wall of a dim, dirty cell. His face swollen, shirt torn, but his eyes spark up as I enter and shine my flashlight beam on him.

Graham.

CHAPTER 46

THE THINGS LEFT UNSAID

"All, everything that I understand, I understand only because I love."

-LEO TOLSTOY

MY ATTENTION IS drawn to Graham, who is clearly worn out, mentally and physically, but trying not to let it show. I have no idea how long he has been here or what they have put him through.

He is panic stricken at the sight of a Dragon Slayer standing in front of him. I see it in his bloodshot eyes, his reflexes, the fight-or-flight horror cutting through him.

Exhausted and bleeding, Graham is still not backing down. He will fight to his last breath. He has no clue that I am behind the mask. To him, I'm just the next threat, and he's ready to meet it head on.

"Graham, it's me!" I yell out.

I rip the mask from my face, dropping it to the floor. Graham's face alters as the struggle leaves him, followed by an overwhelming expression of wide-eyed amazement.

He looks at me as if I've shattered him into pieces.

"Charlie... what the hell... what are you wearing? You're one of them?"

I reach for him before he can pull away, quickly forcing my words out.

"Graham, please. BlackSteel took Lex and countless others, just like you. I'm here, they're here, to rescue everyone."

His stare is blank as he tries to process what I've just told him. I pull myself from his arms and stand, holding my hand out to him. He grabs it, wincing as he manages to straighten himself up. His bruises, cuts and burn marks are endless.

Graham rolls his shoulders and cracks his neck, groaning in pain. He stares at me with a look I have never seen before in anyone.

"You got another gun?" he asks, his voice hoarse.

Tristan steps forward, flipping a pistol in his hand before passing it to him.

"Best I've got."

Graham snatches the gun without hesitation. He cycles the magazine with a practiced hand.

"All I need."

The hallway grows colder as we move forward, faint lighting stretching into slithering shadows along the walls. My grip on the rifle tightens; each step resonates within my mind, a countdown timer ticking away.

As we near a heavy door at the end of the hallway, Tristan raises a hand, signaling for us to halt.

"This is the last cellblock here. If Lex is there, we will find her up ahead."

He looks at me and then signals for his team to take cover.

I follow him as he turns the corner; my heart pounds against my chest.

A bitter smell of antiseptic combined with stagnant air assails me. The cot in the corner is disheveled, but there is no Lex.

"She's not here," my words crack in my throat.

Graham comes in behind me, his face dark with shadows.

"They move people around all the time. They've been taking over parts of these facilities for torture chambers. She could be there."

I turn to him, part of me anticipating the worst.

"Torture chambers?"

"Yeah, admit you're a Dragon Slayer, and they'll execute you. Don't admit it, and they torture you until you do. That's what they were doing with all the people imprisoned here.

"That's what BlackSteel has become. They don't care about innocence or guilt. They just require bodies. It makes them appear to be in charge, grasping straws to look like they are in full control."

Tristan leans against a wall.

"See Charlie. The world's full of monsters. And sometimes it takes monsters to kill monsters."

Graham narrows his eyes.

"I'm sorry, but who the fuck are you?"

"Just someone on your side with a gun, for now."

I step between them.

"Graham, this is Tristan. He's leading this rescue. We wouldn't be here without him or the rest of his Dragon Slayers."

Graham gives a single nod, not complete trust, but enough for us to move forward on better terms.

The alarms haven't stopped, just dulled into background noise. The wreckage from the initial onslaught fades behind us, replaced by gleaming floors and spotless walls. Deep inside this building, nothing has been burned or broken.

Tristan holds up a hand again for us to halt.

"This is the maximum-security block. Last of the resistance should be here."

We come to another door. Tristan signals that we flank. Graham takes one side, his bruised face tense with focus. I take the other side, rifle at the ready. Tristan takes the center, his hand grasping the fore grip.

He steadies himself.

"Ready?"

"Ready," I reply firmly.

Tristan pushes the door open, and the world explodes.

BlackSteel guards were waiting inside, rifles already up. Gunfire tears through space, rounds chewing into the doorframe, walls splintering around us.

Tristan moves in first with precision. His shots land clean. Two down before they can even shift position. Graham pushes wide, dropping another and turning just in time to catch movement at the corner of his vision.

Another guard rushes in from behind a recess. He's fast, but Graham's faster. He sidesteps, strips the rifle clean from the man's hands, and slams him back into the wall hard enough to rattle the room.

The last guard is dug in on my flank, using a column for cover. We trade fire, short bursts ricocheting off concrete. He's good, smart enough to stay low, fast enough to make me work for him. But I've got the angle. One move, and he's mine.

I shift out, just enough to line up the shot.

Click.

Empty.

I freeze for half a second. Exposed and wide open, I'm an easy shot for him.

He's already pulling up the rifle.

Then it happens. Pure muscle memory.

My sidearm clears the holster before I even register that I've reached for it. Bullets ring out, fast and final. He jerks and stumbles before collapsing to the floor.

It's over before my brain catches up with my body. I'm still standing. He's not. The room's gone still; the firefight finished in under ten seconds.

Graham steps over the guard he dropped, eyes scanning for movement that never comes. He checks the rifle once, then slings it over his shoulder.

"Well, looks like I found a rifle."

Tristan barks.

"Good, but we need to keep moving."

I glance over at the dead guards, tangled in wild postures. BlackSteel's manpower lacks experience. Clearly, these unfortunate souls did not have what they needed to survive. They would have been prepared for us, but only with support from Sorakin.

The windows in a control room reveal rows of drones and mutts lined up in perfect formation, prepped for rapid deployment. Sleek black exteriors, armed and ready, designed to neutralize intruders in seconds.

Only now, they're completely useless.

Fortunately, whatever Carter, Merlin, and the Dragon Slayers did, it worked.

I can't help but wonder how many other battles are playing out right now. Teams like ours pressing forward, gaining ground, all because Sorakin's systems went dark at the opportune time.

Tristan motions forward as we follow behind him. The deeper we go into the cell block, the quieter it is. Tension builds, suspended in the air. My rifle grows heavier, its weight biting deeper into my hands.

We're near. I can feel it.

Tristan steps in front of the next door, grasping the handle, but it's locked tight. He yanks it once more, cursing in frustration.

"Fuck. There's gotta be a way to open this. We have the codes, just need to find the access panel."

Graham gestures towards a group of rooms.

"The access control is probably in one of those. We have to split up, there's no time to waste."

Tristan is already in motion.

"Graham, you take the far left, I'll take the center. Charlie, take the other one. Check in if you find anything."

"Got it," I say, moving cautiously into a dimly lit room.

The air is thick with a foreboding presence. There's a faint whir of electronics breaking the silence. Papers and cords are scattered across the desk, signs of a hasty and frantic departure. My boots crunch on debris scattered across the floor, giving my movements away.

Rifle at the ready, I continue to scope the room. The light from the hall spills in behind me as my body casts long, moving shadows. Come on, there must be something here. A panel, a switch.

Then I hear something. A faint shuffle from behind the desk. I whip my rifle in the direction of the noise, eyes locking on the overturned desk.

"Come out," I order, my voice sharp. "Hands up. Now."

A young woman rises, unarmed, with her hands trembling.

"Please I'm not a guard, Please, please don't shoot me."

She's terrified and appears to be telling the truth.

"I'm not going to hurt you. I need to get into the next room. Where's the access panel?"

The woman nods, blinking back tears.

"Yeah… Over there…"

She gestures toward the far wall, toward a door in the corner of the room. But I catch her eyes shifting left. Once, and then again. That's enough to make my instincts kick into overdrive.

I pivot hard, diving into cover just as a burst of gunfire erupts from the left-side hallway. The woman behind me screams as she becomes collateral damage in the barrage. I hear the thud of her body hitting the ground before I even see the shooter.

Heavy plating. It's a BlackSteel commander, wearing the same style armor as Reddick.

I roll into a firing position and squeeze off two clean shots. One slams into his side, the other into his shoulder. The impact staggers him. He grunts, snarling, colliding with the wall like he just got hit with a sledgehammer. The armor stops the bullets, but the impact must hurt like hell.

He stays in the fire zone, trying to push forward, but I'm already moving. I sweep left, wide, and fast, boots pounding the tile, my aim settling just ahead of his recovery.

Two more shots to the gut.

They hammer into reinforced plates, loud and solid. One of them found a seam as blood starts to spread beneath the armor, soaking through the cracks. He drops hard, hands scrambling toward the injury as he groans, a wet gasp escaping him.

He clutches his stomach, blood seeping between his fingers. "Don't shoot. I surrender... I give up..."

Cautiously, I approach the downed tech. She's conscious, clutching her shoulder, tears running silently down her face.

"You're alright," I say quickly. "Help is coming."

I reach for my comm.

"Tristan. The access point is behind a door here. Two wounded. Med evac. STAT."

"Copy that."

Without warning, a loud voice crackles over the PA system.

"Attention... this is Commander Larsen... Execute all prisoners now. I repeat, execute all prisoners!"

Spinning back towards the commander holding the comm, a wild rage surges through my chest.

I pull my rifle up for the kill shot, ready to end him.

Then I notice it.

His other hand clenched firm around a grenade with no pin.

"Fuck."

I throw myself sideways, diving behind the nearest cover, bracing for impact. The blast hits, brutal and blinding. The explosion punches the world into fragments.

A pressure wave tears through the room like a scream made of steel. Glass windows shatter around me as the blast rattles through my skull and detonates behind my eyes. I can't see.

Everything is blood-smeared red and flashing white.

I slam into the wall so hard it knocks everything out of me. Air, thought, identity.

Maybe I'm dead. Maybe this is it.

I have no sense of my body, just static and fire.

Then, a sound? A shape?

A pulling at the edge of my mind, trying to grab hold.

Voices, muted, broken.

"Charlie! Grayson!"

I can't tell where they are coming from, but I feel a presence. Strong hands reach under my arms, dragging me through broken tile and smoke. Tristan and Graham. They've got me.

Everything is spinning. I blink hard. Blood stings. The ringing hasn't stopped, but it's starting to weaken, like a siren fading into the distance.

Another breath. Sharp. Burning.

Then another.

I suck in air, chest hitching, lungs scraping against ribs that feel like they've cracked under the blast. But I'm breathing. I'm still alive.

They carefully lift me into the hallway, setting me down against a wall. I slump hard, fingers twitching against concrete as I rip my helmet off. Caustic air slaps me back into reality.

Tristan crouches beside me, his hands already checking over my gear.

"You should be good. I don't see any major hits. Looks like the mask came in handy."

I glance down at it, and freeze.

A jagged spike of shrapnel is buried in the armor just above my temple. Deep. Twisted. Without the Dragon Slayers mask, I would have been killed.

"I'm fine," I mutter, forcing myself upright.

My whole body protests, but I block the pain. The adrenaline is too strong, flooding through my veins, silencing everything but the need to move.

"We need to get Lex. Tristan. Access panel room. Other side."

He doesn't waste a second, moving in quick, determined strides.

There is a low mechanical whirring sound, disengaging the locks with a heavy clunk. The door slides open as Tristan bounds forward, rifle raised high.

Gunfire erupts, sudden, relentless.

We can't see it, only hear it echoing through the corridor. The massacre has started. BlackSteel is cleaning house. And every shot feels like it's for Lex, each one landing a blow to my chest.

We run down the corridor, the loud cracks getting closer. Two units are moving systematically down the line of cells, shooting inside, one by one. Executing prisoners.

So focused are they on their bloody executions that they

don't notice us. Tristan shoots first, clean, precise. Graham follows up taking out the second guard. The guards fall forward before they can fire another shot.

Tristan releases a brisk command.

"Secure the area. Search every cell."

We spread out, moving down the line. Some cells are empty. Others… I push on, resolute.

My body grows colder, my heart racing as I search faces, hope dissipating.

Then I see her.

At first, just her hair, that unmistakable amber catching the pulsing red light, glowing like fire in the dark.

The shape of her body, curled in on itself, lifeless.

Then the blood.

It's dark, spreading beneath Lex, draining the life out of her. It stains the concrete in a slow, merciless crawl. But she's breathing. Shallow. Strained.

Alive.

"Lex!" I scream." Lex. I'm here!"

Her head rolls slightly, eyes fluttering, unfocused, but when they lock onto mine, she releases a soft, weak smile.

Her voice trembles, thin and fading.

"Charlie… you came for me."

"I'm here, I've got you. You're going to be okay."

Lex emits a soft grimace.

"Damn. That would be…"

Her entire body convulses rigidly, her skin freezing cold under my touch. She reaches out to me, her hand shaking. I take it, holding on firmly.

I push both hands onto her side, attempting to cut off the bleeding, attempting to keep her together. My fingers are already wet with blood. Too much. It's too much.

Lex attempts to move, but the motion causes a visceral, gut-wrenching shudder to run through her whole body. She sucks in a sharp breath, her eyelids fluttering.

"Fuck," she barely chokes out. "Talked too much shit this time."

"What are you talking about Lex?"

Her lips twist into a weak grin.

"Runnin' my mouth... you know me."

She breathes unsteadily, her fingers relaxing in my grasp.

"Told them they're all billionaire simps with small dicks. That's what got me here."

A strangled sound escapes me, part laugh, part sob, raw and trembling.

"Lex."

"Don't," she forces the words out. "This is my fault. Not yours, Charlie."

Even now, she's still trying to protect me. Still shielding me from the guilt, from the weight she knows I'll carry. She's the one bleeding out, and she's worried about me.

Her body convulses again, her breathing shorter, more shallow gasps.

"Thought I'd never see you again." she says, voice barely rising as her breath falters. "Kept thinking, shit, this is it, I'll never see my Charlie again. But now..."

Her fingers clench around mine, feeble but present.

"You're here... just so happy you're here."

I bite back a sob, as tears stream down my face.

"Yeah... Yeah... I'm happy too, Lex."

Words fall from her like a final exhale.

"Just... hold me one more time... okay?" It's so... damn cold."

I wrap my arms around her, holding her close, trying to share my warmth with her, trying to keep her with me.

"I'm here," I press my face into her and let the words spill out. "I've got you. I'm not letting go."

This isn't real. This can't be real.

"Lex," I weep, tears scorching my skin. "Lex, please, please. I need you."

She doesn't move. The one person I had left, the one thing I swore I wouldn't lose, is slipping away in my arms. I can feel her warmth fading by the second, the world peeling her away from me. One breath at a time.

A hand clamps down on my shoulder, thrusting me away from her. My body tightens prepared to battle, to rip anyone limb from limb who attempts to separate us.

It's Tristan, falling to his knees next to me, his fingers digging against Lex's neck, feeling, probing.

His head snaps up, voice tense and concentrated. He runs his hands quickly along her torso, checking entry points, pressing lightly near her ribs and abdomen.

"Her pulse is weak, and she's got multiple gunshot wounds, but it doesn't seem like she's been hit in the vitals."

A noise gets caught in my throat, halfway between a sob and a breath, hope and pain tangled into one.

Tristan applies pressure to the wound with practiced ease. His hands move fast and steady, years of training kicking in as he tears his pack open and begins shouting orders into his comms.

"This is Tristan. We require immediate medical evac, gunshot wound, critical blood loss. No vitals compromised. We need to move now, or it won't make a difference."

He snaps his fingers at Graham.

"Get pressure on it tight. Do not let up."

Graham doesn't protest. He crashes down beside Lex, his

hands closing over the wound without a moment of hesitation. Blood seeps through his fingers, but he doesn't relent.

I'm paralyzed. Can't breathe. My fingers float over Lex's face, grazing her cheek, pushing wet strands of hair back from her forehead.

Tristan is already five steps ahead, tearing through his med pack, calculating as he works, a man racing against a ticking time bomb.

"She could go into shock at any second now, and we could lose her." He growls, more to himself, but I catch it, and my chest clenches.

He continues to work fast, ripping out QuikClot gauze, forcing it deep into the wound with rough efficiency, as Lex's body jerks from the pain and pressure.

"Graham, keep compressing while I wrap," he commands.

Tristan rips open a bandage, wrapping it tightly around Lex's torso, holding the gauze in place.

"Charlie," he says, not looking up. "If you have anything to say to her, now would be the time."

His words devastate me. A sob tears through my chest as I take Lex's hand and press my forehead against hers.

"I love you so much Lex."

My words break free, soft but soaked in everything I should have said sooner.

"Oh God, Lex, I love you. I've always loved you. I was so fucking stupid, so blind. But not anymore. Not now."

Her lips tremble, but her eyes remain closed.

"It's about time… " she murmurs so softly I'm not sure I imagined it.

A laugh chokes out of me, distraught, relieved, and shattered all at once.

"I know… you're everything to me." I reply, every syllable laced with fear. "But you have to stay with me, Lex. You have to."

Tristan snaps, voice rough with pressure.

"She's losing too much blood. We need an exit, now."

A crackle of static comes through on his comms.

A voice answers.

"Nearest friendly hospital, 8 miles away."

Tristan doesn't hesitate. He lifts Lex gently into his arms, muscles bunching, his hold firm.

"Graham, bring the gear. Charlie, keep her awake. We're running out of time."

I nod frantically, brushing tears from my face. I clutch Lex's hand, keeping her with me, with this world, with this moment.

My promise is unwavering.

"We're getting you out of here."

Her breath washes against my skin. It's weak. But it's there. The second we have Lex in the SUV, Tristan is back trying to save her life.

He acts on pure instinct, grabbing more supplies from the back compartments as Graham closes the back doors with a slam. All I can see is Lex, her body limp, her breathing shallow.

Tristan's tone is level, but insistent, a combat medic in the zone.

"She needs her blood volume stabilized, or she's not going to make it to that hospital."

Helpless, I watch while he tears open IV tubing, locates a vein in Lex's arm, and plunges the needle in with ruthless efficiency. His hands move quickly, every motion vital.

I tighten my grip on Lex's icy hand, whispering in her ear.

"Stay with me. Just stay with me."

Tristan secures the IV with tape, ensuring it stays in place.

He squeezes the bag, forcing the fluids to flow faster, then checks Lex's pulse.

"This will buy us some time."

He glances up at Graham.

"You a good driver?"

"Yep," Graham replies, already climbing into the front seat.

Tristan tosses the keys to him.

"South Memorial Trauma. Step on it."

Graham punches the hospital into the GPS and throws the SUV into gear. The tires squeal as we tear out of the lot, sending dust flying as our vehicle lurches onto the road.

I barely notice what is happening. I can only focus on Lex.

Tristan is adjusting the compression repeatedly, monitoring her vitals. I see the tension in his face, but it doesn't affect his movements.

"How fast is too fast?" Graham yells, clenching the wheel.

Tristan doesn't skip a beat.

"No such thing as long as you don't crash. Hit that switch to the left of the wheel."

Graham flips it, and police sirens start to blare, giving us a new lane through traffic. He floors it, not wasting anytime.

Tristan seizes my wrist, yanking my focus away from Lex. His fingers sink into my flesh, hard enough to bring me back to reality.

"Charlie, listen to me," he says, his voice biting. "You have to keep her awake."

My breath catches.

"I... I'm trying..."

His grasp becomes firmer.

"No, you don't understand. If she nods off, she's not waking up.

"Charlie... she will die."

His hands maintain their motion, applying new gauze, securing the bandages, adjusting the flow of the IV.

"Keep her talking."

I grab Lex's face and turn it to mine.

"Lex... hey... hey... look at me."

My words come out as a forceful command, one that won't let her slip away.

Her eyelids twitch. Her lips open, but no sound emerges.

My stomach twists. I hold her tight, willing her to remain.

"You're not going to leave me; do you hear me? I won't let you."

Air escapes her mouth, a few words follow.

"So... dramatic..."

A strangled laugh bursts from me, wild, naked, and devastating.

"That's me Lex. The dramatic one."

"No... silly... that's me..."

I squeeze her hand tighter, holding her here with me.

"Then prove it. Stay awake, Lex."

She blinks slowly, too slowly.

I'm losing her. Panic tightens my chest as words tumble out, revealing the truth I've hidden way too long.

"We're going to travel the world," I tell her, my voice shaking. "You and me. I'm finished with the FBI. I'm finished being their puppet."

Her eyelashes flicker.

"Doesn't sound like you..."

I manage a faint laugh as I sweep her damp hair from her face.

"I think I'm finally figuring out who the real me is... and I know what I want."

Lex's dull eyes meet mine.

"I want you, Lex."

Tristan takes her pulse again, his face impassive.

"Three minutes out," Graham yells from the front, weaving in and out of traffic.

Tristan continues adjusting the IV, checking the clotting agents and monitoring her vitals.

I can sense how close I am to losing her.

Lex's lips move, but her voice is almost too soft to hear.

"Charlie."

I lean closer to her, panic-stricken.

"I'm here, Lex."

"Just know… I love you so much. If I don't…"

Her breathing is weak, her grasp on my hand loosening.

My voice breaks.

"You will live."

She exhales a shaky breath, eyes flickering up to mine.

"Then you… owe me… that vacation…."

Tears well up in my eyes.

"I'll take you anywhere you want."

She gasps out sharply, wincing.

"It better… not be a… shithole."

I weep with a soft laugh.

"Deal. Just don't fall asleep… okay?"

The SUV hurtles ahead, sirens blaring.

Graham wrenches the wheel, turning into the hospital parking lot.

"Go, right to the front!" Tristan shouts.

The instant the brakes squeal, the doors open. A trauma team rushes towards us.

Tristan is out first, seizing the closest medic.

"GSW, severe blood loss, conscious but barely. IV in,

pressure on, clotting agents in effect. She requires a transfusion ASAP."

They work with the efficiency of a fine-tuned machine, pulling Lex from the SUV.

"Charlie," Lex faintly calls out.

"I'm right here," I answer quietly, following close behind.

As they rush Lex through the hospital doors, a nurse blocks my way.

"Ma'am, you need to stay back here," she says.

I pretend not to hear her and automatically push forward.

Graham pulls me back, his voice firm.

"You have to let them work."

I'm suffocating as I watch Lex wheeled through the emergency room doors. Her body limp on the stretcher, blood streaked on the sheets.

Tristan exhales, running a hand through his hair before turning to us again.

"We did everything we could do, now we just have to wait."

He's right. There's nothing more we can do for her but hope.

And more than anything.

I hope that wasn't our last goodbye.

CHAPTER 47

THE ONES LEFT STANDING

"Don't grieve. Everything is according to nature. What matters is not what you lose, but what you become."

- MARCUS AURELIUS

THE MOMENT LEX disappears behind the double doors, my anxiety deepens. The adrenaline rush that carried me through the prison firefight is rapidly dissolving. In its place is a hollow chasm of sorrow and pain.

My entire body grows heavier by the second; it's a strange sensation of sinking without water. I drop down on a waiting room chair, my fingers and legs twitching in nervous unison.

My clothes are stained with blood. Lex's blood. Dried, flaking at the edges, morbid reminders of her clinging to my skin.

The ringing in my ears hasn't stopped since the blast, but my pain masks it. I run my fingers along my shirt, touching the damp fabric, which is warmer than it should be. My hand becomes stained with blood, wet and dark. Must be shrapnel. I didn't even feel the penetration.

I close my eyes, trying to steady myself. There's no sense in rewinding now; what if is a useless ritual. Still, it infiltrates my mind.

If I'd cleared the room faster. If I'd taken the opposite hall. If I didn't show any mercy to that fucking commander who condemned so many prisoners.

Pressing my palms hard against my thighs, I try to bury those defeating thoughts. A subtle cough breaks my focus.

It's Tristan, leaning against a back wall, neck tilted, eyes shut. Stillness cloaks him in restless tension as he clenches his fists. A hard-pressed man waiting for an order that will never arrive.

As I stare at him, realization hits me. Tristan saved Lex.

I was losing her in that cell, resigning myself to the fact that she was going to die in my arms. If he hadn't been there, if he hadn't jumped into action, she would never have made it out of that cell alive.

I stand up too quickly, my legs reluctantly move as I shuffle myself across the room.

"Tristan."

He doesn't acknowledge me; he knows what's coming.

"You saved Lex."

I stop myself, almost not wanting to tempt fate.

"You gave her a shot to make it here alive."

Tristan opens one eye, with a flicker of something deeper behind it.

"I'm just happy I could help. Nice change of pace from so many bad things happening... it always feels good if you can save a life instead of taking one."

He is sincere, a simple truth from someone who's seen too much go the other way.

I see this man for what he really is. Just Tristan, the man who carried Lex through hell. The man who gave her a fighting chance.

Looking at him, I realize the unfathomable.

Tristan is wearing his Dragon Slayer armor.

We're standing in a public hospital, bloodied, wearing the symbol of a domestic terrorist group, and no one's taking any notice. Nurses fly past. A doctor asks for a scan. A security guard leans against the far wall, scrolling through his phone.

I turn back to Tristan.

"Why isn't anybody looking at us?"

"Charlie, they're busy helping people."

"That's not an answer, Tristan."

He opens both eyes and pushes himself upright, grimacing with pain.

"You really want to know?

"It's not just about getting paid. If that's what you're thinking."

"Then what is it?"

He's quiet for a second, like he's relinquishing a secret.

"Doctors want to help people. So do nurses. That's why they're here. Hospitals can't run just on good intentions.

"When BlackSteel tightened its grip, and the government pulled funding, places like this started to collapse. No supplies or funding. They were barely hanging on.

"So, the Dragon Slayers stepped in. Used billionaire money to reroute what they needed fast.

"And in return, when we show up, they don't ask questions. They do what they came here to do."

"So that's why the trauma team was waiting when we got here," I answer with a hint of surprise.

"Yup. They don't work for us or answer to us. We just keep the hospital running smoothly. Some know. Some don't. But either way, they help us when it matters."

I look back towards the double doors where Lex vanished.

My arms feel heavier, the fatigue seeps deeper, causing my heartbeat to pulse behind my eyes.

She is alive for now because of the Dragon Slayers.

Their network. Their belief in helping the people no one else will.

A doctor steps into the waiting room. Instantly, all three of us go still. She doesn't rush. Doesn't look rattled.

That must be a good sign, right?

Her gaze moves over us steady, professional.

"I'm Dr. Patel. Ms. Thompson is stable."

Her words hit harder than expected. My brain knows what that means, but the rest of me can't process it fast enough. Part of me had been preparing for the worst. I had already started fortifying myself.

Graham lets out a low, slow whistle.

Tristan doesn't move. Doesn't say a word. What changes is his posture. It softens, not fully relaxed, just a small release of sorts. He was braced for the worst and, like me, doesn't quite know how to process this bit of good news.

But Dr. Patel isn't finished.

"However, we ran a scan during stabilization. There's internal damage, debris we couldn't reach. She's being prepped for surgery now."

The relief drops. Sharp and fast.

I say nothing. I don't move. Everything inside me is screaming again.

Graham mutters under his breath.

"Jesus."

Tristan's eyes are fixed on the doctor with clinical focus.

"Doctor, when you say internal damage, are we talking liver? Vascular? Deep hemorrhage?"

Dr. Patel changes her stance, addressing him differently.

"Vascular injury near the kidney. We're extracting the frag-ments and repairing the surrounding tissue. But there's a risk of continued blood loss during surgery. Given her condition, it could go either way."

Fifty-fifty. A coin toss between life and everything else.

Tristan holds the doctor's eye for another second.

"Appreciate you keeping us updated."

Dr. Patel smiles back.

"We're doing everything humanly possible for her. Now, we need to get the rest of you checked out. Full medical exam, patching up and a shower. Staff will be out shortly to assist."

Dr. Patel leaves us lost in our thoughts.

"They have the best surgeons here," Tristan's voice is assur-ing. "Nothing more we can do. Let's follow the docs order and get cleaned up."

I don't want to leave. I don't want to look away from the hallway where Lex disappeared. But there's nothing I can do for her just waiting here.

A nurse leads me through a quiet corridor tucked behind the trauma wing. Inside a narrow exam room, she gestures for me to sit.

The nurse works fast: pulse, pupils, blood pressure. She dons gloves and begins peeling back what's left of my clothing, layer by grimy layer.

"You actually walked in like this?"

I bow my head, barely able to hear her words.

"A grenade?"

"Mostly."

She doesn't comment, just gets back to work. My wounds seem second nature to her.

The nurse rattles off.

"Second-degree burns across the left leg and part of the

back. Fragmentation wounds, thigh, abdomen, both arms. Possible fractured rib. Eardrum rupture, right side. Heavy bruising across the torso.

"And you've got a concussion. Eyes are slow to track. You're pale, borderline disoriented. Your brain's taken a hit, semi-shock, so you don't feel anything yet."

I didn't realize it was that bad.

She straightens and meets my eyes.

"If you were under my care, I'd keep you here for at least twenty-four hours."

"But I'm not under your care, am I?"

"No, Ms. Grayson," she says flatly, handing me a set of scrubs. "I'm just the one making sure you don't pass out in the hallway."

She points to another door.

"Go shower. I'll finish treating you after that and get you bandaged up."

The water feels like punishment. My whole body flinches, muscles locking tight before they finally start to release. There is not one inch of me that doesn't hurt. Some wounds sting; others burn.

I brace against the wall and let the water work. I watch it all swirl down the drain, grime, ash, and blood, some of it is Lex's. Drying myself off, I can't stop thinking about her. She's the only thing that matters.

As the nurse finishes treating me, I thank her profusely.

She gives a quick shake of her head.

"Please. I'm just glad I can help. Without your people, this place would've been an abandoned ruin months ago."

The nurse thinks I'm a Dragon Slayer. I still tell myself I'm not one of them, but I honestly don't know exactly who or what I am right now.

Heading back into the waiting room. I find Graham and Tristan relaxing on a couch, both in civilian clothes.

Graham's hands are wrapped, bandages circling his knuckles like he punched through something that didn't give. There's bruising across his face, a strip of medical tape at his temple, and his forearm is freshly dressed, blood peeping through the gauze.

Tristan has tight wraps on his biceps and over one shoulder. The edges are neat, precise, but something about the dressing feels deceptive. Like they're hiding more damage than they show.

Neither of them complains. But looking at them now, I realize I wasn't the only one who took a beating.

We all walked through an inferno to get here.

Graham has lived this before. It's written in the set of his features; in the steadiness he wears like armor.

Tristan too, but I see it in the way he listens to the quiet.

How many times have they sat like this? Waiting. Knowing they did everything they could and still might lose someone anyway.

I think of my father. The man who built his life around saving others.

How many times did he sit waiting for news he couldn't change? How many missions ended with silence and hope tied in knots?

My dad thought he sacrificed his life for something bigger than himself. And now I know it was nothing more than a brazen deception.

And then I think of my mother.

God, I won the lottery with her. Kind. Patient. Tougher than anyone I've ever met. She held everything together, even when it was falling apart.

She made me promise her one thing.

Don't be on the front line.

I said yes. I meant it.

But now I understand the full meaning behind my mother's request.

It wasn't just the danger she wanted me to avoid.

It was this.

The waiting. The helplessness. The endless fear of loving someone who might not come back.

My father's legacy forced my mom to live this. Over and over. Knowing this makes everything worse.

Graham and Tristan look at me but don't say a word. I crumble into a chair, sitting across from them.

The clock on the wall ticks forward in steady, rhythmic beats, a slow march that doesn't match what's happening in my head. Time feels broken. Stretched too thin and crushed all at once. Every second without an update pulls me deeper into a space I don't know how to exist in.

I stretch my fingers open, close them, repeat. Again. Again. It's the only rhythm I have left. The only thing that keeps me from splintering as I slowly drift into a light sleep from exhaustion.

Murmurs wake me. It's Graham and Tristan conversing, trying to keep their voices low. There's something under it. Recognition. A shared language they haven't spoken yet.

"Three tours. Middle East mostly." Graham says, massaging his shoulder. "Spent some time in the Pacific with a Recon unit."

"Marine?"

"Yeah. How'd you guess?"

"You've all got that look. Like you could take someone's head off with one finger if you had to."

"Fair enough.

"Tristan, you had to be a medic at some point, but the way

you moved during the breach, that's more than support work. You're a doc, aren't you? Embedded."

Tristan's lips twitch into a smile, the kind that says Graham nailed it.

"Navy Corpsman. Attached to a Marine unit for 3 years."

Graham lets out a slow whistle.

"Knew it. No matter what's going down, you're already prepping on how to keep someone alive."

"Always craved more. So, I got pulled into SEAL and later on transferred to black ops, until everything fell apart."

Graham's expression is less guarded, more open.

"Yeah, crazy, thinking back about all that shit back then."

I see their deep-rooted connection. Brothers in arms. That same worn-out edge that comes from watching too many people die, while somehow you manage to live.

The only difference is Graham found a way to try to preserve the system. Tristan found a reason to burn it down.

I'm still half-listening to Graham and Tristan, caught in the quiet rhythm of two men who understand each other without needing to explain it.

A sharp knock at the door startles us.

Dr. Patel walks in. Her face is unreadable.

She looks at the three of us. War-torn statues waiting for her to speak.

And then Dr. Patel smiles. It's the kind of smile that reflects good news.

"Lex pulled through."

Those words change everything.

Relief courses through me. All the emotions I've been carrying, every worst-case scenario I prepared myself for, every wall I tried to build, all collapse in an instant.

I stand up too fast. My legs buckle, and my vision goes

blurry. The release is too big to contain. Uncontrollable tears flow down my cheeks.

Emotions collide inside me. I rush forward to the only people who've lived this moment with me.

Tristan instinctively wraps his arms around me, as I press my face against his chest. His hug is strong, comforting and reassuring. I turn and pull Graham into our embrace. He doesn't flinch, just folds us in, solid and unshaken.

They saw me through this nightmare. The ones who kept her alive long enough to make it here.

When I step back, wiping tears from my face, Dr. Patel is waiting.

"She's unconscious, but stable. The surgery went well."

A ragged breath slips out of me, and suddenly I am stretched between the earth and the sky.

"Lex needs lots of rest. Give her time. She should make a full recovery."

Graham falls back on the chair, his body flopping like a rag doll, taking a breath that fills his lungs. The weight he has been carrying for way too long has been lifted.

Tristan's eyes close briefly, his face embracing a heartfelt smile. A small part of him is letting go.

Tristan has stood on the other side of this too many times, relieved that this time it has not ended with another body for him to bury.

"Please, Doctor," I implore her. "I need to see her."

"You can. But you'll need to stay outside the ICU doors. Come with me."

Our walk to the unit takes far too long. Every step stretches the distance between fear and hope.

We stop in front of a wide observation window, protecting Lex from the outside world.

And there she lies.

Too pale. Too still. Covered in wires and tubing, her body dwarfed by the white of the bedding and the machines that keep her stable. Her face is marked with bruises and cuts, with a line of gauze wrapping beneath her collarbone.

She looks incredibly fragile; one wrong move could shatter her.

I decompress myself, trying to process what I am seeing.

But she's still Lex. And I know I love her more than anything else.

Dr. Patel touches my shoulder.

"Your friend is heavily medicated. She should be awake in eight to twelve hours. She'll be disoriented. This whole process takes time. Nothing more you can do here."

Without another word, we head back to Graham and Tristan.

The waiting room is quieter now. Dimmer. The chaos has dulled into the late-night lull where even time feels sedated.

Tristan pushes off the wall towards me.

"Lex is in good hands, Charlie. There's nothing we can do for her right now. We all need to get some rest, or we won't be of any use to anybody, especially ourselves."

He reaches into his jacket and pulls out two hotel key cards, holding them out, one in each hand.

"I had someone get these while we were getting checked out."

Of course, Tristan would have been thinking ahead. I check Graham's expression, and it tells me everything; he's not surprised. Neither of us had thought about where we'd go next. I hadn't let myself think past this hallway.

He passes the key cards to us, then reaches into his pocket and pulls out two small envelopes. One is pressed into my palm, the other into Graham's.

"This'll make things easier till we get your gear back."

It's Dragon Slayer logistics.

I look down at the envelope. I don't even need to open it. I already know there's a lot of cash inside.

Graham flips the key card between his fingers, looking at Tristan with unspoken gratitude.

"After being locked in a BlackSteel cell this long. An actual bed sounds pretty damn nice."

I don't answer. I'm not going anywhere.

"Guys, I'm going to stay here."

Tristan doesn't argue. This is not a fight he will win.

"Charlie, I don't blame you. I'd do the same."

He clasps Graham on the shoulder and tilts his head toward the exit.

"Come on. I'll drop you off."

Graham looks at me for a moment, a questioning glance requesting reassurance. I meet his eyes and give a small, firm nod. He walks away without pursuing it any further.

Tristan joins him in heading for the doors. I rush up to him, not yet ready to let him go.

"Tristan…"

He stops, looks back over his shoulder.

"Thank you. I mean it. For all of this. For what you did. You don't know what it means to me. I don't know how I can ever repay you."

Tristan stares at me a second longer than he should. He smiles knowingly, almost humbly.

"You know what, Charlie? There is a favor you can do for me. And for a lot of other people, too."

A sense of unease crosses my mind.

"What is it?"

His smile lingers as he turns back toward the doors.

"Don't fret about it now. We'll talk later."

Tristan walks away, leaving me standing there, alone, tired, and unsteady as I hold onto something I don't yet understand.

Lex is alive.

And that's the only thing that matters.

Whatever Tristan asks, I will do. My debt to him runs deep.

CHAPTER 48

THE FINAL MOVE

"And again, I say unto you. It is easier for a camel
to go through the eye of a needle, than for a rich
man to enter into the kingdom of God."

-GOSPEL OF MATTHEW 19:24

THE HOSPITAL IS unnervingly quiet, and so am I. The fear that has plagued me since the moment BlackSteel abducted Lex has diminished. Still, there is a part of me that is wrecked, raw and exhausted, but at least I'm not bracing for the next blow anymore.

She's alive. That truth brings much-needed comfort. But it also opens a space for everything else I've been holding back to come rushing in.

The individuals both BlackSteel and the Dragon Slayers murdered. And the lives I took as well. It all haunts me, even though I try to justify my actions. At least, that's the belief I find myself embracing.

Death comes with the territory. I've personally signed off on it more times than I care to admit. But this time, I delivered the kill, and that changes everything.

Peeling myself off the waiting room couch, I head to the cafeteria. It's almost empty, except for two exhausted nurses staring at their phones. The only sound is of the coffeemaker in the corner, brewing a pot no one will touch.

A cold bottle of water from the vending machine revives my fingers. I should drink. Eat. Rest. All I can do is sit, locked in place.

Everything is different. Prior to the recent turn of events, I viewed the Dragon Slayers as ruthless killers, extremists, a threat to everything I was meant to protect.

That version of me wouldn't recognize the one sitting here now. And yet, I feel more like myself than I have in countless years.

One thought remains.

"You know what, Charlie? There actually is a way you can really make it up to me. And a lot of other people too."

Tristan's words loop in my mind, an unanswered question that continues to pester me.

What does he want? What did I promise to fulfill? Will more lives be lost?

I do owe Tristan that favor for saving Lex. No matter what the cost, it won't matter.

A dull glow catches my eye from the corner of the room. It's an empty TV screen mounted on the wall. I hesitate and then push to my feet, grabbing the remote.

The screen lights up, displaying SLY News. It has always been a broadcast machine, a relentless, twenty-four-hour cycle of propaganda, spun and controlled by the billionaires who own it.

That didn't make SLY News unique. Every major news outlet has been bought and reshaped by billionaires with different political labels, different supposed agendas. Left, right, moderate, it didn't matter.

They were distractions. Different flavors of control, all designed to keep the masses occupied while the real power stays untouched.

Watching the broadcast, the graphics are the same, the branding unchanged, but the administration's polished talking heads have been replaced. I don't recognize a single face. The billionaires who owned a majority of the networks have left, gone missing, or have just given up to appease the Dragon Slayers.

The anchor's tone is soothing, professional, with no manufactured tension, no desperate attempt to steer the narrative. It's just news. Hard facts, delivered without spin.

"Mass uprisings have taken over the streets and are no longer isolated events. They've become a nationwide movement, peaceful, organized, and driven by a group calling itself the Union Guard.

"Since the Sorakin Tech network was disabled, multiple attacks have been carried out on detention centers across the country. Some are calling them liberation missions. Others claim the Dragon Slayers were involved. But regardless of who's behind them, one thing is clear: the tide has shifted."

She pauses as footage rolls showing massive crowds flooding the streets, holding homemade signs, and waving American flags.

We will vote!

Tuff's the terrorist!

End Government Privatization!

They're ordinary people, veterans, teachers, nurses, and doctors demanding the reinstatement of free elections. For the first time since the crackdowns began, the resistance is solidifying.

The Dragon Slayers lit the fuse, now, The Union Guard is carrying the torch.

The broadcast expands coverage, displaying rallies in every major city, demanding the reinstatement of elections, the removal of the billionaire-controlled administration, and the dismantling of BlackSteel's private military.

These are carefully coordinated demonstrations.

Then comes the line that lands like a hammer.

"We have confirmation that several BlackSteel facilities have been breached, and key political prisoners have been freed."

My breath catches in my throat. Political prisoners.

Not terrorists.

Even SLY News is announcing it loud and clear. The same network that once parroted every lie, which helped justify the mass arrests, the crackdowns, the censoring of dissent. They're calling it what it is. The narrative has cracked. And once it breaks, it never goes back.

The footage cuts to a series of interviews playing across every major network, clips of generals, governors, and legal experts going on record. No more mincing words.

"The Tuff administration is an illegitimate regime," one general says frankly, his medals catching the studio lights. "We are committed to restoring the democratic process. No matter the cost."

Another clip, this time, a state governor's press conference.

"We've withdrawn all recognition of federal directives from this administration. Our allegiance is to the Constitution, not the billionaires' fantasy of power."

And then it cuts to Attorney Miles Archer.

He's standing on courthouse steps, well-starched and composed as ever, not a wrinkle on his face or high-end suit. His

voice is slick, words exact, like he's delivering the winning closing argument and loving every minute of it.

"The law is clear. It's on our side. That's why I'm here, and I
am not going anywhere until we get justice."

Cutting back to the anchor, she speaks with severity.

"The question now is how long the President of the United
States can pretend the country is still behind him, especially after
BlackSteel and the administration redirected all manned support
to reinforce the billionaire Freedom Zones. That enforced measure effectively abandoned the rest of the nation.

"Without Sorakin systems, it's clear the President and his
administration no longer have the resources to hold everything
together."

They've been pushed back, not defeated. At this very
moment, Alexander Sorin and his engineers are buried deep in
some underground facility, working to reboot their entire network, drones, surveillance, and enforcement systems. It's only a
matter of time before they do, and then the game will change
again.

Tuff isn't gone. His strongholds are still in place. The billionaires still have their bunkers, their stockpiles, their unlimited
resources.

The screen shifts. There he is…

President Tuff.

Tucked away in a secure bunker, with no press, no audience,
his voice echoes in the dark gray space. The usual bravado is
still there, but his skin looks sallow under the studio lights. His
forehead is covered in beads of sweat, and his hair has turned
completely gray. The President is disheveled, tie off center, suit
wrinkled.

His words echo as he growls.

"Don't listen to them. These so-called leaders, these traitors to America! They are stealing your country! They are trying to take away what is rightfully yours!

"I am the President of the United States! I hold the power! The American people voted for me and thus stand with me!"

His fists slam against the podium. He's unraveling as he lashes out.

"Do not give in to fear! Do not let these criminals take your possessions! If they come for you, if they try to steal your home, your future, you fight. Fight, fight, fight!"

He repeats it like a mantra, fists pumping, his face turning beet red.

"We will not back down! We will never surrender! Forget your fake elections, your lies, your treason, because I am still your President! And I am not going anywhere!"

The camera lingers too long. Tuff's heavy breathing is audible, his eyes wild. The screen finally breaks to a commercial.

The entire world is breaking apart at the seams. Tuff's administration is losing control. The billionaire class is still fortified, but cracks are starting to appear on their walls. The people are no longer theirs to control.

And Tuff? He knows it. He's backed into a corner. His words aren't commands anymore. They're pleas.

My mind is too tired to process what I am witnessing. Even the hard steel chair I'm sitting on feels comfortable, a solid base beneath me. My body tries to sink into it, my limbs heavy, my mind slowing as more images flash on the TV screen.

My eyes close, and I succumb to sleep.

Suddenly, I am shaken awake. A familiar voice is rousing me. My body protests, stiff and sluggish, mind foggy, energy depleted.

"Ms. Grayson."

For a moment, I forget where I am.

It all comes rushing back as I struggle to raise my head. The person disturbing my slumber is Dr. Patel.

"Lex is awake; you can see her now."

My mind is foggy; the doctor's words are incomprehensible. Then it registers. A live wire snaps me to life, energy surges through my body, wiping away every ounce of exhaustion.

"She's awake?"

Dr. Patel nods and suddenly I'm sprinting. Out of the cafeteria, into the hall, pushing past medical staff, offering no apologies. The only thing I focus on is getting to Lex as fast as possible.

Reaching the ICU doors, I stop.

For the briefest moment, I hesitate. Lex is awake now. And that means facing whatever comes next, together. The fear, the trauma, the pain that she has experienced may scar her for life.

Impacting her body. Her mind. Her soul.

What if my beautiful, free-spirited Lex is gone? The kind of trauma she has been through can have lasting negative effects.

It doesn't matter. I will stay by her side. No matter how long it takes. She would do the same for me.

Pressing the ICU entrance button, the doors slowly open. I close my eyes, take a deep breath and step into my new normal.

Lex is there. Bandaged. Bruised. Monitors beeping, wires running from every part of her frail body, machines blinking in sync. Her skin remains pale, frame appears smaller, but she is breathing.

My throat tightens.

"Lex."

Her head shifts, sluggish, eyes heavy-lidded as she turns toward me. Her movements are in slow motion as she fights the cocktail of pain meds they have pumped into her.

And then she sees me.

A faint smile tugs at her lips, barely there, but ever so real. Even through her drug-induced haze, her eyes twinkle when they meet mine. And in that single look, I know, she's still herself.

Still Lex. Still mine.

"Hey, you," she murmurs, barely above a whisper.

My heart shatters.

"Oh my God, Lex, I…"

The emotions are too much, too tangled, and I can't hold back anymore. I lean in, wrapping my arms around her, pulling her into the gentlest embrace I can manage.

Pain flickers across her face.

"Ow, ow, that hurts," she weakly moans.

"Shit! I'm sorry, I just…"

A mix of relief and release slips through my lips. We just stare at each other, as if meeting for the first time.

Brushing a strand of hair away from her face, Lex absorbs the sensation, her face peaceful. I press the gentlest kiss against her lips. It's quick, careful, just enough to remind myself that this is real. That she is real.

"I thought I lost you," I whisper.

"I don't remember much," she continues. "But… I thought my life was over… that I was going to die in that cell."

She pauses, a flicker of something unreadable crossing her face.

"And then I saw you."

Her few words split open my vulnerabilities.

"I wasn't going to let them take you from me."

Lex studies me for a moment, her gaze locked onto mine, something deeper flickering beneath her exhaustion.

"Charlie, I can't believe you rescued me."

"Well, it wasn't so simple."

A faint crease forms between her brows.

"But… how?"

I hesitate, knowing this isn't the time to explain everything.

"It's a long story. Let's just say the Dragon Slayers helped me find you."

She fixes her gaze on my face, processing what she just heard.

"You were with the Dragon Slayers?"

"They saved you."

Her lips part slightly, like she's about to say something, but she just exhales, sinking further into the pillows.

"That's insane. I need more morphine."

I let out a quiet laugh.

"Yeah, well… like I said, long story."

Lex gives a slow response.

"I'll hold you to it."

She shifts slightly, grimacing as she tries to get comfortable.

"Hey… one thing I do remember."

"What's that?"

Her lips curl into the faintest smirk.

"Someone owes me a vacation."

I chuckle, shaking my head.

"Deal."

A soft voice from behind makes me turn. Dr. Patel stands at the doorway, watching with quiet patience.

"Alright, I think that's enough excitement for one morning. She needs rest."

I hesitate, glancing back at Lex, who's already fighting to keep her eyes open.

"You're gonna be okay?"

"I think I'll live."

Her voice is already fading, the exhaustion winning out. Within seconds, her body relaxes into the bed, her breathing steady and even.

I don't move right away, instead watching the slow, steady rise and fall of her chest.

Leaving Lex's room, I feel lighter. Dr. Patel leads me into the hallway. For a moment, neither of us speaks. We will share a lifelong bond, another person I am indebted to.

"Doctor, I can't thank you and your team enough. The way you saved her, everything you've done."

"It was our pleasure. We're just happy we could help. Especially in an opportunity like this one. We should be the ones thanking you and the others.

"Before the Dragon Slayers interceded, we were at wit's end. Every day was a struggle to get the bare minimum care for our patients.

"Health care corporations, insurance companies, and hospital board members forced us to do more, with less. Cut corners, push unnecessary treatments, reducing those that were too costly. Patient pushing to make quotas. It wasn't about quality care; it was about profit."

Dr. Patel's words are full of frustration and exhaustion from the years spent fighting a system designed to squeeze people dry, before it lets them die. Money over humanity.

"Now? We don't have to deal with that anymore. This is the funding we need. The supplies. The staffing. It's been a complete turnaround. Better pay, work hours and, most of all, respect. We're able to do our jobs. Helping people heal."

Now I'm experiencing firsthand the change Lancelot spoke about in real time. It's here. In the hospitals. In people's lives.

Dr. Patel guides me to another waiting room. I stop short.

Graham is there laughing. A hearty one.

He doesn't laugh like that, not with people he doesn't trust. The only time I've ever seen that expression on his face is after a mission, when he's back with his team, cutting loose in those rare moments of peace.

Sitting next to him is Tristan.

The cold, calculated Dragon Slayer who's spent years toppling the world order? He's sitting there, enjoying the company, like an old friend.

"Well, you two seem to be having a good time," I say, announcing my presence.

Graham coughs, straightening as if I caught him stealing something. He wipes a hand across his face, still shaking with quiet laughter.

"Hey Charlie. Just sharing an old combat story."

Tristan grins.

"One where someone thought it was smart to take a shot at a squad of marines' Doc."

Graham chuckles.

"Bad call. You don't touch the medic. You do, and the whole unit makes sure you regret it. How's Lex?"

"She's doing okay. Dr. Patel says she's on the road to recovery."

"Good to hear."

Tristan reaches down and grabs a backpack off the floor. He tosses it to me, and instinctively I catch it.

"Got all your stuff in there."

Unzipping my bag, I check my gear and personal items from the campsite. My phone is in there, and as I turn it on, the screen lights up with notifications.

Thirty-three missed calls from Carter. Too many texts to count.

Fuck. In all the turmoil, I completely forgot about him.

Tristan gives a dry half-smile.

"Don't worry. Carter knows everything's fine."

"Great. He's still going to kill me for not telling him sooner."

"So now that everything's good, do you have a moment to talk?"

My mood changes sharply.

The favor.

I straighten a little, bracing myself.

"Of course. What is it?"

Without missing a beat, he gestures to Graham.

"I've already spoken to him about this. He's all in."

I turn to Graham. He's watching me steadily, the lightness gone from his face. He is fully committed to whatever is planned.

Tristan sharpens with intention.

"Something big is going down, Charlie. I can't give you all the details, but it's probably going to be the final move."

"Final move?"

"We're taking down the White House."

Surely, Tristan must be joking. The White House has been excessively fortified to the point of absurdity. The blocks around it were sealed off months ago; roads were closed and all entry was funneled through BlackSteel checkpoints.

Sorakin Tech may be offline, but going after the White House is a tactical nightmare.

"You want me to be part of that? To attack it with you?"

"No. This one is Dragon Slayers only. I told you before. We need people like you to put it all back together when we're finished. And for the better."

"And you need me there… because?"

"The second we take Tuff and his administration out, we need to make sure Washington doesn't spiral out of control.

We need governors, military leaders, anyone with power to be ready to pick up the pieces."

"Tristan, you're planning to cut the head off the snake and hope the body dies?"

"Removing Tuff and his inner circle will be the catalyst to make the billionaire cities crumble. Citizens aren't on his side anymore. We make this move; we make it count, and hopefully it saves a lot of needless bloodshed."

"I want to be there... but Lex..."

"I get it. Lex will be more than fine. Charlie, we leave soon. You'll be back in 2-3 days tops."

What Tristan is asking me is beyond belief. How dare he ask me to leave her, not now. But then the Grayson in me resurfaces, reminding me to do what must be done.

I know he's right.

"Okay, I'm in."

And just like that, everything is set in motion.

CHAPTER 49

SHADOWS BEFORE THE FLAME

"When dictatorship is a fact, revolution becomes a right."

-Victor Hugo

TRISTAN RISES FROM his seat, adjusting his jacket.

"Alright, well, unfortunately, it's time to start getting packed up. We have to head out soon."

"Right now? I haven't even said goodbye to Lex."

Tristan reaches into his pocket, pulls out a phone, and hands it to a nurse walking by.

"Excuse me. Can you give this to Dr. Patel?" he asks politely . "It's for her patient in the ICU. Alexa Thompson."

The nurse takes the phone without hesitation.

Why am I not surprised?

"You Dragon Slayers really do think of everything."

"When you've got a lot of money, you can give away a lot of stuff. Honestly, I don't know how many phones I've given out at this point."

Collecting our gear, we head for the hospital lobby. Outside, a flatbed is waiting in the loading zone. Standard issue military, weathered green paint. The same type of vehicle used to haul troops through conflict zones.

The soldier behind the wheel is in full military fatigues, boots polished, expression unreadable. The flag patch on his shoulder surprises me. The insignia of the United States of America.

Processing the sight of the patch makes me blink a few times.

"That's... actual military?"

"Yep, Union Guard."

Tristan climbs up onto the tailgate as Graham pulls himself up next to him, and I follow. The tailgate slams shut behind us with a heavy clunk as the engine growls to life, thick and powerful.

We sit in the back, pressed shoulder to shoulder, surrounded by the scent of oil, canvas, and gunmetal.

"So, we're just driving straight in?" I ask.

"Charlie, we're heading into a siege. It's worse than we thought. The whole capital is locked down. Machine guns, barricades, sniper nests... it's a military fortress."

Tristan adjusts his rifle strap.

"Even without Sorakin Tech, BlackSteel continues wrestling for control. They're desperate. They know if the White House falls, it's over. That's the last stronghold they've got left, the final illusion of power."

Graham shifts beside me.

"They're going to defend the Capitol with all their might. It doesn't matter if it's working or not. They'll burn the city down before they ever let it go."

Tristan adjusts his grip on the side rail, eyes scanning the interior of the flatbed before settling back on me.

"It's gonna be a few hours. Now's the time to catch some sleep."

There's no argument from me. He's right. There's nothing to do but wait, and my body has made the decision for me.

I shift against the canvas wall, finding the least uncomfortable spot, letting my legs stretch out. The hum of the engine, the constant rattle of the road beneath us, merge into a calming current, far removed from whatever is waiting at the end of this ride.

D.C. is a fortified city. BlackSteel is bleeding but remains extremely dangerous. If this is truly the last stand, there's no pretending we're walking away clean. The mission isn't here yet. I close my eyes and let the weight of it all prod me to sleep.

A jolt awakens me, a sharp bump in the road that rattles through the flatbed. My neck aches, my back is stiff. I must've been out longer than I realized. My eyes struggle to adjust to the dim evening light seeping through the canvas flaps. We're not alone anymore.

Through a narrow opening, I catch glimpses of armored transports ahead and behind us. Dozens of them. A full military convoy stretches in both directions, tires grinding over cracked pavement as we roll forward in unison.

Graham is fully awake, posture upright. Tristan glances at me to check if I've woken up.

"We linked up with the main force. They're locking down every entry point to the city."

Outside, the scenery is unsettling. Abandoned vehicles are pushed to the side of the road, sandbag barriers shield the area, and warning signs flap in the breeze.

The skyline of D.C. looms ahead, broken by cranes, scaffolding, and the hard angles of barricades. The convoy slows as we approach a checkpoint.

Soldiers in standard U.S. military uniforms move to intercept. There is nothing flashy about them, no special markings on them . Just crisp gear, rifles slung tight, and eyes that know what to watch out for. No question these individuals are Union Guard.

One of them steps up to the driver's side, leaning in for a quick exchange.

After a few seconds, the soldier steps back and waves us forward. Another guardsman lifts the barrier and signals to the others.

We're in.

The truck rumbles forward, crossing into the heart of the siege.

Tristan taps the metal wall behind the cab.

"Left at the next junction."

The flatbed turns off the main convoy route and rumbles down a narrower access road flanked by barricaded storefronts and shattered glass. The deeper we move into the city's skeleton, the more abandoned it feels, a world where only soldiers and silence remain.

The truck comes to a halt beside a dark alley. As the engine idles, a gray SUV pulls up alongside us. The vehicle has no plates, just heavily tinted windows encased in dull armored panels.

Tristan hops down from the flatbed and gives a short wave.

Two men step out of the SUV. The first is tall, lean, a stature made of angles and precision. His gaze sweeps the area before landing on Tristan with a sharp salute.

The second is shorter, stockier, built like a wrecking ball. His shoulders are thick under a faded tactical jacket, scars marking his cheek and knuckles, signatures from past battles. He moves with authority, and the second he sees Tristan, a grin splits across his face.

"Tristan," he says. "Good to see you made it."

Tristan clasps his hand.

"Roland, good to see you too."

The taller man stands silently behind Roland, eyes scanning the area with military precision.

Roland shifts his attention to us, giving Graham and me a once-over.

"So, you're Cross and Grayson. Glad you kept Tristan alive for us."

He jerks a thumb toward Tristan.

"We need him a little longer."

Tristan chuckles.

"Alright, Roland, enough… let's move."

The SUV we're in pulls away from the checkpoint entrance. Floodlights cut through the thickening dusk as we weave through deserted streets.

"Lancelot's having the meeting tonight," Roland states. "We're executing the siege first thing tomorrow morning."

"How serious is it?" Tristan asks.

"It's happening"

There is no room for uncertainty. The Dragon Slayer's decision has been made.

Tomorrow, they strike.

BlackSteel banners hang from buildings, high and defiant, rippling in the wind. The last remaining symbol of a billionaire empire clinging to power. The White House is their last line of defense for those unwilling to relinquish their stronghold.

Somewhere in there, Tuff is hiding.

The SUV navigates the outskirts of the city, winding through industrial roads, stopping in front of an unobtrusive warehouse. Nothing about it would suggest it's anything more than an abandoned storage facility.

But the second the doors open, the atmosphere bursts into action.

Dragon Slayers move in coordinated rhythm, conversations filling the space, weapons being checked, maps laid out across tables.

And now, I'm standing in the middle of it. Taking it all in.

I hear my name ring out across the massive space.

"Charlie!"

Carter barrels towards me, embracing me in a tight hug. His energy is infectious, and his excitement is completely unfiltered.

"Boss. You're alive! Fuck, thank God you're alive!"

He releases me and turns to Graham, his face lighting up.

"Oh wow, Graham! I'm so glad to see you!"

Graham's expression hardens, cutting through Carter's enthusiasm.

"So... You are working for the Dragon Slayers."

Carter's face shifts, nervous energy replacing his excitement.

"Well, now yeah... I guess, but before? No... I swear!"

Graham lets out a very faint laugh, shaking his head.

"Listen, Carter, I was an ass before. I was frustrated with everything, so I just hope it can be water under the bridge for us."

He extends his hand to Carter, who looks surprised but relieved as they shake.

Carter steps back, his face still full of amazement at the whole situation.

"How crazy is this shit? Look at all this, look at everything going on! You have no idea what we've been up to. This, all of this, is history in the making!"

He spins around dramatically, arms gesturing wide as if he is showing off a new amusement park instead of a war room. Then he leans in, voice dropping to a conspiratorial hush.

"Merlin and I completely wrecked Sorakin's systems. I mean, we gutted them. The only reason we got in that deep was because of BlackSteel. Those idiots linked everything, so their overreach is what gave us the backdoor. We buried code so deep it'll take them a while just to figure out what broke, let alone how to fix it."

I raise an eyebrow.

"How long are you thinking?"

Carter proudly shrugs.

"If they want the system back up to full operational control? They're gonna have to rebuild the entire framework. Rework it from scratch. Could take months if they even have the manpower left to do it.

"So yeah. We didn't just take the legs out from under them… we ripped out the damn spine."

And by the look of our surroundings, the Dragon Slayers are not done yet.

Carter is completely in his element. This is a far cry from when he was stuck behind an FBI desk, frustrated with the bureaucratic machine we both endured. But here? He's thriving.

Tristan stands off to the side, enjoying our unexpected reunion. One of the nearby operatives tells him that Lancelot is ready to brief us. It's time to move, as an overjoyed Carter falls into step beside Graham and me.

"Listen, you two. After tomorrow, things are going to get… well… fucking intense. Between the Dragon Slayers' assault on the White House and what we're doing on the network side, this could be the final blow."

I don't miss the could part.

"Could or will. Carter, you don't sound completely convinced."

"Boss, BlackSteel is way too quiet. Either their network is completely down, or they're hiding something. We're not picking up any chatter from them."

"Carter, that doesn't make sense. If they were scrambling to hold their ground, there'd be some intel."

"Exactly. So, either we've got them completely backed into a corner, or they're planning something we can't see."

"And we're walking into it either way?"

"Yeah. And imagine if the White House is cut off from the other billionaire cities. What they would do in that kind of desperation, with Tuff leading them…"

Tuff has always been erratic, self-obsessed, but he's never faced the likes of the Dragon Slayers or the Union Guard. If he's out of options, if he knows the end is coming, what does that make him capable of?

Mutual annihilation is a strong possibility.

As we pass a row of worktables and crates, Guinevere strides by in the opposite direction, her presence, as always, cutting through the space. Without breaking pace, she tosses a glance and smiles our way.

"Hey, Carter."

He lights up right away, voice a slight pitch higher.

"Oh hey, Gwen…"

I give him a look, half amusement, half curiosity.

"I see you and 'Gwen' have hit it off."

Graham leans in with a low whistle.

"Damn, Carter."

Carter waves it off, straightening his jacket.

"It's not like that. Right? Like… I don't actually have a shot?"

"Nah, you got this," Graham chuckles. "You're a real Romeo."

We keep moving, weaving through gear and operatives locked in prep mode until the buzz of activity begins to fade away, and then we see him.

Even in a room full of men built for war, Lancelot stands

out. A masked statue carved from iron, fully armored, while his comrades have long since shed their gear.

"Sir," Tristan says with deep respect.

Lancelot turns, gravity itself bending to accommodate him.

He grips Tristan's hand firmly, then clasps a hand on his shoulder, the force behind it unintentionally strong. Tristan tenses for a second. It's barely noticeable, but I catch it.

Lancelot speaks, his words rolling thunder.

"Tristan, glad you made it back safely. Your success should be celebrated. But there is no time. I need you to take Graham and head to the armory. Find Asher. He needs your assistance."

Lancelot turns his focus squarely on me.

"Grayson, I'd like to speak with you privately."

Tristan reads the room in an instant. He claps Graham on the shoulder and gestures to Carter.

"Come on, Graham, you can help me out, and pretty sure Merlin could use your help too, Carter. We're on a strict timeline here."

That leaves me alone with Lancelot.

He turns, leading me toward a back corridor. I follow, my pulse steady, but my thoughts spinning out of control. It's probably not an everyday occurrence that someone gets summoned for a private talk with Lancelot.

His quarters are unremarkable, as expected. A large cot, a metal desk covered in tactical maps, and stacks of documents. No luxury or warmth, just a space built for efficiency.

In the corner, a single framed photograph catches my eye. It's a woman holding a baby. The image is old, and the colors are faded, but it's the only personal item in his room.

Lancelot sits, his voice quiet as he addresses me.

"Tristan told me he gave you the news about your father."

"He did."

It's strange how much saying those words stings. With everything else I've experienced between the violence and Lex, I haven't had time to dwell on Bill's betrayal. But hearing it from Lancelot is a wound ripped open again.

"Your father was a true hero, Charlie."

My eyes narrow, studying him more carefully.

"Did you know him?"

His response is respectfully firm.

"I served under his command. We were in the same unit for a tour. I was with him on Operation Silent Aegis.

"That day, we were set up. Your father saved my life and the lives of a lot of brave men and women, buying us time to escape.

"James Grayson was one of the best soldiers I ever served with. Not just because he was skilled, but because he defended the people beside him. Your father stood up for what was right, what was just, even when it cost him his life."

It's strange hearing that from someone I consider to be a monster.

The eyes behind his mask stay fixed on me, unreadable.

"And that's what they used against him. They knew exactly what kind of man he was, someone who wouldn't run, wouldn't leave anyone behind. Set the whole thing up knowing he'd go down in a blaze of glory protecting others.

"And, he did just that."

It makes me sick. Not just what happened to my father, but how they used him as a pawn. How easily the system weaponized his loyalty, like it's done to so many others, so many times before.

"Why are you telling me all this?" I demand. "What do you want from me?"

"Charlie, we've been monitoring you for a while now. Your

track record. Your skills. The way you think. To put it simply, we need good people, people like you.

"We've caused too much damage in our role. Too much pain. Even the ones cheering for us out there don't understand. They think this is justice, but it's only another turn of the wheel of violence. We were simply a swing back on the pendulum.

"If the Dragon Slayers are part of what comes next, then this doesn't end. We'll just become the new target. The excuse for the next wave of bloodshed.

"This mission was never about taking power. It was about breaking the cycle of corruption. But if we stay in it, if we try to carry this into the future, it will only guarantee that the pain will continue."

His tone lowers as if he is talking to himself.

"The Dragon Slayers are shaped by violence. Molded by the system until it was all we knew. This is the only peace left for us, knowing we did everything we could to stop this institutional madness.

"We weren't always like this. I wasn't always like this."

Then, without another word, he reaches up and removes his helmet and mask.

The scars are the first thing I notice.

Deep, jagged, carved into his skin like the history of his pain was written there. Some look like burns, others like blade wounds, some aged with time. His entire face is a roadmap of war.

In that moment, I understand why he wears the mask. It's not just to conceal his identity. It's because whatever life he's lived, whatever wars he's fought, he no longer looks like the man he used to be.

But his pale blue eyes… his eyes don't match the brutality of his face.

"After Silent Aegis, something in me cracked.

"We were left to rot out there. That's exactly what it felt like. And when I got home, it was like the world had already moved on without me.

"But I tried. Got out of the military. Met someone who could tolerate me and all my baggage. Emily."

His hand absently runs over his face, a self-aware smirk tugging at the corner of his lips.

"Back then, the scars weren't this bad."

The humor doesn't reach his eyes.

"I didn't deserve Emily. She was the most incredible person I've ever known. And eventually, we had a kid. A little girl. Samantha... she was everything to us."

Her name shadows his face, and I brace myself because stories like this don't end well.

"She was four when we found out she had cancer. It wasn't some rare, untreatable death sentence. It was curable.

"But curable meant expensive."

Lancelot struggles to continue.

"We drained all our accounts. Every cent we had. Sold the house, sold the car, sold anything that wasn't nailed down. And it still wasn't enough.

"She died, Charlie. Not because the doctors couldn't save her. Because an insurance company decided she wasn't worth saving."

I feel the fury crawling up my spine, slow and suffocating.

"Emily never recovered. She tried, but she couldn't escape her grief. She took her own life less than a year later."

Lancelot sighs deeply.

"And me? I thought about it. I had the gun in my hand more nights than I can count. But I couldn't do it. Couldn't bring myself to pull the trigger."

There's nothing for me to say.

Lancelot sinks back into his chair.

"So instead, I joined a mercenary force. I didn't care anymore. Figured if I couldn't end myself, maybe someone else would do it for me."

He lets out a humorless chuckle.

"But they didn't. Somehow, I kept surviving.

"And in the meantime, I started telling my story. And the more I told it, the more I realized I wasn't alone.

"That's where it started. Every person I met had the same story. A handful of powerful and greedy people had ruined millions of lives, and no one could stop them."

His voice grows heavier.

"So, we became the thing that could, not to fix it, but simply to destroy it.

"We never thought it would be a revolution. We just wanted to burn as bright as we could before someone snuffed out our flame, but they never did.

"Luck. Skill. Tactics. Call it whatever you want. But now we're here. And we're finishing this."

"Finishing this?"

"Tomorrow, we're giving everything we have. The Dragon Slayers will strike one last time."

The way he says it makes my stomach twist.

"You make it sound like you're not expecting to come back."

"Because we're not, which is why you're critical to what comes next. When we're gone, they will try to regain power. Maybe not the billionaires we're facing now, but someone else will."

My heart pounds. The meaning is clear now. This is a suicide mission. Lancelot doesn't expect to live through it. None of them do.

"Charlie, what do you believe about what we've done?"

"I honestly don't know. You've done horrible things. And those are just the things I know about. I can only imagine the rest."

"You're right. The actions of myself and the other Dragon Slayers have been heinous.

"But what do you think of our cause now?"

I hesitate. My thoughts are tangled, shifting, trying to settle into something tangible.

"The system wasn't right. I don't know how long or when things went astray, but its obvious something needed to be done."

"I just wish there was less bloodshed. Honestly, I don't know… it all depends on what comes next."

A shadow of regret crosses his face.

"I wish there was less blood spilled as well. It's sad what these battles do to people, to all of us."

He studies me carefully.

"And that's exactly why we need you. And others like you. Tomorrow, we may not be here."

I close my eyes. It's not that I didn't expect casualties. I knew this battle would be brutal and that not everyone would walk away alive. But the way Lancelot says it leaves no room for hope.

My thoughts switch to Tristan, the way he helped me, the way he risked everything to save Lex. The way these Dragon Slayers, people I once considered terrorists, keep proving to be something more.

I contemplate all scenarios before meeting Lancelot's gaze.

"Okay, I'll do it, you have my word."

Lancelot stands, his movements slow and deliberate. He extends his hand out to mine. His grip is made of steel, and I shake hands with someone who is more than just a man.

His smile is unmistakably warm, his reply one sincere word.

"Good."

In that moment, I know my answer holds special importance to him. Perhaps more than either of us expected.

Then, without hesitation, he reaches for his mask.

The second it slides back on, something shifts, the mere mortal in front of me is gone. The symbol, the force, the leader of the Dragon Slayers has returned.

"Now, I must address my team," he commands.

Without another word, he turns and strides out of the room. I follow a few steps behind, preparing myself for what comes next.

Lancelot moves to the front of the war room, his massive frame casting long shadows across the Dragon Slayers surrounding him. The air is thick with anticipation, the kind one feels before an approaching storm.

Everyone here knows what's coming.

No one dares speak, not when Lancelot stands before them. He begins with a voice that careens through the space like a force of nature.

"I want to start by thanking you all. For your commitment. For your sacrifices. For your belief in this cause."

Lancelot's armor doesn't hide the impact of his words. He speaks like a man with nothing left to prove, only something left to finish.

"We have always known that the Dragon Slayers were only the spark. The fire that followed was not ours alone. It was everyone's. This movement was not built on the shoulders of a few; it was built on the backs of every person in this room. On the backs of those who fought, those who gave everything to ensure others wouldn't be crushed by a system that viewed them as disposable."

He doesn't rush, each word balanced and firm.

"We are here because of you. Because of all of us."

The energy in the room shifts, a clock spring being wound up tight.

Lancelot straightens.

"Now, it is time. Time to strike at the beast and cut off the head of this treasonous snake.

"Tomorrow, I will lead my Dragon Slayers in a direct siege of the White House. The last true stronghold of the billionaire class. The final bastion of those who sought to own this country instead of serving it.

"The Union Guard, those stepping forward to rebuild, have cleared the path for us. The military has blocked off the surrounding area, allowing us to pass through. We will not be stopped."

Lancelot's tone darkens.

"They know the blood to be shed should not be on their hands. They know it has always been meant for ours.

"We have burned the old system to ash. And now we finish the mission. This is our burden to bear. Not theirs."

There's no stirring in the crowd. Just unyielding attention and acceptance.

"Tomorrow's battle will be more than just an ending. It will be a message.

"The billionaire strongholds still stand. They are waiting, watching, hoarding the last remnants of their empire. But they are fractured. They are leaderless."

His voice is ironclad, final.

"Once we take Tuff, the last head of this beast, the rest will fall. Without him, the billionaire cities will crumble under their own weight. There will be no need for a prolonged war.

"This is why we fight. This is why it ends tomorrow. This

most likely will be the last time we see some of our brothers and sisters in arms. This will be our last stand."

An uneasy pull twists through me as I subconsciously look towards Tristan. He's standing near the edge of the crowd, arms crossed, listening.

He's already done so much for me. Saved Lex. Stood by me when I least expected it. And now, just as quickly as he entered my life, I could be watching him walk into something he never comes back from.

As if Tristan can feel my thoughts, his gaze turns toward me. He shows no fear. Instead, he sends me a small, knowing smile, filled with the reassurance that it will all be okay.

But how can it be? Tristan stands there unshaken, like this is just another mission.

Lancelot continues his speech, his words sealing the gravity of it all.

"But that is not what matters. What matters is that we ensure that the legend of the Dragon Slayers lives on.

"Because long after we are gone, there will be others who seek to rebuild the corrupt empire we are tearing down. There will be others who try to claw their way back to power. And they must remember what happens when greed goes unchecked.

"They must remember that the masses will always rise up."

A suspenseful pause before his last words lock everything into place.

"It has been an honor and a privilege to serve with all of you, and tomorrow…

"We finally slay the dragons."

He raises his fist, and the crowd explodes. The sound is thunderous. These Dragon Slayers, the ones who know this could be the end of the line for them, are shouting with all their might.

Their faces hardened by war, eyes lit with purpose. They're ready to finish it.

And with that, Lancelot's inspirational rally ends.

Carter steps up beside me, stretching his arms with a long sigh.

"Damn, man. That was… intense."

I don't answer right away. My mind is tangled in everything Lancelot said, in Tristan's words, in what tomorrow will bring.

"Well, boss, I don't know about you, but I'm gonna at least try to get some sleep. Not sure if that's actually possible. But hey, come on, I'll show you where the bunks are."

I follow him through the warehouse, my legs and body are sore, my mind refusing to slow down. The corridors are quieter now, fading as Dragon Slayers prepare themselves in their own way. Some are strategizing, others eating what might be their last meal, while some, like Carter, are trying to grab whatever rest they can.

The bunk room is dimly lit, lined with rows of cots, nothing fancy, just a place to crash.

Carter gestures across the room.

"Take whatever's open. Not like they're picky around here."

I find a cot next to him and run my fingers over the rough fabric of the blanket.

"Thanks, Carter. After everything with Lex, I haven't had much sleep."

Carter flops onto his own cot, letting out a deep sigh.

"Yeah… well, good luck getting any rest, boss."

I don't have the energy to respond.

I lay back, staring at the ceiling, willing my body to shut down, to let me sink into whatever bits of sleep I can get before it all implodes tomorrow. But my mind won't stop. Lancelot's meeting. Tristan's words. The thought of what lies ahead, if they don't come back.

Then, my phone buzzes.

My breath catches as I grab it from my bag, glancing at the screen.

Lex.

Instantly, sleep becomes the last thing I need.

"Hey, how are you feeling? Are you okay?"

Lex's voice comes through, groggy and weak.

"Hey, yeah, don't worry, I'm fine.

"I hear you're off saving the world again."

Guilt tugs at my chest.

"Lex, I…"

She cuts me off with a quiet chuckle.

"I'm just kidding. I'm sorry, Charlie.

"Dr. Patel filled me in on everything. And honestly? I probably wouldn't be here without the Dragon Slayers. So, I'm more than happy to loan you out for a little bit."

Then, softer.

"But… please, please be safe."

"Lex, don't worry, I'm not going to see any combat. The Dragon Slayers are going to complete their mission tomorrow. I don't know any details, but they said they wanted me here."

Lex's tone sharpens instantly.

"Why do they want you there?"

"I think it's because they know this is the end for them. Whatever happens tomorrow… they're not planning to make it out alive. The Union Guard is the future now. They'll be the ones left to pick up the pieces."

"Okay, I guess. It's almost morphine time for me, so I'll be out, but…Charlie, I want text messages… please?"

"Don't worry, Lex. I promise to keep you updated."

"I'm going to hold you to that.

"Hey, Charlie… one more thing."

"Yeah?"

"I love you."

The warmth of her voice spreads through my body, anchoring me. It cuts through chaos, through uncertainty, through everything that tomorrow may bring.

There is no hesitation from me.

"I love you, too."

I set my phone down on my chest, staring at the ceiling, letting my thoughts drift away.

It's not war or death that fills my mind. It's Lex and me. The thought of getting away together, taking that dream vacation, of finally being free of everyone and everything.

The idea is enough to quiet the fear inside me, enough to push the worry aside.

Enough to close my eyes, as sleep pulls me under.

CHAPTER 50

RECKONING

"When a long train of abuses and usurpations…evinces a design to reduce them under absolute Despotism, it is their right, it is their duty, to throw off such Government."

-THE DECLARATION OF INDEPENDENCE (U.S., 1776)

THE SOUND HITS before my eyes even open, boots pounding against concrete, gear snapping into place, sharp and focused, no one bothering to be quiet.

Bolting upright on the cot, I catch my breath, heart already beating out of control.

This is it. The final push.

The Dragon Slayers are prepping to enter the serpent's den.

Shaking off the last haze of sleep, I head to the staging area.

Tristan stands near the far end of the warehouse, speaking with three Dragon Slayers. He's fully suited up, battle-ready. If his mask were not off, he would have blended seamlessly with the others.

His hands try to keep up with his words as he points out

strategic marks and delivers his orders. Even now, at the edge of whatever the hell happens next, he is remarkably calm.

Heading towards him, I slow my steps. There is no need to interrupt him. Every moment with his unit is more important than speaking with me.

Then, as if he feels my presence, Tristan turns his head. He gives one final directive to his men and strides toward me.

He knows why I'm here. And he wants to talk just as much as I do.

"Looking for me, Charlie?"

"Just wanted to wish you luck, Tristan. Do you know what's about to happen?"

"Maybe. Maybe not."

"Please be serious, Tristan. Is this a suicide mission?"

"Charlie, this whole thing has been one giant suicide mission. It was supposed to end for us with every battle, every raid. But this may be the one that does."

"Does what?"

"Exactly what we came here to do."

"Which is?"

"Be the force that changes everything. Charlie, you of all people know this. The Dragon Slayers are merely the spark.

"And you don't have to worry about me."

"Tristan, you make it sound like you're already gone."

"We'll find out soon enough. But thanks, Charlie."

"Thanks for what?"

"That you care about me. There aren't many people left like that for us."

Tristan steps forward, his expression sobers.

"Don't waste your time on me. You have Lex, Graham, and Carter to be concerned about. Focus your attention on them.

"Speaking of which, go round them up. You three will be in the second section of the convoy."

"Tristan, you promised nothing dangerous for us, right?"

"Trust me. You'll be completely safe. We've got the Union Guard handling the perimeter. It's only the Dragon Slayers that will see some action today. You have my word."

Tristan's hand rests on his mask, his eyes searching for mine, releasing a silent goodbye. He flips the mask down, and the soldier returns.

I stand there, our moment together slipping into a memory, one which could hold our last conversation.

Beginning to make my way toward the front, I hear a familiar grating voice.

"Well, if it isn't FBI Barbie."

I stop mid-stride and turn to face Donovan Pierce. He's leaning against the back of a truck, cigarette dangling from his tobacco-stained fingers, smoke curling at the edge of his mouth. He looks like hell, but he's alive.

"You're still breathing, Donovan?"

"Yeah. Crazy, right? Guess I am just too damn stubborn to die."

He flicks ash to the ground.

"Glad to see you made it through this circus, Charlie."

"Donovan, what the hell are you doing here?"

"Apparently, the Union Guard decided they wanted the best of the best."

He takes another drag of his cigarette.

"No fucking clue why they picked me. Maybe they're out of options. But hey, still kicking, so I guess I've got something left to do.

"Not surprised to see you here though, kid. Always figured you'd stick the landing."

"Well, best of luck with whatever happens from here on. Donovan."

"Yeah. Hate to say it, but we're all gonna need it."

He turns and walks away, fading into the background.

Donovan didn't just wander into this. He made himself valuable somewhere, and I can't shake the feeling he's downplaying how much he's really involved.

It's unclear if I can trust him, but I'm damn sure he's earned his seat at the table.

As I continue moving forward, the entire space is alive and bustling as I scan for Graham and Carter, I spot them near one of the waiting transport vehicles, ready to go.

Carter notices me first.

"Hey, boss, did Tristan spill the beans?"

"He gave me nothing. I still have no clue what they're planning, but it's time to load up."

Graham folds his arms, skeptical as ever.

"I'm all set. You ready, Carter?"

"Same here, although I'm armed with just a laptop. No gun, right?"

Graham can't help but laugh at him.

"Damn right. Last thing we need is you slipping and shooting yourself in the foot. Guinevere would be heartbroken."

"Good to know you've got my back."

"Enough, guys," I interject. "Time to load up."

We climb into the truck waiting for us, doors slamming shut and locked. Our convoy moves through the streets, emitting a steady rumble of heavy machines. There are three transports full of Dragon Slayers ahead and one more behind us. We're boxed in, and that makes me uneasy.

On both sides of the street, the Union Guard stands at

attention, silent, unmoving, like sentinels posted at the edge of history.

These are all former soldiers. Men and women in uniforms, a collage of military branches.

They're people who served. People like me. People who believed in this Nation, who followed orders, who never expected to be standing on the other side of this fight.

The system used Bill, and he knew it. He had seen the corruption, knew exactly what it was, and embraced it, carving out his portion of control.

Still, the question remains: would Bill have made the same decision if the billionaire's chokehold on power weren't there?

Would the system have ever rotted this badly if unchecked greed hadn't been the defining factor?

Why did 3000 people need so much power that they squeezed life out of the rest of the world?

It was foolish of them to even think this could last forever.

Carter lets out a nervous laugh.

"Hey, when we all first met, who would've guessed we'd end up in a Dragon Slayer convoy heading to the White House? Fucking crazy, right?"

"Crazy?" Graham replies. "We passed crazy with Lancelot's first video. Try batshit insane."

The moment of humor fades quickly, replaced by a heavier burden.

Graham shifts his focus, his tone pragmatic.

"Thing is… we know this will not be over, even if whatever the hell the Dragon Slayers have planned works out."

Grahams right. The Dragon Slayer mission is brazen and extraordinary. The system is broken. And now? Power vacuums don't stay vacuums for long. This administration may fall, taking some billionaires with them, but that leaves the nation up for grabs.

Revolutions don't always lead to positive change. After the dust settles, those with alternative motives will stake their claim. We need to make sure that this doesn't happen.

Sorin is working around the clock to bring his system and robotics back online. BlackSteel is mobilizing its dwindling forces, retreating into any remaining strongholds. Wounded predators waiting for the opportunity to strike again. None of this is far from over.

The truth is ugly, but it's all I can think about. I speak next with sincerity.

"Listen, guys. Whatever happens, we work together. The Dragon Slayers sacrificed too much to let our country slip back into chaos."

"Well, boss, no matter what, I'm in it for the long run."

"Thanks, Carter. And you, Graham?"

"You know, Charlie, I was thinking of retiring to a remote island, off the grid. But yeah, I'm in. Not gonna let what's left of this country fall apart even more."

The convoy comes to an unexpected stop. We're here. An uncomfortable silence settles over us.

As we step out, the first thing that registers is how close we are to the White House. Fifty yards, if that.

BlackSteel's White House fortifications are menacing. The heavy metal fence that surrounds the grounds has gone up dramatically in height. Behind it, reinforced bunkers and turret nests jut out like hardened scars, each angled to kill.

Just silent, fortified intent.

The whole place is locked and loaded, waiting for someone or something to cross the line.

Tristan's voice reverberates in my head.

Trust me. You'll be completely safe.

From my vantage point, I can see everything clearly. Dragon Slayers line up in perfect formation, standing at attention, their black and gold armor glistening in the early morning light. Leading them, the symbol of the war itself.

Lancelot.

Next to him, Tristan.

Is this the last time I'll see both of them alive? I shake off the thought and focus on what's in front of me. Dragon Slayers, thirty loyal soldiers, marching toward the White House, risking everything. Not for wealth, fame, or revenge, but for the chance to be the force that shatters a corrupt system.

No one ever believed they would come this far in their quest for freedom. Yet, here they are, walking toward the White House.

I anchor myself, preparing for the worst possible scenario. Gunfire, snipers, an ambush, the possibilities are endless.

Is this the Dragon Slayers' plan? To get cut down in broad daylight, force the world to watch, turning themselves into martyrs?

It's reckless. It's insane. What I'm witnessing is less like a plan and more like an execution in motion.

Suddenly, the front gates slowly begin to open.

This is it. Shots will be fired. The question is, who will take the first bullet?

My whole body goes numb as BlackSteel guards step into view, rifles in hand, formation tight. It appears that they're preparing for a fight, ready to meet the Dragon Slayers head-on.

Then, they abruptly halt.

One of them waves back, signaling, and that's when the momentum shifts.

A line of people approaches, hands above their heads, wrists bound. The BlackSteel guards step aside, letting them pass without incident.

It takes a second for me to comprehend what I'm seeing. Who I'm seeing.

The blood drains from my face.

Victor Hargrove. Dr. Hart. Eugene Laskey.

And then, President Tuff.

They're all being escorted out at gunpoint.

The BlackSteel soldiers surrounding them aren't guarding them. They're turning them in.

And then, one by one, the remaining BlackSteel guards drop their weapons to the ground. They kneel. Hands behind their heads.

They've surrendered.

Lancelot and the Dragon Slayers keep moving forward, completely unfazed. Entranced by what I am witnessing, I start walking towards them.

And I'm not the only one.

Graham. Carter. The rest of the convoy. We all start moving, drawn in by the sheer magnitude of what's unfolding in front of us. I don't stop until I'm close enough to see the fear on the faces of the people who built their world, destroying ours.

They believed their wealth could protect them, that money would keep BlackSteel loyal to the end. But dead men can't collect a paycheck.

Their loyalty to Tuff, his staff and the billionaires was not worth dying for no matter how much they were compensated to do so.

It was not supposed to play out this way. The people who owned everything are now on their knees.

The Dragon Slayers break formation, moving with urgency toward Lancelot. Their backpacks are held low, their movements quick and precise. The rest spread out, forming a tight perimeter around the kneeling captives. A human wall, a final barrier between the establishment and the commoners, who are no longer at their disposal.

Weapons are secured and packed away efficiently. No one resists. No one dares.

Tuff, Hargrove, Hart and Laskey are paralyzed in disbelief.

Two of the Dragon Slayers start removing video and audio devices to capture this historic moment.

Lancelot is about to make a statement.

The image forms in my mind before it even happens.

Lancelot, standing in front of the White House. The most powerful figures in the country kneeling, bound behind him.

History is being written in real time.

The camera clicks on. The live broadcast begins.

Lancelot looks directly at the camera, his baritone voice resonating across the White House lawn.

"When we, the Dragon Slayers, started this movement, we knew it would only succeed if you, the masses, embraced the truth.

"That this planet, this world, belongs to all of us. Not just a select few.

"For generations, they have told us there is no other way. That their hoarding of wealth, of power, of control, was necessary. That their success was earned.

"They pitted us against one another while they thrived off our blood, our sweat, our suffering. And when we cried out for justice, for something fair, they mocked us.

"They held themselves up as idols, when they should have only been seen for what they truly are."

Lancelot's tone darkens.

"The greatest plague upon humanity is unchecked greed."

He continues with conviction.

"Because of that realization, we have succeeded. Now... it's time to finish our mission."

The Dragon Slayers raise their rifles in unison, stepping forward in controlled formation.

Lancelot turns to President Tuff, still kneeling and bound. The world watches with bated breath.

Dear God... is this about to be a mass slaughter? Is this the real plan?

Lancelot positions himself next to Tuff and roars

"There is no longer a need for us.

"We, too, have committed atrocious and horrible crimes. We, the Dragon Slayers, are surrendering to whomever becomes the newly elected administration. They will decide our fate."

The Dragon Slayers begin to kneel, placing their weapons beside them. They slowly remove their masks, rifles, and side-arms.

Lancelot remains standing.

He continues, his voice dropping even lower.

"We carried these weapons with purpose. But violence should never be the answer. It can never be the tool that builds a future. The greatest victories require no battles.

"Thus, we accept our fate. We deserve to pay for the heinous actions we have committed."

Without hesitation, he reaches up, fingers gripping the edges of his mask.

And removes it.

For the first time, the world sees the grotesque figure beneath it. The weathered, battle-scarred face of the man under the mask.

A man who has seen war. A man who has lost everything. A man who has burned a system to the ground and now humbly accepts the consequences.

He kneels.

There is dead silence as The Union Guard moves forward with procedure.

Soldiers process the Dragon Slayers as they would for any other surrendering force.

I watch, unable to speak, unable to move.

The Dragon Slayers surrendered. There will be no last stand. No blood spilled in defiance.

My feelings are indescribable. Relief? Disbelief? Fear? Pity?

This was never about winning for the Dragon Slayers.

This is about the world never forgetting why they fought in the first place.

The Dragon Slayers set out with a purpose, a mission. Whether the world sees them as revolutionaries or criminals, no one can argue that they accomplished what they set out to do.

They never wanted power. Never sought to rule. They only wanted to shatter the illusion, to wake the world up, to force a nation to ask the questions it had been too afraid to confront.

Why do we suffer under rules and laws that only benefit a few?

Why do we accept a system that was never built for us?

Why were we not louder?

Maybe, if citizens had spoken up sooner, had they demanded change before it went too far, the Dragon Slayers would never have come into existence. There is no doubt that they were the spark. And sometimes, a fire must be lit under people to ignite them into action.

Movement catches my eye. Tristan.

He's being led away, hands bound as he walks with purpose, as if none of this fazes him. As the guards escort him forward, he turns his head, eyes locking onto mine.

Tristan gives me his classic smile, sharp, easy. He maintains the same cocky confidence, the invisible armor that makes him immune from any consequences.

He always had a plan. A next move. A way out.

But this time, I can't guess what's running through his mind.

Is it the confidence of a man who believes he'll walk free? That the world will judge him fairly?

Or is it something else?

No matter what happens next, Tristan's already done his part. He served his purpose, and now, he can finally rest.

Everything feels strange and muted, like the aftermath of a violent storm. The remnants of what was once a revolution, now a quiet surrender.

So much has changed.

I'm not the same person who accepted that promotion just a short while ago. I was on the right side of the law. I believed in the mission. I believed in what I was doing.

Even now, I'm still trying to figure out where I stand… but one thing is certain.

This isn't about duty or survival or chasing someone else's version of order. I see the true cause. Working to restore a nation worth believing in, one built on justice and equality for all.

Something right. Something fair. Something sustainable for everyone.

I realize the hardest part has yet to start.

Lancelot understood that. A man who seemed incapable of fear, feared what comes next. It's always easier to destroy than to build.

That's why he wanted me. That's why he wanted us.

We will be on the side that picks up the pieces. The new government will need people to make sure that it doesn't fracture the second it's built, to ensure no one just grabs the power that's been left behind.

But how long before people start reaching for it again?

Before greed tries to creep its way back into control?

Even worse, was this system broken at all?

Or is it the only system we can produce, destined to rebuild itself no matter how many times we burn it down?

I take a slow breath, letting my mind settle down.

This is the turning point, the start of something different... for better or for worse.

No matter what rises from the ashes, I'll keep fighting. Legacies are not handed down; they're carried forward.

If this is truly a new beginning... then let it be one that dares the world to do better.

AFTERWORD

Based on the current trends, by the time the median person's wealth doubles, the fortunes of billionaires will have multiplied tenfold, ushering in a new class of wealth, and with it, the age of trillionaires.

AUTHOR'S NOTE.

Thank you for reading this book. It truly means the world to me, and I hope you enjoyed the experience.

If you enjoyed this concept and story, the best way to help is by leaving reviews, as it makes a tremendous difference.

I plan to continue writing this series no matter what, but your support can help expedite the timeline and allow me to focus even more on it.

If you want to follow the process be sure to check out our Discord channel to get early access and updates for all future works.

I enjoy interacting directly with those who make this possible, as I am very grateful for your support.

Thank you again for taking the time to read this.